Spirit of
Prophecy

SPIRIT OF PROPHECY

First Edition June 2018
ISBN 978-1-9995867-9-9
Published by Money-Magnet Global
Typesetting by FormattingExperts.com

BOOKS BY J.J. HUGHES
Crime, Mystery, Spiritual Adventure Parables
www.moneymagnet.global/booksbyJJHughes

* * *

FREE OFFER!

SIGN UP AT bit.ly/2pgEfiW for the FREE BONUS chapter and discover who committed unspeakable atrocities in the past, and why. Things are not always as they appear on the surface, indeed current day villains, victims and rescuers may have switched roles. Find out how the past life events play out. Read the book then solve the clues, by signing up for the BONUS chapter.

Spirit of Prophecy

J.J. HUGHES

PRAISE FOR SPIRIT OF PROPHECY

Engrossing and thought provoking, Spirit of Prophecy *takes readers
not only on an exciting murder mystery but to a much deeper level of
engagement. It explores, in these momentous times of change, how human
awareness is expanding – not without challenge! – to remember
a greater understanding of who we really are. And in inter-weaving
the ordinary and extraordinary experiences of its heroine, it shows that
her empowering intuitive and 'super-normal' perceptions are innate
capabilities of all of us, if we choose to be open to them.*

**Dr Jude Currivan, cosmologist, planetary healer,
futurist and author of *The Cosmic Hologram***

* * *

Calling all Indie Authors

To become a No.1 Bestselling Author, get all the top marketing tips
and insider secrets, FAST TRACK your way to success with Geoff
Affleck's amazing on-line training course.

Visit bit.ly/2sqC6mx

* * *

Follow J.J. Hughes, No 1 Best Selling Author, on Twitter, Instagram,
Pinterest, Facebook – @booksByJJHughes
or get in touch via her website:
www.moneymagnet.global/booksbyJJHughes

ACKNOWLEDGMENTS

This work has been a long time bringing forth, timing as they say is everything, but probably not linear in the way we believe or currently imagine. So, I'll take this opportunity to express my deep gratitude to my collaborative team as without their input, and endless encouragement this book wouldn't have manifest itself out there [here?] in cyber space or on the shelf:

A big thank you to Ian Large, for coming to the rescue, and getting the formatting back on track before the Formatting Experts rallied to the cause. Thumbs up to Rebecca Baker and Claire McGowan at The Literary Consultancy [TLC] for cracking [if at times painful!!] editorial input. Kelly Martin for amazing cover design, my friend and fellow Indie author Ken Fry, [if only my output could match his! I highly recommend you read 'The Lazarus Succession']. My very on-the-ball, incredible multi-tasking VA: Shari Sant, and the truly creative, and ever upbeat web-designer Paul Chantler, and Steve Shellard for his unstinting support and feedback during the long hard-slog that a novel can [did] entail.

Thanks also to Samantha Dakin who ensured my Americans stayed in tune!

To the out-there-guys Yuri Milner, who is funding the Breakthrough Listen search for alien civilizations beyond earth, Elon Musk an original inspiration to us all, a phenomenal visionary who aims to colonize Mars. Jeff Bezos launching the Blue Origin rocket company… awesome… Star Travelers rock!

The incredible Psychic Sisters, especially Sheila Young who at my reading at Selfridges, London advised me to finish my novel, and that it would be a worldwide best seller: wow! And they organized amazing workshops on their fabulous cruise – thank you lovely sisters: Jackie Cox, Carole Holiday, Tess Khalil, Sue Philips, Georgi Simpson, Geraldine Sullivan, Jayne Wallace, Sheila Young, and special thanks, to Ann Thomas whose guided past life regression sessions were truly inspirational and pivotal for me, and her wedding on board the ship; was unforgettably 'wild and free.' Ah, also Bev Ward a brilliant medium, and Jen G our beckon of light guide, and my adorable, bubbly friend Jackie Whelan – a Yorkshire lass too, east to my west.

Here I mention but a few, finishing with a special thanks to my parents Margaret and Arnold Simpson, and somewhere out there in the black hole, Sir Fred Hoyle, visionary scientist and politically incorrect thinker. Your time is finally now, and may they rightfully, albeit posthumously award you the Nobel Prize that was your due.

To all my dear readers near and far, if you enjoy this book please share, spread the word, and post a review at your favourite store and GoodReads:

Books2Read.com/sop

GoodReads: bit.ly/2LihFPJ

This will really help me improve my work, and help other readers to discover the book, and explore the themes for their benefit too.

THANK YOU!

ABOUT THE BOOK

Sometimes, a book comes along which ignites a spark, which speaks to the unconscious, and stirs a deep inner knowing – this is intended as such a work. It is not designed to be shoe horned into a specific genre, although there are elements of crime mystery and romance going on here. If you liked *The Celestine Prophecy*, *The Secret*, *The Alchemist*, or *The Arrival*, then you'll love this.

Spirit of Prophecy is ultimately an adventure parable, written for all of you on a quest for spiritual insights, and those aiming to actualize the next level of human potential.

Some of it may seem a little farfetched. All that is asked is that you keep an open mind, [events have a habit of playing catch up]. Already, computers have transformed our lives in ways which we might have dismissed in our youth as outlandish, crazy fantasies from the wildest shores of sci-fi. The pace of change going forward will be exponentially accelerated. Ahead, we have the new frontiers of Artificial Intelligence, and many other challenges and also benefits arising from technological advancement. The ego doesn't like change. It prefers what it knows to feel safe and secure. But, how do you see the world? Are you afraid of the future, or excited by it? Remember, radical change is not rare… it's the norm.

We start from a place where there's an in-built desire to believe what we know is true, and indeed that truth is the central one, and that the world is going to remain exactly the same. Also, many people are heavily invested in maintaining the status quo. Where egos are over invested in outcomes, often truth suffers or is suppressed. So, when someone or something comes along to challenge that belief by outlining a vison of the past or the future that deviates from that, we're inclined to dismiss it, even if the alternative is better!

Some of the greatest inventors in human history, for example Tesla, had ideas which were considered bizarre, even 'out there.' Sir Fred Hoyle believed in panspermia. In 2013, two scientists working on the Human Genome project argued that 97% of non-coding sequences in human DNA is genetic code from alien life forms – and this was intentional not accidental. They also concluded that evolution is not entirely what Darwin thought it was, or as a consequence, what we may think it is. The pair of scientists from Kazakhstan published 'Icarus,' their research theory that our species was created by a higher power, a more advanced alien civilization, and the ET's signed the genetic code with the number 37. As with Hoyle before them, they were ridiculed, and their ideas were debunked, and branded as crazy. The alien origination detractors grew annoyed, believing that somehow mankind is dumbed down by this theory. Not so, of course. Mankind has advanced, and increased vastly in sophistication, and deserves much credit for the multitude of awesome, incredible accomplishments.

However, it only takes a few amongst you, the visionaries, to believe, and kick start the process so that new concepts can take hold and gradually become accepted as normal. Even the Vatican has been positive about aliens for years, with Pope Francis offering to baptize Martians. Now that would be some serious christening party, eh?

So, here's to the new norm. This story is offered as a nudge towards the new understanding, the new paradigm. If it resonates with you, please spread the word, so that we can all collectively learn and grow.

Please post a review on your favourite store after reading the novel:

Books2Read.com/sop

Spirit of
Prophecy

CHAPTER ONE

Magic is just science that we don't understand yet.
Arthur C. Clarke.

Rosetta
19th December 2021

Sleep, Rosetta told herself, as she burrowed deep under the duck down duvet. *It was a time of rest and rejuvenation, right?*

Wrong.

For starters, she couldn't actually get to sleep. It was a classic catch-22 situation which so far, no amount of hot baths followed by endless mugs of cocoa would fix. As for calm inducing essential oils, obviously she'd been there, tried that. It had now reached the point where one whiff of camomile made her want to puke. She lay on her back staring at the ceiling, thinking how weird it was that when your eyes adjusted, they could perceive different shades of blackness in the dark. *Spooky*, she thought, *how the mind would begin to interpret things which the eyes struggled to see. Like those grey swirls of nothingness lurking near the window.* Just thinking about it made her skin grow prickly.

'Shit!' she gasped as something darted out of the corner. God forbid it was heading towards the end of the bed. A horrible surge of anticipation made her catch her breath. As soon as the thing landed on the bed with a soft, ominous thud, she knew she'd made a mistake moving into this flat. It backed onto a wooded copse, and fuck knows what lurked in that. Heart pounding, Rosetta slithered under the duvet, covered her head, and clamped her eyes tight shut. A slight

1

rancid smell of stale smoke and perspiration reached her nose, and she realised that death smelled like this only a lot, lot worse. Right now, the recurring nightmare didn't seem nearly so bad; that was mere spectator sport compared to this. The thing was padding across the duvet, and it was heading her way, intent on evil. What if it drained her life force? The knot in her stomach tightened, and then her guts began to churn. The silence in the room was heavy and oppressive. She decided she didn't fancy hanging around to find out what the thing had planned. No, she had to escape, and get out fast. In a whoosh, she flung the duvet off, leapt out of bed, and hit the light switch. Atone, her large black cat, blinked, his eyes glowing yellow as he stared at her with a bemused look on his face which said: *Rats, and stone the crows, what's all the fuss about?* Realising he was the zombie-like thing that had landed on her bed, Rosetta let out a sigh of relief and chuckled at her own drama queen stuff. She scrambled back into bed. For a while she scratched the cat's chin. Soon he began to dribble and purr, and against all odds she finally drifted off to sleep.

And then it began, as always; running on and on, repeat. Rewind. Here it comes again, the never-ending nightmare.

Around five hours later, Rosetta woke up with a jolt. The premonition of something terrible about to happen began unravelling in her mind yet again.

'Help, get help!' her scream reverberated harshly into the darkness. No help arrived, no backup came.

'No,' Rosetta gasped, 'stop.' The real hell was about to begin. Terrible images tumbled through her mind: the horse rearing, tyres screeching, and the twisted metal of a car. The smell of smoke filled her nostrils, and then… then… the high-pitched shrieking started. Dripping in sweat, she threw back the duvet and gasped for breath. She needed air, and little by little, part of her brain realised that the image wasn't real, it would pass. Gradually her laboured breathing slowed, and got back to normal, whatever that was. She sat up in bed and rubbed her eyes, blinking at the luminous green numerals on the radio alarm clock. She'd woken at 5:22 a.m. on the dot again, but this time it had a sinister finality to it. The attack would happen soon unless she did something.

But what?

What was she supposed to do? With a heavy sigh, she swung her bare legs over the edge of the mattress. Her feet found her slippers of their own accord. From the end of the bed, Atone, her familiar, opened one eye and emitted an indignant high-pitched meow, but otherwise he didn't stir. Rosetta rolled her neck from side to side, desperate to relieve the tension that had taken hold. *If only Daniel was here to offer support,* she thought. He would massage her neck, and more... but he was undercover somewhere. Maybe he was in Pakistan, or Lord knows where. Anyway, for weeks now, contact between them had been limited: actually non-existent. They knew when they signed up for the project with the Office of the Director of National Intelligence, and when they'd taken the Oath of the Galactic Realms, that on occasion, they would be required to sacrifice their personal lives for the ultimate cause. But this was the first time they'd been apart for so long, and now her muscles ached from the sleep that yet again had delivered zero rest.

She'd experienced too much sleep deprivation; a total bummer this. It was torture after all.

Not for the first time since she'd been recruited by the Elite Paranormal Intelligence Service, or EPIS as they were called, she wondered if the sacrifice was really worth it. The pay was decent enough, but her work was all-consuming, talk about being married to the job. She could be posted anywhere in the world, which meant she couldn't provide a settled home life for her two children. Also, being a regular police officer and working for EPIS meant she didn't really fit in anywhere. Right now, what she longed for was some rest. Horrible as the vision was, it wasn't exactly a matter of national security. Life and death, yes, but an accident on a country road was relatively low-key. Rosetta rolled her neck, trying to ease the tension that threatened to unleash a bad headache. There must be far more buried, something sinister further back, and ultimately that was the crime to be absolved and atoned. But when did it occur and what exactly took place?

The temperature in the room had dropped sharply, which set her shivering. So, she hurried over to the door to grab the thick dressing gown hanging from a hook. Wrapping herself in it, she sensed that time was running out. She'd been having the same nightmare for two weeks now, belting out in her sleep like a cheap Christmas CD stuck on a loop. She knew her premonitions could go either way, and sometimes the outcome wasn't entirely signed, sealed, and delivered, so things could be prevented, altered, maybe even diverted. This precognitive vision fell into the preventable category. Rosetta sighed, trying to make sense of things as she headed for the bathroom across the hall. The inevitable ones were easier, as there was nothing she could do to alter events, but this kind required her involvement. Somehow, she had to figure out who the victims were and get a warning to them before it was too late. It became a kind of crime prevention in a way, she supposed. The foot soldiers in the force would investigate the who, the what, the how. But it was her job to intervene and stop serious incidents happening where ever possible, but the over-arching mission was to determine the BIG 'why'. Why do some crimes which defy sanity or reason have a thread to be unravelled and followed to the source in order to discover the real karmic cause? However things appeared on the surface, she had to determine how events in past lives had impacted the present.

The bathroom mirror had disappeared behind a shroud of mist. In the corner she'd stuck her affirmations on yellow Post-it notes: *Your words are your wand. You're a star! You're the best, always rate yourself.* Rosetta wiped the surface clear with the sleeve of her dressing gown. She recoiled at the sight. *Yuck.* Her lustrous dark auburn hair shot out in random unruly spikes from what was best described as a halo of frizz – a seriously bad case of bed hair. Fit, fabulous, and forty, was supposedly the new twenty-something. Really, who were they kidding? Apart from the plastic surgeons, her gay best friend, her mum, and maybe her Aunty Mabel, who really believed that shit? Her eyes weren't too bad, big, bright emerald green and almond shaped, framed with thick lustrous lashes. Rosetta blinked as she huddled over the sink and splashed cold water over her face. She longed for a hot shower to ward off the cold and soak away the aches and pains of another long night. But there was too much to do, too much at stake, and a deadline looming.

She headed downstairs to the kitchen and lingered in her study over a large mug of black coffee. What she really needed, post the welcome caffeine hit, was inspiration. She stared into the cup that now contained only dregs and grounds, it had been drained. *Just like me,* she thought wearily.

Fourteen nights of interrupted sleep, imagine torture and then some.

Screw it, she thought, *I've got to do something.* An adrenaline rush cut through her exhaustion, and Rosetta set about retracing her thoughts going over the things she'd seen. At some point in the nightmare she recalled that she'd been plotting to 'do in' Peter, her evil ex. *Hmmm, dreaming of revenge, nothing new there, then?* Still, she could always cast a spell on him, but then she chuckled to herself. *Now that would be a waste of a perfectly good spell, wouldn't it?* Why did Peter suddenly appear? Was there some significance? He now had a new wife with a neat blonde bob, who played tennis, and frequently flashed her tight butt at the coach, no doubt. This Patricia woman, who had flaunted herself at Peter, whipped her knickers off – *whoosh* – and was rewarded with an expense account, a McMansion which had once been Rosetta's matrimonial home, plus her darling kids came as part of the package. Rosetta sighed at the sheer bloody injustice of it. *Focus,* she chastised herself, shaking her head. She was digressing, and she needed to think straight, so she checked her notebook. What else? Ah yes. She'd dreamed about rewriting the ending of *Wuthering Heights*, about Cathy and Heathcliff.

Rosetta opened her dream journal and scribbled this down, and added: *The Yorkshire moors, the cobbled main street of Howarth, the parsonage where the Brontë family lived, the graveyard opposite.*

What was she missing?

Jane Eyre... Rochester. Guardian Angels, give me a clue, please.

Novels, novelists, what had that got to do with it? She got up, and flipped the switch on the kettle, refilling her cup once it had boiled, and all the while her brain began circling like a hawk about to swoop on an unsuspecting field mouse. She took another glug of the strong stuff. Then it came to her in a flash. *Gothic novels. Gothic.* Swiftly, propelled by a sense of urgency, and mounting apprehension, she darted back into the study. She plonked herself in the office chair, a smart ergonomic one with backrest and neck support. After she got herself comfortable she flipped the lid of her laptop which she positioned on the left side of the desk, then she switched on the Mac PC, and logged into the Eclipse system.

As she typed, words in the violet spectrum appeared on the screen:

Charlotte Brontë
Emily Brontë

Graveyard
Gothic
Wuthering Heights
Jane Eyre

Eclipse presented images in 3D, an incredible visual collage, on an interactive whiteboard that filled half of the office's main wall. For the clairaudient, there was an optional sound dimension, currently switched off, and for the clairsentient, Eclipse could be programmed to create atmospheres and emotions. Simultaneously Eclipse sent prompts to the Mac screen:

Charlotte Brontë, born 21st April 1816 – died 31st March 1855
Emily Brontë, born 30th July 1818 – died 19th December 1848

Is this significant?
Rosetta drew a sharp intake of breath as she typed: *Yes – today is the 19th December.*
Eclipse reconfigured:

Emily Brontë
Dies: 19th December of tuberculosis
TB
Gothic
Wuthering Heights

The Eclipse extrasensory database was the most sophisticated in the world. EPIS employed only prophets, masters, and adepts, the caretakers of the secrets yet to manifest. They also had incredible predictive architecture systems, and Rosetta never ceased to be amazed at the possibilities Eclipse came up with.

She typed: *configure possibilities, priority = 'urgent'* and pressed the Enter key.

On a conscious level, what Eclipse came up with seemed bizarre in the extreme, but to her subconscious, it made perfect sense.

Gothic – four-star event horse, Irish Thoroughbred – TB
Dies: 19th December 2021.

'Shit,' Rosetta muttered, scraping a strand of hair off her face. *Not if I can bloody well help it.*

She typed furiously, *Call someone.* Her index finger jabbed the Enter key.

Owner or rider? Eclipse asked helpfully.

Both. She stabbed out the instruction. *Now!*

On command, Eclipse started dialling like an ultra-sophisticated Echo device. Rosetta checked her watch, 6:45 a.m. *Come on, come on,* she prayed to herself, *answer the God damn phone. No one calls you at this Godforsaken hour, unless it's urgent. Pick up the phone, please.* She drummed her fingers on the desktop and checked her watch again. She hated being late, and she really needed to get ready for work. She couldn't be a no-show, as she was leading a training session for over twenty officers. But she had to warn the riders. The dilemma made her breathing quicken, and she cleared her throat several times.

I'm torn, as in should I stay, or should I go? she pondered this as she scratched her chin. *I know, leave a message and tell Eclipse to broadcast it. Ok, here goes.*

'Hi, this is Rosetta, DS Rosetta Barrett. Please listen carefully, get off the road, now! There's a car crash about to happen. The driver will try and mow you down. Call me back urgently, please.' She replayed the message, satisfied that if the horse rider picked up or dialled back she'd at least know what to expect. With a sigh of relief, Rosetta hurried to the bathroom and dived in the shower.

Later, still dripping and wrapped in a towel, she went to the study to see if the outgoing call had connected. So far, no luck, Eclipse was still dialling out as she headed to the bedroom. Ditching the towel and grabbing a dark navy suit complete with a pale pink shirt, she quickly got dressed, ready to go to work at Yorrex police station. The training session kicked off at 8:30 a.m., so she couldn't hang around too long. She checked the Eclipse call display status message, one more time. Still no luck, but the system was synched to her mobile so at least she wouldn't miss anything.

It occurred to her that the situation was too ominous to leave to chance. The best thing would be to send a couple of uniforms out to the rider's home address. After a few minutes Eclipse came up with: *Luckenham Park, YO6 7DD.*

'Phew, thanks.' She sighed with relief as she called the station to dispatch someone as a matter of urgency.

Rosetta pulled on a pair of black designer boots, knotted a scarf round her neck, and was about to leave. Then she changed her mind, dashed upstairs, and grabbed the duvet off the bed, dislodging Atone in the process. The haughty cat looked rather peeved. Rosetta dashed downstairs and rattled his food dish. Predictably, he swiftly graced the kitchen with his presence, and wound himself between her legs, announcing his arrival with his distinctive raspy mewling.

'Out-the-way, oh mighty Mouser,' she said, bending down to stroke the top of his head. She cleared her throat as she stuffed the duvet in a black plastic bag. 'Right, off to the dry cleaners with you.'

With that, she let herself out the back door, locked it behind her, set the home security system via her mobile, and scurried to her car. Clicking the remote, she chucked the bin bag on the back seat of her car. She thought about the prophetic dream which had the potential to ruin Christmas for an awful lot of people. One minute they're just riding down a quiet country lane, and the next, normality is flipped over into blood, guts, and hospital visits. Outside, daylight hadn't yet penetrated the thick blanket of grey fog, and Rosetta cursed when she realised that all the car windows were caked with ice. After a furious rummage under the passenger seat, she unearthed the de-icer spray and went on the attack. Then she sat in the car with the heater blaring, trying to clear the icy mist on the inside as she pondered the motive. There was a growing trend where vehicles were used as lethal weapons. ISIS and Al Qaeda had called for followers to use trucks and 4X4s as weapons – the ultimate mowing machines to cut down the enemies of Allah. Was this incident terrorist motivated or inspired?

With a knot in her stomach, she wondered how the day would unfold. Sometimes unexpected things happened, and the reasons were only revealed with the passing of time. Rosetta shook her head as she remembered their call to the cause: *if you can make a bomb you're a bomber. But if you can't, use a gun or a knife. And if you can't find a knife, use a car.* Innocent victims lined up like skittles. Would there be enough time to warn them, or would she be too late?

'Please, God, spare them,' she whispered under her breath.

CHAPTER TWO

Peter
19th December

The children, Alice and Edward, argued over the TV remote control. Each shriek and yowl which erupted from the breakfast room tightened his nerves like a band of brittle steel. Why did they have to have a TV in every room, for Christ's sake? Nowadays, if they weren't glued to Netflix, they were texting on their iPhones, bought courtesy of Bank of Dad, or uploading Lord knows what onto Instagram or Snapchat. Even one of the senior Facebook former employees said social media was ruining society.

Too bloody right, Peter Marshall thought, *social cohesion my arse.* He couldn't stand it any longer. He gritted his teeth and the painful knots across his shoulders shot down his arms, contorting his hands into fists. *Teenagers,* he thought, shaking his head. *Why don't they ever act like responsible human beings? A bit of respect would be nice for a change.* In fact, he was going to bloody well insist on it.

He pushed the cereal bowl away and sighed. The trouble was that Patricia just didn't rule them with a firm enough hand. They weren't her children, so that didn't help, but she overindulged them and had no idea about discipline. She found it easier just to give in – couldn't be arsed with the arguments, no doubt. As soon as they got to St. Petersburg and he had more time, he would take them all to task. Peter rose and pushed his stool away from the central island so roughly it scraped across the wooden floor.

He winced, temples throbbing, as he made his way to the utility room where the medicines were kept. After a rummage in the cupboard, it became apparent that no aspirins remained, only the empty foil with all the bubbles popped.

'Damn it,' he muttered. Why couldn't Patricia get things organised? *Damn her.* He provided for the family, and she ought to jolly well get these things sorted. Standards had to be maintained. What on earth did she do all day, anyway? *It wasn't as if she was the one who'd been woken up in the middle of the night by the phone call from the States,* he thought bitterly. *How would she like Commander General Rathbone, who reported directly to the President, yelling down the phone at her in the middle of the bloody night?*

What an arrogant jerk. Why are Americans so infuriating? They elect actors and TV reality stars as presidents yet think they're superior – how does that work exactly? Then he chuckled. *After all, the world was a stage, so maybe they had a point?*

Presumably, his position in proximity to power made Rathbone feel justified in barking orders and demanding confirmation from the British Intelligence sources that the Russians had hacked the Pentagon. What bloody cheek. It reminded him of Obama's fit of pique in 2016 when he'd expelled all thirty-five Russian diplomats. *I mean really, if the Kremlin had hacked US national security, quite feasible this, why not just get their house in order and maybe hire the young autistic British hacker lad to seriously upgrade their spyware? Russo-West relations were supposed to improve post the cold-war, but what with the former Russian spy nerve gassed in Salisbury and the like, it hadn't quite panned out that way. Who'd want my job, the diplomatic equivalent of a raging Ebola epidemic, he wondered with a sigh? Mind you he'd been lucky to escape the firing line after Mrs. May followed Obama's lead and she too expelled diplomats.* Needless to say, with Rathbone's ranting, followed by Patricia's snoring, Peter hadn't got much sleep.

It didn't seem possible, but the noise in the breakfast room had risen in volume. He poked his head through the archway and glared pointedly.

'Will you two be quiet!' he yelled. His head throbbed, and he felt quite drained.

The children fell silent for a moment until Alice stuck her tongue out and Edward retaliated.

'For Christ's sake, sit down, the pair of you, and finish your break-fasts,' he snapped. Peter dealt with everyone the same way: he yelled, and invariably they listened.

Alice arched an immaculately threaded eyebrow. 'Did you know Mum's been in touch? She's in the UK, in Yorrex, working with the local police.'

Peter made no attempt to hide his contempt. 'What does she want, the –' he stopped himself just in time. Abusive thoughts and Rosetta were hard to separate. Oddly enough, he'd dreamed about the mad bitch only last night until the phone call had woken him up. Thank God.

'She wants to meet. She's got our Christmas presents.'

'Absolutely not, I forbid it.'

Alice opened her mouth to protest but then thought better of it.

'Heaven forbid, what on earth's the matter with you? You've been in a foul mood all weekend.' Patricia assumed her most martyred expression as she deposited a stack of cereal bowls into the sink and attacked them with Fairy Liquid.

Peter shot her a look of pure contempt. She had no idea of the pressure he was under with the latest Kremlin vs Whitehouse spat, leaving him dancing a fine line along a very precarious tightrope. Yet she cared nothing for any of this. He let out an exasperated sigh. What was the point of trying to explain? Patricia, his former PA and now his second wife, would never understand. She'd been a decent enough PA, an expert at blow jobs, but now her life consisted of school runs, lunches, and tennis tournaments. As for the blow jobs, they were a bonus long since forgotten, of course.

'I don't know why I bother paying the fees to send these two to private school. They don't teach them any manners at all. Complete waste of bloody money, and if you two don't learn how to behave properly, you'll be off to Glebels.' He could have added that educating both his children privately was a great asset for them and a serious financial sacrifice for him and the Foreign Office, but there didn't seem much point. Peter sighed and took a large swig of lukewarm coffee.

Alice pulled a face and stuck her tongue out at the prospect of attending the local sink-pit comprehensive. Perhaps it would do them good? Let them have it hard for a change. Lord knew he hadn't had any privileges himself, born and dragged up on the infamous Hoylem Estate in Glasgow, and he'd clawed his way up inch by inch.

Peter glanced at his watch and cursed under his breath. If he was sharpish, he might catch the 7:35 a.m. fast train. Not that he usually gave train timetables much thought. Ordinarily he flew home from Russia for the odd weekend, and there would be a chauffeur-driven limo at his beck and call. But today the limo driver had phoned, complaining about a five-mile traffic jam on the M29, and consequently Peter had decided to take the train and sample the commuter misery that he'd read so much about in the dailies. Anyway, it would give him a good excuse to berate Spiers, the incompetent Minister of Transport.

'Where've you put my briefcase?'

Patricia scowled. 'I haven't touched it. It's probably in the study where you left it.'

After a rummage in his office Peter found his briefcase, snatched it up, and slammed the door behind him.

CHAPTER THREE

Juliet
19th December

The day began with promise but ended with a full stop the colour of blood.

When Juliet Jermaine came to the end of the bridle path, she steered left towards the road, dropping one rein to fiddle with her jacket zip. The raw air stung her cheeks, and she drew in a sharp breath. Ahead, on the telegraph wires, two magpies perched, hanging in the air like elevated music notes.

'One for sorrow, two for joy,' she muttered through clenched teeth. One of the magpies cocked its head as if observing her progress. As the other magpie took flight the wire reverberated, dislodging a pair of fang-like icicles that hurled to the ground and shattered. Startled, Juliet braced her back, and gave the reins a squeeze so that her horse, Icon, came to a halt. Above, on the quivering wire, a large ominous-looking bird, black as a witch's cat, took up its sentry post. *A raven*, she thought as it emitted a loud squawk. In Greek mythology they were associated with prophecy. With a tiny shudder, she turned to check on Isabella.

'You okay?' Juliet called. The teenager's black velvet cap bobbed up and down. A nod, she assumed, although Isabella's pretty face looked paler than usual, and her straight blonde hair spilled out from her hat in a crazy flurry. Gothic, the magnificent white stallion, bounded towards his stable companion in a series of bunny hops.

'Yikes, is he always this fresh?' Isabella's expression was determined, but her voice sounded hollow, and thin.

Maybe they should turn back, Juliet wondered, but with Tracy the

13

groom off sick, she had so much to do. All the horses needed exercising to get fit, ready for the start of the competition season in March. Juliet hoped the road would be quiet. The last thing they needed was a bunch of trailer trucks whizzing past. Just then Gothic sprang alongside them with a clatter of hooves.

'Argh,' Isabella gasped, her eyes widening. 'I'm worried I won't be able to control him.'

Juliet nudged Icon onwards with her heels. Predictably, Gothic leapt forwards with an almighty snort.

'That's why I put him in the gag snaffle, just in case you need extra brakes.' *Serious stopping tackle, this.* She mentally checked the bit that comprised three hanging circles of metal. She had attached the reins to the second ring to afford Isabella more control and brakes. Gothic started chomping on it and tossing his head. *Terrific, trust him to get himself worked up.* They continued at a brisk trot.

'Whoa.' Juliet braced her back to signal Icon to stop at the end of the drive. She sensed that he was not going to, so she blocked with her hands and sat deeper into the saddle. Icon responded by rearing up. He paddled his jet-black forelegs in the air, conducting an invisible orchestra with his feet. Juliet coaxed him back down to earth with a series of tugs on the reins. However, the second his front hooves touched the ground, he lunged forwards and shot halfway across the road, then changed his mind, twisting in corkscrew fashion, ducking, and diving all the while as he tried to get back towards the drive.

Juliet gasped as the horse keeled over to the right, lurching sideways on the frosty asphalt. *Thank heavens,* she thought, as he staggered back the other way, and managed to right himself and regain his footing. *That was a close shave.*

'Steady, boy.' Juliet gave him a pat. Instinctively, she turned to check on Isabella and Gothic.

'Take it easy. I can't risk either of these two going down on the road.' She had a peculiar apprehensive sensation knotting the pit of her stomach. She checked her watch: 9:45 a.m. They'd left later than usual, hoping the frost and ice would thaw, but maybe it was still too early?

Isabella peered at the ground, tension etched on her face as Gothic pranced along, tossing his head and snorting.

'It's a long way down.' A faint quiver in her tone betrayed her nerves.

'He can take care of himself. He won gold at Tokyo last year, re-

14

member?' Juliet said in a pacifying tone. 'Three years to the next Olympics, and here we come.'

'Yes, but…' Isabella spluttered. 'I mean, he's so valuable and well, he's a stallion… Is it safe?'

'Don't worry. Gothic will take care of you. He's a perfect gentleman, but if Icon were human, I reckon he'd be a supermodel, or maybe a tennis brat.' She flashed a broad smile at the young girl, then, on hearing a vehicle approaching, turned and craned her neck. 'Oh, move over, cargo van coming.'

She waved Isabella onto the grass verge and signalled for the vehicle to pass. It inched forward, one of those do-it-yourself hire vans. Icon rolled his eyes and shook his mane, reminding her of a petulant king signalling to his cringing courtiers. It made her chuckle. The driver crawled past, nice and wide, and Juliet flashed him a dazzling smile.

Meanwhile Gothic decided to act up and came to an abrupt halt. A bout of furious kicking by Isabella, a tall but slight thirteen-year-old, had no effect at all. Gothic planted himself and refused to budge as he peered through a gap in the hedge into a wide murky ditch beyond. *Holy shit,* Juliet thought as she scanned the prickly hawthorn, a stonker of a hedge, the kind guaranteed to sort the men from the boys out on the hunting field. Then something caught her eye, a glint of silver amongst the green.

Razor wire.

Mo-fo, she thought. *If Gothic spooks and leaps forwards, he'll run right through the wire.*

Disaster.

And Isabella might get slammed bang in the middle of the hedge. She might break her neck… her back…

'Pick your reins up! Turn his head away from the hedge. Good. Now kick him on,' Juliet barked. She'd seen a horse caught up in wire once. Horrific – flesh ripped to the bone with blood spurting everywhere. The more the poor animal had struggled, the more the barbs had taken hold. She shuddered at the prospect.

'I can't, he won't,' Isabella wailed, as the stallion gathered himself together and pricked his ears. Her eyes catapulted open. 'Oh no, he's going to jump.'

The nice quiet hack to Halfway Heights was not turning out quite as envisaged. Juliet gnawed her lip and her mind raced. Gothic could easily clear the ditch with her on board, but Isabella might not manage it. The only thing was to try to distract him.

15

Quickly.

'Yank the right rein in really short. That's it, get his nose around.'

Suddenly, a pheasant crashed out of the undergrowth, emitting a loud *phwork, phwork* distress call. It scuttled in front of them, first this way, then that.

'Jeez,' Juliet muttered under her breath. 'That's all we need, a pheasant with a death wish.'

Gothic gave an almighty snort and sprang about six feet into the air.

'Aargh... help!' Isabella shrieked, wobbling and pitching sideways out of the saddle.

'Quick, grab hold of his mane and get yourself back up!' Juliet commanded. Meanwhile, her mount, the highly-strung Icon, tossed his head and bounced up and down on the spot like a homicidal balloon.

Somehow Isabella managed to haul herself upright.

'Good job, Spiderwoman,' Juliet encouraged, as Isabella slumped in the saddle with a traumatised expression etched on her face.

'He's pretty fresh this morning,' Juliet said. *Understatement of the year*, she thought. 'Hmm, we'll get off the road and take the track along the ridge.' The tension in Juliet's neck muscles eased a fraction, but it occurred to her that perhaps they ought to turn back. For some reason, the bad feeling had returned. At that moment, her cell phone rang. With difficulty she fished the iPhone out of its holder and glanced at the screen: *unknown caller*. Probably some robot telemarketer from Nigeria or Pakistan, so Juliet hit the red *End Call* button.

CHAPTER FOUR

Juliet

'Are you okay?' Juliet yelled.

Isabella managed a tiny gesture that sufficed for a nod, so Juliet decided to carry on, nudging Icon into a brisk trot. The powerful gelding arched his neck and dropped his nose in response to Juliet's quiet signals. As the horse's hindquarters swung rhythmically from side to side, her thoughts drifted. Her cell phone rattled off, shrill and insistent, the same thing again, a blocked number. Irritated, she turned the phone off and sent Icon into a burst of trotting. Interval training, especially up hills, was good for improving a horse's fitness level. After a while, she realised that Gothic wasn't keeping up. She twisted in the saddle and saw Isabella fiddling with her chinstrap.

'What the heck are you doing?' Then, as Isabella removed her hat, Juliet's tone crackled with a mounting sense of urgency. 'Be careful! For God's sake, put your hat back on!'

* * *

The winter sun hovered low in the sky. The driver yanked the visor down but still had to squint to see the road. The lane was full of twists and hairpin bends, not to mention potholes. The safe, solid Range Rover presented little problem, and although it tended to roll a bit at speed, it handled fine at fifty miles per hour. He took the bend in a smooth glide and scrunched his eyelids as the full impact of the sun's rays hit him in the face. He blinked repeatedly as he struggled to adjust his vision. His foot accidentally pumped the accelerator, and the vehicle lunged forward, picking up speed. Suddenly, the sun lifted, and he saw blurred shapes. It took a while to recognise them as horses. A white one and a black one, side by side like pieces on a chess board.

'Shit. Where the hell did they come from?' His brain whirred, trying to work it out. They weren't supposed to be here now. *WTF? They must have set off earlier than anticipated.*

Without him thinking about it, his foot moved to the brake and the heel of his hand hit the horn with an ominous bleat.

The horses' rumps loomed up fast.

What a load of crap, he thought, gripping the steering wheel with sweaty palms.

One of the riders turned in the saddle and scowled. As the Range Rover hit ice and slithered sideways into a skid, the rider's expression changed to fear. His mind raced. Out here on this stretch the roads hadn't been gritted. How on earth could he reduce his speed without losing control? His stomach lurched as he dropped down a gear, and he eased the steering wheel a fraction back to the right.

Towards the horses.

If he overcorrected, the car would go into a spin and slam through the grey stone wall that jutted out of the ground like a row of neglected tombstones. He'd end up in the ditch, as had happened once to a mate of his. A bad number, that – life support, a ventilator, you name it. *Keep calm,* he told himself. He engaged the clutch and dropped down another gear, beads of perspiration breaking out on his forehead. The Range Rover's engine growled as it drew level with the horses.

'Get off the road. God damn you, you idiots. Move!' His pulse throbbed. 'Too close, too close,' he muttered. The wing mirror clipped a stirrup.

Metal on metal.

He checked the speedometer, willing it to drop.

At last. Thank the Lord.

Finally, the horses disappeared from his peripheral vision. He eased the car back onto the right side of the road. He let out a sigh of relief and wiped the sweat from his brow with the back of his palm. In the rear view mirror, he saw the horses skittering across the road. He couldn't risk taking them out here – too damn icy – he'd tackle them a bit farther along where the road had been gritted. He'd checked the route earlier on one of the many reconnaissance missions. Leave nothing to chance. He was thorough, and he didn't plan on getting caught. Not this time.

'What?' he gasped in disbelief as the girl on the black horse shook her fist. He eased off the accelerator and sat upright with a jolt.

'What the devil?' He peered at the rider's image again. He recognised her from somewhere. He'd encountered that lip-curling challenge to his authority before, but where? He racked his brain, trying to recall a fragment of memory.

The rider mouthed the F-word and tossed her head.

'Pah! You stuck-up cow!' The muscles in his neck strained, and his face contorted. Something welled up deep inside, something old and primitive.

Hatred.

Two hot flares shot up his cheeks as his blood pressure soared. He slammed on the brakes until the pads bit together with a furious shriek. The force of the emergency stop pitched the Range Rover forwards with a screech, slewing the front end onto the grass verge. He braced himself against the steering wheel.

'Right, it's over, bitches! Now you'll be sorry – you're dead meat.' His eyes narrowed to slits. A tiny speck of white spittle hit the windscreen. He rammed the gear stick into reverse and pumped the accelerator. The Range Rover shot backwards.

'Ha!' he laughed gleefully as he checked the mirror and saw the anger evaporate from the rider's face. Her angry expression gave way to one of total confusion. The surge of a testosterone rush kicked in when her eyes widened in panic.

'Yes, taste the fear, bitch. I'll teach you to mess with me. I'm the man.'

* * *

A wave of shock and disbelief rose in Juliet's chest. Her breathing came in short, harsh bursts. She stiffened in horror as the car hurtled towards them in reverse. For several moments she remained motionless, not believing what she was seeing. *He isn't really trying to run us over, is he? Any second, the car will stop,* she reassured herself. The horse quivered beneath her, and she sensed his desperate urge to flee. *Once a horse runs for its life, everything it's ever learnt is forgotten. Icon will bolt with no sense of anything that might get in his way.* She had to keep calm, make him feel safe. Surely the driver would stop in time?

But the car picked up speed. The jerk-off had his foot to the gas.

'What the hell are you doing?' she yelled. 'For Christ's sake, stop!' The Range Rover's progress seemed relentless.

19

Isabella looked dazed and confused as Gothic tried compressing himself against the hedge. His eyes sprang wide open in panic and foam spilled from his mouth. He was panting in quick nervy bursts.

'Isabella, Isabella! Move!'

She didn't seem to hear. Juliet screwed her eyes tight shut.

'Think, focus, breathe,' she commanded. 'Get a grip.'

When she opened her eyes, nothing had changed, and she knew with gut-wrenching certainty that the driver was not going to stop of his own accord. There was no sidewalk, and the hedge would not offer enough protection to save them. Her breathing quickened. The harsh rasp of the Range Rover's engine filled her ears. By now, it was less than thirty metres away. *Not only do these dumbasses drive on the wrong side of the highway, they can barely work an automatic.* Juliet shook her head and swivelled her neck around, searching for an escape route. Agitation gripped her in the pit of the stomach. If she and Icon jumped the hedge, Gothic might follow. After all, horses were herd animals. With a professional's eye, she assessed the hedge at around five feet high, but a horse of his calibre could clear it from a standstill.

Twenty metres.

An outside chance, but she had to try. She had to save them. What could she do? *Please God, I need your help.* She screwed her eyes tight shut.

'You motherfucker, why don't you stop?' she wailed.

Isabella's sobs turned into a pitiful mewling sound as fear gave way to sheer panic.

Something inside Juliet snapped. The look on Isabella's pale, wretched face stirred up her protective instincts. Teeth gritted, and jaws clenched, she kicked Icon's sides like something gone demented.

'Icon, you pig. Move!' she howled. Every sinew, every muscle in her neck and shoulders strained with the effort, but Icon refused to budge. She went weak with nervous tension, and somewhere under her ribs a wave of panic surged.

'Isabella, move. Damn it. Get out of the way. Jump!'

The vehicle homed in, the trunk looming towards them.

Isabella and Gothic remained rooted to the spot. Juliet let out a whimper of dismay. No time to clear the jump. Only one alternative remained.

Juliet took a deep breath, pressed her booted calves against Icon's flanks and squeezed with all her might. She must get between them and save Isabella and Gothic from the worst of the impact.

This time Icon responded.

Thank the Lord.

She felt the energy gathering in his haunches. The crest of his powerful neck rose up in front of her as he sprang towards his stable companion.

* * *

The black horse leapt sideways towards the white one. The driver registered confusion for a second or two. It appeared to be the equine equivalent of a suicide mission. The stupid cow had deliberately tried to block his path. *How dare she?* He slammed his foot onto the accelerator pedal so hard the engine let out a high-pitched squeal.

'Damn you,' he spat as the black horse twisted itself clear at the very last minute with a peculiar corkscrewing movement. His anger intensified, and it made him even more determined to inflict some damage on the remaining pair. He had to take the target out, otherwise he'd fail, and his family didn't do failure. The big white horse stood on its hind legs, twisting and contorting in a desperate bid to escape. He wanted them wiped out, obliterated, then all his problems would be solved.

A loud *thud* rocked the car.

A high-pitched shriek pierced the air. Everything blurred out of focus. He blinked in quick succession until he could just make out the jerky image of the horse careering sideways. He caught a glimpse of the rider, her mouth wide with fear as the animal toppled over. It crashed through the hedge towards a wide ditch.

'*Yes!*' He punched the air and let out a whoop. He'd done it, he delivered. Only then did he apply the brakes. 'Ha!'

A wonderful wave of excitement washed over him. Job done! By God, putting rich, privileged a-holes in their place was a sweet thing after all. Serve them right for looking down on him and his sort. He rammed the car into first and drove off at speed with a huge grin spreading across his face.

* * *

A sound hung on the air, a terrible high-pitched scream that would haunt her dreams forever. Juliet hung onto Icon's mouth. His whole body quivered, and terror erupted in the whites of his eyes. She yanked on the reins, battling to get his attention.

Can't let him bolt, hang on to him. The mantra ran through her mind.

21

Icon's ears flattened against his skull, and Juliet realised that if he couldn't go forward, he'd probably stand up, maybe even throw himself over backwards, crushing her in the process. She swallowed, her mouth parched and filled with a taste that reminded her of two-day-old garlic. She hauled the right rein in until his nose rammed against the toe of her boot. Now the only place he could go was round in a circle. She held him like that until little by little his fear begin to evaporate.

'There, good boy,' she croaked, licking her parched lips and gulping. Where in the name of God was Issie? Her heart crashed against her ribs, and another wave of panic surged. Surely, they must have jumped clear? Her heart slowed a fraction as she twisted in the saddle. Panic swept over her, leaving her drenched in a cold sweat. *Please, God, let them be safe.* She had never wanted anything so much in all her life. Out of the corner of her eye, she thought she saw something move.

Her stomach gave a queasy rumble. She sniffed the cold country air and screwed up her nose. The arid pungent aroma of sweat mixed with fear made her feel nauseous.

In the ditch, something twitched.

A horse's leg.

Don't be silly, she told herself. The horse's leg is over there, in the middle of the road, a white foreleg with a black hoof. The metal shoe glinted in the wintry sunlight. Her mind worked on the image again.

Juliet clamped her eyes tight shut as her thoughts pinged around like some crazy video game. The image of a gory mass of sinew, bone, and tendon erupting from the top of the bloody limb filled her mind.

No! Please God. It can't be. Her whole body shook, and her guts heaved.

'No,' she sobbed, her throat constricting until she feared she would choke.

Blood spurted a pool of scarlet across the tarmac, oozing and squirting from Gothic's freshly severed arteries. Her teeth clattered in the first wave of shock. Her stomach lurched, and its contents, jelly toast and bile, surged into her throat.

'G-Gothic?' Her face contorted as she emitted a high-pitched wail. A howl of indescribable pain.

A few minutes later, a driver stopped. Shortly afterwards, two police cars arrived at the scene, then the ambulance.

Dah-da-dah-da-dah, came the fire engine with its sirens blaring. *Thank the Lord. Help,* she thought. *Help them, please.*

22

Weak and jittery, Juliet dismounted, and one of the officers led Icon away. Her stomach churned, and her legs buckled. She clutched at the police officer's arm. As she looked at her hand, it began to shake, a slight tremor at first that soon came in uncontrollable waves.

'Shock,' another police officer explained, wrapping his jacket around her shoulders. 'Can you tell us what exactly happened?'

Juliet forced herself to recount the horrific events. She pleaded with him, 'Help them. My horse is wedged in the ditch with Isabella trapped underneath.' Her voice sounded far away, as if she was on autopilot. 'I have to c-call Michael, my vet.' She switched her cell phone back on and it went crazy with missed call messages, at least twenty pinging in rapid-fire succession. Then it started to ring, and a breathless voice came on the line.

'Juliet, is that you? My name's DS Rosetta Barrett. I've been trying to reach you all morning. Am I too late? What happened – are you okay?'

Juliet let out a deep sigh. 'Who the fuck, are you? I don't have time for this. Get off the line!' She aborted the call and dialled the vet. Then somehow, with her mind in a whirl, she managed to explain to the police officer what had happened. Next, she called her boyfriend, Matt.

'Come on, damn it. Pick up the fucking phone,' she cursed. Eventually she ended the call. Time difference, what time was it over there? He was in Miami and had probably switched the phone off when he went to bed. She paced up and down the grass verge at the side of the road with the cell phone glued to her ear. First of all, she called her parents, her best friend, Todd and then, with her heart thundering against her ribs, Orla, Isabella's sister.

'Orla,' she croaked. 'There's been an accident. Isabella and I were out riding…' Her voice cracked with emotion, and she couldn't continue.

Orla fired off a series of questions. 'What happened? Where are you?'

Juliet managed to mutter a few details.

'Where's Isabella? For the love of God, is she okay?'

'I don't know.' Juliet rocked backwards and forwards, swaying on her feet. 'I don't know. Please, just get here as soon as you can.'

The firefighters hacked a large hole in the hedge and swarmed into the ditch. Juliet wanted to rush to her horse and comfort him, but the police officer held her back.

'Now, love, don't get yourself in a state. The vet's on his way. Take a deep breath.' The officer gave her a hug. 'Look, they've got the winch round him. It won't be long now.'

Terrible images floated through her mind. 'Oh, Jeez. Jesus.'

The flickering lights from the assorted emergency service vehicles made her feel faint, and she leaned against the nearby patrol car. The early morning winter sun had disappeared behind a cloud. Dense greyness descended all around.

Metal clanked, and cogs turned as the winch engaged. Juliet forced herself to look towards the ditch. Inch by inch, they raised the twisted, mutilated body of her beautiful horse to the surface of the shallow grave.

Juliet sprinted to him. The brittle grass crunched beneath her boots and her footprints etched a trail in the silvery frost. Close up, she knew, a terrible knowing, that she could not save him now. How could she have failed them both? First it had been Totem and now Gothic. She should have turned back after the incident with the pheasant.

If only, if only…

Juliet bit her lip, desperate to contain the despair that threatened to overwhelm her. A low moaning sound escaped from her lips as her legs grew weak, and she sank to her knees. How could she bear to look at him like this? She screwed her eyes tight shut. Eventually she opened her eyes and, blinking back the tears, scratched his brow and stroked his cotton-candy mane the way she had a thousand times before. Only this time his skin was cold, and a dark green canvass shrouded his body. She took up position on the damp grass that felt as coarse as a kitchen scrubber, and, with the horse's head cradled in her lap, she rocked backwards and forwards, moaning softly.

Juliet was still slumped over Gothic's body when Michael, the vet, arrived. He touched her elbow gently to signal his presence.

'What the hell happened?' Concerned yet professionally calm, he led her away by the arm. His voice nudged her out of her daze.

A fireman removed his hat, revealing a mop of hair that was drenched with sweat, and approached her. Juliet tried to explain to Michael as best she could in between sobs.

'As bad a case of road rage as I've come across, and believe me, I've seen some real horror stories,' the fireman said, shaking his head.

'Road rage?' Michael looked aghast as it began to sink in.

'Yeah, the girls were riding down the road, and this idiot came past way too fast. Juliet waved her fist at him, and the guy flips. Shoves it into reverse and –' His words forced home the terrible inevitability of the truth.

24

'*Girls?* Why, is there someone else involved?' Michael looked at Juliet, searching her face for clues.

She nodded. 'Isabella took her hat off. I yelled at her to put it back on, but…' Tears welled in her eyes, and her mouth twisted in agony. 'Why would she do that?'

'Isabella Levine?'

Trembling, Juliet pointed towards the ditch. She grabbed Michael's arm and clutched it for support.

'Heaven forbid.' He shook his head. 'Heaven forbid.'

One of the three paramedics working frantically in the ditch called for a stretcher. Two of the men took up their positions, one at Isabella's head and one at her feet, and they proceeded to ease her slowly, by degrees, out of the ditch.

'Isabella,' one of the ambulance crew said. 'This is John Clayton. I'm a paramedic.' He had his arms raised above his head, holding a plastic bottle of fluid attached to a drip tube inserted into the back of Isabella's wrist.

'Isabella, can you hear me?'

They set her down on the stretcher. Mud and slime matted her fine blonde hair and every breath rattled in her chest. With each laboured breath, a blood-filled bubble escaped from her nostrils.

CHAPTER FIVE

Rav
20th December

The investigation was taking shape thanks to the mind maps and photographs linked by inky squiggles spread out across the multiple whiteboards at the front of the incident room. DCS Rav Patel had summoned the team of investigating officers for an early morning update. Strewn with Christmas cards, tinsel, and a real Nordic pine complete with a sack of Secret Santa presents, the room had a jaunty feeling. The uplifting aroma of spice and cinnamon plug-in air fresheners completed the festive effect.

Rav headed up the team. Smartly attired, in his own assessment, in a well-cut dark navy suit and a crisp white shirt which he'd ironed himself, he addressed the group. His father had taught him from an early age that first impressions and appearances were crucial. He glanced around the room at the assembled motley crew and concluded that the idea had been wasted on them – with the sole exception of DS Barrett, who at least made an effort to always look presentable.

'Right, what have we got? Olympic event rider Juliet Jermaine, uninjured, prime witness.' He tapped the photo pinned to the whiteboard. 'One badly mutilated dead Olympic horse called Gothic, and a thirteen-year-old girl, Isabella Levine, who died of crush injuries in hospital not long ago. Now it's at least death by dangerous driving, but I'm conducting a murder investigation on the basis of the car being used as a weapon.'

He paused while they took in the update. Most of them had children of their own, and the death of a child invariably affected them all deeply. Initially when he'd first been transferred here from the

Met, he found the humour rather colloquial, and on occasions inappropriate, but gradually he realised that his team's gallows humour was simply their way of coping. Who couldn't feel the tragic pain of parents losing a child? He wasn't a father, not for want of trying, but he would do everything in his power to get justice for the family. Rav pointed to the board, skipping from right to left and back again with his indicator. 'Isabella Levine, probably just in the wrong place at the wrong time, but we need to close this assumption down. Shirley, you take this one up, and can you organise a family liaison officer?' He glanced at the thickset Scottish detective, big-boned, in her late thirties. She was an experienced, determined detective with an exemplary clean up rate, but whether that compensated for her brisk, rather charmless style was debatable, he thought.

'Right, boss. I'm on it. I've got Stuart Simpson in mind as FLO. I've already met with the parents, Patrick and Ann, the twins, and the elder sister, Orla. God love them, they're in bits as you kin imagine. I'll follow up all leads, obviously, but from what I've gleaned from the older sister, who's known Juliet for a number of years, it seems more likely that Juliet was the target. She's made a few enemies on the way to the top as it happens. A thought, sir, shall we look at social media sites and WhatsApp?'

Rosetta leaned back in her leather swivel chair and turned to face Shirley. 'Good idea, Hodges. I'll get hold of GCHQ and get the encryption codes they cracked. That'll save time as we won't have to keep making repeated requests for access and Special Services clearance and the like.'

'Can you do that?' Shirley looked suitably impressed.

Rosetta made a steeple with her hands. 'Sure, EPIS not only owns all the targets, they run the entire shooting range and all matches across the globe. Do we have a good techie at our disposal?'

Rav nodded. 'Young Flanagan works for SOCO, but we can borrow him.' He didn't know what to make of Rosetta, as she'd been seconded to the unit by the commissioner, so he figured she was a spy in the camp, but worse than that, and to make his brief even more complicated, she was Secret Services. Rav sighed: just managing this lot, plus the expectations of the powers-above was a full-time job, without adding a secret spy to the toxic mix. *It's going to be a tricky swamp to drain, this, isn't it?* he thought, his shoulders sagging a fraction.

'Cheers, guv,' Rosetta said. 'Okay, Shirley, can you elaborate? So why is it Juliet? What's the possible motive?' She lifted the lid on her laptop and crossed her legs.

Shirley flicked through her notebook, squinting at the pages through a bouffant swell of blonde hair. 'Well, according to Orla, Juliet is at the top of her game, but she trampled many a one along the way. She's an American, a tough cookie by all accounts, initially funded by her mega-rich parents who live in Rhode Island, New England, but since her gold medal success she's in high demand for advertising and sponsorships, and the like, so now she earns a fair whack in her own right.'

'Now she can cut the strings to Bank of Mum and Dad,' Dennis observed wryly. 'If only my lot would follow suit.'

Shirley laughed. 'No, disrespect, Denny, but your bairns, they're nay gonna have the genetic blueprint of Olympic athletes, right?'

Dennis conceded the point with a broad grin.

Rav checked his watch and frowned. Glancing at Dennis he noted that his middle age spread was advancing at a rapid pace. *Strange,* he wondered, *why some men thought it was acceptable to let themselves go?* Rav, who prided himself on his dapper good looks, made a vow: *if I ever let myself get like that, shoot me please.*

Shirley picked up her thread. 'Erm, right, where was I? Ah, the parents worked hard, and built up chains of fast food outlets, and such. From the age of seven, she was raised over here, mainly by her grandparents, went to boarding school here, and stayed in Britain to train, and it's remained her base ever since. When it comes to winning, she's pretty determined, and she's trampled over a fair few wellies and riding booties, no doubt –'

'The posh ones are called Hunters, aren't they? And the toffs wear those Barbour wax jackets to walk the compulsory spaniels,' Dennis interjected.

Rav cleared his throat. 'Hmm, sorry to say this, but my knowledge of horses goes about as far as a once-a-year flutter on the Grand National. So, what is this eventing stuff?'

Shirley nodded in sympathy. 'Eventing's not quite as cut throat as other equestrian sports such as show jumping. It's blue-blooded and quite a close-knit, albeit extended, family affair, Orla reckons. Well, I'm not an expert either, guv, but apparently there are two individual Olympic disciplines. Show jumping, remember wee Nick Skelton at Rio? Then there's dressage, like a fancy sort of horse gymnastics, all dancing and prancing about. Well, eventing combines those two disciplines, plus they do a pretty stiff cross-country course. You'd need a wee dram or ten of Scotland's finest to get over some of those fences, mind. Princess Anne was a top eventer in her day and so is her daughter Zara Phillips, now Zara Tindall.'

'Thanks, Shirley, for explaining that. So, let's get back on track; possible enemies, competitors who have it in for Juliet? Is there anyone else that merits follow-up?' Rav asked.

'Well, there's definitely the boyfriend, Matt Lebaine, and according to Tia Carter – she's the housekeeper, on long leave at the moment visiting her folks up North, they had nay been getting on too well recently. He took an assignment in the States to give them some both some breathing space. He's also Juliet's coach and fitness trainer, so she did nay take kindly to him pissing off right before the season was due to begin again in March. Apparently, eventers…' she scrutinised her notes, 'turn their horses away in October for a few months, then bring them back into work in December, slowly rebuilding horse and rider fitness levels, ready for the start of the new competition season. Juliet was livid with her chappie, as she felt that Matt, as their coach and fitness trainer, should have been here for that, but he went abroad instead, dumping her in the lurch, mind. Then there's the head groom, Tracy Mathews. She called in sick the day before the accident.'

'Okay,' Rav said, scribbling on the board. '*Tracy Mathews, Tia Carter, Matt Lebaine*, the BF. Get a mug shot up here on the board, pronto. Anyone else?'

Shirley flicked through the pages of her small black book. 'One of Juliet's closest chums is top New Zealand rider Todd Hammond. He can probably give us the lowdown on the competition and anyone who might have it in for the lassie, I reckon.'

Rav scribbled in big, bold letters, *Todd Hammond*. 'Right, Charlie, prepare the warrants to obtain the phone records of everyone named here.' Rav tapped the whiteboard for emphasis.

Charlie was in his early thirties and had recently sprouted one of those tufty beard things that were all the rage a few years ago.

Charlie sighed. 'All of them? I mean, seriously?'

Irritated, Rav narrowed his eyes, and sighed to himself. Babes and rookies being slow on the uptake was bad enough, but seasoned officers ought to know better, so he summoned up another of his famous death stares to convey his displeasure. 'Yes, seriously, and pull out all the stops, do I need to remind you lot that the clock's ticking. The bigger the time lapse, the harder it'll be to close the case.'

'Right, boss.' Charlie looked suitably chastened and scratched his beard.

Rav continued. 'Okay, Shirley, you've already got a good handle on the horsey sorts, so can you follow this line further?'

'For sure,' she said with a smile.

'Great,' Rav continued. 'As luck would have it our foot patrol were busy yesterday, and they found a vehicle abandoned about two miles away on Farley Heath. Forensics are at the scene now, but the vehicle was torched, and left as a complete burn-out.'

At that moment Josie, his secretary, came in and handed Rav a few sheets of paper. He told her to add two pages to the whiteboard, the other one he kept.

'Right, update from SOCO, hot off the press, thanks,' he said as Josie turned and left. 'They've recovered a dark four by four, a recent model Range Rover. Coincidentally, a two-year-old vehicle fitting the description was reported stolen from Shirley Heights railway station car park at around 7:50 p.m. last night. Owner and registered keeper, one Peter Marshall, diplomat, currently our envoy to the Kremlin, got off the 7:30 p.m. London train that evening, went to the car park where he'd left his vehicle that morning, and found it missing. Vehicle registration…' Rav went to the board, and added, 'Vehicle Registration number 252D100. 'Those are diplomatic plates. Marshall phoned in, and reported the vehicle stolen, call logged at five to eight last night. Okay, so, lines of enquiry, house to house, and send two uniforms to the railway station this evening at rush hour to ask commuters if they saw anything unusual yesterday morning. Pull the CCTV footage. I'll ask for the registration number to be run through the Automatic Registration Plate Recognition system to see where the vehicle went, from there we can try CCTV searches to see if we can identify the driver.'

DC Dennis Johnson took a swig out of a Costa takeaway cup and scrutinised the board. The Christmas reindeer horns perched on his head were flashing like a set of demented traffic lights. 'Is that our e-fit next to the photo of Marshall?'

Rav nodded.

'Shit,' Dennis groaned. 'It looks like the scarecrow out of The Wizard of Oz.'

The group of officers cracked up laughing.

'I mean, you can just imagine the headlines, can't you? PC Picasso quits before he gets the sack!'

DC Charlie Boyd shook his head. 'That one's not too bad. But if it's meant to be Marshall, no doubt he'll be filing a complaint, and suing for damages for hurt feelings, and ruining his chances on Tinder and the like.'

Shirley looked irritated. 'Why the devil do we need an e-fit, we've already got a photo?'

Rav shrugged. 'SOCO works in mysterious ways, I guess.'

Rosetta groaned. 'Anyone remember the Portuguese thing when little Madeleine went missing? That was a real cracker, just a blank blob shape with a few strands of hair. What did the press nickname it?'

'Egg-head,' Charlie replied. 'Hilarious, if it wasn't so bloody tragic.' He took a bite of fruit cake with a thick layer of icing on top.

Rosetta looked at him, aghast, and shook her head. 'You eat Christmas cake for breakfast, WTF?'

He nodded and wiped the crumbs off his shirt. 'Me mam gets a bit carried away, like. I reckon it's that Mary Bloody Berry's fault. We've now got a nation of pensioners going do-lally with icing bags, fretting over fancy nozzles, and needing urgent treatment for sugar addictions.' He patted his considerable belly. 'And, as you can see, I don't even like cake, me.'

Rosetta rolled her eyes to the ceiling. 'Lord, have mercy on us. Okay, back to business. So, the perp loses it on a quiet country lane, does a runner, torches the car, then reports it missing. Or it's the thief who stole the car, maybe to cover up the real motive for wiping out a horse and rider, whatever that may be?' She trailed off and sighed. 'One other thing you need to know. Peter Marshall is my ex-husband...' her voice trailed off.

Rav noticed that the colour had drained from her face. No wonder, he thought, as it would be an almighty shock to discover your ex was potentially mixed up in the very crime you were investigating. Rav shook his head, and then there was the impact on the kids, she had two, as he recalled. Plus, he'd have to make a decision whether or not to keep her on the case, but then again, the decision wasn't entirely his. Rav sighed; why did life have to be so darn complicated?

Rosetta coughed before continuing. 'You'll gather this means my impartiality is potentially compromised.' She paused as if trying to gauge the mood in the room. 'I suggest that you don't bring him in for questioning at this stage. He's a career diplomat, so getting charges to stick might prove, well, shall we say, a tad tricky. He's very well-connected, so ensure all enquiries are discreet, and dot all the I's and cross all the T's. Does Marshall's alibi stack up, because right now he's looking like an obvious suspect?'

'On it, that's being checked. So far, his story is consistent, but not bulletproof or infallible,' Rav confirmed. 'So, Dennis, you pull the CCTV footage from the railway station, the platforms, ticket office, and the car park, plus run searches on our crime database covering all vehicle thefts in the area over the past five years, and see what patterns come up.'

'Right, guv, I'm on it,' Dennis replied. 'Another possibility, just a thought, but is it possible that Marshall's the real target?'

'Interesting, go on.' Rav looked thoughtful as he mapped that theory on the board. Then, as he turned, he shuddered slightly as he caught a glimpse of Charlie picking cake crumbs off his lap and popping them in his mouth. *Gross. What the heck has happened to manners and etiquette?* he wondered.

Dennis scratched his chin. 'Well, it just occurred to me that if he's involved in politics and foreign bigwigs, and all that, he might have pissed off quite a few important people. And they might have decided to set him up to teach him a lesson.'

Rav looked impressed. 'Good thinking outside the box, DC Johnson.' He started to clear the papers on his desk. 'Okay, get cracking. Good. Right, off you all go and report back at 1700 hours.' Rav waved everyone out. As they trudged out he indicated for Rosetta and Shirley to stay behind. The other officers shuffled to their feet and left the incident room.

CHAPTER SIX

Rav

The three of them moved to Rav's office, where he pulled the door shut, closed the blinds, then stood on the other side of the desk and studied the two policewomen.

Rosetta spoke first. 'So, sir, what do you reckon?'

Rav sat down with a thump and rested his hands on his head. 'We've got a well-known Olympian plastered all over the advertising boards, a career diplomat and his ex-wife on the investigation team…' His voice trailed off as Shirley threw him a conspiratorial what-the-fuck look. 'It doesn't get any better than that really, does it?'

'If you're a bloodhound reporter on the scent it does, thanks to our very own witchy-psychic here,' Shirley groaned.

Rosetta swivelled in her chair, and the two women exchanged a flash of hostile glances. Rosetta folded her arms across her chest with a snapping gesture.

All I need now is these two stabbing one another in the back, or worse still, slinging spells around, Rav thought, trying to loosen his collar a touch. 'Actually, I'm thinking about the press; the last thing we need at this stage is them on our backs.' He jabbed the phone on his desk and barked down the speaker to his PA. 'Order four more reception robots to man the frontline calls, please – urgent.' With that, he hung up.

'Seriously?' Shirley groaned. 'I loved my Roomba vacuum, and now I wouldn't be without my Housebot, but the general public hate interacting with those bloody bot things.'

Rav couldn't help glaring at her in annoyance. The commissioner wouldn't condone a head count increase, so the bots were all he could throw at the problem.

'Well, one of the things we're working on at EPIS is controlling AI. Take driverless cars, or rather self-driving cars, for instance, and how to make them ISIS-proof, amongst other things,' Rosetta chimed in.

Rav groaned inwardly. Why did he have that sinking feeling that life was about to get even more complicated?

Rosetta continued, brimming with more enthusiasm than a time share salesman. 'Car accidents alone kill over a million people world-wide every year, okay so there have been fatal accidents with driverless cars that need totally ironing out, but can you see the pros of driverless cars, as in fewer human error accidents?'

'That's right,' Shirley enthused. 'AI can't get drunk, distracted, or lose its temper.'

Rosetta nodded. 'Yes, but there's still some way to go to improve fatality rates. Then at some point, the AI is going to have to be programmed to make a moral judgement. That's where it gets complicated. Let's say three school kids dash out into the road in front of the self-driving car, which has three passengers on board. Does it swerve to avoid the children, and put the passengers at risk, or save the passengers and hit the kids?'

Rav scratched his chin. 'I see where you're going with this, and how it leads to some big moral questions, because when the machines start making decisions about who lives and who dies, what happens to us?'

Rosetta nodded excitedly. 'Exactly, it's precisely these big questions that EPIS is helping to solve, and they also provide global regulatory framework and oversight for all AI development. It's okay right now, with narrow AI only focused on specific tasks. But what happens in thirty or forty years' time, say in 2050-2060, when it's predicted that general/broad AI will be fully developed and widely implemented?'

'Go on.' Rav said, impressed at her grasp of new technological frontiers.

'First and foremost, it's essential that all broad AI has inbuilt controls, so we don't let the genie out of the bottle that comes back to haunt us. We have to ensure that AI won't outsmart humans and become an uncontrollable threat. So, for instance there will be tripwires installed that detect dangerous activity and close it down.' Rosetta sighed, and her shoulders sagged. 'See, if Peter's car had been self-driving, the tripwire would've cut the engine, and Isabella and Gothic would still be alive.'

'Right,' Shirley let out a low whistle, 'so this clever AI stuff will save lives, and lower crime rates?'

Rosetta smiled. 'If it's properly programmed, I sure hope so, that's precisely why I joined EPIS. We have a huge amount of data on road rage, traffic violations, you name it.' She laughed. 'High-speed car chases will be a thing of the past, although our boy racers in the force might not be so chuffed. Self-driving cars can be programmed to safely perform an emergency stop-on-command and lock the doors, so the perps can't do a runner. That's just one example of where technology is heading, really the potential's incredible.'

Rav had been chewing things over from several angles. 'I'm just wondering, though, about jobs, hmm… If crime rates go down, logically fewer police are needed, then where does that leave us?'

'Better off in terms of world peace and harmony, but maybe financially screwed and twiddling our thumbs?' Rosetta chuckled. 'Mind you, on a serious note, one consequence of more AI, as Rav pointed out, will be job losses, and not just low-skilled work. In tests, the Computational Pathologists or C-Paths were more accurate with diagnosis than highly skilled doctors. A US company called Enclitic has an algorithm which was put to the test against four world leading consultants – they had a seven percent false positive rate, whereas the machine had none. As the robots take jobs there's going to be a lot of stagnant incomes, mass unemployment, a massive divide between the haves and the have-nots, leading to social unrest, then guess what?'

'Crime shoots up,' Shirley concluded. 'Thank goodness I'm not in Traffic about to get Tesla-fied, and my job and my pension are safe.'

Rosetta concurred. 'The powers that be need to seriously start thinking about creating the new jobs now. As for our pensions, well, financial advisers are another group who'll get replaced. This year alone, the robo-advisors have £323 billion worth of funds under their management. Even the UK government, who aren't exactly known for innovation or radical forward thinking, are looking at this.'

Rav shook his head. 'Do you have any good news?'

Rosetta cocked her head to one side and looked thoughtful. 'If we're not careful, robots could be more dangerous than nukes.'

'That's the good news?' Shirley looked aghast.

'Let me finish,' Rosetta admonished. 'The doomsayers are predicting all kinds of impending catastrophes, when AI matches the human brain, and remember humans have a slow biological evolution, whereas machines could redesign themselves at exponential rates. The Future of Humanity Institute reckon that one day AI could turn against us, unless we instil core values like empathy, compassion, morality, and the finely nuanced controlling methods necessary to avoid them turning treacherous. We have to get it right at the onset, that's imperative.'

'Such a thing as Future of Humanity Institute actually exists?' Shirley's jaw dropped open. 'Holy shit!'

'Yeah, I know,' Rosetta agreed. 'Mind-blowing, but on a happier note, the Associated Press uses AIs to generate over six thousand stories a quarter, so the journalists' days are numbered, and then I predict that our jobs will be a hell of a lot easier. Ta-da!'

'Good bloody riddance,' Shirley laughed.

Rav agreed. 'Indeed, bring it on, but on that note, Shirley, can you get Charlie to call our PR lot in, on overtime – if that's what it takes – to try to control the situation, and keep the lid on things for as long as possible? Rosetta, can you alert Juliet not to make any announcements, and try buy us some silence?'

Shirley squirmed in her seat. 'Ah, um, it's a bit late for that, sir. She has an agent, and she's released a statement already.'

'Go on.' He fixed her with a steely gaze.

Shirley cleared her throat and read the press release:

Saddled-with-Sorrow:

Olympic equestrian Juliet Jermaine released a statement today expressing her profound grief at the death of her horse. It said:

"I'm heartbroken that I had to say goodbye to my greatest friend and the horse of a lifetime, Gothic. He made my career and I'm so grateful for the amazing times we had together. Gothic, I'll miss you forever."

'Struth.' Shirley sniffed. 'I know what she's going through; I felt devastated when Digger, the family mutt, died last year.'

Rav shook his head. The OTT sentimentality when it came to pets. Some people even created obituary pages for hamsters. *Whatever next?* he wondered, *Tadpoles?*

'Okay, Shirley, that's all for now.' He watched her back as she left, then turned his attention to DS Barrett.

'Rosetta, can you get the agent's name, and obtain some silence? What about social media?'

'Gothic has his own Facebook page, with thousands of followers,' Rosetta said.

Rav looked up at the ceiling. 'That figures, but this is supposed to be about Isabella, a young teenage girl whose life was brutally cut short, not a candy-rush for all those pony mad little poppets. Rosetta –'

'I'll have EPIS shut it down for a while, guv.' Rosetta stared at Rav, and she squirmed. 'I'm gutted. Isabella was the same age as my youngest, Alice. As a mother and a cop, I really want to see this case solved as soon as, but about my ex… do you want me off the case?'

Rav leaned back in his chair, his arms folded, and returned her gaze. 'Do you think he did it?' He stood up. 'Is he capable of such a thing?'

She rubbed her forehead. 'Honestly, I don't know. He's got the kids. A few years back, he abducted my son in the middle of the bloody night, and a fat lot of use our own were in helping me get him back.' Rosetta grimaced. 'Apparently, thirteen-year-old lads with influential fathers can stay abducted, and no one gives a monkey's.'

Rav took a deep breath, not quite sure how to broach this. 'Did you lose custody of your children?'

Rosetta's face filled with pain, and in that instant Rav wished he'd never asked. She nodded, looking downcast.

'But, I thought mothers always got custody of the children. And you're a police officer, an upright citizen. Surely, that must count for something?'

Rosetta shrugged. 'No, apparently not when you're also a psychic, and a… metaphysical practitioner.'

'A what?'

A hint of a faint smile touched her lips. 'Yeah, well, I'm reluctant to say witch, as you can imagine what a field day Social Services had with that!'

Rav nodded sympathetically. 'I guess.'

Rosetta clasped her hands under her chin. 'My main concern is protecting my kids, but we're estranged; Peter made sure of that by drip feeding them with poison.' She looked despondent.

'I think it's called parental alienation, but why? I've never understood why any parent would do that to their own kids.' Rav twiddled with his pencil and proceeded to sharpen it.

'Payback, I suppose. That's part of the reason I joined EPIS and moved away. Losing my kids was too bloody painful, still is,' she said with a sigh. 'They've been through enough already with the divorce, losing their mother's influence, and if it gets out that their father is mixed up in this… it… it will be devastating for them. I do know he'll be a hard bastard to nail if he did do anything. His scruples make Harold Shipman look like the patron saint of medical ethics. Do you want me to take a backseat? Really, solving the current crime's technically not my main objective. Well, it is, and it isn't. I work on the bigger overarching crime prevention strategy.'

Rav looked at her quizzically. 'What exactly is it that you do? And what brought you back here?'

'Fair cop,' she said, 'I can't go into too many details, but suffice to say that I've been having premonitions about this incident for over a fortnight. Sadly, it panned out pretty much like my visions foretold, although the outcome could have been prevented.'

In that moment he caught the tailwind of her anger as she continued. 'How uniform failed to intercept the two horse riders that morning beats the shit out of me –'

Rav raised his palm, signalling her to stop. 'Ah yes, sorry about that. It was the robot that took the call. It decided that Luckenham Park was a low crime risk address, in a low crime area – so... the patrol car was diverted elsewhere.'

'Take that, you bitch!' Rosetta looked livid. 'I gather you've installed Predpol?'

Rav nodded. 'Well, the commissioner felt it would be a more cost-effective use of manpower –'

Rosetta cut him off. 'You realise that robots use deep learning, and they become self-teaching, in ways that no human can really comprehend? In due course, their algorithms can introduce race and class biases, and God knows what else. That's precisely one of the things that EPIS is working to rectify and prevent. We can't have a proliferation of robots swapping ill judged, random, and highly inaccurate information, because it will be very difficult to erase, and the consequences will be detrimental and discriminatory, and damn tricky to override.'

Rav processed this. 'You were about to explain a bit more about your... your role.'

'A number of police forces in the US have abandoned Predpol for the time being because it ended up with the high crime areas being over-policed, and the low crime areas under-policed. That's known as the feedback loop or FBL, which rolls out like a self-fulfilling prophecy. That's a big area that EPIS uses psychics for, in the effort of eliminating FBL. The experience with Predpol hasn't been particularly positive to date, and it's in for a major re-vamp. The public weren't happy, and the force themselves felt controlled and undermined which had a negative impact on morale. So, you might like to mention that to your boss.' Rosetta pursed her lips, and she appeared deep in thought. 'Well, every cause has an effect, and usually when I have visions it means there's a serious past life crime to be solved. That's what I need to investigate, so the karmic ripples stop being repeated endlessly.'

Rav shook his head, and his face softened. 'Ultimately it's atonement rather than justice that you're after?'

'Correct, that's pretty much it.' She looked impressed. 'If past wrongs are righted and the ripples stop spreading, then overall that should loop back into good FBL,' she said with a grin. 'And translate into lower overall crime rates, a win-win. The fascinating part is that things are never quite what they seem on the surface.'

'That's crime for you,' he laughed. 'So, if you have visions, premonitions, do you prevent crime, like in *Minority Report?*'

Rosetta raised an eyebrow. 'Ah, so you think I'm a Precog – a mutated human? Cheers, for that.' She scrutinised him carefully, as if weighing her next move.

'Oh dear, no… not… well,' Rav said, feeling rather mortified.

'Would you like a shovel, you know, so you can dig yourself in even deeper?'

'Pass. What I meant was, is the future set, and known in advance?'

Rosetta considered this for a while. 'Only to a certain extent, and sometimes, as in this case, the crime could have been, but wasn't, prevented. The outcomes aren't pre-determined, and things playing out today aren't always what they seem on the surface. Quite often the villain was previously the victim, or the rescuer, and unless lessons are learned, and the original wrongs are righted, it just goes on spiralling out of alignment.'

'Is it a sort of tit-for-tat?' Rav chewed this over, strangely relieved that she wasn't a spy after all, even though he didn't fully understand what she was exactly. He sensed that her brief was something far more important and set on a far bigger stage. Suddenly he felt reassured, and glad of her involvement.

'Stay on the case. We're short-staffed as it is.' He nearly added, *besides I like having you around,* but he checked himself just in time. 'It won't be long before it's all over the dailies, the BBC website, the Mail online, and we need to keep ahead of the game. Shirley and I will handle all the media stuff.'

'I get the impression that she doesn't like me much. Actually, the Precog mutation angle might not be so far-fetched after all.'

Now it was Rav's turn to raise his eyebrow. 'Go on.'

'Well, back at EPIS HQ there are people who think that life on Earth originated from outer space, that humans have some ET DNA.' Rosetta stared at Rav as if trying to assess his response, which would be tough as he really, really didn't know what to make of that.

Time for a change of subject, he thought.

'I wouldn't worry about Shirley. Besides, you must come across scepticism all the time?' Not for the first time, Rav appraised her with interest. Slim, with lustrous dark auburn hair, that reminded him of conkers or horse chestnuts, also she had luminous clear skin. In summary: strikingly attractive with amazing eyes, but it was more than that. She radiated a kind of energy that was hard to define, like a magnet that drew you in even though your head was flashing warning signals and trying to resist.

Rosetta shook her head and groaned. 'You bet. Eventually telepathy, healing, all those things that are currently deemed out-there will become the new normal. I call them supernormal actually. Bring on the paradigm shift, and not a minute too soon. I'm getting a bit weary of being the odd one out.' She scooped up her briefcase and turned towards the exit.

'You'd better keep a low profile. Meanwhile, get onto that agent,' Rav called after her. *Fat chance of Rosetta staying under the radar,* he thought as he waved her off; why did he even bother wasting his breath? She was a law, a code of conduct, and a complete rule book unto herself, that one. Before long he'd be bailing her out of trouble. He stared at his fingers and picked at his neatly manicured nails one by one. What firecracker would Rosetta let rip next?

Only time would tell.

CHAPTER SEVEN

Juliet
19th – 20th December

Juliet tossed and turned. She couldn't get the accident out of her head. Something perverse compelled her to keep running terrible images over and over again, like a bad B-movie on a loop at the local movie house. After a while, she snapped on the bedside light, and peered at the clock. It flashed the time: 12:15 a.m. The luminous green display hurt her aching eyes. What a difference a few hours had made to her life, she thought miserably. There was still no word from Matt, *why the hell is he messing with me?* She heaved herself off the pillows and turned her head a fraction, calculating every movement with precision, desperate to avoid the lurking headache that threatened to take hold at any moment. The feelings rose up from somewhere deep inside, wave after wave – terror, devastation, agony. Here comes a tsunami of heartbreak which threatened to leave a permanent stain on her soul. What she really wanted right now was to put the clock back. Stop time and rewind.

Propped up against the pillows, she glanced around the room where her clothes lay strewn across the old pine floorboards. In the corner the doors of the closet, an antique French armoire that had belonged to her grandmother, burst open. Its contents, old back issues of *Horse and Hound* – the equestrian Bible – spilled out. She swung her legs out of bed and shuffled across the room. *Oh my God, what a mess. Room-life metaphor,* she thought, wriggling into a heavy sweater and throwing on a pair of thick sweatpants. With a sigh, she picked her way downstairs and snuck outside barefoot, the way she used to as a child.

41

Sharp pangs of cold pierced between her toes. She liked the feeling. It made her feel real, somehow. In the stable yard, with its absorbing sounds and smells, she felt a kind of peace. The odd water bucket rattled, but otherwise the silence was strangely comforting. She made her way slowly towards Gothic's stall at the end of the row. Her legs felt wooden and heavy as if they were no longer attached to her body. As she paused and held her breath, she could visualise his magnificent head, ears pricked and eyes alert, framed in the doorway like a spectacular oil painting. Juliet drew an intake of breath so sharp and harsh that it hurt her chest. She bit her lip, and tears filled her eyes.

All her life spark and vitality seemed to drain away as she took a faltering step forwards and clutched at the door for support. Eventually, with a supreme effort, she forced herself to peer inside, into the darkness. She could sense his powerful presence all around. In her mind's eye, she could see him struggling to his feet, his eyes large and liquid, blowing softly to signal his irritation at being disturbed. Juliet bit her lip harder and sniffed. His smell wafted over her. All her horses had their own smell that she recognised instantly, but none was as distinctive as his, the sweet musk of stallion pheromones mixed with meadow hay and freshly laid shavings. Tears spilled down her cheeks.

'Oh, God, how could you take him from me? Why?' She shoved her fist in her mouth to stifle a sob. She switched on the light, blinking until her eyes adjusted.

No Gothic, of course.

In the right-hand corner of the doorframe, a silken web shimmered, and a spider launched itself on a single thread like a terrorist on a suicide mission. Juliet shuddered with revulsion. She turned off the lights and, with that, she hurried back indoors.

Two hours later, the shrilling phone jolted her awake. Irritated and ragged from lack of sleep, she snatched at the receiver.

'Christ, Jules, are you okay?' Matt asked in his characteristic clipped, almost nasal drawl. His tone was firm and no-nonsense, the voice of a man who was always on top of his game. 'I've been trying to reach you nonstop.'

Juliet wanted to scream at him, to hurl a torrent of abuse down the phone. When she needed him most, he'd let her down. But rapidly, her anger gave way to grief, and grim pockets of despair. 'It's a… a total nightmare.' A strange gurgling sound came from her throat. She couldn't bear thinking about it. Yet, somehow, she was going to have to bring herself to utter the words. 'She's dead! They've switched off

Isabella's life support machine, and Gothic... He was so jittery, you know, like he sensed something.' Juliet screwed her eyes tight shut as it all came flooding back. 'Jesus... Jesus.'

'Shush, don't go there. Don't beat yourself up.'

'I tried to save them. Poor Isabella, she was just a kid. How could I have failed with something as important as this?' Her voice disintegrated into a tortured mewling sound as she slumped back against the pillows. 'I should never have let her ride him. It's... it's all my fault. That's what you think, isn't it? That's why you haven't called me sooner.'

'No, of course I don't blame you. Don't torture yourself. Oh, I don't know. Maybe sometimes, some of us aren't meant to be saved.'

A band of pain tightened across her forehead, and she grimaced. She took a deep breath. Opening up did not come easy to her.

'For the first time in my life I feel like a complete failure. I don't think I can cope. It's too much. Please come home.' There. She'd said it. But would Matt get it? Could anyone comprehend the horror of what she'd seen? She'd always thought of herself as someone strong and capable, and now she had to face up to the fact that she was as fallible and vulnerable as everyone else.

'It's been a nightmare booking a flight, but I should be back early tomorrow morning. Look, I know it's not brilliant timing right now, but you need to give serious consideration to the planning application.' His tone was cajoling, that of a parent dealing with a stubborn child. 'The developers won't wait around indefinitely. Ours is only one of a number of potential sites they're considering.'

'As if I give a shit about that right now!' she snapped. What an insensitive jerk, what planet was he on? He was obsessed with selling the estate, her legacy from her grandparents, to make way for a housing development. She wasn't interested in the finance stuff. That was his department and he was always looking for a bigger bang for his buck, or her buck, if it came to that. *Screw you,* she thought.

'But...'

'Not now. I really, really don't have the capacity to deal with this,' an unmistakable note of accusation hung in the air, 'not now. Why are you even going there?' She had no intention of listening to something she didn't want to hear. Even she had to admit she was remarkably like her mother in that respect. Her temples throbbed, and blood pounded in her ears. She blinked, trying to clear the white dots and dashes that blurred her vision. 'Matt?'

'What?'

'This is really driving me nuts.' Juliet screwed her eyes shut and gritted her teeth as she recalled her vet's expression when she'd put this to him, the way he'd shifted from one foot to the other and refused to look her straight in the eye. The bond between her and that horse was closer than anything she'd ever experienced. 'Do you… do you think they suffered?'

There was an awkward pause, presumably while he groped for a reassuring response.

'Oh, Jules, no, of course not, it would have been quick and painless.'

'You think so?' Despite all her resolve, her voice cracked. She couldn't bear it if they'd suffered. 'Maybe not,' she said with a twinge of desperation, and she tried to reassure herself, 'maybe not.'

'Absolutely, now try and get some sleep.'

'Bye then.' She hung up and switched off the light. *Sleep,* she told herself. *You must get some sleep.*

Later that morning, later than usual, she dragged herself out of bed. Her breath tasted gross and metallic as she shuffled to the restroom to brush her teeth. The reflection in the mirror came as a shock. The last time she'd looked this bad had been after forty-eight hours non-stop partying in Ibiza for her twenty-first birthday. Her lustrous black hair hung limp and lifeless as cotton candy mixed with seaweed. Her eyes wouldn't have looked amiss on a sick bloodhound, and her lips were pale. The only thing that didn't seem distorted was the beauty spot at the corner of her mouth. Juliet sighed. It was the face of a woman who had won the lottery and lost the ticket.

'What a state,' she muttered as she slipped on her dressing gown, and trudged downstairs with a sigh.

Since the accident the phone had hardly stopped ringing, and the answerphone's memory had reached capacity. Juliet shuffled into the study, jabbed the *Play* button, and collapsed into the swivel chair to listen to the messages.

Wearily, she deleted all the messages except the one from Tracy, her groom, timed at just after 7:00 p.m. yesterday. She replayed it to make sure that she'd heard it correctly.

'Hi, Juliet, it's Tracy. God, I'm so sorry about the accident. Matt phoned me from the States. It's terrible. I don't know what to say. Look, I'm still not fully recovered, but I'll come in tomorrow, and cover the morning shift so you can have a lie-in. Catch you later.'

At first the full significance didn't register, but when it did, Juliet gasped. *Oh my God.* Surely there must be some mistake? Automatically, she clasped her throat. Why on earth would Matt have phoned Tracy hours before he'd called her? *It can't be possible.* Matt would never do a thing like that. She glared at the timer on the machine and decided that it must be playing up.

Yes. That was it, she thought, and her heart rate slowed a fraction as she slumped in a chair and crossed her legs. Who had called immediately prior to Tracy? A quick check revealed that it was Todd, her best friend and fellow event rider. He was in his thirties, a Kiwi, and like her he had been based in the U.K. for years. Juliet knew his number by heart. She dialled.

'Todd, it's me,' she sniffed, trying to hold it together.

'Darling, how are you?'

'Oh, you know, bitch, moan, whine, that kinda thing.'

'Really, that good huh? How's Isabella? You poor thing, I bet you didn't sleep a wink last night. I bet you need a hug,' he said kindly.

'Oh God, what a total fucking nightmare,' she growled. Somehow, she was worried that if she mentioned Isabella, it would make things even worse, like drawing down a curse. Yesterday when she went to the hospital she learned that there had been serious damage to her internal organs. An image from the room flashed up, a deeply disturbing sight, with a proliferation of tubes, bottles, bags and electrodes. Juliet shuddered as she recalled fragments of the conversations that she'd heard. 'Patient has a ruptured spleen, spinal compression, a fracture at C1 and C2 vertebrae, bleeding on the brain.' At the time she'd thought, *oh my God, what if Isabella never walks again?* That had sent her skittering in a panic. She couldn't imagine anything worse than being confined to a wheelchair for the rest of her life, unable to walk, let alone ride. But now she knew there were worse things; far worse. She took a deep breath. 'Isabella… didn't make it. They switched off her life support… she died.'

'Shit, I don't know what to say. I'm so sorry, petal. CIO?'

'Sorry?'

'Cry it out.'

'Yeah, I have been.' Juliet gulped, trying to hold it together. 'I got your message from yesterday. What time did you call?'

'Ooops, Saffy, you wicked cow. She's just spooked at a pigeon in the hedge and nearly had me off. Sorry, cupcake, what were you saying?'

'What time did you call me yesterday evening?'

'Oh, I don't know. You know me, I'm gluing to my mobile.'

45

'You mean glued?'

Todd let out an indignant huff. 'Every time you correct my grammar, I love you a little bit fewer.'

Juliet rolled her eyes towards the ceiling. She loved Todd dearly, but he did tend to digress rather like an unruly sniffer dog hot on the scent. 'Try and remember. It's important.'

'Well, now, let me see. We always watch *A-list Highway*. Barrie never misses an episode. I'm a bit more take it or leave it myself...'

'Todd!'

'Sorry. Well, it would've been before *A-list Highway* and that starts at eight, so, between seven and seven thirty, I'd imagine.'

'Oh,' she gasped. 'I don't know what to think. Matt called Tracy hours before he even spoke to me. He said he'd been having problems with his network. It doesn't make sense.'

'That sucks,' Todd huffed indignantly. 'Ah, and that's in your hour of need too. Oh dear. Still, there must be a plausible explanation.'

'Such as?' she snapped.

'Such as Tracy made a mistake, and Matt didn't phone her, or Matt didn't call her, and she's causing trouble, or...'

'Or?'

'He phoned her just like she said.'

'But why? Why would he do that?'

'Hmmm, I'm not sure. But, if I were you, I'd confront them both separately, so they can't confer and then see if their stories stack up.'

Juliet stood up and paced the room. She couldn't bring herself to speak. She couldn't bear it, betrayal on top of everything. She'd never felt this strung out, maybe she was paranoid?

'Hello,' Todd said. 'Can you hear me?'

Matt would never betray her, not at a time like this, for sure. Her cheeks grew hot, and her heart beat with peculiar little jerks. Could she trust him?

What if...?

Juliet forced herself to speak. 'Do you think Matt is into Tracy? Could there be something going on?' A thought whistled through her mind so fast and so unsettling that she couldn't quite grasp why it left her feeling so perturbed.

There was a long silence.

'Todd, are you still there?'

'Sure, sorry Barrie's got me hooked-on Twitter. I was just re-tweeting, "lovehugs-hashtag-kiwicutie." Don't you just love it?'

'Kiwi cutie, are you serious?' Juliet couldn't help emitting a disgruntled snort. 'What about Matt and Tracy?'

Todd gave a cackle of laughter. 'Heavens, you're asking the wrong person. I mean, what would I know about the relative charms of women?'

Juliet checked her watch, a diamond and pearl Ebel which she'd bought with the prize money from her last Badminton win. She shook her head. 'I gotta go. I need to make a phone call, and the police are coming over any minute.'

'*Ciao*, keep me posted.' He blew a kiss down the phone.

CHAPTER EIGHT

Juliet
20th December

Shortly after noon Juliet let the woman detective in and showed her through to the living room. Juliet proceeded to curl up on the old brown leather sofa, wrapped in her fluffy bathrobe, nursing a cup of weak tea. Juliet traced her fingers over the familiar ruts and scuff marks in the leather – the scars of family life, plus the cat's wicked claws.

Opposite her sat DS Barrett, who had stylishly short, neat glossy hair, and a figure as sharp and striking as an exclamation mark. She sported a slash of red lipstick. *Weirdly garish for a police officer,* Juliet thought. She scrutinised her closely as she took a sip from the mug and grimaced at its sweetness. It occurred to her that what she really needed was a large slug of Jack Daniel's to numb the pain. Actually, probably a bottle was called for.

'I'd offer you a cookie,' she said apologetically, 'but I'm afraid I chowed them all down last night plus a family sized tub of mint-choc-chip ice cream, washed down with soda.' Juliet sighed. No doubt if she kept going like this, she'd turn into a super-blob. As if she didn't have enough woes to deal with already.

'Sugar,' the detective said. She looked like a tough, no-nonsense sort. 'Plenty of sugar after a shock, that's what you need.'

Judging from the size of DS Barrett, there couldn't have been much that ever frightened her, certainly nothing that sent her raiding the cookie jar. Juliet smiled faintly. *Oh well,* she thought, *at least my sense of humour has survived intact, ha-ha.* Without thinking, she rummaged behind the large tapestry cushion for the jumbo bag of M&M's and stuffed a handful into her mouth. When she chewed, her mouth tasted nasty and metallic. *Fuck it, who cares if I turn into a fatso? Everyone knows that M&M's are addictive.*

DS Barrett continued, her voice even and her face blank. 'Just to give you an update, we've recovered the vehicle. It was abandoned and burnt out. Our forensic team are running tests. I can't release any more details at this stage. Now, I know this is difficult, but I need to ask you a few questions.'

Juliet rolled her eyes. Her cheeks were stuffed with hard candy, and no doubt she resembled a greedy chipmunk. She took a gulp and swallowed. 'I gave a statement yesterday afternoon at the station. No one wants that asshole caught more than me, but I can't give you a better description. I only saw the back of his head. But he was a big son-of-a-bitch.' She shifted uncomfortably in her seat but did not add that she'd had a strange nagging feeling she knew him from somewhere. That notion sent a shudder down her spine.

'Yes.' DS Barrett looked stern. 'Now, you mentioned that you were a three-day eventer. Can you elaborate on that a bit?'

'Oh God,' Juliet said. Weariness had seeped into her bones. Nothing really mattered anymore, so why couldn't they just leave her alone?

Instead, she had to endure a grilling from DS Barrett, who had now assumed the look of a tenacious terrier shooting down a rat hole. *Huh,* she thought indignantly, *weren't the police supposed to be sympathetic in circumstances like this? Someone ought to remind Ma'am here. Send her on a course to freshen up her victim support routine.* Aware that DS Barrett was staring at her, Juliet acquiesced.

'Eventing's a demanding three-discipline sport involving show jumping, dressage, and cross country. It's the ultimate test of a horse and rider's skill and nerve. Plus, it's one of the few sports where men and women compete on equal terms.' Her gaze drifted to the cabinet filled with cups and trophies, and a sharp pang of loss pierced her chest. There would be no more triumphs for her and Gothic. Without him the gold medal seemed meaningless. At that moment she felt sick, as if she might throw up. She wished she hadn't stuffed down so much candy. She tried her best not to think about Issie, her friend Orla, or their parents. That whole sink pit of grief would suck her under, and she might never come back up. It was easier just to grieve for Gothic. The English were sentimental about animals and they could relate to that, but a young girl cut down in her prime? Way too complicated for most people to process. How were they supposed to respond to that? It seemed to her that blocking it out might help, for now, anyway.

'A bit like the force.' DS Barrett paused. 'That's why I joined. You know, to give the boys a run for their money. Do you mind if I smoke?' Her look was direct and assertive.

Juliet crinkled her nose, but she couldn't muster the strength to object. DS Barrett could probably get an innocent man to confess in, oh… about sixty seconds flat.

'No, go ahead.' She waved her hand in the air. 'Whatever. I couldn't give a flying flamingo.'

'That's another reason I joined. The force is one of the few remaining places on Earth where the smokers are still in a majority.' She lit up and took a long drag. 'Do you have an ashtray?'

'It's a no-smoking establishment.'

A silence had fallen between them.

'Oh, fine. I'll get it.' Juliet heaved herself off the sofa to fetch an egg cup.

When she returned, DS Barrett commented, 'Nice place. Is it yours?'

Juliet ignored the question and just glared at the policewoman.

'Do you compete against the Whitakers?'

'No, that's show jumping, where the top riders are mainly professionals. Eventing tends to attract serious amateurs from all over the world. It's pretty blue-blooded too, what with Princess Anne and her daughter Zara Tindall.' Juliet cleared her throat. 'Look, I hope this isn't going to take much longer, because I've got horses to see to.' Soon enough she would have to apply herself to the difficult business of finding a replacement four-star event horse. The glowing tip of the detective's cigarette dipped and swooped and reminded Juliet of a swallow about to migrate south. Juliet found it irritating. *If only what's-her-face would flap her wings and fly away soon.*

'Was the horse insured? A horse like that would be valuable, I imagine?'

A weak nod sufficed for a reply.

'How much was he insured for?'

Juliet scowled. 'I'm not getting into that.' The truth was she didn't actually know, that was Matt's department.

The detective arched an eyebrow. 'What about third party and employer's liability insurance?'

'Say what?' Juliet swallowed hard. She felt under attack, as if she was a suspect. Were they going to arrest her on a charge of out-of-date paperwork, insufficient insurance?

'I gather you were employing Isabella while your groom was off, right?'

'Isabella's my friend's sister. Pony-mad, she offered to help out during the school holidays and, you know, earn a few bucks over Christmas.' Juliet squirmed and shifted uncomfortably in her seat. Her throat hurt, and her eyes felt scratchy from crying and lack of sleep.

'A stallion must be difficult and quite unpredictable to handle.'

A pause.

The detective continued, 'Especially for an inexperienced thirteen-year-old girl.'

An exasperated strangled sound escaped from Juliet's lips. 'Jesus, this is bullshit. Gothic was the quietest horse in my yard, the best behaved by far. What exactly are you saying?' Juliet felt two red dots flaming up her cheeks like mini-missiles. Being made to feel guilty was the pits. She needed to get busy and find a replacement.

'Do you honestly think I'd have put him at risk, never mind Isabella? How fucked up is that?' Her voice trembled with anger and frustration. The only good thing this time was that at least she could bury Gothic. With Totem, there'd been no body, and no closure. She covered her face in her hands.

'I didn't mean to upset you, far from it. I called you on the morning of the accident.'

Juliet lowered her hands and stared at the detective in disbelief.

DS Barrett relented, and assumed a sympathetic expression. 'I called to try and warn you. I'm gutted that we never had chance to…'

'You… you called me?' Juliet's jaw dropped, but she vaguely began to recall the string of missed calls. 'Who the hell are you?'

The officer leaned forward and handed Juliet her card. 'Here, now you've got my personal number.'

Juliet scrutinised the card. 'Psychic CID, my ass. What the…?'

'The police use psychics more often than they let on. I'm a detective, a psychic, and a psychologist. I have this gift, like a… a sixth sense. I have visions, I saw what was going to happen to you, but this time I couldn't stop it. I can't always. I'm so sorry.' She shrugged. 'Bringing criminals to book, that's part of it, but also what my team does is ensure that karmic debts are paid. Well… atoned, really.'

Juliet took a sharp intake of breath and crossed her arms over her chest. 'You mean you called me with some ominous warning that I failed to heed? Jesus, are you saying it's all my fault? I'm not following.

Please give me a break.' Then she let out a little snide kind of laugh, a laugh of disbelief.

DS Barrett gave a quiet low tut. 'No, of course I'm not.'

Juliet glared at her. 'I really don't want to hear any more of your crazy theories.' Her tone had a ring of harsh finality to it.

The detective looked chastened. 'Okay, but... okay, well now I need to ask if either of you were wearing anything reflective?'

'What? You've gotta be kidding –'

'Look, I'm really sorry, but I have to ask you these questions. The crime scene investigators had the scene taped off, and they gathered evidence. They've recovered the burnt-out vehicle, and they're testing it for mechanical faults to determine if there were any defects that contributed to the accident. That's standard procedure.' She paused. 'We also need to establish if you or Isabella placed yourself in a position of danger,' she paused again, 'as the person responsible will probably try and claim that the horse was out of control, and it was impossible for him to avoid you.'

The room became hot and airless, and for a moment Juliet felt dizzy, and light-headed. She took a deep breath and snapped upright.

'Jesus Christ, that's sick!' she spat. 'That evil dipshit deliberately backed into us.' Her cheeks and neck flushed hot with anger. 'What's happened to justice nowadays? Has it all gone totally *Alice in Wonderland*? I want you to promise me that you'll catch that asshole, and that he'll pay for this. He can't be allowed to get away with it. I want him to rot in jail. You've got to do something. All that technology, all the DNA... I mean...'

The detective raised her palm in a pacifying gesture. 'Of course, we'll do everything possible.'

Juliet slumped back into the squashy folds of the sofa. 'I'm sorry. I didn't mean to take it out on you.'

'That's okay. Please understand I have to try and pre-empt all avenues; when it goes to court, and believe me it will, the defence will try to deflect the blame any way they can.'

'Well, you have to catch him first,' Juliet moaned. 'Did you see his face, you know, in your vision thing?'

DS Barrett shook her head. 'No, I saw it from your perspective. I saw what you saw, except, I didn't get the impression that he was overly tall.'

'That's freaky!'

The detective nodded. 'However, there's an angle I'd like to explore. I understand that the driver aimed at you initially, but you managed to get clear. Is it possible that a rival wanted you out of the running? Is there anyone you can think of who might harbour a grudge against you?'

Juliet sprang to her feet and paced the room. She had been sitting around inside way too long. 'Look, this is pointless. You've got the car so why haven't you arrested someone – the owner?'

DS Barrett nodded sympathetically. 'The car was reported stolen, so it's not quite that simple. Sometimes it can be an advantage to keep an open mind. Has anything untoward happened to any of the other horses or riders recently?'

Juliet pondered for a moment. 'Well, when Jolly Jove got eliminated from the World Equestrian games after a positive dope test, my friend Pattie swore that he'd been nobbled. Then last year the Clayton-Farmers stables burnt down in the middle of the season when they were on the brink of finalising a lucrative sponsorship deal. Arson was suspected, but nothing was ever proved.' She thought about Totem and bit her lip. 'A couple of years ago, my top horse, Totem, went down with colic. I was in the Midlands competing at the time. He'd never had colic before.'

'But horses do get colic, don't they? It's like a bad stomach ache?'

'Yes,' Juliet agreed, staring at nothing in particular, 'but,' she continued with an ominous sigh, 'they don't usually disappear. Vanish into thin air.'

DS Barrett got to her feet. 'Unless they're Shergar. Was it reported as a crime?'

'That's not funny, but no, and I don't want to get into that now. I have enough on my plate.'

'Okay, I'll be off now. Don't worry, I'll let myself out. Remember, if you think of anything, anything at all, please don't hesitate to give me a call.'

Juliet stalled a moment. 'Well, there is one thing. Weird, and I can't explain it really, but I always felt that Totem and Gothic were one and the same. Does that sound crazy?'

The detective shook her head, her big emerald eyes filled with compassion. 'Not at all. Ah, just one other thing. I need a copy of Gothic's insurance policy, please.'

Irritated, Juliet drew a sharp breath. 'Matt handles all that stuff.' She made a shooing gesture and ushered the detective out of the room.

'How is it that Mr. –' the detective scrutinised her notebook, 'that

Mr. Lebaine handles all your financial affairs?'

Juliet tried not to let her irritation show. Did anyone really have any idea what being an Olympian actually entailed? It was relentless dedication and hard work. 'Well, on an average day, without media engagements and travel, I spend eight hours a day in the saddle, plus an hour a day being whipped into shape by the personal trainer at the gym. So... not much time left for the math stuff, I guess.' Annoyed, she ushered the detective towards the front door.

'Right-o, when's he back?' DS Barrett asked as she departed.

'Soon,' Juliet said, and with that she slammed the door shut. What had she done to deserve this hell? And when would it ever end?

CHAPTER NINE

Rosetta

Rosetta was holed up in her office and typing her notes, deep in thought when a junior came in and handed her a pile of papers.

'What's this?' she asked.

'Phone records.'

'Okay, thanks,' Rosetta said, waving her off. She finished typing, saved her case notes, then turned her attention to Matt's phone calls. It transpired that he hadn't called Juliet until very late, actually the early hours of the 20th, whereas she had been endlessly calling him, as you'd expect. It seemed strange that the BF appeared to have gone AWOL in Juliet's hour of need. Rosetta reached for her notebook and scribbled, *'Follow up timing of Matt's call back to Juliet.'* Her eyes flicked up the page and she noticed the instruction underlined for emphasis.

<u>Shut down Juliet's press agent.</u>

'Shit,' she muttered. She'd forgotten all about that.

Shit. She packed her bag, grabbed her coat, and headed for the car park. *Bloody Bugger,* she silently cursed.

She figured that it would be better to talk to Juliet in person about publicity and her agent, so she arrived unannounced at the stable yard to find Juliet busy tacking up a big dark horse that was tied up outside its stall. It looked highly-strung and excitable. Her daughter Alice had gone through that pony mad phase, so Rosetta knew a bit about the unpredictable nature of equines, and she kept her distance.

'Hi,' she announced breezily, noting Juliet's pained expression. 'Sorry, but I need to ask you to close the publicity machine down for a bit, while we focus on the investigation. I forgot to mention it this morning.'

Juliet shook her head. 'That won't exactly be easy.'

'No, I appreciate that, but the media spotlight will just get in the way right now. Can you just fend them off for a few days? Later, when the initial enquiries are well underway, it will be easier to manage.'

'Someone's already hacked Gothic's Facebook account, and all my favourite pictures have suddenly disappeared off Instagram and Snapchat – that wouldn't have anything to do with the police "managing the media" now would it?'

'I can't comment.' Rosetta took a step back as Juliet rummaged under the horse's belly, grabbed the buckle, and then tightened the leather girth. The horse grunted in response. Juliet retrieved a blanket that was hanging over the stable door and covered the horse's quarters, fastening the buckle at the front and arranging a thin rope under the tail.

'Tracy?' Juliet yelled. 'Can you lunge Icon for ten minutes, please, and get him warmed up?'

A blonde-haired woman poked her head out of the stall next door.

'As you can see we've got company.' Juliet grimaced.

'Sure.' Tracy nodded, resting a fork against the stable wall.

'Thanks. Okay, come with me. I don't have long so stick to the point,' Juliet instructed.

She's quite assertive, actually pretty curt, more like a New Yorker, than a New Englander, Rosetta noted, but her accent was more a lazy soft transatlantic drawl. One thing for sure was that she didn't sound like a typical American, and Rosetta had come across plenty from all over the United States back at Dulce, the EPIS HQ.

'What's your accent? Where in the States are you from?' Rosetta asked. 'I can't quite put my finger on it.'

Juliet gave a faint half smile. 'It's complicated. God bless America. I was born in Rhode Island, New England. Ironically, I guess, seeing how it panned out. But I was raised here in the UK since the age of seven, so in a way it's a hybrid accent. It confuses the hell out of everyone, as I tend to switch from an American twang, to stiff upper lip.' She gave a short laugh. 'Still, I'm pretty much an affiliated Brit by now, but...' The smile was gone as quick as a flash flood in Florida.

'Ah a pity you're not nationalised, that'd help our medal count hike up a few notches.' Rosetta laughed at her own joke. 'Still, can you make the call to your agent now, please?'

Juliet bristled as she reached in her jacket pocket for her mobile and dialled.

'Hi, Becky… fine. Well, not really. The police are here, and they've asked me not to talk to the media until further notice.'

Rosetta followed Juliet to the office where she proceeded to put the kettle on, her phone cradled in the crook of her shoulder as she listened intently. Apparently, Becky the press agent had quite a bit to say. 'Well, cancel it,' Juliet sighed. 'Look, at the end of the day the most important thing is that the police nail the bastard that's responsible, for Issie's sake. Her parents need justice, they deserve some closure first and foremost. Gothic's replacement will just have to wait a little while.'

There was a pause.

'Sod the sponsors! Look, I've got to go now. Yes, I'll keep you posted. Bye.' Juliet rolled her eyes and pointed to a sofa, complete with an assortment of dogs of various shapes and sizes. 'Take a seat.'

The prospect of getting covered in pet hair and smelling like a dog didn't appeal too much, so as Juliet elegantly poised her tall athletic frame onto the low soggy settee, Rosetta remained standing, only to be confronted by a big black Labrador who gamely stuck its nose right in her crotch. Rosetta squirmed and managed to discourage the unwanted attention. Across the room, Juliet disappeared under a barrage of adoring licking and squealing mutts.

'Okay, that's enough, guys,' Juliet chuckled. 'Hardy, get off! Now, lie down. Thank you, good boy.' She turned her attention to Rosetta. 'Besides the media thing, what can I do for you?'

No point beating around the bush, Rosetta thought. Anyway, her style was also fairly direct. 'I'm interested in exploring the kind of choices you make, and I'd like to explore if there are any patterns that you're experiencing as a consequence.'

'Is that really relevant?' Juliet grabbed hold of a collar in the vain attempt of fending off a terrier's tongue. 'My parents hate dogs and I was never allowed to have one as a child, so to discourage them from visiting too often I decided to rescue a few strays – and, well, the numbers kind of swelled.'

'So, I see,' Rosetta observed. 'I'm more of a cat person myself.' She thought of Atone, who really, since Daniel had gone silent, and the children weren't responding, was all the companionship she had these days. A wave of sadness welled up inside. Loneliness was never something that she'd foreseen for herself, and now she was stuck in it. *How do you block out blackness?* she wondered. *Stop wallowing in self-pity, just focus,* she scolded herself. 'Reading between the lines I get the sense that you're not all that close to your parents?'

Juliet got up and made them both some coffee. 'That's right,' she said, handing Rosetta a "Keep Calm and Carry On" mug. 'My father was consumed by work and building an empire, and my mother suffered from depression. So, after a while, they sent me here to live with my grandparents and I was shipped off to boarding school, which I hated, by the way. But I guess I benefited from their work ethic, so that's something positive, I guess.'

'Did you benefit from anything else?' Rosetta asked, leaning back against the chaotic work surface that was littered with horse bandages, rubber bands, and horsey things.

Juliet eased herself back onto the sofa and crossed her long, slim legs.

'Their money came in handy,' Juliet admitted. 'Top level equestrian sport needs mega bucks and the pay's not nearly as lucrative as tennis or golf. In fact, it's like at the minimum wage end of sport, I'd say. So, I was lucky to have unlimited financial backing and access to the top horses, a team of world class mentors and coaches, plus a retinue of grooms, stable hands, and trainees. So, I get to focus on what I do best, which is riding and creating partnerships. I'm eternally grateful for that. Who wouldn't be? But still, at the end of the day, it's down to me. Success doesn't just fall into your lap.'

'No,' Rosetta agreed, taking a sip of coffee. 'So, what's the key to getting to the very top. What makes an Olympian?'

Juliet thought for a while. 'Well, when I'm not travelling, giving masterclasses, being photographed its endless hours in the saddle. Plus, the gym sessions, not for the faint hearted, this.'

Rosetta couldn't fail to be impressed. That was serious dedication and then some. 'And, what else?'

'Well, a positive attitude, and optimism, amongst other things. But you have to start with the right mind set.' She gave a weak smile. 'I'm finding that pretty tough right now.'

Rosetta nodded in sympathy. 'Loss is a bummer, especially when it's totally unexpected and not of our choosing.' *I should know,* she thought to herself, wondering how she'd attracted her current situation and experiences. She had supposedly cleared all her negative karmic energy and attachments; done all the work. Yet, here was still more stuff showing up. She turned her attention back to Juliet.

'I've been wondering about this, why didn't you answer my call that morning? Why did you choose to ignore it?'

Juliet looked rueful. 'My strategy for success involves dealing with distractions. I'm pretty stellar at planning and organisation and I can't afford to get side tracked. If it doesn't serve the end goal, it tends to get ignored. I guess I'm sort of ruthless about it. You have to be single-minded to keep on track.'

'Makes sense,' Rosetta agreed. 'What else gets you to the very top?'

Juliet flinched and took a gulp of coffee as if she were forcing some dark feeling back down. She paused and stared at the toes of her black leather boots. 'I'm pretty fanatical about routine. I like things running on auto-pilot. Heaven knows horses are unpredictable enough, so I like everything else under control as far as possible. But…'

'But?'

'If only I'd ditched the routine that morning. If only I'd stayed off the road, hadn't been so obsessed with getting the horses fit – the outcome would have been so different.' Her body sagged back into the cushions. 'After all, what's better? An out-of-shape horse, or no horse, and a dead girl?'

'Yeah,' Rosetta said with a sigh. 'Coping with adversity is tough, yet here you are carrying on, getting back on track. That takes guts.' Rosetta shot her a smile of encouragement. Being a detective meant that you encountered people in the raw mess of life at its worst. Everyone had different ways of reacting and working through the process, and often it wasn't a pleasant experience.

'One thing I know for sure, is that managing my emotions is key to success, especially as horses are so sensitive, and they can pick up on small feelings. I always had a very clear purpose and a bold mental vision. I visualised myself bringing home that gold, knowing that there'd be challenges and failures along the way, but I was totally focused. But this… all the years of discipline, training in all kinds of weather, and the sheer grit required just to keep going, let alone improving, now…' Juliet stared ahead blankly as her voice trailed off.

'What?' Rosetta asked softly.

Juliet uncrossed her legs and let out a long sigh. 'Each time life knocks us down, are we supposed to bounce back or sometimes are we supposed to change direction? Is the price we have to pay really worth it?'

'Good question. That's something only you can figure out, by listening to your intuition. Over time, we can accumulate the patterns and consequences of negative choices, and actions, and these need to be cleared before we can move forward and transform.'

Juliet narrowed her eyes. 'What are you getting at exactly?' Her body language began to close down and tighten, and Rosetta realised that she would need to proceed lightly to avoid alienating her further.

Rosetta put her mug down on the work surface and cocked her head to one side.

'Earlier, you mentioned that you thought that Gothic was a reincarnation of one of your previous horses.'

'Well, that makes me sound like I'm nuttier than a fruit cake and anyway, I didn't mean it. I was distraught at the time.' Her face had set, and her eyes had narrowed. Her look said, *don't you dare go any further with this line of enquiry.* Resistance was a common defence mechanism, it was the ego's way of trying to reassert control whenever a person made a shift to a more spiritual path. Rosetta had encountered similar responses many times and she knew it was simply a phase that had to be pushed through.

'You're not crazy at all, quite the opposite. In fact, I'd say you're pretty well attuned. Do you think what happened was some entirely random accident, or do you feel there's more to it?'

'I'm not answering that, I'm not going there. What's important isn't why this happened, it's moving forward, and finding a replacement horse. Do you know how difficult that will be?'

'Sometimes we have to embrace the pain in order to grow.'

Juliet slammed back against the sofa and snarled, 'Who the hell do you think you are coming here to lecture me about pain? I compete at the edge, and all the time there's risk. Risk of injury, paralysis, broken bones, death – you name it: loss and losing. Look what happened to poor Isabella. Argh…' Juliet screamed, and her legs started thrashing until one by one the dogs flew off the sofa and scarpered.

Rosetta waited until the angry outburst had run its course. 'Feeling a bit better now? It's good to get it out of your system.'

Juliet sniffed.

'The thing is, when I have visions, particularly so vividly, as I did with your accident, it usually relates to past life events and karmic consequences that are showing up in the present,' Rosetta said in an even tone. She really needed Juliet's co-operation, and she wondered how to broach the subject which she knew may not go down too well. 'Would you consult a past life regression therapist, is that something you'd consider?' Rosetta crossed her fingers behind her back. Ordinarily, this wouldn't be necessary, as EPIS could travel backwards via the time portal. But it was still out of action thanks to the unwanted guests that had arrived.

'Whoa... whoa... not so fast,' Juliet held her palms up. 'I'm not signing up for any of that paranormal stuff.'

'That's fine, there's nothing to worry about. I've brought you some literature, and I can recommend several excellent reputable therapists.' Rosetta passed her a clear folder with some leaflets inside. Juliet tossed it to one side, and although she still looked disgruntled and shut down, Rosetta sensed that her barriers had shifted a little.

Almost as an afterthought, Juliet glared at the literature. 'Wait a minute. Stop right there. You're saying that something in my past has something to do with... with the accident? Like a ripple that went splat, and spread crap everywhere?'

'Yours and Gothic's pasts, I imagine, but I can't say for sure unless someone accesses your Akashic records.' Rosetta studied Juliet's body language to see how receptive she might be to the suggestion. 'There's nothing bad or spooky about it, quite the opposite.'

'Why in the world would I sign up for any of this stuff?'

One of the terriers jumped up onto Juliet's lap and started nuzzling into her armpit.

She leapt to her feet, dislodging the terrier in the process. 'I've had enough of your mumbo-jumbo, and if you come here again, spewing this trash, I'm going to make a formal complaint. Do I make myself clear?'

'Perfectly,' Rosetta said. She needed to shift the exchange back onto more neutral and predictable police and victim lines of enquiry. 'I checked some phone records earlier and it seems that Matt wasn't very responsive and only phoned you very late. Why was that?'

Juliet stiffened and sat bolt upright. Rosetta observed that she'd touched on a raw nerve.

'Oh, he was busy and then there was the time difference.' Her tone seemed forced and unconvincing as her voice trailed off. She picked at her nails.

That doesn't stack up, Rosetta decided.

'Ah, right, did he call anyone else that you're aware of?'

Juliet hesitated and licked her lips. 'He called Tracy first.'

Rosetta noticed the slightest of squirms before Juliet rapidly regained her composure, and she concluded that she'd just witnessed an Olympian master the art of thought re-framing: closing down negative pathways and focusing on positive outcomes.

Rosetta chewed the end of her roller ball. As far as she could recall there were no calls from Matt to Tracy on his phone records. 'Which hotel was he staying at in Miami?'

'The Blue Dolphin on Ocean Drive, why?'

Rosetta shrugged as she scribbled a reminder in her notebook: *Pull Lebaine's hotel phone records from the Blue Dolphin, Ocean Drive.*

Juliet stood up and put her coffee cup in the sink. 'Are we done here? I have to get back to work.'

'Sure. Thanks for your time.' Rosetta added her cup to the stack. 'Just one more thing – in my latest vison I dreamed about Gothic's funeral. He was buried beneath a large oak tree overlooking a beautiful meadow. You were there, so were Tracy and Matt and two men I didn't recognise and a vet – yes, a vet, I think, called Michael. A small private ceremony which was videoed, and the link was embedded in an email. The email went viral and caused you great distress, so may I suggest...'

Juliet gasped. 'That's exactly what I have planned. How did you know?'

Rosetta put her notebook in her bag and turned to Juliet. 'I'm not trying to interfere. I'm only trying to help. With information you can make a different choice and decide not to embed the link in an email and save yourself more grief.' Rosetta set off, about to leave, then she stopped at the doorway and called out softly, 'Meanwhile, if you change your mind about the past life regression reading, just give me a call. I think it would really help tie down some of the loose ends and nail this case.'

Juliet did not look convinced.

CHAPTER TEN

Rosetta

Out in the yard, Rosetta watched the horses' nostrils steaming over the stable doors and into the crisp winter air. Some were munching on hay and shaking their heads impatiently, as if they were waiting to kick their heels out in the fields. To her right as she walked away from the yard she saw Tracy cantering around the school on the big black horse.

Tracy was attractive, with her blonde pony-tail bouncing under her riding hat, but she was nothing special compared to Juliet. If there was something going on with her and Matt, it begged the question, why? Sex, perhaps, there was always that, the lower part of the anatomy leading the way. But why would he risk losing a rich, famous, elegant girlfriend for her? But then again, Rosetta had to admit the inner workings of men could be unfathomable. She'd totally believed that she and Daniel, Danny-boy, would end their days together. He was her best friend. They confided everything to one another, giggled at the same things, and they were madly, deeply in love, or so she thought. But without warning, he simply withdrew. No explanation, nothing… just a total shutdown. He'd left her high and dry with an unsolved cold case, and he damn well knew how much she'd hate that. Daniel knew just how tough this assignment would be. Her going back to the UK, being so close to her children yet emotionally still so far away. She gathered from her good friend Professor Romanski or Gandalf, as she affectionately called him, that Daniel was fine. No car accident or sudden death, nothing that drastic, just business as usual, and he was still working at the base, carrying on like she didn't even exist. That came as a shock, and really messed with her head. She must be some really sad bitch, if she was not even worth properly finishing with.

'You bastard,' she muttered through clenched teeth. 'How could you, you of all people, do that to me after everything we've been through?'

Why me? she thought bitterly. *What I have done to deserve this?* Her life had come off the rails five years ago during the divorce. The first blow was the kids, now Daniel, so apart from Atone she'd lost everything that she'd ever cared about. Rosetta was alone with all the stigma that entailed. Her family was broken, shattered into a thousand pieces, and she'd invested so much emotional energy into the relationship with Daniel, and she'd done so much clearing work on herself; all for what?

So much for meditation, spiritual cleansing, heightened awareness, radiating love and peace. And positive thinking, what did any of that get you? Big fat zero. Ah, let's re-frame that like a good Olympian, so from loss I have the opportunity, the chance to learn a lesson.

Her phone pinged, announcing a message. She fished it out of her pocket and glanced at the screen. She felt a flicker of excitement when she realised it was from Alice. The pleasure was short lived in the usual tsunami of pain.

Alice: *Stop texting, you're pathetic! We don't want anything to do with you. You weren't there for us when we needed you.*

Me: *I'm sorry. I want to try re-build our relationship. Will you meet me halfway?*

Alice: *No. Go away and never come back.*

Me: *I love you, always remember that.*

When their conversation ended, Rosetta felt a surge of guilt mixed with grief at all the lost connections and the lack of communication.

Ha, ha. Rosetta threw her head back and gave a bitter laugh. *Why do I need to learn that loss is part of the human condition?* she fumed. *I already bloody well know that. I see it in my job on a daily basis. That's bloody hard, so do I really have to be so disconnected from everyone I love? Do I really have to be brought to my knees?*

Rosetta glared up at the dull grey sky. 'Well, do I? Earth to spirit guides, aliens, and angels, where are you when I need you? Argh, sod the lot of you!'

Soon it would be Christmas, and all those family festivities, a logistical nightmare for divorcees, of course. How she wished she could return to Dulce, the EPIS HQ, where she could finally confront Daniel, spend time with friends and like-minded spirits. But instead, she was stuck here trying to solve this case. Stuck somewhere where she didn't fit in, and certainly didn't belong.

Rosetta shivered, tightened her scarf around her neck, and jutted her chin out, determined not to break down here. But the thought of happy Santa reunions just made everything worse. *Why was life on Earth like the school of hard knocks without a truancy pass?* As she pondered on this, the horse cantering round the schooling area snorted, quiffs of steam coming out of its nostrils. She noticed that its coat had been clipped so only the hair on the legs remained. To stop it from sweating, she assumed.

Rosetta took a deep breath and inhaled the assorted smells of the stable yard. It came in layers, along with memories of happier times: first leather polish, then fresh hay, hot horse. It felt like entering another intoxicating world. Rosetta gripped hold of the enclosure fence, and she wondered if things had been different if she and Alice could have bonded over her love of ponies. She had been pony-mad for a while, but Peter would not entertain it, and eventually it phased out.

Another relinquished passion, and a missed opportunity, Rosetta thought with a sharp pang of regret as she scurried back to her car. She should have fought Peter, held her ground, and insisted that Alice deserved a pony. It was so many little girls' passion, but in truth she'd been too busy and consumed with the divorce battle and her career, so she hadn't been there for her children. Not really, and not in a fully supportive way. A lump rose in Rosetta's throat. It occurred to her that things could be worse. There'd be no text messages from Isabella to her family, no teenage rebellion, no birthday celebrations, nothing. She swallowed and took a deep breath. Masking her true emotions behind a brave face, that was one of the things she did best. She was a detective after all, not a bystander rubbernecking at pileups. Detectives had to wade right in there and deal with dark life events at the very edge... right on the brink. But now, cocooned inside the vehicle and out of view, she turned the engine over and a large tear trickled down her cheek, then another, until she couldn't stop sobbing. *There now,* she told herself, *just let it all out.*

The radio crackled into life as she whacked the volume up to drown out the noise and distract herself. *Don't try holding it in, leaving it to fester,* she thought, clutching the steering wheel as she collapsed forward, burying her head on the rim. *No matter what it takes,* she thought, *I'm going to catch Isabella's killer. After all it could have been my daughter, my beloved Alice, in the wrong place at the wrong time. No parents deserved what the Levine's were forced to endure. They'd been dealt a life sentence with no prospect of parole.*

The radio belted out the tune "Cry Me a River," and pretty soon, the words were drowned out and washed away.

* * *

At 5:05 p.m., the team had gathered in the incident room where Rosetta stood and turned to face the group. The collective mood in the room was sombre, this was now a cat-A crime, and they didn't yet know how high the chances were of a reoccurrence.

'I'd like to give you an update on road rage attacks. Can you spare me a short while for that?'

Rav nodded and took a seat. Really, he didn't have much choice at this stage, as he didn't exactly know what her brief was. 'Sure. Fire away but keep it short and sweet. We've a long night ahead of us as it is.'

'Okay. I've printed summaries.' Rosetta pointed to a pile of A4 papers on her desk and picked up one to read from. 'Grab yourself a copy on the way out. Essentially, road rage is a criminal offence, where classically an angry motorist injures, threatens, or kills another person. That might be another motorist, a cyclist, or a pedestrian. It's not usually pre-mediated, and it's not the same as aggressive driving, which includes speeding, tailgating, and the like. That's a traffic offence. So, here we have a road rage incident that went badly out of control, and what we need to determine is who, and why. As you know, I'm a trained psychologist, but I'm not responsible for perp profiles on the Yorrex force so I don't want to go stepping on anyone's toes. But I have other gifts... erm... abilities.'

There were a few snickers.

Rosetta continued, unperturbed. She was used to being hassled. 'The first thing to determine is, was it a purely random, circumstantial event, or was there motive involved? According to the statistics, this wasn't your typical or most common kind of rage attack. What records indicate is that most events occur on Friday, twenty-one-point-one percent are afternoon in peak rush-hour travel times, twenty-five percent in urban areas, when there's moderate congestion, and in good, often sunny and fair-weather conditions.' Rosetta shuffled the papers in front of her and turned over a page. 'Ours took place between ten and ten thirty in the morning. That's not the peak morning travel time, and the records show less than ten percent of episodes happen in this period, compared to twenty-five percent at peak afternoon rush-hour time. But what's interesting is this took place not in an urban area but on a rural country road, and that accounts for only seven-point-nine percent of recorded incidents in the survey, whereas urban freeways rank as the most common location, with twenty-three-point-seven percent. Now, we can draw some conclusions from the statistics. Drivers get more short-tempered when they're fatigued, stressed, and in a rush, and this is likely to be more so at the end of the week on the way home, rather than on a weekend when they're not even going to work. That's substantiated by the statistics. Plus, there tend to be more incidents when congestion levels are moderate rather than high. Any ideas why that is?'

'Well, more horn honking and obscene gestures fly around in a traffic jam,' Shirley suggested. 'But in heavily congested conditions, I guess they're stuck?'

Rosetta nodded. 'Exactly, the difficulty of escaping damps down the anger levels somewhat. Bad weather has the same effect. In snow and ice, road rage is very rare, the theory being that motorists are distracted and drive more carefully. In fact, there are zero road rage incidents recorded in similar icy conditions. Overall, the day, the time, the rural area, and the bad driving conditions make this a very unusual attack compared to the survey charts. The notes cover this in more detail. Help yourselves later, but meanwhile can I have your thoughts?'

The room fell silent. Then, finally Dennis piped up, 'To summarise, it was either a totally random encounter between the victims and the perp, that's the sort of thing the public really hates, the inexplicable, arbitrary meaningless stuff, but in which case it's a highly unusual case, or it's the thief making a getaway in a stolen vehicle. But there's a motive and for some reason, he wants the horse riders wiped out.'

Rosetta laughed. 'Pretty good assessment, yes, and as statistically it doesn't fit the random road rage attack pattern at all, I'd say we're definitely looking to find a motive. This was a brutal attack, in broad daylight. We need to explore every avenue and nail the bastard. Anyone else got anything to add?'

DC Boyd took a deep breath. 'Maybe the driver had a motive, and wanted Juliet and the horse out of the running, but made it look like a random road rage attack thingy?'

'Thank you, Charlie,' Rosetta said. 'That's an interesting twist that we can't discount at this stage, and for what it's worth, that's my favourite. On that note, I'd like to add a profile of the typical road rage attacker. Usually male, but females are catching up on the aggression stakes.'

'Och, right,' Shirley interrupted. 'There was that high-profile one who murdered her fiancé, poor laddie, and she covered it up with the story about road rage attack by a stranger – what was her name?'

Dennis opened up a Google search on his PC and reported back, 'Tracie Andrews. She went down after killing her fiancé in his car on a country lane in 1996. She stabbed him repeatedly but then concocted this complex story about how they got involved in an argument with another motorist who killed Lee in a road rage attack. She went on *Crime Watch*, with Lee's parents, appealing for witnesses to come forward. But, the evidence didn't stack up. Lee's blood was splattered in the back of the car, and he had clumps of her hair in his hands. There was no other DNA. She went down for fourteen years.'

'Hmm, interesting,' Rosetta said. 'I'll check, as her psych profile might shed some light on current investigations. You never know. Okay, well, here's the classic psychological profile that might fit a road rage individual. There's typically anti-social personality disorder or narcissistic traits, or someone with borderline personality disorder, essentially the types who lack empathy and show zero remorse. What else?'

Rosetta studied her notes and stretched her neck before continuing. 'As promised, here's a list of characteristics: impulsive, reckless, prone-to-risk-taking. Sensation and attention seekers, but they may hate to be late. They're obsessive but only about things that are important to them. Often bizarrely about time keeping –'

Charlie interrupted. 'OCD-like? I'm like that about boiled eggs, I canna stand 'em too runny.'

'Hard-boiled mine, all the way,' Dennis muttered.

'Excuse me?' Rosetta rolled her eyes. 'As delightful as it is to learn that you two culinary geniuses are not in need of Delia's egg-boiling cookery book, and we can cross that off the Secret Santa list, can we just get back to the subject please?'

'Talking of Secret Santa, mind, I'd quite like an egg timer, hint, hint.' Charlie chuckled.

'In your dreams, man, we got you a sign: *Everyone brings joy to this office, some when they enter, and some when they leave.* And guess where we reckon you fit?' Dennis joked.

'Yee are nay a wee bundle of joy,' Shirley added.

'Okay, children, settle down,' Rosetta said tutting. 'This is a criminal investigation, not a flaming rom-com! Now, as I was saying about the rage road profile, maybe it's part of the control thing – they tend to be manipulative, domineering, and controlling. These types like to dominate, and they have an innate sense of their own superiority, and a big sense of entitlement. They're hostile to authority, and rules, except rules of their own making. They tend to have a complete disregard for their own safety, and the safety of others, so will have no qualms using a vehicle as a weapon.' Rosetta paused. 'Any questions so far?'

Charlie shook his head. 'Well, no disrespect, but that sounds like every fucked-up shit already serving time.'

Rosetta burst out laughing, and the others joined in too. 'That's true, us shrinks always label violent killers as narcissists or psychos,' she chortled, 'but this one's still out there, very much at large. Check crime records; look out for a history of traffic violations: speeding fines, not wearing a seat belt, a general I'm-above-the-law attitude. Be on the alert for someone who brags about driving at an early age, or who has previously resisted arrest. Watch out for that sort of thing. Oh, and finally, remember we always think our sixth sense will detect a psychopath, but that's rarely the case. They're conmen, superb actors, prolific liars, and they'll fool you just like…' she snapped her fingers, 'just like that.'

'Cheers,' DS Hodges said, frowning. 'So, never mind swiping right, I won't even get as far as that since I'm now too terrified to even bloody well log on.'

'Never mind Shirley,' Dennis commiserated. 'Why look further afield when this here station is a deep mine of rich untapped man-pickings?'

'Argh,' Shirley growled, hurling a notebook at his head and then a pencil.

'Please –' Rav admonished, looking exasperated. 'Can I remind you that a young girl is dead? Now, let's get back on track, and just crack on. Charlie, you go first.'

One by one the team reported their findings. Rav updated the board accordingly.

'So,' he said as he stood back and studied it. 'What've we got?'

'Well,' Shirley cut to the chase. 'We're nay really much further forward, are we?'

69

It took balls to lay the truth right on the line like that, Rosetta thought, resting one elbow on the desk and her chin in her hand. She chewed over how events had rolled out so far, and the lack of progress left her feeling flat and dejected. Juliet hadn't answered her call, no bobby on the beat went out to intercept her because the Bot said no, but could she have done more? *I'm like the keeper of all things karma and confidential who's lost the key. What am I missing? Ah, of course,* she thought, *maybe there were patterns.* 'Any other unsolved similar cases?' she asked.

Rav shook his head. 'No, Charlie checked that angle already.'

'So, it's not a serial killer.' She ran her fingers through her hair and frowned, wondering where all the blind alleys were heading.

'Not unless he's just hitting first base, in which case, no MO,' Dennis observed.

'Has anyone claimed responsibility?' Rosetta asked.

'What do you mean?' Shirley said with a puzzled look.

'I mean like the soldiers of the Islamic state.'

Shirley shook her head and groaned. 'Shit, that's all we need. Someone mutters *Allahu Akbar* and the counter terrorist unit will be swarming all over us like a rash.'

There was a collective groan.

'That could be a classic come-to-Jesus moment, eh?' Dennis quipped. 'Still, look on the bright side, that'd mean they'd take over, and we'd be stood down, and Christmas as usual is delivered unto us. Amen! An' I get to watch all me best telly programs without interruption.' He held his crossed fingers up and grinned. 'So, Santa, can you cough up a few Koran martyrs or radicals for us please?'

'That ought to do it,' Shirley clucked like the resident mother hen. 'Our big break is to get relieved of our own cases, wow. Just one problem... they dunna do isolated country roads for a start and they're usually quick to take ownership.'

'True,' Rav concurred. 'They go for crowed streets, parades, mass gatherings, that sort of thing.'

'The more infidels the merrier,' Charlie said.

'Keep your infidels, MI5-ers, and tank loads of intrepid crime reporters, ta very much,' Stuart, the family liaison officer, shot back. His shoulders slumped, and he had a look that indicated he was not too impressed and verging on being pissed right off. His normally laid-back demeanour became taut. 'Imagine having to explain that lot to the Levine's. I mean, *Sorry to have to mention this, but it appears that your lovely thirteen-year-old daughter was on some jihadi hit list. Brace yourselves for the media invasion of the century.* Never mind a come-to-Jesus moment, this is embracing the lavatory bowl. Positively puke making. Cheers for that, guys!' He threw Rosetta a look filled with burning indignation.

Rosetta raised her hands, palms outwards, in a pacifying gesture. 'Okay, sorry, I didn't mean to ruffle feathers with the terrorist theory, so let's just put that one to bed.'

But really, if you don't like that, she thought, *you're going to hate what's coming next.*

CHAPTER ELEVEN

Juliet
21st December

Juliet drove to Gatwick first thing to meet Matt at arrivals. She got there early, parked in the short-stay car lot, and fretted trying to remember the level number. Once she'd parked in some grey concrete multi-storey and had to call the breakdown services just to locate her vehicle. *Talk about embarrassing.* She took the elevator down to the ground floor, then the walkway. En-route she grabbed a latte and a muffin and went to wait in line with the relatives and taxi pick-ups with names on notice boards. At last Matt came into view, dragging his suitcase on wheels, making her heart flutter, and she caught her breath at the dimple that came with his broad smile. She'd missed him so much, she just hadn't realised until now. He wore a dark green T-shirt with a checked green shirt over the top, and a pair of ripped, frayed jeans, plus a pair of dark designer shades: the shabby-chic rockstar look but hardly ideal for the UK in winter. As he came towards her, he looked up and raised his chin in greeting.

'Hi,' he said, grinning.

'Hi,' she said with a mixture of joy and relief. 'I'm glad you're back. How was the flight?'

'Long, but I did manage to fall sleep. Then there was this kid, a total little brat, kicking the back of my seat. Remind me never to have kids.' His finely chiselled features were the colour of light golden toast.

'Well, not right now anyway,' she agreed. It seemed an odd thing for him to say, as they'd discussed having a family at some point and she thought the matter had been settled. She wouldn't have accepted his marriage proposal if he seriously never intended to start a family.

She'd been thinking after the 2024 Olympics, but that had all gone wrong now. She made a mental note to follow up about it later and meanwhile she gave him a big bear hug, hanging on as if she'd never let him go. She so needed physical contact and support, a broad shoulder to cry on and someone to cheer her up when things got really bleak: like now.

Close up, he smelled fresh and clean, as always. She inhaled deeply as he kissed her on the cheek. 'Are you wearing new aftershave?' It smelt of pine, citrus, and notes of vanilla musk. *Delicious.*

'Yeah, Marc Jacobs, it was a… erm… I got it in duty free.'

'Yes,' she said, feeling a tiny twinge of hurt that he wasn't more affectionate. Didn't she deserve a hug? After all, they hadn't seen one another for over two weeks. And what had he been about to say about the aftershave? That it was a gift? Who from? Immediately, her thoughts launched into disaster mode.

Stop it, she told herself, *now you're really getting paranoid. Get a grip.*

'Did you meet anyone interesting?' she said as they made their way to the car park. On cue he rattled off a list of places, people, and parties. All crap that she didn't want to hear. She wasn't listening. It was impossible to concentrate, and the more enthusiastic he sounded, the more he flashed that smile and those perfect teeth, the less she cared. He loaded his suitcases in the back and they exited the airport.

At the traffic circle, she checked the fuel gauge. They would need to fill up with gas on the way back. Matt had his eyes closed, and he seemed to have drifted off to sleep. *Un-freaking-believable.* He hadn't even mentioned Isabella or Gothic once. How messed up was that? The spoilt brat, did he really think it was okay to act like nothing had happened, what planet was he on? This wasn't anything like the loving reunion she'd envisaged. She'd imagined that things would improve once he got back. *Yeah right, in my dreams,* she thought. This snoozing loser slumped next to her was hardly your Average Supportive Joe, not even close. *Ha,* she thought, *this part is proving to be way beyond his meagre acting capabilities.* In that instant, with anger mounting, she wanted to slap him, pound his chest with her fists – anything to provoke a reaction. Resisting temptation, she set her jaw sullenly and fell into silence, staring at the highway. Eventually, he stirred.

'What's the matter?' he asked.

'Nothing.'

'You're very quiet.'

'I'm tired.' Juliet frowned. 'You could have got a taxi from the airport instead of having me pick you up.'

Matt opened his arms and looked up as if appealing to the Dali Lama. 'But you offered.'

'You could have refused,' she said tersely. 'I've got more than enough on my plate.'

'Look, Jules, I don't want to get into an argument over this.' He sounded weary. 'I'm tired too. I've been worried sick about you.'

Juliet sucked in her cheeks and silently fumed. Supposedly he had bought himself aftershave, but nothing for her. No thought of acknowledging her pain or trying to cheer her up. Either that or someone had given him aftershave as a rather intimate gift. Frankly, she didn't know what was worse.

'I… Oh, forget it.' She assumed her best "screw you" expression.

'Come on. I can tell there's something on your mind. Just talk to me, please.'

Silence.

'I want to help. Help you in any way that I can, but I can't if you shut me out.'

She didn't know why it was so difficult to get the words out. After all, she'd been rehearsing all morning on the drive over. She paused, searching for the right opening. Then she said, 'Okay, there's something I'd like you to explain.' Finally, she was about to give in to the nagging dread which had been building inside her since yesterday.

'What?' he asked, scrutinising her closely.

Oh Lord, she'd been dreading this. She grew flustered and her palms grew sticky.

She'd sensed it on the voicemail messages, something deeply disturbing. Something was definitely not right. Try as she might, she couldn't quite put her finger on it – an affair, perhaps – but her instincts suggested it ran deeper than that. She took a deep breath. 'Is there something going on between you and Tracy?'

'What in the devil's name gave you that idea?'

'It was something she said.' Juliet paused, not wanting to continue in case she didn't like his reply. She felt shivery and apprehensive. 'Did you call her on the day of the accident?'

'Probably, I was worried sick. I must've phoned half my address book.'

Juliet glared at him, not knowing what to think. Following Todd's advice, she had already quizzed Tracy, who'd stuck to her story. 'You called her hours before you called me. Why? Just tell me the truth.'

She hardly dared to breathe.

'Jesus,' he spluttered. 'Are you going nuts? I didn't cut my assignment short to rush home and listen to this rubbish!'

Juliet's chest rose and sank in rapid succession. Could anyone who looked so hurt and indignant possibly be lying? Either that or he was a better actor than she'd thought. She really wanted to believe him.

'Okay, I'm sorry.' She raised one hand in a pacifying gesture. 'Forget it. I guess I'm pretty paranoid at the moment.'

'You can say that again. Are flamingos pink or what?' he growled, turning away and staring out of the passenger window. They continued the journey home in silence.

Later that morning, when Matt had given in to his jet-lag and gone for a nap, Juliet called Todd from the kitchen with the phone wedged in the crook of her shoulder as she loaded the dishwasher. From the window, she watched two workmen with a small earthmoving digger across the paddock, near the giant oak tree.

'Hi,' she said, turning away, not wanting to dwell on it. 'They're in the paddock digging Gothic's grave, right now.'

'Oh… ah… Oh dear,' Todd said. 'Is that allowed? I mean is it legal?'

Juliet gasped. 'Yeah, it's fine, horses are classed as pets. So, you can… can bury them at home as long as the… the site's not on a water course, or something.'

'Right, well, Barrie and I will come over and we'll give him a proper send-off. Just let me know when you're ready.'

'Thanks. Will Barrie be here for the burial on the twenty-seventh? I thought we'd better get Christmas over with. But isn't he away filming?'

'Auditioning, but he doesn't leave till the 29th December. Oh, my dear Lord, move over Idris Elba, Barrie's set his sights on being the first black James Bond. Can you imagine him with his tackle in a tight Speedo strutting along the beach? That's all I need. Frankly, I know I sound like a total bitch, but I'm so praying he does not get offered the bloody part. Imagine all that adoration going straight to his head. He's already insufferable as it is. You can't imagine what I have to put up with. I'm working through a self-help book called, "How to Change Your Life in Seven Days." I've been at it for over a fortnight now, so it doesn't bode too well, does it? Anyway, enough about me, how did it go with M and T?' he enquired in a conspiratorial whisper.

'Oh,' she sighed. 'Matt denied everything and got kinda aggressive. Honestly, I can't think straight anymore. Why would he risk everything we've got?' She set the dishwasher's timer and took a seat at the table.

'Perhaps it's the Essex-girl peroxide hair, East Ender chav manners, or the voice of a throat cancer patient in remission?' Todd cackled wickedly.

'Todd!' Juliet snapped as she lightly caressed the table's worn surface.

'Barrie reckons it could be an ego thing. Matt rates himself highly, and he needs a lot of attention and constant devotion. And babe… my Barrie should know. If he lands that 007 thing he'll be like a dog with two dicks and my life will be hell just pandering to him.'

'Attention that I'm too busy to give him, you mean?' Juliet frowned. Perhaps she was guilty of being complacent, of treating him like an old familiar piece of furniture. She stroked the table, deep in thought. It needed a good wax and polish. *Same as me*, she thought. *It's been forever since I shaved, plucked, let alone primped and preened. Still, who has time for all that?* she wondered.

'Maybe, I mean really what the fuckety-fuck do I know? It's only a theory, but what if he finds someone in awe of him? Someone inferior to the obviously desirable girlfriend, but who'll lavish him with loads of attention? Voila! Enter the nearest employee. It happens quite often, apparently, you know, knocking off the nanny, so, why not the groom?'

'Thanks. You've made my day,' she moaned. 'What am I supposed to do?'

'Hire male grooms,' Todd squealed. 'Do you think I'd have pretty young boys wandering round to catch my Barrie's eye? Do bears do their do-dahs in the woods? I mean, really! My grooms are all fat, ugly, and female.'

'Argh,' she groaned. 'Did I mention that I called the developers and put the deal on hold?'

'Really?' he gasped, clearly interested. Todd loved gossip. 'Matt's not going to be too thrilled about that, is he? That project is his baby. Talking of which, did I mention Craig's new man? He's barely old enough to be doing a paper round. I wish he'd just grow up and stop getting tingles in the old tingle-wingle for guys half his age.'

'How old is he?'

'Oh, late twenties I suppose. Craig's no cradle snatcher but he must be sixty if he's a day. Although he's had a face-lift, does Botox, and lies about his age, of course.'

'I'm feeling pretty old myself these days,' Juliet sighed.

'It'll pass, and you'll soon be back to yourself. OMG, the police called me into the station yesterday, for questioning! Just imagine. What an ordeal. I took Barrie with me obvs, I mean, I hope they don't think I'm a suspect.'

'Really, what did they want to know?'

'Well,' he sounded cagey. 'This and that, they seem quite interested in your eventing rivals, fallouts, Matt's relationship with Tracy, and was there anything going on between them.'

'What did you say?'

'That I hadn't got a clue, of course.'

'But who would mow us down like that?' Juliet muttered.

'Dunno,' he sighed. 'It beggars belief. Look, I've got to dash. I'm teaching in a minute. Call me tonight and give me all the gory details.'

'Okay,' she agreed, 'I just don't know what to think anymore.'

'Well,' he murmured, 'try not to overthink things. Just keep calm and try to get back into a routine. You know, to take your mind off things. You used to be such a stickler for routine.'

'I guess.' She shrugged. 'But why does it take so long to nail the bad guys?'

'Well, that's understandable, the police have to follow all leads and make sure the case is watertight. Call me later, babe, and keep calm. Bye babe, love you loads.'

'Love you too,' Juliet said, and she hung up.

* * *

Matt surfaced in time for lunch, a sandwich and a bowl of soup. Juliet had her favourite, pastrami and Swiss cheese with deli mustard on rye bread with plenty of pickles. Matt ambled across the kitchen and flopped onto a chair, looking groggy.

'I told you it'd be better to try and stay awake,' she admonished gently as he stifled a yawn.

'I was just too knackered.' He yawned again to emphasise his point. 'How did the teaching go this morning?'

'Fine.' She bit her lip and her cheeks grew hot. 'But I've got a problem. I took one of the youngsters out, and I had a really bad panic attack. I had to turn back. I can't handle going past the spot where… where it happened.' She squirmed uncomfortably. It seemed so wet and pathetic. If she couldn't get out of her own driveway, what chance did she have of getting to the Olympics?

77

Matt nodded. He didn't interrupt. Instead, he gave her hand a re-assuring squeeze. 'Try not to dwell on it. You can't change what happened. Remember, if you've made a mistake in your dressage test, you don't dwell on it, do you?' He took a bite out of his wholemeal ham roll and chewed.

'No, I try harder, and think about where I can gain extra marks to catch up.' She studied a spoonful of minestrone soup, trying to decide if she was hungry anymore, and decided that she wasn't. She wrapped the sandwich and stuck it in the refrigerator for later.

'Exactly,' he said squeezing her arm softly and giving her a kiss on the side of her face. 'That's why I'm trying to get you to focus on finding a replacement horse.' He was watching her with concern. 'I know you think I'm being insensitive, but we've got to keep the big picture in sight, keep moving towards the main objective.' He stood up. 'Have you finished? You haven't eaten much.'

Juliet nodded, so Matt cleared the dishes then sauntered over to the sink and deposited them with a clatter. With a low whistle, he filled the kettle and set it to boil.

Juliet shook her head, the lump in her throat made speaking difficult. 'Maybe you're right.' She shrugged. 'But there'll never be another horse like him.' She caught her breath and clapped her hand over her mouth, worried that she would break down. Memories flooded her mind. She pictured Gothic the very first time she'd seen him after the long, gruelling trip over from Ireland by boat and road. It had left the stallion weak and emaciated. His hipbones had been jutting and his tail thin and straggly. His white coat had been thick and matted with sweat and foam. But Juliet hadn't registered any of that. She'd admired the fine sculpting of his head, and there'd been no doubt in her mind he was a thoroughbred – and a very highly bred one at that. He had turned, blowing softly, and fixed his gaze on hers. That had done it. The minute she'd seen those huge, exquisite eyes and the kind expression filled with hope and trust, she'd known that she had to have him. No matter what it cost. Her face had flushed. It had been love at first sight.

Noel Joyce, the canny dealer who had imported the horse, recognised the soppy look on her face and had swiftly launched into his sales spiel in earnest. 'Be jabbers, this hoss is quality. Well, no doubt you can see that for yourself. Why, he was stellar on the hunting field, an absolute star. The Master of Tipperary was all for having him, for sure.'

'Really? So, he's hunted, and he jumps ditches, hedges? What about water?'

'Absolutely. You know it could take years to find one as special as him. Or was it the Master of Limerick? I never can say exactly. 'Tis a bit of a blur.' Then, he'd heaved a most theatrical sigh and added, 'Mind you, I've already refused several offers. I'd really like him to go to a good home, you see.'

That was the masterstroke that had clinched it. Juliet recalled Noel's genial toothy grin and smiled at how easily she'd been ensnared by his whiskey-fuelled spiel.

Gothic turned out to be as green as the Emerald Isles, and he'd certainly never seen hounds. Not close up, at any rate. Still, she'd never regretted that decision for a moment. The very first time she'd ridden him it'd felt as though they were flying. Her eyes widened as she remembered how he had galloped to victory in competition after competition, his huge ground-eating stride making short work of the distance. There must have been some very disappointed men in scarlet coats searching the length and breadth of Eire for just such a horse.

Juliet wiped a tear from her eye with the back of her hand and forced a little smile. She mustn't forget how lucky she'd been to have him.

'I know how much he meant to you,' Matt said, handing her a cup of coffee.

'Thanks.' She stared at the cup, studying the network of hairline cracks that covered the surface glaze. It looked brittle and fragile, as though it might shatter at any moment.

'But you need to get back on track. Moping around won't get you anywhere. What about the Olympics? You'll be better keeping yourself occupied. A couple of sessions with a sports psychologist to over-come the panic attacks and you'll be riding down that road again, no problem.'

'I… I don't know. The thought of it makes me feel sick.' She warmed her hands on the cup and took a sip.

'If you don't do something soon, the horses will pick up on your nerves. You've got to be positive. Yes, it's a setback, but you've got to brush it off. You can deal with this.' Matt's tone softened, and he looked over, trying to gauge her reaction. 'Maybe we can ask Doctor Knightly to recommend some kind of trauma therapist. What do you think?'

'I'll think about it.' She shuffled to her feet and busied herself mov-ing the dishes and plates from the sink to the dishwasher. It felt too soon. She wanted to try and explain to him how she felt, but she never seemed able to convey to him what was so obvious to her. He would look at her with a dazed expression. Then she'd try to explain it another way. Then she'd wait, hoping that he'd get it, but he always said, "Why? I don't understand."

Why?

Until she felt useless and inadequate as well as misunderstood and unsupported. The loneliness and frustration of it made her cry. That set him off. Then, with a look filled with hurt and bewilderment, he'd repeat in a monotone, "I don't understand. Why are you upset?"

Why?

My horse is dead. Thanks to a streak of bad luck and a streak of ill-fated choices. Why the hell do you think I'm upset?

Juliet sighed and shuffled from side to side. Maybe Matt was right about getting help. She always wanted to do everything herself, but the longer she left it, the worse it would get. It was kind of like her phobia with spiders which over the years had magnified a thousand-fold. She set down the last dish and turned to face him.

'DS Hodges asked me to do a TV appeal to get witnesses to come forward, but...'

'But?'

'I really don't know if I can do it. My family doesn't like publicity. It's a kinda mobster-and-lobster thing.'

He paused, resting his head on his shoulder, and studied her for a while. His deep blue eyes shone with sincerity and concern. 'Well, they're happily living it up on Rogue Island, soaking up lemonade with sprigs of mint, and Long Island iced tea. They'll never even know. How many Americans follow European channels on a regular basis? Not many! Did your parents offer any assistance, by the way?'

Juliet nodded. 'I refused.'

Matt rolled his eyes. 'Why? They're loaded!' He shrugged. 'Well, it's entirely your decision. But knowing you, I think you'll regret it if you don't do the TV appeal and everything you can to make sure that bastard is caught.'

'I guess.' Her lip quivered. 'You're right. I've got to do whatever I can.' Grief was a strange thing. One minute she thought she was coping, and the next minute she was back to square one. She bit her lip and tried to compose her features along more positive lines. 'Anyway, I gotta go, I've got four horses to school this afternoon.' Could she rely on Matt for his unwavering support? So far, they hadn't got off to a great start. She grabbed her waterproof jacket and headed out the door. The wind whipped up the rain until it lashed against her face.

That evening, when Matt got around to opening his mail, all fanciful notions of support evaporated, pronto. He stormed into the kitchen.

Juliet looked up from feeding the dogs and caught his expression, lips tight, and his chin set and knew that trouble was heading in her direction.

'Hmm, and when were you planning to tell me about this?' He shoved a letter under her nose.

She paused long enough to compose herself and sound neutral. 'Is it from the insurance company?' She tried to look innocent, but she was a lousy liar, and Matt knew her too well. 'I guess I'll make us some coffee,' she sighed.

'You know damn well what it is!' The muscles in his neck clenched and his cheek twitched.

Juliet took a step backwards, momentarily stunned into silence. She had to be careful how she handled this. Otherwise it would deteriorate into something nasty, and very ugly.

'You sound angry.' She turned away and set the dog dishes down on the floor. 'Good boys, here we go,' she said as the two German pointers, Laurel and Hardy, bounded over with their tails wagging.

Matt's eyes flashed darkly, and he snapped, 'It's a letter from Land Development Ltd acknowledging our decision not to proceed. Our decision... when did you discuss this with me?'

'I meant to,' she sighed, transfixed on the kettle to avoid looking at him. 'I just never got the chance. Matt, please just calm down and listen.'

'Terrific,' he spat as he screwed the letter up and hurled it into the bin. 'You know how hard I've worked on that deal, and all for your benefit.'

That's pretty ironic since he really didn't have anything to lose in this. She was the one who'd suffered the backlash, the hushed whispers when she entered the village store, the fights with her family, and the silent hostility emanating from the local community. How could she be sure that he didn't have any ulterior motives, and that he really was as altruistic as he claimed? The expression on his face made her want to yell, but she held herself back so that she came across as calm and reasonable.

'Yes, I'm sorry. I should have talked to you about it.'

His cheek gave a tell-tale twitch that signalled an inner struggle to keep his emotions in check. Control was his *modus operandi.*

'But I knew it would provoke an argument,' she continued with a weary sigh. 'I'm too tired to fight any longer. I'm tired of fighting my family. My grandparents left this estate as a base for me, not for property speculation. And besides, the entire village is anti the idea of a massive housing development, and I can't say I'm stoked about increased traffic either, especially now. I just want to get back to normal again as quickly as possible.'

'Fine.' He set his mouth in a thin line and gave the table a sharp rap with his fist. 'Whatever. Have it your own way.'

'We can still operate from here.' She reached out and gave his arm an affectionate squeeze. 'And I can still get to the Olympics if you help me find a replacement horse.'

He regarded her coolly as she handed him a cup of coffee. 'I'm not interested. Have you any idea what it's like living with someone as single-minded as you? All you think about is the Olympics, and your bloody horses. Even now you're not really here, are you? Not really.'

His words stung her like a slap, and Juliet gasped. She had anticipated his anger but not his coldness or the steely glint that flashed in his eyes. There was something about that look that made her uneasy. 'Matt, I...' she protested. But he waved his arm to fend her off and stormed out of the kitchen, leaving her staring at his back.

That night they slept in separate rooms for the first time in a long time.

At breakfast the following day, it occurred to her that he might be right. She had been a bit remote since Gothic died, but wasn't that inevitable under the circumstances?

Matt passed the cereal packet and it moved civilly between them in a sort of grown-up version of pass-the-parcel.

A farce, really.

Matt gave out hostile vibes, all prickly elbows and calculated indifference.

Juliet studied her breakfast as if it was a riveting novel she couldn't put down. Eventually, they both stood up at the same time to fetch the toast.

'Excuse me,' they both muttered.

'I'll do it,' she suggested by way of a kind of peace offering.

'Whatever.'

'Matt, I –'

'Not now, Juliet. Leave it.'

She stood in front of the sink and looked out of the window at the old oak tree in the corner of the paddock, where the horses would gather in the summer, glad of some relief from the flies. They would huddle together under its thick, leafy branches, heads in the shade, butts out and tails swishing.

The workmen had finished digging. The hole was covered with board and a tarp, and it had a fence around it with a makeshift gate.

'Oh,' she exclaimed as the smell of burning toast wafted past her nose. *I gotta remember to empty the crumb tray,* she thought as she deposited the slices of charred remains into the bin. 'I've been a bit distracted lately, and I –'

'A bit distracted? You've got a vacant sign hanging on your forehead. As in "the lights are on, but there's no one home."'

How much more fricking insensitive could he be? She had never made any secret of her ambition. It wasn't as if she had misled him on that score. Juliet gritted her teeth. She could walk away and ignore his remarks. That was an appealing prospect right now, anything for a quiet life. Or… she could retaliate.

Right.

She marched to the dining room and stood in the doorway with her hand resting on her hip.

'Get your own shitty toast and jelly,' she said. 'And while you're at it, shove it somewhere the sun doesn't shine.'

With that, she spun around and slammed the door behind her.

CHAPTER TWELVE

Juliet
22nd – 23rd December

The argument continued for several days, building in momentum as time went on.

'Please, let's get this straight.' Matt's shoulders collapsed with weariness. 'Tracy's totally not my type, but she does appeal to some of the owners.'

'But, you did call her from the States? You lying son of a bitch! I knew you were up to something.' She banged her fork down on the table and pushed the plateful of curry away.

'Great, I've been working on Gothic's replacement, and you think I'm up to no good. Terrific, thanks for your vote of confidence!' He looked hurt and indignant.

'I didn't know what to think,' she replied defensively. 'Why did you have to be so secretive?'

'I wasn't going to tell you until I had something concrete. I didn't want to get your hopes up, but I've been working on getting more top horses in our yard for several months now.' He filled her glass with casual precision, and he looked serious and obliging.

'Oh?' Juliet tried not to appear too enthusiastic.

'Yeah. I went through all the Badminton declarations, eliminated the owner-riders, the ones without any real Olympic prospects, and guess how many we're left with?'

'How many?'

Matt did not reply, he carried on eating.

Juliet strummed the table top with her fingers. 'Well, how many?'

'Four.'

'Four?' she echoed. 'You're kidding. Only four horses of his calibre?'

'No, actually there's only one potentially as good as Gothic.' Matt shrugged. 'Anyway, I've been talking to Bert Humboldson to see if he'll let you take over the ride. I reckon he'll go for it.' Matt waved his fork in the air with a triumphant flourish.

'Bert Humboldson?' Juliet spluttered. 'But Todd rides for him. Are you suggesting that we make a move on Todd's rides? Is that what you and Tracy have been up to?'

'Yeah, you got it in one.'

She shot him a warning look. 'No, Matt. No way! Todd's my friend, for Christ's sake. He's been so supportive. He calls or texts me practically every day just to make sure I'm okay. Forget it!'

'Ah, I see. So, were you planning to take a couple of years off, then? Because that's how long it'll be before the Intermediates are ready to upgrade. And there aren't that many Badminton horses around. I reckon Chi-Chi Charlie could win for us, and you could definitely qualify for the World Equestrian Games.'

'Maybe, but right now I need all the friends I've got. Orla's got the idea that I'm somehow to blame for Isabella's death,' she said in a small voice. 'Even if she comes around, which I doubt, it'll never really be the same, will it?'

'No, it won't, but what about Chi-Chi Charlie?' He reached across the table and helped himself to a samosa.

'Forget it, losing Orla's bad enough, but not Todd as well.' She folded her arms as though it was final.

'Well, you can kiss goodbye to the Olympics then. And let's face it, Todd's a New Zealander, so what about team USA?'

Her eyes widened, as she toyed with the notion of taking her best friend's horse. The internal battle raged, doing what was right and nice, or doing what was necessary to stay at the top of her game. Little by little, the more she toyed with the idea, the less abhorrent it became. Todd would understand that it wasn't personal. On the eventing field, they were competitors, both out to win. Juliet had integrity, but she also had ambition. As she searched her heart it seemed that her eventing ambitions transcended everything. Loyalty to a friend was important, but...

'What if Todd lost the ride and you just happened to benefit? Wouldn't Todd want you, more than anyone else, to look after the horse?'

'Well, you might have a point, I guess.' She smiled, but it didn't erase the troubled feeling nagging at her insides. She wanted to be popular, to be loved as a friend, yet she'd spent her entire life on the

Olympic gold medal mission and she couldn't give up now, not after she'd come so far.

'Yeah, I guess. There's just one problem though. To get the ride, we'll have to move.' Matt stared at her over the rim of his glass.

'Move, why?'

'Because the Humboldsons live in Leeds, and if they're driving down to see their horses, they want a yard that's got easy access to the M1. There's no chance of Bert driving to Yorrex, as he's not too impressed with the M29. "As congested as a fat lady's corset," was how he described it.'

'Shit,' she exclaimed as she processed this bit of information. 'But he makes the trip to Todd's.'

'Precisely, and he's had enough of the journey. So, we move and that gives Bert the perfect excuse to change the arrangements. Owners can be flighty as you well know, and the horse's a far better medal prospect with you on board. Bert's hungry for that gold, so it all makes sense.'

'You mean we'll have to sell here after all?' Juliet felt weary at the prospect.

'I just want what's best for you.' Matt briefly wiped the skin under his right eye with his index finger. 'But if you sold to Land Development Ltd, you could afford to move anywhere, not to mention a new top-of-the-range horse box. And you could buy yourself time and you could afford a four-star horse outright, plus a string of talented youngsters to bring on.'

His cheek twitched, and he drummed his fingers on the table. 'You're one of the finest event riders America has ever produced. It'd be a shame to waste such awesome talent. You're a team and individual gold medal winner, Todd won team Olympic bronze, that's it. You deserve the best rides, and Bert wants that gold so bad he can taste it.'

'Well, I don't know –' She sucked her teeth.

'A change of scenery would do you good, so you aren't reminded of what happened.' Matt could be very persuasive, she had to give him credit. 'You look tired. Why don't you have an early night, and sleep on it?'

'Yes, good idea. I feel like a nice long soak in the bath.'

'Sure. I'll clear up,' he said as she left the table.

* * *

The next day, they collided in the kitchen. Breakfast had been a tense occasion. Matt was still sulking over the fact that Juliet didn't trust him, and she had accused him of having an affair with Tracy. Juliet felt a bit bad about that, as it transpired that he had been trying to help her. But things between them were still strained.

Late in the afternoon, the silent hostilities continued in the confines of the car. Matt drove. Juliet studied his profile in silence with little sideways glances. He had this amazing ability of seeming totally unperturbed while inside he fretted. She wondered if it was an act or if he really didn't care that they'd had their worst-ever argument? Did all women dwell on things while men pretended indifference? His chin was set, and with the Roman shape of his nose, he reminded her of one of those heads in profile – all arrogant and haughty, stamped on an old gold coin.

They drew into the Yorrex police station car park, and Matt reversed into a space.

Juliet sighed. 'I'm really not sure about this.' She inhaled deeply, breathing in his smell – Lynx Africa. It filled the car like a continent.

Matt stared at her, his eyebrows arched. 'What?'

'Publicity, it's not our style,' she said, raising her hands in the air. 'Apart from the obligatory announcements in the *New York Times*: births, marriages, and deaths, it's not the way we do things.'

'Lord, you rich Yanks with your ridiculous codes and conventions.'

'Well.' Juliet shook her head and scrutinised him to see if he was joking. She couldn't tell, but on balance she decided that he was probably having a dig. He viewed her family as castles to his housing estate. 'It's not my fault if I fell for you instead of some chinless Harvard wonder, is it?' Her tone sounded a tiny note of pleading. Matt's facial profile was close to perfection – a strong jaw, chiselled chin with requisite cleft and a faint shadow of designer stubble. Even when he was being insulting, she found him charismatic. She just wanted things to be right between them again.

'I guess not,' he agreed. 'But this publicity might even rustle up a replacement horse, and surely Issie deserves justice, don't you think?'

'Of course, I'll do it for her. I'm… I'm devastated,' she said biting back her tears. She needed a distraction, so she checked her reflection in the window of a parked car. 'You don't think this outfit's too bright? Maybe I should have worn the pale green suit?'

'It's fine. Trust me, you look fine. Just hurry up.'

CHAPTER THIRTEEN

Rav
23rd December

The television appeal was being broadcast live on the six o'clock news. Isabella's parents, Patrick and Ann, were placed at the centre of the stage with Stuart their FLO in between. Patrick Levine looked stiff and formal in his Sunday-best tweed suit. Ann was an attractive woman with thick but immaculate make-up disguising her dark shadows and sunken cheeks. Juliet perched at one end of the long table, along with DS Hodges. They faced the crowd, national and daily press cameras, the internet agencies, TV reporters, and they all blinked as the flashes went off.

DS Hodges adjusted her microphone and cleared her throat before outlining the key facts about the incident. She carefully pinpointed the date, time, location, type, and colour of the car – a dark grey Range Rover with distinctive number plates. And she held up an improved artist's impression of the driver – white male, late-twenties to mid-forties, medium build, above average height. She added that Isabella was airlifted to Yorrex General, where she subsequently died. Then, she handed over to the parents to say a few words. Rav observed that under the table, out of the media's view, Stuart, the family liaison officer, had hold of Ann's hand and every so often gave it a reassuring squeeze.

Patrick looked bewildered as the shutters clicked. He took a sip of water from a plastic cup. 'First of all, we'd like to thank the police and the emergency services for their sterling work.' He paused. 'Our precious daughter, Isabella, was just thirteen years old, a lovely sweet girl, a loving daughter, a wonderful sister. It's difficult for us, her parents, to make any sense of this. It's not the sort of thing you expect to happen in a leafy Yorrex lane to two girls out riding. But someone must know or at least suspect who's responsible, and as a husband and a father, I ask you to please come forward. It doesn't matter how small or insignificant your information may seem. Please, come forward to the police.'

Ann bit her lip. She reached forward past Stuart, who was sitting between them, touched her husband lightly on the arm, and whispered something.

'Oh yes,' Patrick said, lowering his head. 'May we ask you all to find a moment in your busy lives to send our daughter your prayers.'

After a respectful pause, Juliet and Ann chorused in unison, 'Amen.'

A reporter announced himself, 'Nick, Sky News. I gather you've recovered the vehicle. What about the owner? Have you had him in for questioning yet?'

Rav squirmed ever so slightly. Of course he was being goaded. The reporter knew damn well they hadn't. 'No, that's not necessary at this stage. The vehicle was stolen, and we're following a number of leads.'

At the back of the room, someone sprang to their feet. 'DCS Patel, you haven't released the car registration details. Why's that?'

Gina Davis announced herself to the room and continued to press home the advantage. 'Perhaps the Yorrex force is hamstrung and understaffed after all the recent cutbacks? Do you have sufficient officers to do the job?'

Rav ducked that question, they were short staffed but announcing the fact would be a political miscalculation, and he had enough years of service under his belt to know that politics and policing were not a brilliant mix; particularly when it came to airing controversy on national media channels.

'Hi, I'm Russell Parks, ITN news. I've been doing some research and apparently through natural shrinkage and transfers your manpower is down by over a third. How do you think the public's going to react if serious crimes go unsolved due to under resourcing?'

DS Hodges opened her mouth to speak, but Rav cut her off. 'I see no point in speculating about public opinion. We're here to appeal to the public to come forward with information for Isabella and her family's sake. We will apprehend the person responsible. I can assure you of that. So, Juliet, would you like to add a few words?'

Patrick stared at the three officers with confusion etched on his face.

Juliet shifted in her seat and chewed her bottom lip. 'It's imperative that the police get new leads, to help find the man who deliberately used his car as a weapon to annihilate my beautiful horse and leave a young girl dying in a ditch.' She paused and took a moment to compose herself before continuing. 'My horse and I were certain to be shortlisted for the American eventing team at the next Olympics. A horse as special as him won't be easy to replace. I'd like to take this opportunity to ask you for your help.'

Pause.

'There are too many horses and riders injured, maimed, and killed on the roads every single day. The statistics are terrifying. So, motorists everywhere, please slow down and give horses plenty of room. Please, kill your speed, not our horses. Remember, horses and riders don't bend – they bleed. Thank you.'

DS Hodges pointed to the Crime Stoppers number. 'Any information, however small, call us. We will find Isabella's killer, that's for sure, but we need your help. Were you in the vicinity of the accident that day? Anywhere near or at Shirley Heights railway station? Were you on Farley Heath? Remember it was the 19th December, that's four days ago. Please get in touch. We need to wrap up now. Thank you all for coming.'

CHAPTER FOURTEEN

Rosetta
24th December

Rosetta had been slumped over her desk for longer than she cared to recall. Despite the massive volume of calls that hit the switchboard after the TV broadcast, or perhaps because of the swamping effect of the same, Rosetta felt as if they were just treading water. The CCTV cameras at the railway station were all malfunctioning and had been for some time, and the vehicle tracking system revealed that the driver had taken a route where CCTV cameras were conspicuous in their absence. From this she deduced he was probably a well-seasoned local car thief, familiar with all the back roads.

Rosetta took a slurp of caramel latte from the recyclable plastic Costa cup and sighed – she had paid for the coffee using a crypto currency app on her mobile. That was progress, as she was decidedly App-adverse. Back at EPIS HQ, big data had long since merged with block-chain, and all the contracts from employment to outsourced goods were strictly smart, but here at Yorrex there was a dearth of high-tech crime detection.

Frustratingly, so far, the trail had gone colder than a polar bear's arse stuck in the north-pole and it would be hard to maintain momentum over the shut-down Christmas holiday period.

To make matters worse, snow was forecast. *A white bloody Christmas,* she thought miserably, and still no word from either of her kids. *Eat your heart out, Cruella De Vil,* she thought with a sigh. At some point she was going to have to come clean about her suspicions that Matt and Tracy had unregistered phones, or burners, as they were called. And that would put a big damper on the Christmas cover rota.

Actually, it would be blown to hell and back. She wondered if she could sit on it till the holiday celebrations had finished.

The landline on her desk buzzed and jolted her into a sitting position. It was Rav, summoning her to his office down the hall, where she found Shirley already in position.

'Okay, Shirley, fill her in,' Rav said, leaning back in his chair.

'Right, we interviewed your ex, and as you'd expect he's hunkered down behind all that officially-off-limits, secret cloak-and-dagger stuff, so not very forthcoming about anything...'

'No surprise there, then,' Rosetta said.

'Nope, and he turned the GPS off on his mobile, so we couldn't track his route. But the first electronic record on the nineteenth was his diplomatic swipe card at the Foreign Office a few minutes before two that afternoon.'

'If his train got in on time that means there's a hell of a gap, or he didn't get on or off the train when he claimed.' Rosetta let out a low whistle. Things were getting a bit more interesting at last.

'Correct,' Shirley affirmed, 'but eventually he filled us in and told us he'd gone for breakfast with an associate, then returned to his flat in Westminster where he'd had a shower, got changed, caught up on some paperwork, and then went to the foreign office. That checks out with the security desk at the apartment block. Mr. M. refused to reveal the name of his breakfast guests. He cited national security, blah-blah. But the interesting part is we tracked him to his private members club. Nay underestimate a determined Scot on the scent, eh?' Shirley let out a loud self-satisfied cackle.

Rosetta looked at Rav and signalled that she was impressed. 'Okay, let's have it.'

'Yours truly only had a wee get together with Pa Riley, our very own Travellers' Chief and notorious Mr. Big of the underworld.'

'What?' Rosetta spluttered, her eye brows knitting together at the prospect. 'Really?'

'Well, the old man was kitted out in his best bib and tucker, mind, but not exactly the kind of company you'd be expecting a diplomat to keep. Do you have any ideas what that might be all about?' Shirley asked.

Rosetta shrugged. 'Not a clue, but what's Pa Riley's area of criminal expertise exactly?'

Rav filled her in. 'Armed robbery, burglary, car theft. He has a number of scrap metal yards that we believe are fronts for money laundering operations. But, it's nailing him that's a –'

Rosetta gasped. 'Well, ordinarily, I'd say Peter would rather be in Liberia during another Ebola outbreak than be associated with someone like that. He's very, very fussy when it comes to his reputation. Yet first we have his car stolen, and then a breakfast meeting with a notorious car theft operator all in the same day.'

'What's your gut instinct on this?' Rav asked.

'It can't be a coincidence, that's too far-fetched even for fiction. So, it seems to me that my lovely Peter hired Pa Riley to steal his car.'

'Why?' Shirley butted in.

'That's the sleeping cobra yet to be stirred.' Rav said.

'Exactly,' Rosetta agreed. 'It's odd that they'd be seen together though. Unless... it all went wrong, which we know it did, and as a consequence they wanted to alibi each other. But that's all pretty random, so it doesn't hang together too well.'

Rosetta pondered on this and concluded that random simply wasn't her ex-husband's style. There had to be more to it, and she had a sinking feeling that it had something to do with her. Working closely with the Russians, and being well briefed on espionage tactics, Peter would suspect that his ex-wife could hack any and all of his bank, phone, medical, and any other records any time she chose. In his job, he'd certainly have some inkling of what EPIS was capable of. That must mean there was a trail linking Peter to Pa Riley, and now they were both potentially mired in a murder investigation. It occurred to her that Peter figured that she'd quickly find the evidence that implicated them both to some extent, so he'd given her a heads up. But why, what was he up to? She wondered if she should discuss this notion with Rav, but on balance she decided to wait, and see what unravelled.

'Rosetta?' Rav waved, trying to attract her attention. 'Do you have anything to add?'

She was jolted back into the flow of things. 'Sorry, well, a couple of things... Do we have a copy of Gothic's insurance policy yet?'

Shirley nodded. 'It's on file, and it's a tidy sum an' all.'

'How much?' she asked.

'A cool million, and guess who's the beneficiary?'

Rosetta waited expectantly.

Finally, Rav spoke, 'Matt Lebaine, and I don't want a word of this getting out of this room.'

'Phew, the plot thickens.' Rosetta shook her head in disbelief. 'And there's more. Matt called Tracy before he phoned Juliet, so she's definitely not best pleased. But I've checked both sets of mobile records, and the phone log from his Miami hotel, all their social media accounts plus WhatsApp, and drew a complete blank. So, –'

She knew where this would go next, and the team wouldn't like it, as Christmas may well end up cancelled.

Rav shook his head. 'You mean, they're covering their tracks and it looks like they've got unregistered pay-as-you-go phones?' Rav checked his watch. 'Shirley, get the team together in the incident room in thirty minutes.'

'Yay, guv,' Shirley said, scowling at Rosetta as they both departed.

Shortly afterwards, Rav briefed the team and a collective groan reverberated round the room. They all knew it meant warrants, searches, and possible arrests right slam bang in the middle of Christmas.

'Right,' Rav enthused. 'Let's get cracking. The sooner we start, the sooner we finish.'

DS Colin Murray had been seconded from a nearby force. He lumbered to his feet with a frown plastered across his face. He was in his early fifties, with salt and pepper hair, and his complexion had the ruddy hue of a seasoned drinker.

'That's it then, if I miss yet another Christmas I'm finished, the wife is fresh out of forgiveness. So, it looks like I'll be getting a decree nisi in my Xmas stocking.'

'Again?' Dennis chuckled. 'I thought she gave you one last year?'

'It's nay funny,' Shirley complained, assuming a surly expression. 'I'm supposed to catch the train to Edinburgh this evening, and if I miss it I'll never get another seat.'

'Sorry, guys, but we need to strike now and find those phones.' With that, Rav marched back into his office.

A quiet mood of gloom settled across the room.

'Thanks a bunch,' Shirley snapped at Rosetta as they left in single file. 'You didn't have to mention the missing phones right there and then. Surely, it could wait till after Christmas? I've nay seen my kin for over a year and now it's blown. Cheers.'

'I'm sorry,' Rosetta said, feeling pretty rotten. She guessed she wouldn't be winning any popularity contests any time soon. She'd be all alone, so it made no difference to her, but she'd hate to ruin anyone's family time. She of all people knew how precious that was. Her brain whirred into fix-it mode. 'If you drop me the details of your ticket, I'll get you on an overnight train.'

'Yee kin do that?' Shirley said with a hint of suspicion breaking through her heavy Scottish brogue. 'You're sure?'

94

Rosetta nodded. 'Leave it with me, and who knows, you might even get an upgrade to first class.'

'Thanks.' Shirley beamed. 'That'd be grand.'

'You're welcome. I know we don't always see eye to eye, but I just want you to know that you're a damn fine detective.'

Shirley blushed. 'Right, mission phone-find, here we come.'

Back in her office, Rosetta chewed her pencil and leaned back in her chair, which predictably gave a loud squeak. 'WD40 please, Santa, while you're at it,' she murmured. *Holy Moses,* she thought, turning her attention to the latest developments in the case, *what the heck was Peter up to now?*

CHAPTER FIFTEEN

Rav
27th December

Rav shuffled across the canteen, eyed up the full English, but decided he should skip breakfast. The waistband of his trousers had been getting a bit tight lately. First, he stared into the mug of black coffee, then up at the TV screen that was fixed high up on brackets near the ceiling. Sky News was running a feature on Isabella's death.

'Yorrex police are investigating a fatal road rage attack,' the studio reporter announced. 'The driver of a dark grey Range Rover deliberately reversed into two horse riders, leaving a teenage girl, Isabella Levine, in a ditch crushed beneath her mount.' Then they switched to a clip of Gothic competing at the World Equestrian Games. 'This horse, Gothic, the American individual and team gold medal event horse, seen here with rider and owner Juliet Jermaine, died instantly.' The coverage flicked back to the reporter in the studio. 'DCS Rav Patel of Yorrex's major incident team is appealing for witnesses. The vehicle involved in the incident was parked, at around 7:45 a.m. on 19th December, at the local railway station, and appears to have been stolen. Now, it's over to our home affairs correspondent, Samantha Fielding, who's at the scene.'

'Thanks, Sandy.' Samantha stood on the grass verge. 'This is where the incident took place, a quiet country lane where the two girls were obliged to travel in order to get to the nearest bridle path. Most horse riders try to stay off the roads, but they didn't make it that far. The car came past them. Then, inexplicably, the driver jammed the car into reverse, and mowed them down. Juliet's horse managed to jump clear, but Isabella and Gothic ended up here.' She pointed to the ditch as the camera zoomed in for a close-up, panning over the flowers, cards, and stuffed toys left by well-wishers, an outpouring of tributes from the public. The cameraman lingered over the scene and homed in for a close-up on a white toy unicorn with sad brown eyes and the message *Take me with you to heaven.* At the bottom of the screen ran a red ticker tape which announced: *Breaking news: the car involved in the incident, a Range Rover with diplomatic plates, registration number 252D100 found burnt-out on Farley Heath. Are the Russians involved somehow?*

'Shit,' Rav muttered as he grabbed his mug of coffee and headed for his office.

Twenty minutes later, with the dailies spread across his desk, Rav buried his head in his hands. He'd had the commissioner on the phone, delivering a sermon about solving crime on the cheap, keeping within his austerity budget, and adopting a low profile. *Clearly the governor had missed his true vocation as an undercover internal auditor,* Rav thought.

After a cursory knock sounded on the door, Rav shouted, 'Come in.'

Shirley entered his office. 'Jesus, boss, what's with the slapped-arse face?'

'What?' Rav snapped.

'Sorry, sir. Erm, it's just that you don't look too chuffed.'

Rav scooped up the newspapers and deposited them in the waste bin. 'The media have published the diplomatic plates, and my phone's been ringing off the hook ever since. The foreign office, the home office, someone's uncle an' all, and the commissioner… well, he's not a happy bunny, is he?' Rav sighed and rolled his eyes. The day ahead held about as much take-off promise as one of NASA's failed rocket launches.

Shirley plonked herself in a swivel chair and gave him a faint smile of commiseration. 'How much longer before he retires and cashes in on the gold-plated pension pot?'

'Not any time soon, alas. He's jumpy, skittish as a hunted yak, and in a state of extreme nervousness.'

'A yak? Come again?'

'Yes,' Rav said. 'It's the ancient animal of Tibet. They live on the plateaus where the air's thin and the temperatures bitter cold.'

Shirley laughed. 'I suppose it's a bit like that in his air-conditioned posh penthouse office up there, but that's nay the animal that springs to mind when I think of himself. He's more of a…'

'There is nothing noble about being superior to some other man. The true nobility is being superior to your previous self. This is an old Hindu proverb my grandfather taught me.'

'Right, very nice an' all,' Shirley said. 'Well, there's nay question over sir's sense of his own superiority, like. Has he always been so objectionable?'

'Yes, but he's excelling himself of late. He is not happy at all the extra overtime, mounting expenses, extra manpower drafted in for the searches that failed to uncover those missing-bloody-mobiles.'

'But we need to get a message up there to planet bubble. We need more phone lines installed, and pronto. The phones are leaping off the hooks like randy bullfrogs in the mating season.' Shirley paused and scrutinised her boss carefully, as if trying to read his thoughts.

'I don't think he'll authorise that. He's even been ranting on about the cost of the extra robots, and he loves A-bloody-I.' Rav scowled and wiped the black newspaper ink from his fingertips onto a bit of tissue paper that he unearthed from his trouser pocket.

'I take it you're not a fan of the botties, then?'

Rav let out an exasperated sigh. 'Call me old-fashioned, but they give me the creeps. It's like unleashing a hybrid that doesn't reason like a human, so how do we control what we don't really comprehend? I think it's just asking for trouble. Next, he'll be trying to pay us in bitcoin.'

Shirley gave him a look of commiseration. 'Like the ultimate irony, you mean?'

'Exactly, imagine if the police get paid in black money. That'd really crack up the crack dealers.'

'We move over to the dark side,' Shirley observed. 'Yes, if we're judged by the company we keep, it would be as clear as muddy crystal meth, right? Mind you, as a single mom I do love my Alani.'

'Your Alani?' Rav felt an overwhelming sense of weariness rising and descending at the same time, a bit like a vice.

'My Homebot, he's a wee treasure, he feeds the cat, cooks meals, vacuums, irons, even helps the kids with their homework. The Robbies are all the rage now, guv. HMRC use them to spot irregularities and flag income vs spending discrepancies, they have voice recognition to ID you and get you through to the right department…'

'Enough, let's just agree to differ on this.'

'Right,' Shirley agreed. 'Still, the big C's going away tomorrow, jet setting off to the Maldives for the New Year, so he'll nay be any the wiser for the time being.'

Rav laughed. 'You are a mine of useful information. Okay, order seven new lines, express delivery, man them with real flesh and blood, and I'll face the music when he gets back.' Rav aimed the scrunched-up tissue at the waste bin. *Bingo,* he thought as it went in, *got something right for a change.* 'I thought the Maldives were sinking? I read it somewhere,' he mused.

'Well, we can but pray it goes down quick before he gets off?' They both laughed.

'Mind you,' Rav added, 'better the devil you know.'

'Debatable,' she said. 'Hmm, I've been thinking about our media problem. Clearly, we've got a leak, which in itself is not good, and those journalists will never reveal their sources... but... do you think it's wise to keep DS Barrett on the case?'

Rav chewed the end of his pen and mulled this over.

Shirley continued, 'Well, she's a cracking detective, mind, and she got me upgraded to first class to Edinburgh and back which I'm well chuffed about, but... she's... well... a witch and... what-not.'

'A psychic seer,' Rav added helpfully.

'Ay, that an' all. But if the sensation-hungry hounds get a hold of it, can you imagine the furore?'

Rav shuddered. 'She reports to the Elite Paranormal Intelligence Service, the ultimate global Secret Service agency. Her brief is big picture and the stakes are higher than we can imagine. It involves karmic clean-up.'

'Karmic wha... what? I'm not getting your drift,' Shirley interrupted.

'They go back, right back to the source, and put right the original wrongdoings.' He could tell by her expression that she was not buying into this explanation. It was easier for him, of course, as karma was one of the pillars of Hinduism. He'd been raised to understand Samsara, the cycle of rebirth. 'Think of atonement. It's like a stone dropped in a river. We deal with the ripples... the effect. But they go after the source – the cause.'

Shirley shook her head. 'Nah, I don't care about that woo-woo stuff.' She leaned back in her chair for emphasis. 'It seems to me the last thing we need is a media feeding frenzy. It'll cause havoc, and I just want to catch the bastard who killed that wee lassie.'

'I know, but there's more to it. Rosetta had a premonition. She tried to warn Juliet on the day of the accident. She thinks the motive goes further back, to previous lives.'

'Christ!' Shirley lurched forward so far that she almost shot out of her chair. 'If that gets out, we'll be crucified. Remember when Wessex police called in that psychic chap. He totally ingratiated himself with the victim's family, and then it turned out he had previous convictions for fraud and they'd never even checked. Wessex police became a laughing stock and the press, those bloody parasites, crucified them and virtually derailed the entire investigation.'

Rav winced. 'Oh, that's a point. We don't want our professionalism to be judged by what's printed in the press. That's not very productive, is it?'

Shirley let out a long sigh. 'They're already saying that we're short-staffed, too busy going down blind alleys. Do we really want the press sticking their oar in, muckraking over the psychic stuff? The headlines will be horrific and then… then we'll be inundated with the all manner of para–'

'Paratroopers?'

'Hardly.' She laughed. 'No, I mean the paranormal sorts; the weirdoes, the fruit and nutters, the Nutellas, and all the wee-willy-wankers that will come crawling outta the woodwork.'

'I see.' Rav's mood shifted from low to glum. He toyed with his lower lip, fidgeted and shuffled his feet under the desk. 'No, that wouldn't be terrifically helpful, I agree. But she doesn't technically report to me. It's just a dotted reporting line. So, we need to tread carefully.'

'Yeah,' Shirley agreed, 'my thoughts entirely. Can't you get the commissioner to get her side-lined due to a conflict of interest over the ex-husband, or something? Anything, but we need to get him upstairs on it before he trots off on his jolly. We need DS Barrett off the radar and quickly, in my view.'

Rav sighed and his lips flat-lined as if he had a bitter taste in his mouth. 'Leave it with me. Meanwhile, see what you can find out about the leak.'

Shirley raised her hands, palms to the ceiling. 'No disrespect, sir, but that's a complete waste of time, a wild goose chase. Those weasels will never reveal their sources, and as fast as we plug one leak, another one will spring up in its place. Meanwhile, what's the update from forensics and the tracking device on the Range Rover?'

'Hmm, glad you asked. The report's here somewhere,' he said, rummaging around on his desk. Then he checked the wastepaper bin where he'd ditched the newspapers. 'Ah, here it is. I had a quick scan through and they traced shopping trips, the gym, the tennis club, but what stands out as odd is a number of repeated trips to the few square miles in that part of the city that are largely Muslim enclaves. Plus,' he paused to find the correct page, 'there were visits, six in total on different days to two notorious jihadi mosques. What are we to make of that?'

'It's odd though, wasn't a terrorist attack one of DS Barret's pet theories? Still, maybe Marshall was doing a little research for our Russian friends.'

Rav crinkled his nose. 'I don't think they have an Al Qaeda problem, do they? Thanks to the Blair-Bush invasive consortium that's our special relationship reward, isn't it?'

'Yeah, I guess. Actually, it was a wee joke. My guess is old Peter-Perfect didn't want the FO lot picking up on that. Did they check CCTV records?'

'Good point.' Rav flicked through to the back of the report. There were a number of still black-and-white shots of the car parked in various grimy underground car parks, stationary at traffic lights, and so on; some images of a few Muslim youths congregating in a skateboard park. 'Nothing there of any particular interest so far as forensics can tell,' he said, handing the report to Shirley. 'Drop it off on Rosetta's desk and ask her to take a look.'

Shirley nodded. 'On that subject, namely Ms. B. and the media hounds... surely, we'd be better taking charge? Why don't we give the press a statement, pre-empt them before the cork pops and lets the genie out of the bottle, so to speak?'

Rav chewed his cheek. 'Thanks. I'll give it some serious consideration.' With that, and a wave of his hand, he signalled for her to depart.

CHAPTER SIXTEEN

Rosetta

Day nine of the investigation. Rosetta grimaced as she tried to locate her cigarette lighter. No easy task as her desk was buried under files and paperwork. *It must be here somewhere,* she thought. 'Ah, at last, the little purple Bic, come to me, baby,' she giggled.

Outside, the weak winter sun was making a rare appearance, and there was a breakthrough in the case at last. She swivelled on her office chair, which emitted a harsh squeak, as she leant to reach a le-ver file. Santa had not obliged with the WD40 she'd ordered. The vehicle, or at any rate the burnt-out wreck of it, had been recovered early on and forensics had given it the complete once-over. Some old guy – what was his name? Rosetta scrunched her forehead. Ah yes, Mervyn Wallace-Smith, retired estate agent and frankly a pompous old git, had discovered the Range Rover while out walking. He had also seen someone running away from the scene, but for some un-fathomable reason it took over a week for the boys in blue to process this detailed bit of information. Even then, it wasn't properly flagged in the system, and DC Boyd only came across it by chance. They had a crucial witness whom they'd managed to mislay, and DC Boyd only managed to trip over it by accident. A total cock-up, and typically no one was taking ownership, how impressive was that?

She remembered her friend's advice, and Juliet's example about how to reframe negative situations, so she re-ran the thought: how lucky was it that they'd reconnected with the buried clue, like pirates of the Caribbean finding treasure in a rucksack? Ah, Mervyn. How could she have forgotten Mervyn? His wife was a short, stout, and very bossy, obsessive dog breeder, and meanwhile, for light relief, the husband was driving her crazy phoning every day for an update, as if his discovery somehow entitled him to privileged information. Rosetta sighed. Thus far she'd managed to keep her temper in check but only just. Mervyn had one of those irritating faces that she just itched to rearrange.

'Eureka!' she'd shouted when Charlie had made the discovery, but her euphoria had been short-lived as there had been a series of less than flattering articles kicking off about police incompetence in the local and national press. There had been a lot of heat from the top after that, but then, in a pissing contest, the biggest dicks always won, didn't they? Thank heavens the commissioner was on his jolly-days and out of the way for a while. Rosetta stubbed out her cigarette and without thinking lit another one. Was it her fault if uniform, who'd taken the call, couldn't put two and two together and come up with four? They'd managed to get forensics mobilised to the burnt-out car on Farley Heath, big round of applause, clap, clap, bravo. But, they'd also buried Mervyn's statement: boo, boo, hiss?

Still, being brutally honest, most of them would be better off escorting hedgehogs and toads across the road, than grappling with serious crime – bless? According to Mervyn, when she'd had the pleasure of taking his statement, he'd been walking his dog, Mary-Lou, across Farley Heath at around 10:30 a.m. on the 19th December. He'd seen the flames and had been distracted as he went to investigate, and Mary-Lou had run off. There'd been an incident with another dog walker, and Mervyn was particularly keen to press charges against the owner of the large dog, possibly an Irish Wolf hound, as he maintained the dog was out of control and had attacked his bitch. "Tried to ravish poor Mary-Lou," were his exact words.

Rosetta took a drag on her cigarette and rolled her eyes to the ceiling. *The things that dog walkers had to contend with as they trekked across the AONB, and the green belt, what with spotting burnt out vehicles, stumbling across decomposing bodies, plus the canine equivalent of rapists, God forbid,* she thought with a touch of sarcasm, *whatever next?*

Still, there was a decent e-fit of the other dog owner, and it was vital to identify and interview him. Mervyn had been uncertain if the dog owner was one and the same person that he'd seen running away from the burning wreck. Had there been one other person at the scene, or two? That was what she needed to find out.

She mentally thanked Mervyn for his input and started on the mountain of forms she had to fill out. Ahead another night alone in front of the telly with a pile of paperwork beckoned, how delightful. Too many lonely nights ahead, and before long New Year's Eve would come around and yet again she had nowhere to go, and no one to stay in with.

An hour later, the paperwork pile hadn't shrunk much. Rosetta peered over the rim of her coffee cup and took a swig even though it had long since gone cold.

'Come in,' she barked in response to a knock at the door. It opened to reveal a man, around five foot-nine, with long dark hair, tinged with streaks of grey, and a goatee beard. *Brad Pitt this was surely not,* she thought, inviting him in with an exaggerated sweep of her arm. 'Ah yes, Mr. Potts. I appreciate you stopping by. Thanks for giving up your free time and coming in so promptly. Please take a seat.'

'Well yes, but your request was hardly a request. More of a summons, and frankly, I don't know how I can possibly assist.'

'The thing is, Bradley... may I call you Bradley?' Rosetta sniffed, detecting a faint odour of fetid goat. 'The thing is, we have a description of someone running away from where a vehicle was abandoned near the Druid Temple at Farley Heath, and this vehicle was involved in the road rage incident that you may have heard about.'

'Yes, a terrible thing, but I still –'

Rosetta shook her head impatiently. 'As Chief Travellers' Liaison Officer for the region, would it be correct to assume that you have a good knowledge of the travellers on the Farley Heath settlement?'

'Of course,' he snapped.

'The thing is, Brad, the Range Rover was reported stolen that day, when the owner returned to the railway station and discovered it missing.'

'That doesn't mean that the travellers had anything to do with it. They're not implicated in every crime committed around here. It's precisely that kind of prejudice...'

'Your loyalty is touching,' Rosetta interrupted, narrowing her eyes to signify her determined resolve. 'But you know as well as I do that there's been a spate of high-value cars disappearing recently and this has their sticky magpie fingers all over it.'

'I take it, then, you don't actually have any conclusive forensics.'

'Look,' she spat, 'let's cut the crap. I've got a dead kid and a dead horse and your desire to protect those people and frustrate our enquiry is beginning to get on my nerves.'

'How typical, this is nothing but circumstantial conjecture.'

'Erm, no, Brad, actually we have a very good description of a man we'd like to question. Curly dark hair, around six feet, athletic build, oh and here's the interesting bit, gold loop earring in one ear. Now what do you think?' She produced an e-fit and placed it on the desk in front of him with a triumphant flourish. 'I'd like you to look at this and see if it's anyone you recognise.'

Bradley Potts removed his glasses from the top pocket of his jacket and perched them on the end of his nose. He stared at the image for a long time. 'Hmmm,' he said eventually. 'I can't be certain, of course, and you must promise to keep this information strictly confidential, but I think it might be one of Pa Riley's relatives who was over from Ireland for a while.'

'Excellent.' Rosetta chewed the end of her pencil and tried to bridle her excitement. She giggled at her chair, which gave a loud squeal. 'Sorry about that, everything in here's falling apart. So, do you have a name?'

'Let me see.' He tugged at his beard as if milking the goat of inspiration. 'I think his name is Rafferty… Tommy Rafferty.'

'Excellent. That's very helpful. A few more questions, if I may? So, this Mr. Rafferty, what relation is he to Pa Riley and is he still in the UK, or has he gone back to Ireland?'

Brad settled in his seat and looked slightly more relaxed. 'Well now, let me see. I believe Tommy is his nephew. I haven't seen him lately, so I assume he's gone back.'

'Back where?'

Brad twisted his beard and gave it a tug. 'I can't be one hundred percent certain, but I believe he's from Inis Cara, on the south-east coast of Ireland.'

Rosetta tapped her fingers on the desk. *This could be it, the breakthrough we so desperately need.* 'And roughly when did he go back?'

'Hmm, well, I can't be certain, but it must have been shortly after the… the incident.'

Rosetta nodded. 'Do you know if he had his own car? Did he take the ferry and drive, or did he fly? I believe he had a dog with him?'

Brad chuckled. 'Yes, a great big grey thing.' He scratched his forehead as he pondered. 'I can't be totally sure, but I think he came over in an old Land Rover, and, come to think of it, I haven't seen it recently. So, I'd say on balance, he probably drove.'

'Thank you, Brad. Is there anything else that you can add? Do you know where Mr. Rafferty works? Anything that might help us locate him?'

'Is he a suspect?' Brad's voice sounded leaden, and he seemed worn-out.

Rosetta picked up on his fears. 'No, he's not a suspect yet, but we do need to eliminate him from our enquiries. He was seen in the area shortly after the vehicle was torched.'

Brad sighed. 'Well now, it doesn't look good, does it?'

'Look, I give you my word that any information you give us will not be linked back to you. I appreciate that would make your position extremely difficult.'

Brad burst out with a rasping laugh. 'You mean extremely dangerous. The Riley's are not the sort of people you'd want to cross, and actually it's not just work. I count them as my friends. Gypsies, ancient Romani and Irish Travellers like them, are much maligned and misunderstood.'

'Yes, I get it. I'm different too, and sometimes others can be really cruel about differences. Nothing whatsoever will be traced back to you, I promise.' Rosetta sighed. At least the Gypsies had their clans, they had their traditions and they had each other. How she longed for that, but increasingly, with Daniel gone AWOL, she had no one.

Brad looked relieved. 'He used to be a very successful show jumper, and he's a horse dealer, so he shouldn't be too difficult to find.'

Rosetta laughed. 'I should have guessed. Thank you, Brad. You've been really helpful, and I really appreciate your assistance, more than you can imagine, perhaps.' She slipped him her card, and then sprang to her feet and ushered the council official towards the door. Someone really ought to take his armpits to task, and the sooner she removed him from her room, the better.

'I need to run some checks on Pa Riley, and his nephew,' she explained.

'I see.' He pondered. 'Well, I have to warn you that Pa Riley does not hold the police in very high regard. I think it's unlikely that he'll cooperate with you at all.'

'Really?' she grinned. 'I figured that one, but we'll just have to see about that now, won't we?'

She stared at Brad's back as he departed and reached for the file at the top of her bulging in tray. She quickly scanned the cover and determined that it was the forensics report on Peter's car.

How did I manage to miss that? she wondered.

Shirley had dropped it off yesterday, as she recalled, so maybe the endemic incompetence was catching, it seemed. *Sign me up for hedgehog patrol too, take me to your prickly leader.* Rosetta flicked through the report, speed reading as she homed in on the conclusion paragraph. There were a *number of visits to Muslim hotspots and visits to known jihadi mosques. What is the relevance of this? Status: unquantified.*

Odd, she thought, *Peter was hardly the sort to find religion in mid-life, and show up for Koran readings, or whatever – perhaps he was into DIY bomb making classes – ha, ha,* and with that she tossed the report into her "out" pile.

* * *

Later that day, the checks on Tommy Rafferty confirmed that he had no previous form. He was a horse dealer from Southern Ireland, and so far, he'd kept his nose clean. Rosetta opened the file again and leafed through it until she came to the photograph.

'Phew.' She whistled. He's *a good-looking son of a bitch this one... no contest.* He had that intoxicating mix of rough-and-ready and boyish charm that she found impossible to resist. Something stirred deep inside her, and she realised that she knew this man. Rosetta wracked her brain – where had they met, and when? She came up with a blank. Then, it occurred to her in a flash of dazzling recognition that they had a deep connection, not in this lifetime, but further back. In a previous lifetime, they'd been soul mates, perhaps even twin flames. *Wow,* she thought, *now this case is beginning to get really interesting.* How and when exactly had their paths crossed?

DC Charlie Boyd popped in with another irresistible offering – a fresh brew. 'How's it going?'

'Swimmingly... not...' She forced herself to avert her eyes from Tommy. Tricky, as he had a magnetic hold over her. Eventually, she shrugged and accepted the tea gratefully. 'How about you, any updates?'

He grabbed a chair and pulled it to him in an aggressive swoop before plonking himself down. 'Shirley interviewed Todd, the New Zealand event rider. He's probably Juliet's best mate, I reckon. Anyway, he said that Juliet suspected that Matt has a thing going on with her head groom...'

'Tracy.'

Charlie nodded. 'Righty-o. Also, Matt had instigated the sale of Luckenham Park to property developers to build a big housing estate. The proposals are going through the various planning stages as we speak. But Juliet is getting cold feet as there's a lot of local opposition, plus her family over in the US of A aren't too keen. Way back the estate belonged to an Irish strand of the family, and Juliet's mother's quite sentimental about her Irish-American connections, apparently Juliet keeps changing her mind, first she pulled out, now it might be back on.'

Rosetta put her elbow on the desk and rested her head in her hand. 'Give us a break. But really, I don't see what this adds to the mix. If Juliet ends up dead, where does that leave the fiancé? They aren't married yet, so what does he stand to gain? What do you think? What's your gut instinct on this?'

'The Irish, bless 'em, are everywhere, fricking jigging all over us. Well, fair enough, but is Matt her next of kin? That needs checking. Remember the author, Helen Bailey, who was murdered way back in July 2016?'

Rosetta shook her head.

Charlie wriggled and made himself comfortable. 'She wrote teen fiction and was a well-known author, the Queen of Teen they called her. A few years after her husband died, she met a bloke online...'

'Oh, Lord,' Rosetta groaned. 'Spare me from the cruel world of internet dating.'

'Anyway, this Mr. Stewart, her gorgeous grey-haired widower, GGHW, ups the life insurance, makes sure he's the beneficiary, gets her to change her will and leave her fortune of around four million pounds to him. Then, a bit before the wedding, he reports her missing, but actually he's murdered her and her dog and dumped them in a cesspit.'

'Argh.' Rosetta shuddered. 'So, it's a cynically executed murder that had money as its driving force? And you think Matt might be up to something similar that's money-motivated?'

Charlie nodded. 'They're engaged, and who's the beneficiary of the insurance policy on Gothic? I bet it's him, has anyone checked that yet?'

They had, but Rosetta wasn't at liberty to say anything on strict instructions from Rav, who these days was becoming morbidly obsessed with leaks.

'Anyway,' Charlie continued, 'if he was counting on a big pay-out from the property developers, and she pulled the plug on the deal, he wouldn't be happy, would he? Also, it's curious that Tracy called in sick the day of the attack. Think about it, her and Matt could have set it all up.'

Rosetta raised an eyebrow; Charlie had hit the nail on the head, but for now she had to play along. 'You mean the horse was always the target? Crikey, great work, well done. Okay, find out who's the beneficiary of her will and report back shortly.'

'Right-o.' Charlie looked well pleased with himself.

'I went down to interview the Travellers,' Rosetta continued. 'I got a terrific welcome, naturally. Thank God, I took a couple of uniforms, all bully beef, and limited brain as escorts. That Pa Riley's a tricky piece of work. Have you met him?'

DC Boyd nodded and rolled his eyes. 'You bet. He used to be a boxer, and he still looks as wiry as a terrier after a rabbit. He's an old bugger, but I wouldn't rate my chances up against him.'

'Quite! Anyway, it seems that our man Rafferty has definitely legged it back to Ireland.'

'Handy that.' He paused. 'Is it me, or is there a funny smell in here?'

Rosetta rolled her eyes, yanked open a drawer, and gave the air yet another squirt of air freshener, but the Brad smell still lingered. 'Hmmm, the strange thing is that Pa Riley seemed genuinely disgusted at the attack. He kept muttering that none of his kind would ever harm a horse.' She paused and chewed her bottom lip. 'The thing is, it kind of makes sense. I'm not sure that deliberately maiming a horse and rider is their bag of tricks at all.'

'Where does that leave Rafferty?'

'Obviously, I'll interview him.' She took a slurp of tea. 'But we've got to pin him down first.'

After Charlie left, she leaned back in her chair to mull over a few loose ends. As expected, Pa Riley had been very cagy about his relationship with Peter and refused point-blank to be drawn on what they'd discussed over breakfast, or the nature of their relationship. Rosetta had her elbows resting on her desk, and her head resting in her hands. She was missing something, but what? *Think,* she chastised herself.

'Yes,' she said, slapping herself on the head. She reached for the forensic report, and this time read it through slowly page by page. When she got to the conclusion paragraph, she let out a loud gasp. That explained why she'd had the vibes about Islamist militants and terrorists. 'Shit, holy shit.' With that, she scooped up her handbag, cigarettes, and lighter, and left the office.

'Just off outside for a breath of fresh air and a fag,' she announced to no one in particular. Outside, at a safe distance from the building, cigarette in one hand, old brick Nokia in the other, she called Peter on his PAYG dinosaur phone. 'Peter, it's Rosetta, we need to talk… and soon. Call me back on this number, and arrange a meeting, pronto.'

She hung up. Just when she thought her life was entering a calmer phase, now things were going from bad to worse: roller-coaster to hell type of worse.

CHAPTER SEVENTEEN

In loving memory of Isabella Rosetta

The funeral was delayed for ten days owing to the holiday period. Rosetta went to the Levine's house, a square-box modern detached on a new housing estate with a recently mown lawn and tidy shrub borders. Stuart Simpson, the family liaison officer, was waiting for her just inside the gate. Tall, dark skinned and with the kind of physique that screamed karate black belt do not mess with me. Stuart ran his fingers through his recently cropped jet-black hair. 'I'm having a nightmare trying to keep the press at bay. I might have to call for backup.'

'Do that,' Rosetta said, offering him a cigarette. 'They don't need those bastards swarming all over them today of all days.'

'Thanks,' he replied as they both lit up. 'I take it you're none too fond of the press?'

'Nah, I confided in a journalist once, a favour for an old school friend, and I got turned over. Rolled in the hay, in fact, and it was right in the middle of my divorce, where I also got stitched up, this time by the old boys' network, so I needed that like a hole in the flaming head.' Rosetta shrugged. 'Where are you from?'

'Camden Town, 'He flashed a set of impressive white teeth, which had somehow managed to escape nicotine stains.

Rosetta chuckled. 'No, I meant, before, further back'

'Ah.' He shook his head. 'You mean what's my ethnic origin?'

'Yeah, I guess. Everything nowadays is a politically correct minefield.'

He nodded. 'Even he or she is getting tricky these days with the trans-gender thing. My folks are from Barbados, the land of palm trees, churches and rum shacks.'

'Right, rum shacks, nice. How are they holding up?' She pointed her chin towards the Levine's front door.

'Not great.' Stuart sighed.

'What does the dad do?'

'He's a solicitor.'

Rosetta took a long drag on her cigarette. 'Hmmm, not one of my favourite sorts, then. When I think of that lot in my never-ending divorce, I think of sharks circling blood and it makes me retch. Are you married?'

Stuart shook his head.

'Good. Best way to avoid a divorce. I'm going to tell my lot I really don't care who's got what. Get a pre-nup, if only to stop the blood-sucker lawyers bleeding you dry with their fees. Just split it fifty-fifty and keep the law-mongers at bay.'

Stuart laughed.

Rosetta continued, warming to her theme. 'No, I mean, what other profession gets paid regardless of results? Win or lose, the client pays. What's that all about?'

Stuart shrugged. 'I take your point. Patrick's a recovering alcoholic.'

'Let me guess, and he's relapsed, poor sod?'

Stuart nodded. 'Shirley reckons that he should be made a suspect. She's trying to get the boss to investigate.'

Rosetta felt irritated, and she stubbed her cigarette out with the toe of her shoe. 'He's a suspect just because he's got a drinking problem? Jesus, then she's going to have to haul in half the Yorrex bloody police force.'

Stuart laughed. 'I guess. Mind you, I'm teetotal myself.'

'Right, well done you,' she said with a sniff. 'But spare us the sermon. Who needs that with a long, drawn-out Roman Catholic funeral looming? I don't know what's worse, the pie-eyed lot or the sanctimonious abstainers. What do you reckon?'

'Tough question, I'll take the fifth.'

Rosetta chuckled. 'That reminds me. A few years back, when I went to watch Alice, my youngest, in the carol concert at the local church, there was a sweet old dear serving refreshments during the interval. Anyway, she got a bit muddled. Dementia, perhaps, but somehow… I doubt it. Anyway, she gave us yummy mummies Ribena, and guess what she dished up to the little songbirds? I'll never forget the kids' expressions. They were all making "yuck" faces. I think one of those five-year-olds actually puked up. So then we were forced to swoop in to rescue the Merlot.'

Stuart shook his head. 'Oh dear, that's not great. I don't have kids myself, but...'

'You can just imagine the headlines, can't you? A *Roman Catholic priest leads five-year-old carol singers on a bender.* That'll be a first... or then again, maybe not, knowing that lot?'

Stuart checked his watch. 'I gather you'd like a word with the Levine's. Are you sure you don't want to speak to them here? It might be more private?'

'No. I'll meet them at the path leading to the church. It won't take long, and I'd rather not disturb them right now while they're getting ready. They need time to compose themselves.'

Isabella's funeral took place at the Church of Our Lady of the Angels. Rosetta arrived early and waited for the Levine's. She intercepted Orla and asked her to take the twins aside while she had a quiet word in private with their parents.

'Excuse me, I'm DS Rosetta Barrett. I'm so sorry for your loss,' she said. 'Sorry to trouble you today, but I just wanted to pass on a message. This is my card.' She handed one to Ann and one to Patrick.

Ann scowled, and Patrick spat, 'We're Catholics. We don't believe in this sort of crap.'

Rosetta winced. 'I don't see dead people. I didn't choose to do this. I have a spirit guide who passes on messages.'

Patrick's eyes flared with rage. 'How dare you come here on the day of our daughter's funeral and insult our intelligence?'

'I'm sorry for your loss, truly, I am. I had a premonition. I was calling Juliet that morning to try and prevent it from happening. You can ask Juliet, and she'll confirm it. Please –'

'Pah,' Patrick said with a look of disgust. 'You crazy bloody woman, next you'll be asking for interviews. Then, in six months' time no doubt, there'll be a book published. *How I Solved the Shirley Heights Crime.* Get out of our way now, or I'll call the police.'

Ann reached out and touched him gently on the arm. 'Patrick, she is the police. She's a detective.' She turned to Rosetta. 'Please, I'd like to hear what you have to say.'

Rosetta let out a sigh of relief. 'Thank you. I know how difficult this is for you and I feel for your loss...'

'No parent should have to outlive their own child can you even begin to imagine how that feels?'

Rosetta nodded and bit her lip. 'I have two children myself. My son's seventeen, and my daughter's the same age as Isabella. I just wanted to pass on her message. Isabella says, 'Papa and Mutti, don't fret. Be brave. Be strong today like you always were for me.'

Ann gasped. 'That's what she called us. How do you know this?'

'I'm just the messenger, that's all. She wants you to know that's she's fine. Acceptance is the thing. She wants you to carry on and be happy. She sends hugs to Orla and the twins, and she says Gothic needs to go home. He's trying to get back home. But she says, "Please don't worry about me too much. I'm happy in my new home. Love you. P.S. can you put my unicorn in with me?"'

'What bloody unicorn?' Patrick asked. 'Why are you doing this today, of all days? Why today when I challenge God to explain why he took her from us?'

'Peggie, that's her favourite stuffed toy,' Ann gasped. 'Can you tell her yes, we will. I have him right here in my handbag. Tell her we love her, and we always will.'

Patrick shook his head, his shoulders collapsing. He looked overwhelmed, like a man going under and slowly drowning. 'Who would take our beautiful girl from us? Can you help us with that? Can you catch the person responsible and give us some closure, at least?'

'I can't interrogate the spirit world, and they reveal only what they deem important. We have a number of lines of enquiry, and Stuart, your family liaison officer, will keep you fully briefed. But I can assure you, we will catch the person responsible.' Rosetta hesitated. 'I don't know if this will help or not, but Isabella was definitely not the target. Her death was a tragic accident. She was in the wrong place at the wrong time.'

'So, what are you saying? What are you getting at? Patrick and Ann both stared at her in astonishment.

Rosetta shrugged. 'Gothic was the target. That's all I know right now. It was the horse.' And she remembered her enquiries after the dream. One of the links was Wuthering Heights, and it turned out the car came from Shirley Heights. The strands were slowly knitting together piece by piece.

'Good day.' With that, Patrick ushered his wife and signalled for Orla and the twins to join them down the well-trodden path towards the church.

The mourners filed into the nave past the beautiful and moving photograph of Isabella set on an easel and adorned with strands of white flowers, trimmed with violet and pink ribbon; her favourite colours, apparently.

Ahead, near the altar, Rosetta caught sight of a white coffin with brass handles, also draped with flowers in the same theme, and a large wreath spelling out Isabella's name. She caught her breath and swallowed. The sermon lasted over an hour, with many prayers and the congregation up and down on prayer benches, and much belting out of many fine hymns.

Orla and Patrick gave readings to celebrate their beloved sister and daughter. Rosetta was aware of many people dabbing their eyes. A sensation of loss and regret permeated the church. In a way, she had lost her own children, but today this loss was final and irreversible. She mouthed a silent prayer, asking that her children remain happy and healthy and that they outlast her by many years.

After the ceremony, the mourners filed out slowly, heads bowed as they muttered in low respectful voices, with Patrick, Ann, and Orla leading the way.

Later, across the gape of a hole, Rosetta could make out Ann's tear-stained face behind the veil of her wide-brimmed hat, an epic Grand National-style thing that had everyone behind it ducking and dodging. Ann appeared oblivious to the hat mayhem. Next to her, Stuart looked smart and sombre in his dark suit and dark raincoat. Patrick held himself upright and rigid, his jaw set, and his fists clenched, and grief etched on his face. In between them, the twins, Katie and Noel, stared at the ground. Noel began fidgeting as though he was anxious to get it over with. Meanwhile, Orla, their big sister, was gently holding their hands and telling them to shush from time to time.

What has this family done to deserve this? How does the life lottery system really work? As the heels of her shoes sank into the damp spongy grass, Rosetta thought of the family photos and video clips on YouTube of Isabella four years ago, at her first gymkhana, whooping in delight with her pigtails flying, her face red from the heat and exertion. More recent pictures showed her competing in dressage and show jumping. How far away that all seemed now. Rosetta bit her lip, acknowledging that it had been in another time, another world, now in the past. It didn't seem fair that there would be no more summers for Isabella. No summer proms, no first kiss, no boyfriend, never a husband… no children. Rosetta sniffed. *What bollocks,* she thought.

The rain came.

The freshly dug mound of earth piled at the side of the grave smelled of clay and compost. Little orange rivulets of water trickled down the sides. It seemed so sad and pathetic that Rosetta looked away. She glanced at Juliet, who looked distant and expensive. Here was a beautiful woman with clear skin, a delicate nose, and faintly arched eyebrows. She possessed the sort of beauty that age would not diminish. But Rosetta could sense Juliet's restless nature; the reined-in passion beneath the calm exterior. As they congregated at the grave-side, Rosetta thought about different religions and their respective words of wisdom. Buddhists believed that hatred led to more hatred and suffering. The Bible said, "Forgive, and you will be forgiven." *Still, what are we to make of the senseless loss of innocents? Fine theories,* Rosetta thought, *but what of mothers who abandon their children?* Hers were not so much abandoned as indefinitely estranged, and it hurt. She felt Ann's loss as keenly as if it was her own.

A large crowd, two hundred or more, had gathered to pay their last respects. They stood quietly under their umbrellas as Father Gerald O'Ryan, the family priest, commenced the reading. He had baptised all four Levine children with the word of God and into the Catholic church, and now he was seeing one of them out.

The rain came thick and fast like an outpouring of collective grief.

Rosetta noticed the tears spilling all around, blending with the inclement weather. She glanced over at Juliet and Matt who stood beside her, tall and erect as Juliet clung onto his arm and sagged against his chest. She sobbed until she wore herself down. Afterwards, a cold sense of desolation settled all around. According to the priest's version, life could be reduced to a series of remote, unrehearsed entrances and random exits. That seemed so pointless, and Rosetta wondered bitterly what sort of a God had designed it that way.

Rosetta clenched her jaw, afraid that if she started crying again, she'd never stop. Staring blankly into the grave, she sniffed and mouthed a soft prayer.

'Hail Mary, full of grace...'

As the small coffin commenced the slow descent into the grave, Ann's shoulders began to heave. Soon her sobs drowned out the priest's words. Her legs buckled, and Patrick struggled to hold her upright.

Rosetta stared up at the sky, the rain splattering her face and no doubt smudging her mascara beyond repair. Ahead of her, the sea of black umbrellas waved in unison as the mourners tried to keep their smart attire dry and save their Sunday-best shoes from the endless drench of silver droplets from the sky.

'Lord,' she whispered through clenched teeth, 'please give this family the strength to get through this. Give us all strength.' It occurred to her that all funerals were dress rehearsals for when the time came to part with our own.

Rosetta reached for the gold crucifix around her neck. Slowly, she undid the clasp and removed the necklace. The crucifix, the rosary beads, all the trappings of orthodox religion. What good had they done? They hadn't spared Isabella from a cruel and senseless death. They hadn't brought the maniac responsible to justice yet.

Please, for pity's sake, let us have justice, if nothing else.

The chain slipped through her fingers and fell onto the lid of the casket, next to the stuffed toy unicorn. For a moment, the cross glittered in the weak sunlight. Rosetta stared at it until it disappeared beneath a thin film of earth.

All in your average day, Rosetta thought as she slipped into her car and the church receded in the rear-view mirror as she drove off. She'd miss the wake, but what she had to attend to was important and it couldn't wait.

After driving for thirty minutes or so, she saw the car park and hooked a right. She parked, rummaged in her handbag for some change for the parking metre, sorted the ticket, then went inside. The revolving doors swept her through into the reception area of Mount Osteria private hospital. It seemed as good a place as any to meet, and there was a coffee lounge on the first floor. If they needed to cover their tracks, they could say they were seeing a consultant about one of the children, and it was a confidential family matter. Plus, in the radio-active environment, chances were, listening devices would suffer from interference, she guessed. She got herself a coffee and found a seat in a quiet corner out of earshot and waited. Her mouth was dry. She should have asked for some tap water, but then she'd need to pee before very long.

She hadn't seen her ex-husband for years and hadn't spoken to him since some time before the divorce proceedings kicked off. After that, all communication was through lawyers at a mere £750 plus VAT a pop. That was insane, and now this. She had no desire for things to drag on and she just needed to find out what the hell was going on. She licked her parched lips and decided on balance to ask for the glass of tap water.

As she returned to her seat, she caught sight of Peter and found herself waving as if he were some old long-lost friend. She stood up, but he declined to shake her hand. He was tall, still distinguished-looking but greying and she noticed his hairline was receding: what a shame.

'Coffee?' She offered, like his simpering secretary or something. Actually, the secretary was now the wife, and she was now lower down life's pecking order. *The wife-to-mistress merry-go-round, another of life's crappy revolving doors,* she sighed to herself.

'I don't have time.' He sat down, hitching the cuff of his dark navy suit, and checked his watch. His was a Rolex, of course, while she was relegated to a cheap and cheerful Swatch. If she had featured on anyone's Christmas present list, she'd have asked for a new watch – but no such luck. She took a large gulp of coffee and crossed her legs. At least, she looked presentable in her dark suit and heels, although it was a mystery to her why she cared. Why did she give a monkey's what he thought anyway?

'Look, Rosetta, just cut to the chase.' His phone rang. He picked it up and moved away, presumably so she couldn't overhear.

Rosetta drummed her fingers on the surface of the table. Even now, when she was potentially bailing out his arse, it seemed she still wasn't worthy of his full attention. The same old dysfunctional dynamics between them were still in play. Nothing had changed, then? Perhaps she ought to pinch herself to make sure that she did actually exist?

Actually, she'd had enough. *Screw you,* she thought as she scooped up her handbag and stood up. That got his attention.

'Rosetta, wait.' He cut the call short. 'Sorry, you know what it's like.'

Rosetta narrowed her eyes. 'Being rude to people who have put themselves out, no actually, I don't know what that's like.'

Peter rubbed his forehead. 'Point taken, okay, can you just give me the low-down on how far they've got? What's going on?'

'I was about to ask you the same question. They… you mean us? Well, strictly off the record, you had a breakfast meeting with Pa Riley at your private members club on the nineteenth. How's that for starters?'

'Shit,' he spat. 'Those dumb fucks are sharper than I gave them credit for.'

'Screw you!' Rosetta growled. 'I just happen to be one of those "dumb-fucks," in case you forgot.'

He paused for a moment, swallowed hard, then made a strange strangled sound. 'Urgh, I… I'm sorry. I'm sorry, Rosetta.'

Wow. She breathed in deeply, impressed at all the effort it took. She never thought she'd hear him say that. 'Thanks, apology accepted. Now can you just play it straight with me? You knew darn well that you'd get rumbled, and that's precisely why you set that meeting up. Why? I'm guessing it was to give you both an alibi, so you weren't implicated in a murder investigation. You knew when I was assigned to this case and your car was involved that I'd do some very thorough digging. Am I getting warm, or what?'

He cleared his throat uncomfortably. 'Yes, you're fairly hot. And you're determined, I'll give you that. So, have you dug up any coffins yet?'

Rosetta thought of Isabella being lowered into the ground not so very long ago, and she wondered what she was doing here, putting her position at risk for a man who had treated her so shabbily. "Sorry" was a start, but really it was just dipping a toe in the ocean of despair that he'd unleashed and the tidal wave of devastation that had engulfed her life. What was the point of misplaced loyalty? He didn't deserve saving. He deserved to drown, slowly, and preferably in gut-wrenching pain.

She shook her head and paused for a long while. Really, there was no point in indulging in notions of revenge. 'I can't discuss the case in detail. That would amount to professional misconduct. But you can disclose information to me off the record.'

'Why would I want to?' Peter exclaimed with a strangled nasal mewl.

'Well, if you assume I know everything and have proof or will have any time soon, that wouldn't be far wide of the mark. You're already in way over your head. The only thing I don't get is why. What are you trying to cover up, or who are you trying to protect?'

Peter gulped. 'It's complicated.'

'You don't say? From where I'm sitting, I reckon "complicated" is the least of your worries,' she sniggered.

Peter's eyes sprang open, and his jaw dropped. 'Hypothetically speaking of course, what might the charges be?'

'Conspiracy to murder perhaps, perverting the course of justice for sure, and that's just for starters. Your career will be finished, of course, that goes without saying. And you'll definitely serve time.' Rosetta watched the colour literally drain from his face and for an instant she almost felt sorry for him. But then the instant passed, quick as Usain Bolt beating another world record. But, actually, if she was totally

119

honest, watching the joy seep out of him cheered her up considerably.

'What're you going to do, you wouldn't–?' He reached across the table and stroked her hand. 'Please, Rosetta, think of our children. Don't do anything rash. I did this for… for someone close to us.'

Rosetta sighed wearily. It had been a long day. She ought to be exhilarated at the power she now wielded over this man who had brought her to her knees, practically destroyed her, and worse still turned the children against her. What mother could bear the terrible anguish of losing contact with her children, or what father, for that matter?

'I want to see the kids before they go back to school,' she said, jutting out her chin determinedly.

He stiffened. 'I can't make them meet you. They're old enough to make up their own minds.'

Rosetta shook her head and pointed her finger in his direction. 'Try harder. They live under your roof, and you control the money flow. And first, I want to talk to Ed alone, and get his version, and then you can fill me in. If you want my help, those are my terms.'

His shoulders sagged. 'Okay, it's a deal.'

'Fine.' She nodded, feeling a surge of relief as it seemed she'd finally get to see Alice and Edward. It had been so long. 'I see the kids, Edward first. There are a few things I need to understand, and then we talk.'

Peter looked aghast. 'You have so little trust.'

'And so little time. *Ciao*,' she said, air kissing either side of his cheek, and with that, she left without looking back.

CHAPTER EIGHTEEN

Rosetta

Christmas had been a solitary affair, sharing an M+S TV turkey dinner with Atone. Alice and Edward's presents went unclaimed well beyond Boxing Day and the New Year. She'd already missed so much of their growing up and now the only updates she got were through Facebook. She spent hours shadowing their friends, trying to piece what they were up to in an attempt to recreate the lost mother-child relationship. She'd sent loads of messages: *I love you, give me a call. Mum.* All, as usual, to no avail.

Meanwhile, the decorations had been taken down and the Christmas tree was long back in the box. The New Year celebrations had been equally dismal, no fireworks – just a damp squib. She'd messaged Daniel: *Merry Christmas, sending love* with heart emoticons. Okay, he was Jewish, and didn't celebrate Christmas, but there was no excuse for Happy New Year communication embargo now was there? This was the man who used to send her text messages by the bucket load and tell her without fail that he loved her, complete with emoticons. Yet now there were no blue ticks next to her messages, so he wasn't even reading them. Maybe he'd died, and everyone forgot to mention it. But no, he was still on the EPIS contact board. So, the ongoing lack of contact was entirely deliberate. How humiliating that she wasn't even worth an official ending. Or even a *Piss off I've met someone else,* nothing. She and Daniel appeared to have gone adrift, no argument, no explanation, no one else involved, unless she could count the chap on the internet dating site Plenty of Fish, Plenty of Wankers, more like it – who described himself as "a legend in his own lunchbox." At least, he had a sense of humour, which was more than could be said of most, but even with him, the chat had fizzled out. Her job description alone had them all running for the hills.

The prospect of endless and unredeemable loneliness beckoned. But one beacon of light shone through all the dross. She was meeting the children for lunch at the weekend. Ed first, then Alice would join them. The prospect was exciting, terrifying, and nerve-wracking in equal measure. She could hardly wait, but then again, what if she blew it?

* * *

Back to work on Monday – the lunch with the kids had gone okay. Everyone had survived the ordeal. They'd both grown so much, and mercifully they liked their presents. Edward had passed his driving test on the first attempt, which was impressive as they had that highway-code theory on top of the practical, and she had to own up that she'd failed hers twice. The stories of her terrible reversing had made Alice laugh. They talked about their favourite subjects – Edward was studying RE, business studies, and psychology at "A" level and planned to go to university to study politics. That made her proud. They appeared to have turned out all right with or without her influence in their later years. Edward seemed to be particularly keen on the Koran, and as she thought about that, suddenly, it all began to fall into place. If Edward had been driving the Range Rover, there'd be a number of potentially serious issues: he was probably driving without his father's permission, as the insurance on a car that size would be prohibitively expensive for anyone under twenty-five, let alone a seventeen-year-old who'd just passed his test. In fact, insurance companies probably wouldn't touch it with a barge pole, so he was driving without insurance and he'd been visiting jihadi mosques that would flag up flashing red warning lights at the foreign office.

All told, a bit like lifting the lid on Pandora's box, and she guessed that was why Peter wanted the car out of the picture. He was trying to protect their son. It would have worked, except the thief went off on a road rage attack that threw a whopping great monkey wrench in the mix. She had to figure out how to tread the fine line between her personal life and her professional code of conduct. Tricky, this, as she'd only just had the big reunion with her children, and they'd all agreed to stay in touch. That was so precious that the last thing she wanted was to disconnect and get cut off. Fingers crossed they could re-establish their relationships and rebuild trust again. But if

Peter went to court, that would seriously screw her chances. Did she really want her children to think she was the bitch who shopped their hero dad, who after all was only putting his son first? *What a bloody impossible situation,* she thought as she checked her watch and prepared to leave the station. It had been a long day, and that called for a drink. The White Hart was closer to the office, but invariably full of coppers, so she and Rav agreed on the Brown Bear. On the way out of the station she got a text from Ed on her personal phone, so rare this that she gasped.

> *Mum, dad says I have to cut off all contact with Nazir.*
> *He's my best mate.*

Rosetta sighed. Some cults and religious zealots preyed on young, idealistic, intelligent sorts, they were easy marks of course. She'd heard of groups even using yoga and meditation as a form of mind control, who'd imagine that? For teenagers like Ed, friendships were important, but this friend was a radical extremist and there was too much at stake. She typed her reply:

> *Sorry, but I agree with dad. Write to Nazir, explain that he was a good friend, and you'll miss him, but you don't share his views. Mum x*

Ed sent back a sad-wailing-face emoticon.

Rosetta gave a long sigh, at least they'd got Ed back from the brink, the Marshall family could count their blessings, but no such luck prevailed for the poor Levine's, no regain and restore for them: only loss and is no more.

* * *

'Thanks,' she said as Rav arrived with the glasses. He was medium height, in his mid-forties, she guessed, and trim probably thanks to his veggie diet. She could really do with something to celebrate. Rav didn't drink, didn't smoke, or eat meat. How exciting was that? He had an orange juice which he sipped, slowly. Meanwhile, she'd already knocked back half her glass of wine. *Self-medicating rules, okay?* she thought.

If she had to pick a word to describe Rav, aside from "conservative," she'd choose "distinguished." His dark hair was greying at the temples, and he always wore immaculate suits. Today, as he reached across the table, she noticed his expensive Breitling watch as it glinted silver in the light above.

'How's Chandra?' The pub was crowded, so it came out louder than she'd intended. She wished she'd made more of an effort with her outfit, but it was too late now.

Rav stiffened, and for a moment the mask slipped. Then he quickly recovered his composure. 'Fine. Chandra's fine.'

Rosetta drained her glass and laughed. 'Rav, you're a crap liar. You'd never pass a lie detector test.'

He shook his head and stared at her. His eyes were warm and genuine. 'How... how did you...?' Then, it was his turn to laugh. 'We're separated. Chandra has gone back to New Delhi.'

Rosetta chewed her cheek, twiddled the stem of her wine glass, and waited for him to speak.

First, he looked uncomfortable, and then he looked forlorn. 'She says I'm too engrossed in my work. She always wanted a child, and sadly that never worked out, so I suppose we grew apart.'

'No glue. I know that feeling. Would you mind getting me a top-up?' She waved the glass under his nose. 'I've got an idea that I'm going to need it.'

'Here you go,' he said on his return, planting a bottle on the table. 'What about you and Daniel?'

'Cheers,' Rosetta said assuming a blank expression, then she added, 'who?'

Rav laughed. 'Sorry to hear that.' He looked as if he didn't know what else to say.

Rosetta never had a problem with speaking up. 'In light of the recent Traveller link, I'd like to be the one to go to Ireland and interview this Rafferty chap.' She tried to keep her tone even and neutral, but the thought of seeing Tommy, of meeting him in person, filled her with a curious excitement. She got her feelings back under strict control and did her utmost to appear professional. 'I'll need clearance with the Garda, of course. Can you organise that or do you want my lot to clear the way?'

He took a sip of OJ. 'What do you reckon, I mean, about your ex and Pa Riley?'

'Dunno, there are other more productive lines of enquiry it seems.' She shrugged. Telling a big white lie had been easier than she'd imagined, and she took a large gulp of wine to push down the pang of guilt. Really, she needed time to figure this whole angle out. She knew if she looked hard enough she'd more than likely trace a substantial payment from Peter to Pa and now that she knew the whys and wherefores she concluded it was better that she didn't go poking under any more stones. Maybe the Peter-Pa connection would blow over or get buried in the shit storm. 'It seems the Irish travellers are definitely involved but it'll be tricky getting any of them to talk.' She glanced across the table and their eyes met. 'So, about the Garda, it would be quicker if EPIS sort it, and I'm keen to nail this angle ASAP.'

Rav nodded. 'Okay, get your boss to grapple with our Irish friends. They could mire us in paperwork that could take months if they're so inclined. How are you getting on with the powers that be in the sky, or wherever EPIS is based?'

'Fine, thanks. I'm looking at a number of celebrity, historical, and fictional connections. First, we had Eclipse search and run all the known deaths and serious injuries due to riding accidents in those categories.'

Rav considered the implications for a while. 'You mean like Christopher Reeve?'

Rosetta gave him a thumbs-up. 'Spot on, and that's an obvious link to eventing as he was competing in cross country at the time of the accident. But, we have to create a wide frame, kind of like a wardrobe to hang theories in.'

'The lion, the witch and the wardrobe.' They both laughed at this. 'An obvious question coming next. How did you get –'

'I've always been psychic, from a very early age. I could predict things, make things levitate, so I guess I was always different. In my teens, I did tarot readings for pocket money. I did a psychology degree at Oxford and my masters in Philadelphia.'

Rav looked impressed as she continued, 'Then, in my mid-twenties, I joined the force.' Rosetta snorted. 'As you can imagine, I had to keep my private life very private. Then, there was a really high-profile serial murder case and my boss decided to call in a psychic, so I offered to help. That opened up a whole new avenue of enquiry. I got a lot of Mystic Meg-type ribbing from the lads, but the perp was caught and jailed, so they couldn't argue with that.'

'No, I guess not,' Rav agreed. He leaned towards her and lowered his voice. 'But the witchcraft bit?'

Rosetta reached for the Sauvignon and replenished her glass. 'Mainly FamTrad, as it's called. I have the gift, as did my grandmother, and she passed on what she knew when I was thirteen. Technically, this is more shamanism than today's neo-paganism, but I studied with the Servants of the Light, which is a great organisation for mystical and metaphysical training run by Delores Nowicki and her husband, Michael. They do an amazing job at preserving the West's ancient rites and traditions. It's not exactly a school of witchcraft, although that's part of it. I guess it's more magician craft.'

'You mean like Harry Potter stuff?'

'Well, we're not quite so scary and vilified post J. K. Rowling, but...' she swallowed as she felt tears welling up from nowhere, 'but in the divorce, my ex used this against me. He totally convinced my kids that I'm crazy, and social services had a field day.' She fished out a tissue and blew her nose, tears rolling down her cheeks. 'I lost custody.'

'I'm so sorry.'

Rosetta sniffed. 'I lost everything, really. I didn't ask to be psychic. Who would? It freaked me out, even though my family were accepting. It started when I was around seven and, believe me, I tried everything to block it out. I don't see dead people, thank God, but I have a spirit guide who brings me messages from the other side.'

Rav furrowed his brow as if deep in thought. 'Can't you have a séance and ask questions and find out who did what?'

Rosetta laughed half-heartedly. 'Nope, I'm not a medium or a fortune teller. For me, it's a bit like a one-way radio channel. They send me messages via my spirit guide. Sometimes I hear voices but more often I have visions in my sleep. Then I have to unravel what it means. That's the tricky part, and that's where EPIS comes in. They've made phenomenal advances in all dimensions. The starting point is belief and an open mind. The messages are useless to closed hearts and shut-down attitudes.'

'EPIS is an enigma. Who are they, do they really exist, where are they?'

Rosetta cupped her chin in her hands. 'Everywhere, and nowhere. They don't have a temple, a coven, a lodge, a meeting place, or even headquarters.' Another fib, but justified this time, she told herself. 'EPIS operates in another dimension, a different realm to ours here on Earth, kind of like Narnia beyond the wardrobe. They police the intergalactic spheres. Some say that Earth is so important because the portal, the gateway between dimensions, is here on Earth and consequently there will always be battles to gain control of it. EPIS only interferes if the balance of power tips too far in favour of bad guys.' Rosetta sniffed. She wanted to be totally upfront with Rav, but her initiation oath prohibited it.

'That's, erm, well, pretty far out there,' Rav observed. 'My brain's getting quite scrambled trying to figure it out.'

'Well, yeah, I get that. But it's not so much an intellectual concept as a multisensory experience. You feel it from the heart or the gut, while the head suspends disbelief.' She sniffed again and scooped up her handbag. 'I could do with a cigarette. Do you mind?'

'Of course not, although isn't it about time you gave up?' Rav asked, his face full of concern.

'It never seems quite the right moment, although Peter did manage to quit. He went to a hypnotist. Oh, that's it, how could I forget? Peter said that he regressed during hypnosis and recalled a past life as an Apache Indian called…' she paused, trying to recall '… Mahkota, or something like that.'

'Where are you going with this?' He stood up, his hand lightly touching her back as he moved her towards the conservatory.

'I really don't know yet. Odd though, as Juliet feels that Gothic was a reincarnation of her previous top event horse, Totem. It seems there's definitely some Native American connection. We'll see.' She turned to face him, to gauge his reaction. He was a Hindu, so reincarnation was accepted in his teachings and his belief system. Fortunately, no great clash of values, no unspoken judgements with this man, which came as a relief. She found his company relaxing, and she wanted more. 'It could be there's a link to the Apaches,' she murmured, shrugging her shoulders. 'But I don't know what the link is yet.'

'Ah.' He studied her, and his gaze was light and caressing. They came to a table out of earshot of the other outcasts and smokers, with a patio heater radiating warmth into the chilly night.

'Shall we sit here?' they both asked at the same time. They laughed, as if it was always meant to be.

Perhaps, she thought wistfully, *perhaps from now on things could be different?*

CHAPTER NINETEEN

Rosetta
2019
Dulce, New Mexico

A few years ago, Rosetta had travelled with Professor James Randell to the EPIS command centre, the military-scientific body responsible for the Eclipse project, which administered and maintained the US government-sponsored teams that were working in all branches of psychic abilities, to unlock the sixth senses and develop new capacities in humans. James was a top parapsychologist employed by EPIS to monitor standards. Highly sceptical about psychic powers, his involvement ensured some checks and balances were introduced into all tests and experiment procedures.

As they drove across miles of rocky flatlands and blood-red desert, he explained to her about the base's history and its ethos. The EPIS command at Dulce had first been run by the US forces and the command base consisted of twenty-eight levels, located some thousand metres underground beneath the mountains in New Mexico near the Colorado border. This arrangement provided security from most forms of conventional attack, and the facilities housed at the base were virtually impregnable should some disaster occur. The base was split up into two main sections: levels one through eleven and levels twelve through twenty-eight. Water was provided from above ground at Earth level to supply an underground reservoir deep inside the base with a one and a half million-gallon capacity. Air was drawn from the surface and screened through a system of chemical, biological, and radiological filters to remove harmful germs and/or radioactive and chemical particles.

As they took the approach road to the base, she clocked that there were miles of high wire fences, concrete pillars, road access blocks and warning signs everywhere: *Missile Testing, Danger: Keep Out, Trespassing Strictly Forbidden. Not exactly a warm welcome,* Rosetta thought. The heat continued to build as the day wore on, and it made her sleepy. She wound down the window, hoping that the fresh breeze would keep her awake. The air hung heavy with the threat of thunder. In the distance the horizon was thick with storm clouds rolling in. *Phew.* Rosetta unbuttoned her shirt collar and wafted herself in an attempt to cool down. The atmosphere was building up thick and tepid, layer by layer. It needed to break.

'Hmmm, I hope they have some serious air-con in there,' she drawled.

James chuckled. 'Don't fret, they have every conceivable comfort, and then some.'

'How much farther?' It had been a long day on the road, travelling across arid desert and the like, across the kind of terrain where it seemed probable that murderous hillbillies were lurking. How she longed for a shower and a long, cold beer on ice.

'Not far now, hang in there. It'll be worth it, you'll see.' He smiled reassuringly.

Rosetta sniffed. Even the air out there smelt parched and thirsty. *How would you describe it? Oh, I know, scorched dust.* She stared into the distance, willing the journey to end soon.

Access to the complex was restricted. Only authorised personnel were allowed inside the base, and there were only a handful of administrative buildings on the surface, plus huge satellite dishes scanning the sky above and beyond.

The car was stopped, and their ID checked and scrutinised at barrier after barrier. The mountain entrance consisted of three defence perimeters with ten-foot barbed-wire fences and numerous checkpoints, each of which required authorisation before anyone could proceed. Military personnel were guarding the series of entrances at all times, armed with machine guns and assault rifles.

Rosetta inhaled when one of the guards pointed his weapon towards the car. 'I guess gate-crashing the party out here is not an option, then?'

'Definitely not,' James agreed, 'they're authorised to shoot intruders on the spot.'

'Right. So, this is not a place where tourists are advised to arrive unannounced?' She couldn't help wondering what was the big deal then? What were they so determined to keep under wraps? She was trying not to get too paranoid but at the same time couldn't help feeling apprehensive. What the hell had she got herself into?

They followed the final stretch of road leading into the facility, cavorting with its twists and turns which presumably thwarted any high-speed incursions past the various checkpoints. Additionally, there were cement and steel barriers deployed all along the road to prevent unauthorised access into the tunnels. She learned that the area outside the mountain complex was guarded by two batteries of surface-to-air missiles, with support backup available from a nearby air force base in Colorado.

The journey seemed endless, and she wondered what could possibly be worth this amount of effort. Once access into the tunnel had been achieved. The trip down to the primary staging area took another third of a mile or so. Predictably, it had its own checkpoint security system. Two young officers signalled for them to pull over, and they went through the same standard routine of ID check, fingerprinting, checking their names against their clipboard of expected visitors, purpose of the visit, and expected length of stay.

James seemed to love it all. It was the 007 effect, perhaps? *Men love spies, espionage, intrigue, don't they?* Rosetta had her doubts. It all seemed so macho, and the environment, consisting of endless grey concrete and miles of barbed-wire fencing, totally lacked charm. The landscape itself was harsh, dry and barren. No fertile plains and flowers out here.

'Do you know the access tunnel to this facility can be sealed by a twenty-five-ton steel and concrete composite door, securing the base from the outside world? Every security checkpoint requires personnel to submit to a fingerprint scan before their entry to the base is authorised,' James said breathlessly, obviously impressed.

Rosetta gave a fake, half-hearted laugh. She wasn't worried about the threats they kept out, but she was beginning to wonder how the hell could she escape?

Apparently, according to James, who seemed to have memorised a mine of useless facts, the main level covered four and a half acres of cleared-out stone with steel-lined walls to protect the facility from electromagnetic pulses. Pressure sensors were located at both the north and south tunnel entrances. They detected the presence of nuclear detonation or chemical warfare and at the first hint of trouble would automatically seal the entrance gates.

Levels one to four comprised the bulk of the administrative areas for Eclipse and the North American aerospace defence command, including personnel, payroll, and accounting. All requisitions and authorisation orders were processed through the administration areas, and those levels also contained a waiting room where visitors stayed until they received authorisation to enter the rest of the facility and their designated escort arrived to collect them.

The administration areas included all base routine records and the secondary backup computer system containing data noncritical to the base's operations. In the event of a systems failure, the base could transfer control between the primary and secondary systems, in order to operate the structure's facilities. Level one housed only a small staff presence, mainly civilians, and an access point for the airflow system that pulled air from the surface and shunted it down into the facility through the purification system. Ducts led down to level eleven, where a there was a secondary airflow system to be used in the event of a failure. The airflow units were highly sophisticated and designed so either system could provide limited airflow, around twenty-four hours for the entire facility, until repairs could be initiated. Armed guards covered all access points to the elevators and all stairwells on level one at all times.

'It's the safest spot in the world.' James positively glowed. 'This is an impregnable underground military command post, built to withstand even close-range nuclear blasts, and which, if necessary, provides a high-tech sanctuary for the world's elite.'

'Such as the super-rich Mr. Zuckerberg, Bill Gates, and Lady Gaga to keep them entertained, perhaps?'

James continued, undeterred. 'This command centre has connections to the world's most powerful satellite, tracking and mapping devices. Those radars and receptor devices we passed a bit farther back have ground crews checking, adjusting, and repositioning them around the clock. Isn't it incredible?'

Rosetta nodded weakly as he continued.

'Level three is mainly used for housing the accounting records department and all files are backed up and out-of-date records are transferred to the archives on level twenty-four. On that level there's also a small mess area. The main mess hall is located on level twenty-two. Levels six and seven consist entirely of massive storage areas designed to hold equipment and supplies as required. Level seven

131

also contains a number of specialised non-perishable foodstuffs and astronaut-style rations which would be used during base lockdowns. When properly outfitted and rationed, they can store enough food supplies to last the entire base for a period of six months. These levels can also serve as holding bays for high-profile individuals deemed worthy and beneficial to the survival and continuity of the base. The show must go on, and these people, referred to as Redeemers, can be housed here temporarily until they can be relocated, by transforming the storage areas into simple group accommodations. It's envisaged that this arrangement will enable the base to hold up to two hundred and forty additional people, a hundred and twenty on each level. The Redeemers are designated as the worthy ones: the Nobel prize winners, the linguists, the scientists, the inventors, and neuro-surgeons: the brightest and the best in their fields.'

'Who's in charge here and what's their background?' Rosetta asked.

'Well, ultimately the Director of Research. You only get names on a need-to-know basis. We're going to be met by the base's top administrator.' They approached two receptionists seated behind a bank of curved glass. 'It's bulletproof,' James said. The waiting area was patrolled by several armed personnel, one with a disgruntled-looking security dog.

'Really? I'd never have guessed.'

After further clearance tests – irises and fingerprints – the receptionist made a phone call, then said, 'Take a seat. Major Harris will be with you in a moment.'

Sure enough, the Major arrived with military punctuality. He was good-looking, a broad-shouldered man with an intimidating presence. 'James, it's good to see you.' He shook the professor's hand. 'And you must be Ms. Barrett? I'm pleased to meet you.'

'Likewise,' she said as they followed him to the elevator. After a slick, high-speed ride which left her stomach behind, they made their way to a glass-fronted conference room.

The Major poured them all glasses of water. 'If you'll excuse me, I'll go find Doctor Ashworth.'

After the Major left, James continued on his pet project. 'Isn't it awesome? Levels eight and nine contain the internal power generation plant and the distribution grid. That's the base's entire hi-tech electrical system, which is generated through a small internal reactor during an emergency. But, most of the time, power is pulled down from the surface and surrounding hydroelectric resources. Even when forced to rely on emergency power, the base can operate indefinitely. Until reactor start-up can be initialised, the base can run on emergency battery power, located on level twenty-three. This power is sufficient to keep the based functional for up to forty-eight hours when used judiciously. On level two, the facility consists largely of the base's secondary air processing plant which helps to draw air to the primary plant on level one, and down into the lower levels of the facility. The remainder of level ten holds the purification and storage tanks. Level eleven is split into two areas, but for all intents and purposes they're referred to as one. The primary elevator shaft runs from levels one to eleven. All personnel and visitors must switch to an alternate elevator system for the lower levels, but only after they've passed another security checkpoint which provides an additional level of security to block access to the base's most sensitive areas below. Level eleven also contains further water purification and storage tanks which can provide several months' worth of drinking water as backup when needed.'

'Yeah, that's reassuring. Are you taking a PhD in engineering, by any chance?' Rosetta quipped.

'No. Why do you ask?'

'Forget it.' She caught sight of the Major on his way towards them. He was accompanied by a smartly dressed woman and a man with grey hair and a Gandalf-style beard in a white lab coat.

'Professor Ritchie Romanoff, chief astronomer and linguist,' he said, holding out his hand, which Rosetta shook.

The woman introduced herself as Doctor Ashworth and explained a bit about what happened on the base. 'We have a number of labs here and we conduct a wide range of sixth-sense research and experiments.'

'What's the purpose?' Rosetta asked.

'That really varies based on the paranormal specialisation. Each group has a different focus and the experiments can take years.'

The Gandalf man chuckled. 'Yeah, if any of us seem a little odd down here, that's because they don't let us out much.'

Rosetta responded rather briskly, 'I'm not going to work here, at this place. I'm a detective. I've got a job, a family…' She was about to say *a life*, but that seemed a bit rude.

Dr. Ashworth laughed. 'No, that's okay. You'll be based out in the field, and ostensibly you'll still work for the police, but the reporting lines will change. Effectively, you'll ultimately report to the global secret service.'

'That sounds complicated.' Rosetta looked at Gandalf, who was scowling over a computer printout. 'Anything interesting occurring?' she enquired.

Gandalf nodded. 'Open source data and algorithms, combined with digital innovation and cloud computing.'

Rosetta sank into her chair and stared up at the ceiling. 'Brainiac solving problems, right? But what problems are you lot solving exactly?'

Gandalf looked pleased with himself. 'Some aliens communicate telepathically with images and feelings, so, as the head of linguistics, I have a team of psychics working on that, and we're making great progress with the mind-melding and mind control.'

Rosetta registered shock at this revelation. Poor Doctor Ashworth looked like a sprinter who had just tripped over the starting block and landed sprawled out on the track, flat on her face.

Rosetta let out a low whistle. 'Are you saying that you have aliens here? Are you for real?'

James and the doctor let out a collective groan.

'That's classified information!' Major Harris barked. 'And if you persist in asking questions, I'll have to ask you to leave.'

'That might not be one of your better ideas,' Rosetta retaliated. She was fed up with this pompous ass pulling his power trips. 'Since you're heading up security around here, if this news breaks, they'll bust your arse faster than you can blink.'

'She has a point,' Gandalf said helpfully.

The Major's face drained of colour inch by inch, but, to give him his due, he didn't flinch, and soon Dr. Ashworth came to the rescue. 'There are absolutely no aliens housed here, categorically, none.'

'Well now, that's not strictly true,' Gandalf said, as if slowly entangling himself from an enthralling dream.

'This is news to me,' Dr. Ashworth growled as she glared at her colleagues one by one. Two red dots of anger flashed across her face. 'Well?'

'Telepathy's not your division, so anything they're involved with is on a need-to-know only basis,' Major Harris said with soft but very assured authority.

Dr. Ashworth looked unimpressed at this response. 'How the hell did it get here?'

Gandalf sighed. 'Well, they came through the portal.'

'What? They...?' Dr. Ashworth looked horrified. 'They arrived via the time portal? That's for time travel, not space travel.'

'Yes,' Gandalf agreed, 'but the mind-melding experiment worked a little too well, and they accidentally got transported. We haven't figured out yet how to get them back, but we will, it's only a matter of –'

'Time,' James cut in. 'Wow, a fucking alien, man. That's –'

'Out of this world.' Rosetta finished his sentence for him with a wicked laugh. 'ET phone home? Maybe you should order a few bicycles?'

Dr. Ashworth had her elbows on the table and her hands resting on her forehead. 'Does the Senate Select Intelligence Service know about this?'

'No, according to Director's orders this matter is in a total information blackout and complete lockdown. We have several personnel in quarantine as a precaution,' the Major said with an air of considerable authority. 'Rest assured the situation is under control.'

'Well, hardly, since you've just let the cat out of the bag.' Rosetta assumed an unimpressed expression.

James aimed a sharp kick at her ankle underneath the table and gestured at her to zip it.

'Sorry, guys,' she ploughed on. 'But I'm definitely not getting mixed up in any of this shit.' She folded her arms across her chest for emphasis. 'I'd like to leave and the sooner the better, if you get my drift.'

'That won't be possible, I'm afraid.' The Major leaned forward close to her face and fixed her with a withering look. 'And certainly, not now that you're in the inner circle, as it were.' He shot Professor Romanoff an ominous glare.

Rosetta sprang to her feet and grabbed her handbag. It was Marc Jacobs, very expensive, so no way was she leaving that behind. 'You can't keep me here against my will.'

Major Harris leaned back and snorted. 'On the contrary, my dear, I can, and I will. I don't take orders from civilians. Do I make myself clear? Sit down! Now!'

Rosetta complied and crumpled back into her seat. She realised the situation had become serious.

Dr. Ashworth reached down by the side of her chair and put her briefcase in front of her on the table. She removed a document, some kind of report that was about twenty pages long, and a hardcover kind of handbook. Carefully, she slid them across the table to Rosetta, who instinctively withdrew her hands and put her arms by her sides.

'What's that?' She felt suspicious, as if she was about to get railroaded.

'That's your employment contract.'

Dr. Ashworth had assumed a fake smile that reminded Rosetta of the python in *The Jungle Book*. What was its name? Hissing Sid – no, that wasn't it. Ah yes, *Kaa*. 'No way. I'm not signing that Goddamn thing. Forget it.' A faint wave of nausea rose up from the pit of her stomach into her throat. She coughed. Her predicament didn't look too positive at that moment. Who could she call? Who could mount a rescue mission? She rummaged in her handbag, trying to locate her phone. She pulled it out, keeping it below the desk and out of view, and stared at the blank screen.

Gandalf smiled at her weakly. 'Your phone won't work. There's no signal down here unless we modify your SIM card.'

Rosetta stared at him. 'Ah, you're telepathic. That's neat. Oh, but the phone thing, that's a b–'

He grinned. 'I know.'

Kaa's eyes blazed, the fake smile still holding fast. 'Just one more thing there's a short survey I'd like you to complete –'

'No kidding? How do I rate my experience here at the Dulce dungeon?' Rosetta shook her head. 'Thanks, but I think I'll pass.' She was beginning to feel like an extra in *Game of Thrones*, or was it *Stranger Things*?

Major Harris's eyes narrowed, and he lowered his naturally booming voice. 'You'll find that cooperation is not only the sensible option, but the only option. Now, if you'll follow me, I'll take you to your quarters.'

Gandalf bit his lip as he caught Rosetta's eye and then glanced at the Major. 'Shere Khan?'

Rosetta muffled a laugh. 'You're good, but no. You're wrong, definitely Baloo.'

They both burst out chuckling like a couple of school kids, and as Rosetta and Gandalf fell in behind the Major, they started singing, *I wanna walk like you, talk like you…*

In spite of her unfavourable first impression, she liked Professor Romanoff. He was a maverick for sure, very politically incorrect, but that was undeniably part of his charm.

Later that evening, in her room – a compact bedroom with a double bed, a work station, and en-suite bathroom – Rosetta sprawled out on the bed, scanning the questionnaire Dr. Ashworth had given her. After all, she had nothing else to do and curiosity got the better of her. She read quickly down the list, her pencil poised in her mouth.

EPIS Psychic Evaluation:

Please circle skills which apply and for these skills rate yourself on a score of one to ten, where one is low, hardly any ability, and ten is high, exceptional ability:

Astral projection – the ability to voluntarily project the astral (emotional) body, which is associated with out-of-body experiences in which an astral body becomes separate from the physical body.

Aura reading – the ability to perceive energy fields surrounding people, places, and things.

Automatic writing – the ability to write without conscious thought.

Clairaudience – the ability to acquire information by paranormal auditory means.

Clairsentience – the ability to acquire psychic knowledge by feeling.

Clairvoyance – the ability to perceive persons, objects, locations, and physical events through extrasensory perception.

Divination – the ability to gain insight to a situation by way of cultic standardised process.

Dowsing – the ability to locate water, sometimes using a tool called a dowsing rod.

Energy medicine – the ability to heal with one's own empathetic astral energy.

Exorcism – the ability to get rid of evil entities by a ceremony performed by a shaman or a priest.

Faith healing – the ability to diagnose or cure illnesses using religious devotion.

Intuition – the ability to acquire knowledge without proof, evidence, or conscious reasoning or without understanding how the knowledge was acquired, but instead having direct access to unconscious knowledge, unconscious cognition, inner sensing, inner insight to unconscious pattern-recognition, and the ability to understand something instinctively, without the need for conscious reasoning.

Levitation – the ability to undergo bodily uplift or fly by mystical means.

Lucid dreaming – the ability to remain lucid during voluntary dreams and or to control one's own dreams.

Mediumship (or channelling) – the ability to communicate with spirits.

Precognition (or premonition) – the ability to perceive future events.

Prophesy – the ability to predict what will happen in the future.

Psychic surgery – the ability to remove disease or disorders within or over the body tissue via an energetic incision that heals immediately afterwards.

Psychometry – the ability to obtain information about a person or an object, usually by touch.

Pyrokinesis – the ability to manipulate fire.

Remote viewing – the ability to see distant and unseen targets using extrasensory perception.

Retro-cognition – the ability to perceive past events.

Second sight – the ability to see future and past events or to perceive information that is not present to the senses, in the form of a vision (precognition or remote viewing.)

Scrying – the ability to look into a suitable medium (such as a teacup) in order to detect significant information.

Shape-shifting – the ability to temporarily change form, usually from human to animal, and back again.

Telepathy – the ability to transfer thoughts mentally through extrasensory perception.

Blah, blah, Rosetta thought as she removed the pencil from her lips and scratched her chin. Some of these skills she'd never even heard of. A few of them sounded neat, like pyrokinesis, for instance, which reminded her of Daenerys or Dany, the Queen of Dragons in *Game of Thrones*. That breathing fire stuff could come in handy, especially for an arsonist.

For her own supernormal abilities, she circled *Precognition, Prophesy* and *Second Sight*, although they all seemed pretty similar. What was the actual difference? No doubt they had a Hogwarts down here where they would teach her the nuances of the paranormal realms. As an afterthought, she added *Intuition*. So far so good, but now she'd have to evaluate her abilities and rate herself. The unclear thing about these kind of tests, was how to score oneself in comparison to what, or, more to the point, compared to whom? For all she knew, this could end up like *The Hunger Games*. Then, presumably, she was better off rating herself crap, so she didn't get chosen to get killed, or worse still get mated with one of the aliens to produce a hybrid. *Shit happens.*

Should she score herself as a five just to be on the safe side? Or, if she gave herself a one, would they kick her out for being useless? In which case, surely this was the way to go? In the end she decided on a six and added "room for improvement."

She tossed the form onto the bedside table, made herself a cup of tea, and lit a cigarette.

Immediately, a smoke detector went off, and the monitor on the wall opposite the bed lit up and flashed to life. The monitor emitted an eerie digital computer voice, 'Smoking is prohibited. Extinguish. Extinguish immediately.'

Rosetta stuck two fingers up at the screen and carried on puffing away, like one of Dany's baby dragons.

'Warning, smoking is prohibited. Extinguish. Extinguish immediately. You have twenty seconds.'

Rosetta laughed. Its shrill voice reminded her of a Dalek in *Dr. Who*. 'Yeah, right. Don't get your knickers in a twist, love.'

Suddenly, with a great whoosh, the water sprinklers in the ceiling switched on. Rosetta screamed and leapt off the bed. She grabbed the duvet, her cigarettes, the Marc Jacobs, and legged it into the bathroom. What had she forgotten? Christ, the forms! She dumped her stuff and raced back in to rescue those too. Everything was soggy, her hair was soaking, and she looked like a drowned rat. She undressed, hanging the wet clothes on the towel rail to dry and grabbing the dressing gown from the hook on the door. Sooner or later, it would stop raining indoors. But until then, it was either sitting on the loo in quiet contemplation or hanging out in the bath.

The bath won.

She wondered what level she was on. They'd got out at eleven, or had it been twelve? Then they'd changed to another bank of elevators and dropped down a floor or two. It had descended so quickly, maybe more than two. She wished she'd paid more attention to James when he'd gone off rambling about the base layout. She regretted never actually having watched *Prison Break*. If she could get out of here, perhaps she could join the escape committee.

Fat chance. They had locked her; yes, *locked* her into this flooded room, and no doubt in the morning they'd be presenting her with a heart-attack-inducing bill for the damages. *Mating with the alien might not be so bad after all,* she thought, as she finally drifted off to sleep.

CHAPTER TWENTY
Rosetta
2019

The next morning, breakfast was served in her room, coffee, orange juice, and scrambled eggs on toast. About an hour later, there was a knock at the door. Dr. Ashworth had come to collect her and escort her to another conference room on one of the upper floors. Again, the elevator whooshed, so fast she lost track of where she was.

She followed the good doctor into a glass-panelled room, where two others were already seated. After brief introductions, Dr. Ashworth waved her hand and announced, 'Daniel's our top employment lawyer. So, if you have any questions about the terms and conditions, he's your man.'

Daniel grinned, flashing a set of Hollywood-style teeth. *Good-looking but smarmy,* Rosetta thought.

'Can I have your card, please?' Her tone was neutral, as she kept it matter-of-fact and business-like. For now, at least.

'Daniel Solomon, pleased to meet you.' He offered his hand in greeting.

'Yesterday didn't exactly go according to plan,' Dr. Ashworth said, staring at Rosetta as if trying to gauge her reaction. 'In order to clarify and dispel any false impressions, please understand that we use crack communications specialists and our technology is unsurpassed. Amongst other things our mission is to create first-rate anticipatory intelligence systems.' She paused and took a deep breath. 'The work with alien communication is just a small part of the big picture. Ultimately what we're aiming for is the ability to improve and automate forecasting, and that has all kinds of uses and benefits.

What we're really trying to do is develop highly automated ways of predicting global social and economic unrest for limitation and prevention purposes. That might include anything from terrorist attacks across the globe, to wide-scale disruptive computer hacking, economic crashes, market collapse, nuclear threats, outer-space anomalies… This list is endless, but the aim is totally benevolent.'

The doctor paused, presumably to let Rosetta digest this information.

Rosetta pursed her lips and shrugged. 'Well, that's more plausible, I guess.'

Dr. Ashworth looked relieved. 'Good. I had a quick look at your answers and I gather from the survey you completed that your main abilities are prophesy and premonition. So, if you joined us, you'd be part of my team, and I think you'd be a real asset.' She stood up, went to the bookcase behind her, and removed two objects from the secure glass housing unit. 'Here. I'd like to show you something.' She carefully pushed two sealed Perspex boxes across the table towards Rosetta.

'What am I looking at?'

'You're looking at Nostradamus, the French apothecary and seer. That's his book, *Les Propheties*. It's a 1555 first edition. The other one is a very early mint-condition Bible. The Book of Revelations is also about forecasting through visions. So, we have a long track record in this field, and an illustrious history.'

A twinge of curiosity arose in Rosetta's chest. 'Where do you get information from exactly?'

'We have a state-of-the-art computer system called Eclipse which extracts classified and open-source data, plus we factor in psychic information, and to date, some of the results have been truly remarkable.'

'Such as importing aliens, you mean?' Rosetta arched one eyebrow in disdain.

Dr. Ashworth sighed. 'It's most unfortunate and unintentional, but very occasionally our computer geniuses get a little carried away and even hysterical, it seems.'

Dishy Daniel opened his mouth to say something, but the doctor waved her arm to silence him. 'It's nothing that can't be fixed, and they're working on it round-the-clock, of course.'

Rosetta scrutinised her closely. 'I'm not convinced this is my kind of thing, plus some of the inmates or whatever you call yourselves are… well, beardy-weird-ies or military crackpots.'

Daniel chuckled. 'Present company the exception, I presume?'

'Dunno about that. That remains to be seen.'

'You're joining us, I take it? Excellent. We have a terrific programme where we go back and fix things – karmic clean-up, so the original wrongdoing stops the ripple effect from spreading and multiplying.'

'Digital atonement?' She laughed. 'That's neat. Okay, I'm in, but I'd like to take a look at the time-machine thing.'

'Very well,' Dr. Ashworth replied with starch-like efficiency. 'However, I'll have to run that past our Director, and it will only be possible after you've officially joined us.'

'Okay. I'll have a quick read through the contract, and, Daniel, if you could go through it with me and explain everything that would be great.'

'Sure.' He flashed the knee-trembling grin again and indicated for Rosetta to follow him out of the room.

* * *

The following day, Rosetta was sworn in under the auspices of the Office of the Director of National Intelligence. She took the Oath of the Galactic Realms and enrolled in the two-week induction training course – the first of many. Now that she was one of them, so to speak, she was allowed to join others in the main mess for meals, and she got to explore a bit. She went swimming and sampled the fabulous health spa, complete with sauna and steam room, treatment rooms, and a hair salon. The facilities were impressive; fully equipped kitchens for the budding Gordon Ramsey-types; garages for the quad biker boys, complete with inspection pits; a ballroom which hosted nightly events and games from bingo to casino. Free e-books, music, Netflix, and Sky Box Sets were available on demand, and those who preferred could visit the full-size cinema with plush seats and even a popcorn dispenser, help-yourself ice cream or frozen yoghurt, and an array of soft drinks.

She'd come across the secondary command bunker and security station that kept tabs on the entire facility with video cameras and presumably ultra-high-tech listening devices too. There was an armoury and even an indoor firing range.

In the lower levels, the laboratories – or the Labyrinths, as they were called – were situated. Generally, there appeared to be a hive of activity throughout the base, with personnel working round-the-clock on a variety of key projects which, as far as she could gather, were mainly focused on classifying new discoveries brought through the T-Portal. The time travel device was invented by Dr. Drew Jenson, the world's foremost archaeologist and linguist. He had his laboratory near the metrological unit which contained a number of analysis and dating tools. Interestingly, there were lots of quarantine rooms for monitoring items and personnel which presumably might pose a health or security risk.

Rosetta couldn't help wondering if that was where they had the ETs stashed.

Nearby was the infirmary. It consisted of a medical bay that could accommodate up to thirty patients and housed state-of-the-art facilities and equipment, including several MRI scanners. There were also multiple gyms, physical therapy rooms, and rehabilitation facilities, plus the base's autopsy and forensic science stations.

On level twenty-four, she discovered the mainframe computer, nicknamed Jobs-worthy, or JW, which was self-contained and under constant lockdown. No personnel could enter the computer facility without authorisation from the base commander or the duty officer. The mission command briefing room was located on the same level as JW. It had a large retractable window and was where personnel met frequently with the base commander to discuss mission specifics and conduct debriefings. It contained a large table with seating for up to twenty people, and just down the hallway was the commander's office which had access to all key systems, as well as a direct phone to the Joint Chief of Staff based at the Pentagon, and a special hotline directly to the Office of the President.

All very impressive, she concluded. Like a large industrious town, except no children or pets were allowed.

Finally, they authorised her access to the T-Portal, which had its own elevator. As they reached the floor marked TP, Dr. Ashworth set off at a brisk jog, leaving her and Gandalf trailing in her wake.

'Sorry, but I spend too much time behind a desk, so it's my way of keeping fit,' she shouted over her shoulder. 'Come on. Keep up.'

They went along a narrow corridor which was lit at ground level and from above. It reminded Rosetta of an airport runway at night time. Dr. Ashworth stopped when she arrived at a holding bay behind huge plate glass windows. *How embarrassing,* Rosetta thought, as Gandalf overtook her with his arms going like pistons and his open white lab coat flapping. She huffed and puffed into last place and made an early resolution to take up jogging going forward.

144

The holding bay looked like a scrub-down area in a research hospital. It had rows of sinks down one side, and she noticed men in overalls, masks, and those very fetching plastic shoes.

'What's that for?' Rosetta enquired.

'It the static-free clean room,' Gandalf informed her.

Dr. Ashworth elaborated, 'With time travel, we could unwittingly transport modern-day germs back to the past and inadvertently change past events, or, coming the other way, bringing back the plague or something like that, so scrupulous hygiene is imperative.'

'Oh, I see.' Rosetta nodded.

Dr. Ashworth continued, 'When the portal's not in use, it's kept in a cryogenic state, using liquid nitrogen and hydrogen.' She indicated for them to follow her up a ramp which gradually inclined through a series of thick steel doors, each programmed with iris and palm recognition patterns to trigger the opening mechanism.

They continued through a tight space between concrete walls until they came to a viewing gallery looking down on a huge cavernous amphitheatre. Some way below them, men in the inevitable overshoes and forensic overalls were moving around work stations, studying graphs and all manner of charts.

'Well, what do think so far?' Dr. Ashworth took them through glass doors which whisked apart, and, on the other side, she pointed to a clear cylinder surrounded by tiny blue flashing lights reaching from floor to the ceiling. 'That's the T-Portal.' She looked like the proud mother of the hot-shot athletic kid who had just scooped all the medals at school sports day.

It didn't look like much. Her mother had something similar that she kept spaghetti in, and Rosetta felt a bit disappointed. After all the hype, it seemed a bit of an anti-climax. She inhaled deeply – and it reminded her of hospitals, all disinfectant and cleaning fluid. Her nose crinkled in distaste.

Dr. Ashworth didn't seem to notice. She had a love thing going on. 'I'll never forget my first trip. Words can't describe the sensation, the speed,' she sighed as she reminisced. 'It takes you backwards or forwards in time. We use it, for instance, to go back and locate the ultimate cause of a crime, so those involved can be brought into full awareness and face up to what they've done.'

'That's no bad thing,' Rosetta said. 'Most of the criminals brought to book never really accept responsibility for their actions. Denial rules, it seems to me. What about psychopaths? Does it work with them too?'

'That's a good point and worth investigating. Perhaps, that could be your thesis at some stage? Generally, people can atone for their past wrongdoings, and stop the karmic ripples perpetuating.' Dr. Ashworth paused. 'So, you see, it has profound implications for policing, criminal justice, and the prison service.'

'Wow. I hadn't thought of it like that. Okay, stick me in it.' Rosetta giggled.

Gandalf laughed. 'There's a lengthy training programme and a waiting list. Plus, we're kind of busy right now with the unannounced intergalactic guests.'

'Yeah, I guess.'

'Did you ever hear of a psychologist and eminent scientist called Dr. Kenneth Headley?' Dr. Ashworth asked.

Rosetta leaned back on the barrier and folded her arms across her chest. She shook her head.

Dr. Ashworth continued, 'He's a member of the Society of Psychical Research and he was an adviser for the TV sci-fi series *Out of This World*. Anyway...'

Gandalf flapped his arms in the air excitedly. 'It's about a teenage girl with superpowers, and her father's an alien.'

Rosetta groaned.

'Actually, that programme was awful, but anyway, Dr. Headley predicted that one of the most important scientific concerns in the next millennium will be the illusion of time itself.'

'And now you've solved the puzzle. Wow, I'm impressed,' Rosetta said. 'What's next?'

'Well,' the professor said, turning towards the elevators, 'if we could prove the link between human evolution and other planets or stars such as Sirius, unlocking the secret would mean solving one of life's greatest mysteries.'

Rosetta gave him a big grin and a thumbs-up sign. 'Well, if anyone can crack the code, it's you!'

CHAPTER TWENTY-ONE
Rosetta
2019

Rosetta had to complete six weeks training. She'd settled in quickly, helped by the fact that she and Daniel soon officially became an item and Professor Romanoff was like the adorable, zany uncle you always wished you had. He had this amazing knack of making really complex ideas understandable even for average folks.

'It's laughable, isn't it?' Gandalf said as they headed towards the restaurant for lunch. 'They roll out the head of NASA to tell us they don't have UFOs or alien spacecraft hidden in Area 51.'

'Does it actually exist?' Rosetta interrupted. 'I thought it was just a sci-fi conspiracy theory or something.'

Gandalf laughed. 'When does sci-fi become sci-fact? It exists in Nevada, near Groomlake, and now our government decides to pop up with the no-spaceship-in-the-hanger smoking gun.' The Professor paused and scanned her face, so she concluded that a response was required. 'That's a calculated distraction, of course. These latest revelations are designed to debunk UFO rumours.'

'Well, a number of governments have released their UFO files as I recall,' she ventured. She really didn't care much one way or the other about that out-there stuff. Leave it to the Trekkies and the Star Wars buffs. 'How did you feel when you first saw an... one...?'

Gandalf shook his head. 'Literally scared out of my skin, but gradually we all acclimatised; me to them and them to me. It's ironic really, since the scientists, SETI, and the super-rich from Silicon Valley – they're all searching for aliens that our governments already know exists. From what I can deduce, the aliens have been coming to Earth for a very long time indeed.'

'Hmmm,' Rosetta pondered. 'So why are they still keeping them under wraps?'

Gandalf paused. 'The idea that life on Earth was created or sparked by cells or DNA of cosmic origin challenges the very Earth-centred philosophies, theologies, and all our notions about our uniqueness and our unrivalled supremacy in the galaxy. A couple of decades ago, when astrobiologists came up with the theory of panspermia, that extra-terrestrial microbial life originated in space and spread to Earth in clouds of interstellar dust or meteorites crashing on the Earth's surface, they were ridiculed. Personally, I increasingly go with the idea of directed panspermia. Life on Earth was not some random event. I think it was engineered by an advanced, highly intelligent civilisation, and we are all people of stardust.'

'Seriously, you subscribe to the E.T. ancestry idea?' She paused, kind of at a loss for words. It was too much to process, and surely this was the essence of craziness?

Gandalf changed the subject as if he sensed that she was struggling intellectually and at all levels. 'You know that NASA is launching a mission to Europa?'

Rosetta looked at him blankly. 'What's that? Some post-Brexit utopia?'

'Nope,' Gandalf chuckled. 'It's a moon orbiting Jupiter, complete with a deep salt water ocean. So, they're trying to find conditions compatible with life – extra-terrestrial or otherwise. It will be handy if Europa can support life, since your Professor Hawking reckoned we need to hitchhike off Earth and find other planets to colonise, as we're on a path of self-destruction down here.'

'Kind of spread the eco-un-love around outer space, then?'

'Exactly,' Gandalf agreed as he chose a meal from the conveyor belt.

Rosetta studied his selection. 'Oh, is that why you're vegan?'

He nodded. 'Plastic is choking our oceans. Everything used here at Dulce is biodegradable or recyclable, and that's one of my proudest achievements to date, in fact.'

Rosetta smiled in encouragement. Instinctively she reached for the surf and turf, then with a sigh, she plonked it back and made do with the four-cheese pizza and a mixed salad. The large glass of merlot was calling her, but she passed up on that too and followed the professor to a table in a quiet corner, bringing a large glass of ice water.

'As your Professor Hawking got older, he became more convinced that humans are not alone. He hooked up with a Russian billionaire to create the Breakthrough Listening Project, trying to detect ET radio signals from outer space. Generally, we are beginning to see a much-needed paradigm shift in the conservative status quo.' Gandalf forked up a mouthful of tofu and gauged her reaction as he chewed.

'Right, but aren't we ignoring the elephant in the room?'

He laughed. 'Yes, indeed.'

'According to Hollywood, aliens are either cuddly adorable ETs, or ruthless, dangerous foes up to no good. So, which is it? Where do they come from, and why are they here?'

He shuffled in his seat. 'Here we have the much-needed, top multi-disciplinary teams, biologists, cosmologists, physicists, astronomers, mathematicians, geologists, chemists, theologians, linguists like myself – you name it – all pulling together and working on those very questions.'

'How long will it take to figure it out?'

'It'll take years maybe, decades probably. I had hoped that the astrobiologists could at least prove the panspermia theory. As another Brit, Sir Fredrick Hoyle, said, *"You are derived from something out there in the sky. Seek it and you shall find much more than you expect."* And now, we've made contact, which is an incredible privilege, isn't it? But the questions still remain. The aliens we have are all trans-human.'

Rosetta raised her eyebrows and gawped. '*Aliens*? I thought there was just the one? My God, they're multiplying.'

'Well, we have Blues and Greys, which are quite different entities. But both kinds have evolved to the synthetic AI stage, so sadly there's no DNA to test and trace back.' He assumed a sad expression.

'Fuckety-fuck. Excuse me, but I'm going to go for the glass of wine after all.' Rosetta returned shortly and placed the glass on the table. 'Where's all this going, exactly?'

'Preparation, preparation, and yet more preparation. Think of all the unanswered questions. For starters: can faiths accommodate new beings? Information will have to be drip fed out slowly, so we don't spark a religious war, for instance. I mean, what if they have attained a far more perfect level of spiritual development than us? How will that go down, particularly as all our religious identities are Earth-centric ones?'

Rosetta knocked the red wine back as if searching for inspiration at the bottom of the glass. 'Didn't the guy who works in the Vatican observatory come out and say that a belief in aliens wasn't incompatible with a belief in God, as we are all God's creatures?'

Gandalf raised his hands, palms facing outwards. 'It's a small step in the right direction, perhaps. But think of all the post-detection protocols that now have to be put into place. We need to assess the impact across every spectrum; biological, ecological, scientific, technological, legal, political, religious, and theological. Right now, we're working flat-out considering all the societal consequences of alien contact and putting together a reconnaissance road map. After all, divulging the existence of a phenomenon that we have no power over or understanding of would be extremely bad for public confidence.' He folded his arms across his chest by way of emphasis. 'Meanwhile, as for understanding, well, it's a huge undertaking.'

'Yep.' She drained her glass. 'It sure sounds like you've got your work cut out for you.'

He nodded fervently. 'Then, there are ethical considerations. Let's say we land on Mars and find it hosts simple, single cell life forms. Do we give Martians a helping hand to evolve and flourish, or catalogue-slash-clear them and go ahead and colonise their planet, or do we turn it into a galactic nature reserve and make it off limits?'

'Wow!' Rosetta gasped, her mouth dropping open a fraction. 'I'm beginning to grasp the scale of the problem. Tell me, how are you getting on with cracking the communication angle?'

'A work in progress, and it's critical to establish motivation, bearing in mind that historically contacts generally led to the destruction of the more primitive civilisation receiving contact.'

'Like Columbus and the Native American Indians?'

'Precisely. So, the global powers that be will need a great deal of persuasion not to take up arms and respond aggressively with pre-emptive strikes or whatever they want to call it. Let's be realistic. The military mandate is secrecy, and if the aliens possess anything that can outmanoeuvre or disarm our best technology, the military will assume that they must be a threat.'

Rosetta gave a low whistle, then wiped her lips on a paper napkin and thought about this for a while. 'Are they here on a peace mission or something more sinister?'

His eyes grew wide. 'That's what I'm hoping to find out, because if news gets out there'll be a lot of sticky fingers reaching for the trigger first and asking questions later. Consequently, I kinda feel responsible for them and the future.' The professor raised his eyes to the ceiling as if searching for divine inspiration. 'The Hopi Indians have legends about Star People who were either their ancestors or Avatars who sent down wisdom. But is this all fanciful exaggeration, thanks to Alien Ancestors on the History Channel? Or knowing what I know now, do I think the myths are true? On balance, I'd say true, and I very much hope that the resident Star People, and their absent relatives, view us with love and benevolence. The Blues seem to… but I'm not so sure about the Greys. So, as they say, the jury's out. Watch this space.'

Rosetta and Gandalf cleared their trays and went their separate ways.

* * *

Rosetta and Daniel hung out in the bar till late then retired to bed. They made love, and for the first time in a long time Rosetta finally felt connected to another human being. She lay against his chest and traced her fingertips through the coarse dark hair. *Nice,* she thought, *not too hairy and Neanderthal, but definitely masculine.* She loved the contrast of the smooth plump paleness of her skin against the light mahogany of his.

Lightly, she recounted what she'd learned earlier from the prof and Daniel lay back, his arms folded above his head, and stared at the ceiling, deep in thought. His receptiveness was such a relief, because with Peter, it was as if they were on different planets. Him deeply rooted in the practicalities and political intrigue, her floating in another dimension.

Rosetta raised herself up and propped her head in her hand as she scrutinised Daniel more closely. She mustn't seem too needy, too desperate, as that might scare him off. But she wanted to hold him close and never let him go. She sensed that deep down they were alike. He was estranged from his family because of his beliefs, as they were deeply religious and did not comprehend the path he'd chosen. Good Jewish boys were supposed to marry nice Jewish girls, settle down, have kids, and big noisy bar or bat mitzvahs. Yet, their wilful eldest son had never conformed. Instead, they thought that he had disappeared into some weird American sect and his views were so strange that when his mother saw the dear rabbi coming, she was obliged to hang her head and cross the road. *Oh, the shame, Daniel, the shame.*

Now, here they were in the vast otherworldly cavern. A pair of unmanned and unmoored ships cast adrift on the stormy seas. She knew that she couldn't expect him, or anyone, to save her as everyone was just about keeping their heads above water. Yet, here they were, finally reunited, a pair of dolphins re-joining their original pod. Rosetta felt a wave of intense joy wash over her. *Hang onto this moment,* she thought.

She took a deep breath. The sheets, like everything on the base, were of impeccable quality. Crisply ironed and smelling divinely of vanilla and linen drenched in freshly mown grass. These were smells which whisked her back to memories of childhood, of donuts and jam, finger roll sandwiches and glasses of ginger beer, with sprinkles of green grass shards, and the picnic blanket on the lawn her father had just finished cutting.

At last, she spoke. 'What do you think about the origin of life? Is it possible that we're descendants of life on another planet?'

Daniel sniffed. 'I don't see why not. I mean it's not much worse than us rising from the primordial soup with no explanation, is it?'

Rosetta laughed. 'I guess not. Perhaps miracles are just shifts in perception. But if humans are part ET, that means they're way more advanced than us and the implications of that are quite profound.'

Daniel rolled over and tickled her till she play-wrestled him off. 'Well, look at it another way. Maybe here on Earth we're just acting out a TV reality show to keep them amused up there. Was it a bolt of lightning from the almighty creator or microbes in interstellar clouds falling from the skies? Who knows? But I reckon science and religion make unhappy bedfellows.'

Rosetta buried her face and nestled in his armpit, inhaling deeply to absorb his unique scent. It had been like that with them – instant chemistry, like a bolt of lightning. And she loved how he told her often and without prompting that he could not live without her. She might have been a damaged woman with history, but now she was on the mend, all thanks to him. She had landed an amazing new job, and an incredible new man: at last. Rosetta breathed in deeply and gave silent thanks that she'd finally got lucky. The time had come to turn over a new page and start a new chapter. How exhilarating. After a while she popped up and stared into his deep oval eyes. She could feel her face glowing at all the wondrous possibilities which lay ahead. She sighed with pleasure at the prospect of the brilliant starry future of their enraptured togetherness. They'd grow old together. She felt it deep in her heart and in her gut. In that moment, she felt that all the pain, all the struggle, had surely been worth it. 'It's ironic when you think about it.'

'Argh,' he groaned. 'Please don't overthink it.'

She laughed. 'Let me finish, it's important. What I meant was, outside, out there on Civvy Street, Planet Normal, or whatever you want to call it, people like me are viewed with suspicion and labelled as weird. Yet, here we are in a cave, a commune of like-minded souls.'

'A kibbutz, even?'

'Yeah, something like that,' she chuckled. 'Yet I'm finding it really weird, as in crazy-weird, that some of them are so into aliens. It just seems so, well...' Rosetta hesitated in search of the right description. 'Well... far-fetched, I guess. I mean, do you believe it?'

Daniel stared at the ceiling for a while, considering. 'I think it's a bit beyond my remit.'

Rosetta groaned and gave him a punch on his side.

'Ouch, what's that in aid of?'

'Bloody barrister-speak. You have an opinion surely? Let's hear it, cough it up.'

'Well, if I said yes, affirmative I'd have to defend or deny the position, so I'll settle for... it's entirely feasible.'

'There you go again, doing the lawyer bit. Do you ever give it a rest?' Rosetta found it exasperating how he fenced with words. 'I might, but not right now.' Daniel yawned. 'It's late.' He reached over and turned the light off. 'Now get some rest.'

'Yes, boss.' She nestled deep into the crook of his arm, her fingers entwined with his, and for the first time in a long time she felt safe, loved, and supported.

And above all, connected.

CHAPTER TWENTY-TWO

Rosetta
2022
Inis Cara, South-East Ireland

Rosetta had been reading about the Blarney Stone, and according to legend, whoever kissed the stone was gifted with eloquence and persuasiveness. She wished she could make a detour to join the multitude of pilgrims climbing the steps to kiss it. Some said it was Jacob's pillow, brought to Ireland by the prophet Jeremiah. Some said it had been removed from mainland Scotland where it had served as the Stone of Destiny to predict the royal succession. Whatever the truth of its origins, it was believed that its powers were revealed by a witch saved from drowning.

At 8:30 a.m., the morning after her arrival in Ireland, Rosetta slung her gym bag over the back of her chair. She was hot and sticky from her early morning 5k run, and she headed off to the toilets. She washed her face, her armpits, and hands in a series of rapid efficient movements, and applied liberal squirts of deodorant. She looked in the mirror, combed her hair, and puckered her lips, ready for a slash of scarlet lipstick. *Not bad for forty-one,* she thought, admiring her reflection. A few wrinkles here and there, but that was to be expected in her line of work. Great bone structure, clear skin, her hair had grown a little, softening her angular features, and her cute pixie nose. Then she eyed her reflection one more time in the full-length mirror before leaving.

She got herself ready in the makeshift office kindly provided by the Garda, the guardians of the peace. The suspect, Tommy Rafferty, arrived shortly afterwards.

'Whew.' Rosetta whistled softly. His photograph did not do him justice.

In the flesh, he had an easy grin, twinkling eyes, and a relaxed manner, and she could hardly take her eyes off him. He was *divine*, and more than that, she felt as if she'd known him since the beginning of time. As if they'd shared infinite joy, and deep sorrow too. The shared experiences bound them tightly in ways that she couldn't yet comprehend. As if they were twins long separated at birth, and finally they were reunited at last.

That's enough, she told herself, and she resolved to be brisk and business-like. She couldn't let the swirl of emotions cloud her judgement.

'Take a seat,' she said with authority. 'Now, as Sergeant Murphy has explained, you're here for questioning in connection with a crime committed in England on 19th December last year.'

Tommy nodded and lounged in his chair.

He looked nonchalant as she switched the digital recorder on. 'Mr. Rafferty has just entered the room, at nine thirty a.m., where DS Barrett and Sergeant Murphy are present. Do you have the details of all your bank accounts and phone records?'

Tommy nodded and passed a file across the table.

'Thanks. I have your current address, full name, and date of birth. Where are you from originally?' Rosetta asked, to break the ice.

Tommy leaned back in his chair and looked vague. 'Here, there, and everywhere – all Irish are from that place, aren't they?'

'He's from County Meath, his family own Tattersalls and vast chunks of land, not to mention racehorses, helicopters, you name it,' Sergeant Murphy said, looking pleased with himself. Tommy, on the other hand, did not look too impressed.

'Cheers, Mick. By the way, how's your brother the priest doing? Is he still reading from that book he didn't write?'

The interview was in danger of degenerating before her eyes. Interesting, though, that Tommy here wasn't a born and bred Traveller after all. Rosetta cleared her throat and pressed on. 'Now, Mr. Rafferty, on the day in question, you were in England staying with friends at the Farley Hollow settlement, correct?'

'I guess.' He shrugged. 'It's a while back.'

'Can you recall what you did on 19th December, please?'

'Got up, had breakfast. I usually have porridge.' He grinned, flashing a set of very white teeth.

'Yes.' She let out a long-suffering sigh. 'And afterwards, where did you go? I need you to account for your movements that day.'

'Well now, let me see.' He put his hands behind his head and leaned back in his chair. 'I can't say for certain, but I probably took my dog out for a morning walk between 10:00 a.m. to 10:30 a.m.'

'Did you go anywhere near the railway station?'

'Nope. I took my usual route, which was across the common, and then through the heath.'

He was a cool customer, this one. 'Did anyone see you?'

'I can't say for sure. Ah, wait a minute, yes. There was an old guy walking his dog.'

'Can you give us a description?'

'Wrinkly.'

Sergeant Murphy disguised his amusement with a cough. Rosetta's lips tugged downwards in a frown. 'This is a serious matter. Do you realise that a young girl was killed?'

Tommy looked suitably chastened. 'The dog was a large Labradoodle, a bitch. The old guy should have kept it on the lead.'

Rosetta raised an eyebrow to signal her interest. 'Go on.'

'Well, there was a bit of a commotion. The old guy was causing a scene, and when Gulliver, my Irish Wolfhound set off after the labra-poodle-doodle thing, bejabbers, I thought the old boy was going to have a heart attack.'

Yes, that sounds like the Mervyn I know and love, she thought with a groan.

'Anyway,' Tommy continued turning the gold ear ring between his finger and his thumb, 'I raced off after the dogs and caught them in the first raptures of romance, as it were. The old boy was livid, waving his stick and threatening me with his solicitor.' Tommy chuckled at the memory.

Rosetta bit her lip to suppress a giggle. How heart-warming to know that Mr. Wallace-Smith was so generous with his imparting of grief and threats. She quickly switched back to professional mode. 'Now, for the record, let me get this straight. Are you saying that between ten a.m. to ten thirty a.m. you were walking your dog on Farley Heath and you were running across the heath in pursuit of your dog, who was in turn chasing a bitch which belonged to an elderly gentleman? Is that correct?'

'That's about it.'

'Really, was there anything unusual that day that you've failed to mention so far?' She assumed an intentionally blank and unimpressed stare as she looked at him and held it until he squirmed a little in his seat.

Tommy let out a long sigh. 'Ah, I reckon you mean the bonfire?'

'Correct.' She opened up a silence and left him to stew in it for a while.

'No big deal. Kids everywhere steal cars and torch them quite often, don't they, Mick? It happens here a fair bit an' all.' He directed the question at Sergeant Murphy, who rolled his eyes conspiratorially.

'Oh, indeed, for sure they do. It's a problem here too. There's not much else to keep them occupied, you see.'

'Exactly,' Tommy looked well pleased with himself. 'Do you remember when kids nicked the O' Sullivan's flashy new Jaguar, and all your forces were strung out across the county trying to intercept them? Oh my –'

Rosetta cut them dead. 'Mr. Rafferty, how exactly do you know the vehicle on Farley Heath was stolen and set alight?'

Tommy's mouth dropped open. He recovered quickly, though. Give him his due.

'The old boy told me that a vehicle had been torched,' he said, with a hint of swagger in his voice.

Rosetta had her elbows resting on the desk as she cradled her forehead in her hands.

'Let me get this right, there could have been someone trapped in the vehicle, but you did nothing? Is that right?'

Tommy looked miffed. 'Well, I'm not a fireman, am I?' His voice sounded whiny, like a child's. 'Besides,' he continued, 'the old boy had already called the emergency services and the Old Bill, and I don't make a habit of getting involved with your sort, so I didn't hang around, like.'

Rosetta shook her head to convey her disapproval. She would have liked to ask him what her sort were exactly, but she resisted. 'Apart from the gentleman with the dog, did you see anyone else that morning?'

'Nope.'

'Did you notice anything else unusual at all?'

'Nope.'

'Hmmm, well, I'd be grateful if you'd explain why you left England in such a hurry? You cut your visit short and you left the next day. Is that correct?'

'Ah,' Tommy said with a grin. 'Well, the English don't really like us, do they? They generally want rid of us like, but we're too busy filling potholes and tarmacking drives.'

Rosetta frowned. The last thing she needed was some PC row over racist attitudes against the Irish taking hold. 'I can assure you the British police are entirely neutral on matters of race and ethnic origin.'

Tommy shook his head. 'Right an' all. Well now, I didn't think the old boy was going to be too pleased when his precious pooch popped out a litter of Heinz Fifty-Sevens. That old boy looked like he had a pretty short fuse.'

'Can you confirm for the record that you left England on the 20th December, a mere one day after the incident?'

'Yeah.'

Rosetta continued, 'And your reason is because of a litter of puppies that may, or may not, arrive in a few months' time?' She shot him an incredulous look. 'Really, is that the best you can come up with?'

'I always planned to be back here for Christmas. I've got horses and dogs and the like. Feel free to check.'

'We will, rest assured of that.' Rosetta checked her watch. 'Can you explain how you knew that the vehicle was stolen?'

Tommy grinned, 'Hard not to know, it was all over the Sky News an' all.'

'When was your previous trip to England?'

'Well now, let me see. Probably April-time a good few years ago. In 2017 maybe, for the funeral of the King of the Travellers, Pa's mate Simon Docherty. It was a grand affair with the ponies and trap carrying the coffin and a convoy of Rolls-Royces. The press called it Big Fat Gypsy Funeral. It went on for days, as I recall.'

'Very well, the interview is terminated at ten a.m.' She switched off the recorder and turned to Tommy. 'I've no further questions for the time being, Mr. Rafferty. Although you're free to go now, please don't leave Inis Cara without informing us. If you have any plans to travel in Ireland or abroad, you are advised to keep us informed of your movements. And once we've typed up your statement, we'll need you to sign it.'

* * *

Later that day, Rosetta had DC Boyd re-check Mervyn Wallace-Smith's statement, and it transpired, as she suspected, that he confirmed Tommy Rafferty's story.

Back at home, there'd been no further mention of Peter. That line of inquiry had gone cold. Really, as much as she disliked her ex-husband, she was relieved. Him being accused, let alone convicted, of a crime would be terrible for their children, and her mother's instinct dictated that she'd protect them first above all else. However, the dilemma was if they didn't identify the driver soon, like it or not she'd have to bring Peter in for questioning. She'd checked all Tommy's accounts, and phone records, and there was nothing untoward. No new leads.

So that left Matt, and persons as yet unknown, as the main suspects. Matt had motive, and it seemed quite contrived that both he and Tracy, his possible accomplice, were absent on the day of the crime. It struck Rosetta as unlikely that Tommy had committed the attack – for starters, if he had the Wolfhound with him when he stole the 4x4, that would be pretty hard to miss, yet Juliet had never mentioned it. Rosetta re-traced her vision and concluded that there hadn't been a dog in the car. Did he torch the vehicle, then go back to the Travellers' camp, get the dog, and set off on the walk to ensure that the fire was still raging? The timing didn't seem right – far too tight. It would depend on how long it would take to get from the abandoned vehicle to the camp and back again.

She made a note for someone to check the journey time, first at a brisk walk, then running. Somehow, she wasn't convinced that Tommy was guilty. But then again, she suspected that Tommy knew more than he'd let on so far. Maybe he was protecting someone? She filed an update report and e-mailed it back to Yorrex police station. She sent Rav a WhatsApp message.

Ro: *Hello I've sent you my report.*
Rav: *Yes, got it. What r u up too this eve?*
Ro: *Apart from being abducted and abused by the Christian Brothers?*
Rav: *Nothing newsworthy there then? LOL.*
Ro: *It's a bit dull round here, so maybe I'll go out dressed as Lady Gaga.*
Rav: *Really?*
Ro: *Joke!*
Rav: *Ah, well I hope you can give the Brothers the slip. Gotta dash. Have a good evening.*

* * *

With the rest of the day at leisure, she pondered on the backstory that was her real concern. What dark tale of historical betrayal and revenge lurked behind the scenes?

That evening, after work, she went for a drink with Sergeant Murphy at the bar in the Silent Inn. He had the red, florid face of a drinker, and it didn't take too many pints of the black stuff and a few whiskey chasers to loosen his tongue.

'Hey, tell me about Mr. Rafferty,' she said, sipping her iced Baileys.

'Ah, when he first arrived here, there was a lot of talk, a lot of rumours and so forth.' He scratched his bulbous nose.

'Oh.' She tried to look uninterested. 'What kind of rumours?'

'Apparently, he comes from a wealthy family in County Meath, but he quarrelled with his family after some kind of scandal, and he left. He took up with the Travellers and has never been home since. You proper know what I mean?'

'Any trouble?'

Murphy chuckled. 'Only with women. He was wild in his youth, a bit of a hell-raiser. But he was always popular with the ladies, the lucky devil.'

'Yes,' she muttered. 'I can imagine.'

* * *

About an hour later, after a refreshing shower and a change of clothes, Rosetta went for a drive, and as if on autopilot, found herself turning into Tommy Rafferty's drive. She took his statement with her – the perfect cover. As she drew to a stop, she questioned her motives. She knew that what she was contemplating was deeply unethical. She should turn around, right now, and drive away. Yet, she felt compelled to spend time with him, to find out more about him. To reconnect with a part of herself that had long since been lost.

'*Céad míle fáilte,*' he said as she got out of the hired car. 'Well now, to what d' we owe the pleasure of this visit?' This guy was straightforward, so at ease, and self-assured. He flashed a smile her way.

She paused, wondering what to say. She could hardly say she was attracted to him, although she was usually quite direct and forthright.

So, she said, 'I was passing on my way back to the Silent Inn and I thought I'd call in with your statement for you to sign.' She cringed at such a transparent lie.

'Ah,' he replied. 'Are you here on police business or is it a social visit?'

'Oh.' She laughed. 'Both, I guess. But I just wanted you to know that we corroborated your story.'

'That's good, DS Barrett.' He shoved his hands into the pockets of his jeans.

'Call me Rosetta.'

'Rosetta, right.' He laughed. 'I'm not sure being on first-name terms with a policewoman is going to do my street cred much good, if you know what I mean.' His tone was flirtatious, and that gave her encouragement.

'I guess not.' She flashed a dazzling smile at him. 'So now that we're acquainted, how about inviting me in for a drink?'

He studied her for a moment in one appraising glance. 'Okay.'

As she followed him into the house, she couldn't help admiring his taut rear. What a physique. How she craved male company. How long had it been? Far too long for sure, but what about the professional ethics? He was still a suspect, after all. She needed some space to get her feelings under control.

'Do you mind if I use the bathroom?' she asked.

He directed her through the living room. 'First on the left,' he indicated.

She went upstairs, turned left as directed, and posed in front of the mirror. She reached into her handbag, puckered her lips, and applied a coat of lipstick. She put the lipstick down, used the loo, washed her hands, and sprayed herself liberally with perfume.

'Cheers,' he said when she returned.

'Cheers.' She accepted a glass of sparkling wine and took a sip. 'Have you lived here long?'

'What star sign are you?' he said. 'Now let me guess... Scorpio?'

'Gosh, did that sound like a chat-up line?'

He licked his lips in tiny darting movements, and his eyes twinkled mischievously. 'Well, was it?'

She stared at him over her glass and shrugged. 'Yes, I guess so,' she giggled. She nodded as she handed him a copy of his statement. 'I'd like you to read this and sign it, before –'

'Before what?' He flicked through the couple of pages and signed with the pen she'd provided and handed the paperwork back to her.

Rosetta licked her lips and smiled. 'Well, that rather depends on you.' It had been so long since she'd made love to anyone, and she longed to be caressed. To savour the closeness of human contact.

'Ah, I see.' He reached across and stroked her wrist, sending a spark of insatiable hunger and desire flashing through her. 'So, do you have your handcuffs with you?'

161

'What?' She had never surrendered totally to anything in her life, yet perhaps now was the time. Why not just go with the flow? She longed to kiss him, to feel his strong life force. The chemistry between them was like an electrical spark. '*Shades of Grey?* Okay, lead me to your dungeon.'

Tommy responded with a kiss that would have melted ice. As their lips parted, she drew a deep breath. For the first time in a long time, she felt fully alive again.

'You guessed right. I'm a Scorpio. How about you?'

'Are you now? I'm a Leo, and ready to roar.'

Rosetta sensed where this was heading. She knew she must resist or she would regret it in the morning. Nothing would be worth jeopardising her career, yet she wanted him so badly. Luckily, as if he could read her thoughts, Tommy took charge. Slowly, as if he had all the time in the world, he took her by the hand. All notions of resistance disappeared as he led her up the stairs.

CHAPTER TWENTY-THREE

*'May you have all the happiness and luck that life can hold, and
find at the end of your rainbows a pot of gold.'*

Juliet
2022
Inis Cara

While Matt focused on the road ahead, Juliet gazed out of the car window at the rolling leas and fields. There was a seductive sameness about this part of the Irish countryside. In the distance, a flock of sheep huddled together against the backdrop of mist that clung to the hills. The sheep opened their mouths to bleat. One ran, others followed. The sun was rising, peeking out over the clouds to promise a fine warm spring day. The mist began to dissolve. Then she saw the sheepdog, slung low to the ground, pushing and nudging the flock until they did his bidding. They broke into a run, and she watched them until they disappeared out of sight. *Goodbye, my friends,* she thought smiling fondly.

'Yikes, watch out! You just ran the light.' On occasion, Matt's driving veered between flamboyant and erratic. Juliet shook her head in disbelief. 'The lights were red, that's a real stop, not a half-assed kind of thing.'

Matt gave an exasperated sigh. 'We haven't seen a soul, let alone a car for hours now. Besides, have you even read the Highway Code?'

Juliet bristled with irritation, she was a way better driver than him. 'No,' she replied sarcastically. 'I'm just downloading it on my cell phone.'

She turned away from Matt and tried not to let him ruin the moment. She loved Ireland – the boozy poetic passion of the Irish, and especially the way they were with horses. Juliet sighed. She was sure they would find Gothic's replacement here. The Irish bred fine event horses. She rested her head against the windowpane and closed her eyes.

They arrived shortly after 10:00 p.m. at Inis Cara, a small village close to the peninsula that jutted out into the magnificent Irish sea. Inis Cara was unusual by Irish standards as it only had one pub, the Silent Inn, which doubled up as a hotel and restaurant. The Inn was situated a short way inland, overlooking the moors in one direction, with far-reaching views of the sea in the other. In the distance, she heard an immense wave crashing against the beach.

The rooms at the Silent Inn were basic but comfortable. Juliet would have liked a sea view, but the hotel was full because of the forthcoming horse sales, so their room overlooked the moors instead. It had been a tiring day travelling. Matt took a shower and Juliet collapsed on the edge of the bed with a cup of Earl Grey tea. When he emerged from the bathroom with a towel wrapped around him, she smiled.

'Do you want a cup of tea?'

'Coffee, thanks.' He gave his hair a rub and collapsed onto the bed.

'I've been thinking.' She paused to see if she had his attention. 'What if Totem and Gothic's deaths were connected?'

'Have you seen the remote control for the TV?'

Actually, she had hidden it under a pillow to make sure that he listened to her.

'What if Totem came back as Gothic to give me a second chance, and you know… get the ending right?'

'Jesus, Juliet! Not that again. Goddamn it. Listen to yourself. A dead horse that came back to life?' He looked up at the ceiling and sighed. 'When we get back from this trip, I think you should see someone.'

'See someone… What do you mean?'

'What about Lou Fitzgerald, your mother's friend?'

'Lou Fitzgerald, he's a shrink… Oh, I see. You think I'm crazy, is that it?' She fiddled with her engagement ring, new and unfamiliar on her finger. If she couldn't share this with him, perhaps agreeing to get engaged had been a mistake?

'Well, you have to admit that you're not really yourself.' He propped himself up on a pillow and discovered the remote control. Predictably, he switched the television on, a bona-fide conversation killer.

Juliet took a bath, and afterwards read her book.

164

Later, Matt fell into a deep, untroubled sleep. The bickering kept Juliet tossing and turning all night as she replayed his words over and over in her head. *How weird,* she thought, *that we can lie here in the same bed yet inhabit different worlds.* His was all rational, mechanical, rooted in the physical and all its laws. Hers was a realm of vision and imagination. They occupied the same time, the same space, yet both of them had a very different perception of reality. So different, in fact, that he thought she had totally gone nuts. With a sigh, she closed her eyes.

* * *

Later, Juliet stirred, still somewhere halfway between waking and sleep, but then as her mind cleared, she recognised the sound of hoof beats. The wind carried the echo of her longings through the crack of the open window. She listened, with all her senses alert, and waited without daring to breathe.

Matt had his back turned to her, and he seemed angry and hostile even in his sleep. Juliet slipped out from under the comforter and tiptoed over to the window, like a child on Christmas Eve hoping for a glimpse of Santa Claus. The moonlight cast a pale, wan beam across the heath, and the stars glittered frosty and bright. She smiled delightedly at the galloping figure. Across the heather, a carpet of purple and grey, the brown and white horse came. *A skewbald,* she thought. She'd never had a horse that colour. Its proud bearing and the spirited swish of its tail made her think of the poem *Tribute to the Horse,* by Robert Duncan:

> *Where in this wide world can man find,*
> *Nobility without pride,*
> *Friendship without envy,*
> *Or beauty without vanity?*

The horse had a back as straight and supple as a young oak, and a playful manner that suggested it was wild, young, and free. It had the look of a horse that had never been ridden and perhaps was never destined to be. *Where've you been, my friend? Thank you for coming back to me.* She could hardly take her eyes off the skewbald as she wondered how long it would take to reach her. Its stride was even and rhythmical, a ground-eating stride. The skewbald had supernatural ability, clearing the enormous five-bar gate without even missing a beat. Speeding across the heather, the horse drew closer.

Juliet smiled, and her heart filled with joy.

Then, in an instant, no more than the blink of an eye, the vision unfurled, slipping away like a half-forgotten dream before it is fully grasped. A horse created from the stuff that wishes are made of disappeared, like Cinderella at the stroke of midnight.

'Oh, no, please don't do this to me,' Juliet pleaded as she scanned the moors.

The horizon was empty apart from some jagged rocks jutting out through the purple haze. Perhaps it was teasing, playing a game? But all she could make out were the writhing tentacles of the early morning mist. Slumped against the window, she prayed that the horse would return. Meanwhile she'd lost all track of time.

Dawn broke, and she felt cold and stiff. She wrapped her arms around herself for warmth and comfort. Eventually, the sun emerged, burning off the mist and warming up the morning. In the background, the alarm clock went off, shrill and insistent. Juliet half registered the sound. Matt stirred, but she gazed out of the window, wondering if the horse would ever return.

No sight, no sound.

Her heart sank. She felt like a mermaid washed ashore far from the smell of the sea. As if, she was a sad out-of-the-water thing that raises a conch shell to her ear, full of longing and yearning for that which was not to be.

Seven in the morning on Saturday, and she wondered for the hundredth time why it took him so long to get ready. She checked her watch, over half an hour had passed before Matt had showered and got dressed. He wore beige chinos, casual, but always well put-together. They went downstairs to the dining room. The French doors were ajar, opening onto the patio and beyond that to the moors. Juliet was tempted to sit outside to breathe in the marshy moors and the salty sea air, but Matt sat inside, out of the draught.

They'd been to the Silent Inn several times before. Juliet had discovered it when they'd come over on their very first trip. Now it was part of the annual pilgrimage when they would buy young horses, ship them back to England, and spend a few months backing and schooling, before selling them on for a decent profit. Of all the places they stayed in Ireland, Juliet loved this the most. The Inn stood miles from anywhere, totally isolated and forgotten by time. It was the closest thing to solitude in the modern world and in complete contrast to their hectic lifestyle back home in England. She found the tranquillity soothing, almost seductive. So, she thought, and not for the first time, that after she had departed this world for the next, she would like her ashes scattered here, where they might be carried away on the breeze that caressed the early morning dew. Perhaps, that was where the horse had gone – spirited away by the wind. It was then that it came to her... the horse's name.

'Espiritus,' she breathed.

Matt looked up from his cornflakes and raised his eyebrows. 'What?'

Now that the horse had a name, surely it had to return? She tried hard to contain her excitement. 'Nothing, just thinking out loud,' she said, a smile tugging at her lips.

'Hmm, are you going to eat that?'

Juliet shook her head as he speared the remaining sausage off her plate and popped it into his mouth.

'Will we be stopping here on the way back?'

'Depends how well it goes today. It's getting nigh on impossible to find anything decent at the right price these days. If they're not careful, the Irish are going to price horse flesh right out of existence.'

'Maybe we should look abroad.'

'And where exactly did you have in mind?'

'I hadn't really thought about it, Eastern Europe, maybe? Oh, I know... Poland.'

'You've got to be joking. In this business, contacts are everything. Who do you know in Poland, then?'

'It was just a suggestion.'

'You should stick to what you know, riding horses and leave me to manage the business,' he said, with an unmistakable condescending edge to his voice.

'Isn't this a partnership?'

'Sure, but how often do I tell you how to jump a fence?'

'Practically every time,' she fumed. 'And without Gothic, and no advanced horses in the yard, it doesn't look too great, does it?'

'Well, there's Icon. You could upgrade him. Still, like I said, I'm working on finding you a replacement and Tracy's doing her bit too, so can you cut her a bit of slack?'

Juliet sighed. 'Icon's not ready yet.'

Matt shook his head. 'It would help if the bloody insurance company coughed up. That would at least pay off the overdraft until the property deal went through. What's happening?'

Juliet looked at him, aghast. 'That's your department. Why are you asking me? You handle the business, and the finances.'

'Well, you shouldn't have penny-pinched on the premiums,' he said.

She glared at him, and her mouth fell open. He had complete financial control. She found money and maths boring beyond belief, so how could he be so insensitive? The insufferable jerk! He knew how much she'd adored that horse. Why had he started an argument about what Gothic was worth? She took a deep breath and bit her tongue, certain that if she said anything, it would degenerate into a full-scale war.

Silence.

'And let's face it,' he continued, 'you really haven't applied yourself to getting your career back on track or securing the sponsorship deal. You've left everything to me as usual.'

That did it.

Her eyes blazed in fury as she picked up a fork and stabbed the air.

'You bastard. How dare you blame me?' she yelled. Out of the corner of her eye, she saw the other guests turn and gawp. 'For the record, let's be very clear. You took care of the insurance stuff. I don't know anything about it. So, don't stop taking the asshole pills anytime soon.'

'Huh, well, I'm surprised one of your psychic mates couldn't have predicted that he was going to snuff it. That would've been handy. We could have whacked the premiums up.'

She inhaled sharply as if she had been kicked in the ribs. Somewhere inside her, the slow embers of a fire began to glow, and grief gave way to rage.

'You dipshit, don't you ever talk about my horse like that again!' Juliet, in the heat of the moment, registered a side to Matt that she really didn't like. He'd hidden it so far in their relationship, but now she'd encountered another dimension to him, and she didn't approve. She reached for the coffee pot to pour herself a refill, but something inside her snapped. 'Take that, you pathetic shit!'

Such a rage bubbled up inside her that it blotted out everything in its path. Juliet took aim straight for his head and let him have it.

Matt's eyes widened in momentary confusion, then, as he saw the coffee pot flying through the air, he ducked.

Just in time.

The white china, standard hotel fare, hit the wooden floor with a resounding crash. It smashed into a thousand smithereens, and the dark brown pool of coffee dispersed like a pool of blood.

Satisfied, Juliet stood up, tossed her head, and stormed out, leaving Matt to deal with the mess.

CHAPTER TWENTY-FOUR

Juliet

Later, when they set off to Moneygall, Matt's bad mood infiltrated the car like a virus. She hated the feeling of tension hanging in the air and those prolonged periods of accusing silence. Nothing said. Nothing resolved. He boxed things away. She didn't. Matt had the looks and he certainly had the movie-star attitude, but she had to ask herself, was there any more to him than that? What really did he have to offer her? She glanced at him out of the corner of her eye. A black mood had settled across his features.

They drove for several miles without saying a word. Juliet was determined that she wasn't going to concede her position. As they passed a farmyard of goats, pigs, and mules, Matt broke the silence.

'Relatives of yours?' he asked sarcastically.

'Yes,' she agreed, 'my future in-laws.' It wasn't entirely a joke and a part of her wondered about his mother. She'd met her once and it hadn't exactly gone well. Orla, her friend, had claimed that Matt's mother been convicted of fraud and she'd tried to warn Juliet about Matt, but Orla had just been jealous, of course. Who wouldn't be? Matt was divine-looking.

He laughed.

That broke the ice a little, and she felt a bit less hostile. Matt had gotten what he deserved, but she knew him well enough to know that he wouldn't apologise first. Juliet sighed. She couldn't bear any more turmoil. She badly needed to get things back on an even keel so that she could just concentrate on her riding again.

She bit her lip and took a deep breath. 'Look, about the coffee pot. Well, you were really pushing your luck.'

'Are you kidding? If I hadn't ducked, you'd have split my head open.'

'Let's just forget about it.' Juliet had no intention of apologising either.

'Jeez!' Matt braked hard and sharp as two dark-haired urchins darted across the road in front of the 4x4. 'Watch where you're going, you idiots,' he yelled through the open window.

The children, two boys of about eight or nine, threw their heads back with squeals of laughter, and then the larger of the two made rude and defiant gestures in Matt's direction.

'Gypsies,' Matt spat like a curse, as if there were no lower form of life.

* * *

Easter Friday every year, Moneygall was alive with the bustle of the Honeygale horse fair, and as they got closer to the show ground, they caught up with the Travellers' convoy. A slow procession on the move, like the Sidhe – the fairy people – as they migrated from this world to the next. Tinkers, Gypsies, show folk, a few ne'er-do-goods, a string of barrel-topped camper vans, battered trucks pulling trailers and gaudy silver campers inching forward. Juliet watched them, her eyes wide and bright. Meanwhile Matt cursed under his breath and scowled.

Along the way, some had set up camp on the wide stretches of grass verge at the side of the road. Washing flapped in the bushes, hung out to dry, and ponies – skewbald, chestnuts and piebald – were tethered everywhere. Little clusters of children chattered and chased dogs of every kind – terriers, whippets, and some unknown varieties too. The Honeygale horse fair was the biggest event of its kind that the County hosted every year. Matt usually managed to find some good young stock at a decent price here, and she hoped this prospect would put him in a better frame of mind.

When they arrived at the show ground, the unmistakable smell of horses greeted them full-on, horses everywhere. *What a wonderful sight.* Her eyes drank them in, large ones, small ones, and a few mares with early foals at foot. Matt employed a buying agent, Shamus O'Byrne, and had done so ever since he'd discovered, a while ago, that the Irish were a canny bunch. The merest hint of an English accent sent the prices rocketing up. As always, they found Shamus in the beer tent, a spit-and-sawdust sort of place where Shamus was doing a first-rate job propping up the bar.

At first, Juliet had disapproved of all this drinking to excess, but now she realised that it was sort of a ritual in Ireland, where deals were lubricated with plenty of Guinness chased down by Irish whisky.

'It's a pleasure to be seeing you all,' Shamus said in a lilting Irish brogue. He tipped his hat. 'Top o' the morning, Juliet. You're as lovely as ever. You're a balm for me old eyes.'

'Thank you, Shamus.' She laughed as he puckered up his lips and ceremoniously kissed her hand.

A thin, spry man of advancing years with a shrewd old face weathered and etched with lines. He had a face full of wisdom, with kind eyes which smiled at her until the skin creased up and they almost disappeared. If the eyes were the window to the soul, Juliet observed, then Shamus had seen a great deal over the course of many lifetimes. He had the bright, inquisitive eyes of a jackdaw. They shone brightly as if a deal or a bargain would rarely escape his attention. He and Matt embraced with genuine fondness. By now, Shamus had a very clear idea of the sort of animal that Matt required, but that didn't stop Matt from launching into a lengthy tirade. Some sort of male-bonding ritual, Juliet presumed, since they repeated it every year, and indeed, practically every time they met. *Here we go again,* she thought, with a chuckle.

'Shamus, are you paying attention?'

'Aye-aye. I'm all ears, I am.'

'Four good clean legs, no lumps or bumps, and four good-sized, even-shaped feet. No pigeon toes and no knock-knees.'

'No, none of that, all right.'

'No coloureds, skewbalds, piebalds, patches, or roans, in short, no tinkers' nags at all.'

Shamus stuck his tongue out and made a shuddering face. 'God's pyjamas,' he spat.

'Yeah,' Matt agreed. 'We definitely don't want mares under any circumstances, not after that Tommy Rafferty's shifty lot.'

'Oh aye, I remember,' Shamus chuckled. 'Mother of sorrows, they were all with child, as I recall.'

Juliet laughed. Matt did not look amused. 'Ten foals. That lot dropped cart horses, everyone. I had foals coming out of my ears, and I'm still paying off the ruddy vet's bills.'

'Are you, now? Well, Tommy's all right an' all, and I'm sure he never knew nothing was wrong.'

'No mares and especially not Rafferty's mares,' Matt said, wagging his finger.

Juliet wondered if they would ever pause for breath.

'Sorry to interrupt,' she said, giving Shamus a sly, envious look. He always had Matt's full attention even when he spouted nothing but nonsense. Why didn't she deserve that unswerving loyalty and comradeship anymore? 'I think I'll go and take a walk around.' As she kissed Matt on the cheek, Shamus tipped his hat again, and she headed out of the tent.

She loved the hustle and bustle of the show ground, with horses being tried and trotted up wherever she looked. The day had started out fine, and it looked full of promise for the time of year. Juliet's spirits lifted as she sniffed the distinctive aroma of horse, the odour of dung with top notes of leather polish filling her nostrils. She wandered around, watching people and absorbing the assorted sensations and the smells. She went to dozens of shows but always as a competitor, with so much to think about. There were show jumping and cross-country courses to walk, strides to count, advice to consider and nerves to battle with. What a pleasant treat, just meandering around for a change. The tempting aroma of fried onions and hot dogs mingling with sweet, sticky doughnuts wafted across the fairground, causing her stomach to rumble. She glanced at her watch. Too early for lunch, so she settled on some doughnuts dusted in cinnamon instead.

She wandered about, nowhere in particular, cramming one doughnut in after the other. Then out of the corner of her eye she saw the sign prominently displayed outside a shiny silver trailer.

Katya – Romany Psychic Seer:
Tarot, tea, and palm readings.

Curious, Juliet peered through the beaded curtain and into the caravan. It reminded her of a jackdaw's lair, full of brightly coloured pots and copper-bottomed pans.

'Come in, m' dear. I've been expecting you.'

A kindly voice, neither old nor young, coaxed her inside.

'Would you care for some nice fresh-brewed tea?'

Juliet swallowed the last of the doughnut. Did she really want to gain insight into her future? Things couldn't get much worse, surely? No, she decided, wiping the sticky snack residue on a paper tissue fished out of her pocket. Katya looked around fifty. Her face was etched with the kind of lines and crags that suggested a hard kind of life. She had long dark hair, peppered with grey. *It probably wasn't easy poking around in the stuff of people's souls,* Juliet thought. *Time to exit,* she decided. But the fortune-teller had other ideas.

'Sit down, sit down, and make yourself comfortable.' Katya pointed at the bench, scattered with jewel-coloured cushions, on the opposite side of the table. Her fingers were long and surprisingly elegant. 'There now, what sort of a reading for you today, my dear?'

'Um, tarot, I guess,' Juliet said with a mounting sense of unease. This was a mistake; a big one. 'Is it okay if I record the session?'

Katya nodded, and Juliet set her cell phone to record and placed it on the table.

'There now, give me your hands.'

Juliet inched her fingers across the smooth surface of the silky tablecloth. For a long while, Katya studied her upturned palms in a way that made Juliet squirm. She should never have got into this. She glanced around the room, looking for an escape route.

'Ah, I see that you're a horse rider, and a brilliant one too, with tremendous talent and determination. You're a professional, maybe?'

'Yes.' She wondered how Katya knew but then figured she must have seen her photograph somewhere and recognised her.

'Your sixth sense is well developed.' Katya pressed the fleshy mound below the thumb. 'Hmm,' Katya empathised. 'Sometimes, if we ignore a whisper, it becomes a shout. Do you have doubts about the man who you're with now?'

Juliet paused, wondering how much to reveal. 'I recently lost my top event horse. This has put my relationship under strain, I guess.' She sighed and leaned back into the cushions.

'Sometimes some of the challenges that we deal with in this life can be traced back to our past. I hear a voice and it says: "No gun will ever kill you. I will take the bullets from the Mexicans, and I will guide your arrows."'

'I don't get what you mean, so what am I supposed to do about that?' The bench was hard, and her butt began to ache. Juliet wriggled in her seat.

'Well, you need to connect with your past, although you may not always like what you find out. Disassociate yourself from the negative energies once and for all. It may well be that righting a wrong in some way breaks the pattern. The pattern seems to be Native American, actually… it's Apache, I believe. Does that ring any bells?'

'No. I don't get it. I had a horse called Totem, but what's that got to do with it?' A wave of irritation washed over Juliet. She wanted answers, not more mind-numbing problems and speculation.

'Indeed.' Katya smiled indulgently. 'But I can only tell you what I see. And what I see is a young Apache chief on a mountain ridge, mounted on his horse. He is staring into the distance and shouting at the wind: *"Sin bala, sin fleche, sin lanza, pero fuego."* Ahead there are eagles, circling as the sun is about to set. He is calling to you, his mother. He is sending you a horse called…' Katya paused as if waiting for a message to come through. 'The horse is called Spirit of the Wind. He sends her to you with his blessings and asks that you help him return the remains of Geronimo's beloved horse, to his birthplace, in his tribal homelands, so that his spirit can be eventually laid to rest. The boy says his father forgives you, and when the horse is restored, he will too.'

Katya let go of Juliet's hands, and she snatched them to safety under the table.

'I don't understand.' Juliet's heart fluttered like a trapped bird as it pounded against her ribs, trying to escape. Something deep inside her stirred. She wanted to answer the call, but fear came stalking her.

Katya looked at her with empathy as she removed the tarot pack from the lavender velvet wrap and shuffled the well-worn deck before passing the cards to Juliet. 'Now, cut the pack in three and think of the main question that you'd like to ask.'

Juliet concentrated hard, intent on willing up the perfect card, as Katya placed them face down on the table one by one until she had shape of a cross – the ancient Celtic cross. She wanted to ask Katya a question, something that she needed to know. She opened her mouth, but no words came.

Questions had to be phrased correctly to elicit the right response. While she pondered this, the moment slipped away. She thought about finding a replacement horse, picked a card and held her breath. *Don't let it be the grim reaper of death. Please, not that one.* She'd had enough tragedy to last her a lifetime.

Her mouth felt dry, and she cleared her throat.

With studied precision, Katya turned the cards over one by one. 'Ah,' she breathed, 'the Tower.'

Thank God for that. But relief was short-lived as Katya frowned and let out a sigh. No wonder. The card depicted a tower struck by lightning, and underneath people were screaming and running for their lives.

Terrific.

'This card signifies chaos and upheaval.' Katya looked thoughtful. 'And destruction. I see your world collapsing around you.'

'Really? No shit?' Juliet scowled and glared at the older woman. 'How about you tell me something that I don't already know?'

'The energy that I sense, is not harmonious, nor conducive,' Katya muttered.

Conducive to what? a voice inside Juliet's head wanted to shriek.

'Ah, that's better.' Katya smiled as the second card was revealed. 'The Sun, this combination indicates that while old structures will be swept aside, this is to make way for something better.'

'Like a sort of spring clean?' Juliet chirped. 'Can you elaborate a bit?'

'I see an emotional experience of great joy and harmony.' Katya paused, studying the rest of the cards. 'You're about to meet someone – *something* maybe – you've been looking for a long time. Yet, you already know them very well and have met many times before. I believe it's a reunion, a homecoming of sorts. Does that make sense?'

Juliet shrugged. It sounded a bit far-out. But then, she seemingly had an Apache son that she knew nothing about. So...?

'It appears as a light... small but very bright and dancing. It's a dancing light which represents – not a husband or a parent – but a child, a friendly child. How very strange. Oh, silly me. Now I see. It's a soul light. The light of your soul friend. Your *anam-cara*.'

'My what?'

'You're afraid you won't find each other again and you're impatient.'

How the heck did she know that? Juliet hugged herself and whispered, 'I miss Totem and Gothic so much and no one understands.'

'Is there anyone you can talk to?'

'Well, not my fiancé. He thinks I'm crazy. My friend's sister, Isabella, and my top horse were both killed in a hit-and-run accident a few months ago. But he wants me to see a – well, you know – when we get back to England.'

'I see. I'm sorry. How do you feel about that?'

She shook her head and groaned. 'I thought we knew each other, but...' Juliet gave a shrug. 'Maybe I am going crazy.'

A shadow briefly flickered across Katya's careworn features then disappeared. 'I doubt it. You seem perfectly fine to me. You've just been through a great deal. Anyway, good news, there is someone who can help you.'

'Who? Where can I find them?'

'I'm not sure, but it's a man, a man with a love of words, and horses.'

Who in the world could it be? Not Matt, for sure, as he'd only ever read one book in his life – *Lady Chatterley's Lover* – and he'd only read that for the steamy parts.

'Where's Espiritus?' Juliet asked, leaning forward.

'The horse is close by. I can sense it.'

'Oh.' She slumped back against the cushions with a thud of disappointment. Then, she sat bolt upright and gasped. 'Whoa, how did you know that?'

'That's part of the way. I just know things.' Katya paused, her expression seeming troubled. 'Well,' she said at last, 'there are some difficult choices ahead. But I sense that you already realise that.'

'This is really freaking me out.'

'Just relax and don't chase after outcomes and force things your own way. Let things come to you for a change. Well, now, that's the end of my reading.'

Relieved, Juliet brightened. 'Oh, I get it. This time it's her turn to find me. Yes, I see. Thanks.'

Juliet counted out a bunch of crumpled Euro notes and handed them to Katya. As she reached the trailer door, Katya called out after her.

'Wait, before you go. Your past is filled with betrayal and revenge. You need to turn the other cheek. Break the circle, find the horse he sent you, and be sure to help your son with the mission.'

Juliet shivered. It all sounded a little vague yet ominous. She was supposed to do something, but what, and more importantly, why?

'Just one more thing... What the boy, my son, said...' she hesitated, 'what does it mean?'

Katya paused as if trying to gather her thoughts. 'I can't give you an exact translation, but my sense of it is this...' she paused and stared at the crystal ball in front of her on the table. 'I'll need to ask the spirits for guidance. Oh, I see, oh. Something terrible happened, and the man involved was Mexican. I think he was related to the boy in some way, but I can't be sure. There was an ambush by the Apaches. It means no bullet, no arrow, no lance, but fire. And you're not going to have a quick death.' Katya's hand flew to her mouth and her eyes grew wide. 'No, no!' Katya yelled, springing to her feet and recoiling away from the table. The colour drained from her horrified face. 'I'm sorry, I can't continue. I must end the session. Please go.'

'But –' Juliet felt a wave of nausea rising in her throat. She swallowed. 'What did you see?'

Katya shook her head as she went into her compact little kitchen and returned with air freshener. She sprayed the room in a frenzied fashion. 'What I saw, I cannot un-see, but worse still was the smell.' Katya took a deep breath and continued. 'All I can say is that what happened back then is linked to what happened recently with the car. I'm sorry. I didn't mean to scare you. Everything will be okay, but there are some things that need to be laid to rest. Here, take my card. I'll help in any way I can.'

Juliet recoiled in shock. She staggered to the door gasping for breath. On the way out, she tripped and almost fell down the stairs. Her legs felt weak and she grabbed the railing to support herself. Her mind was in a complete whirl. She ended the video recording on her phone and wondered if she should erase it. Somehow, the session had been so disturbing that it felt like a bad omen.

Get a grip, she told herself. *After all, it wasn't all bad news. You're going to find the replacement horse.*

Juliet slowed her breathing until she began to feel calmer. She really needed to talk to someone about this and get it off her chest. Who could unravel what it meant, someone open minded, not Matt, maybe Todd? Then in a flash she thought of DS Barrett. She would probably understand. Surely, she'd know what to do?

* * *

Later that evening, back at the hotel, Juliet fished out the detective's business card and sent her a quick email marked "Urgent."

CHAPTER TWENTY-FIVE
Juliet

There are those who believe in unicorns, fairy folk, magical realms, and indeed all things mystical. Secretly, Juliet did too. After Matt left on a fishing trip just before dawn, she found herself heading out towards Tommy Rafferty's place. Matt never had a good word to say about Tommy, as he had a bad reputation when it came to women and horses. Yet, Juliet thought he might understand about Totem and Gothic. Not that they had ever discussed such things, but Juliet sensed a kinship. Tommy Rafferty was a Traveller who flitted on the fringes of settled life. For now, he lived on a hill farm in the shadow of a mountain within hearing distance of the sea. For a living, he did a trick here, a deal there. Could he really be as bad as people made out?

Tommy was crossing the yard with a huge Irish wolf hound following obediently, and he did not seem at all surprised when Juliet pulled up in his driveway. He was wearing jeans, jodhpur boots and a V-neck jumper with a white T-shirt underneath. He had a way of sauntering that was quite different to Matt's decisive strut. It made her knees go weak.

'*Céad míle fáilte,*' he said. 'Well now… to what d' we owe the pleasure of this visit?

'I… oh…' Oh my, she was stuttering like a schoolgirl with a serious crush. And now that she was here, this no longer seemed like such a terrific idea.

'Cat got your tongue?' He grinned, his eyes twinkling.

Juliet stared at him like a thing devoid of speech, mouth gaping. He had a Roman nose and the most amazing eyes, blue with a hint of amber, like fireflies skating on ice. He was altogether striking for a man. His face had character, and a certain kind of knowing that came with age and experience. He must be around thirty, she decided, possibly older than that. She couldn't tell exactly, since he had an ageless quality. Not as technically good-looking as Matt, but Tommy had an allure, a magnetism that drew her in. With those full lips and that chiselled chin, he reminded her of the young Byron, intense and brooding, or mad, bad, and dangerous to know?

Or was he like Heathcliff, perhaps?

Juliet closed her mouth and quit gawping. It seemed so stupid to show up here without any real reason. Matt would be furious when he found out.

She would just make her excuses and leave.

'I had my tarot cards read yesterday.' Obviously, he would now conclude that she was both dumb and gullible.

'Katya?'

'Oh, you know her?'

'Of course, Travellers are a clannish lot. Mind ya, Katya's a Roma, not a Traveller.'

Juliet didn't quite know why, but she had the impression that he was teasing her. 'There's a difference?' she asked. He had an ear ring, she noticed.

He nodded. 'I'm an Irish Traveller. The Roma are mainly European. There are broad similarities. Both are nomadic, for instance, but the ancestral origins differ. However, both ethnic groups are subject to discrimination, sadly.'

'Oh, yes, I guess so.' She remembered Matt hurling insults and curses. 'Well, she suggested that I pay you a visit.' There, she'd said it. Not exactly a lie, she thought. He was a man, and, as far as she could tell, his livelihood revolved around horses and he was Irish – they tended to be smooth talkers, didn't they?

'Ah, I pay her, you know. It works like a charm. She sends all these lovely young women to see me. In our tradition, only women can be fortune tellers, and beggars, of course, so they have their uses.'

This one was a smooth talker all right, with the serious gift of the gab. She sensed that somewhere under the surface, he was kind of a chauvinist. He had that air of total self-assurance that presumably came as his birth right.

'I'm looking for a replacement horse, something really special, with Olympic potential.'

He gazed at her until their eyes locked. Juliet thought she would melt.

Tommy ran his fingers through the wavy jet-black hair that curled just past his collar and he pondered a while. 'Well, you've come to the right place. How about we talk about it over a spot of breakfast?'

She drew back in an instant and was about to turn on her heel and disappear, but she stopped herself. *You're holding yourself back. That old protecting yourself trick. Come on. Get a grip. What have you got to lose?* Juliet nodded, and followed him to the house.

She noticed his hard, taut rear in his tight, faded jeans and decided that he was extremely crushable. He moved in an energetic, alluring way, yet at the same time he seemed languid and self-assured. *This guy's one sexy hunk,* she thought, admiring his broad shoulders and straight, strong back. Strange notions entered her head. Her stomach gave a little flutter. *Heathcliff, it's me, it's Cathy. I've come home.* Then, she remembered, she had felt exactly the same way the very first time they'd met, almost a year ago to the day. Her cheeks grew hot. She knew she shouldn't be so attracted to a man she'd only met twice, and yet...

The ramshackle farmhouse suggested Tommy had little interest in material possessions or static things. He waited for her at the top of the concrete steps, holding the door open. Juliet looked around and observed a state of amiable chaos. *A haven for spiders and creepy crawlies,* she thought, with an almost imperceptible shudder. The walls were lined with photographs of horses of every imaginable shape and size. Her keen eye couldn't detect any evidence of a woman's presence and no sense of a woman's touch. She guessed that, apart from the dogs, Tommy lived alone. She breathed a sigh of relief. Then it occurred to her that he might be gay. He might be living in bliss with a male professional rider. Had there been any rumours like that? The delightful frisson of anticipation was duly reined in.

The very dark slate kitchen floor made the kitchen cold and rather unwelcoming. Particularly as the kitchen was situated at the back of the house, where there was not much sunlight.

Juliet shivered.

Tommy saw that. Little escaped Tommy Rafferty's attention.

'Would y' fancy a bowl of oat bran porridge with grated apple, and wildflower honey?' He indicated for her to pull up a chair at the old pine table and shooed the dogs out into the hall.

'Great.' She sat at the table with one leg curled under her. A stray wisp of her ebony hair flopped over her face, and she flicked it to one side. She watched him as he prepared the oatmeal. He seemed so absorbed and yet she sensed that he was aware of her. He seemed to be all knowing, and all seeing.

At that moment, he turned. His sapphire eyes sparked from under his coal-black hair. *Wow, he's definitely hot,* she thought. She regretted the thought as soon as it popped into her head. *Stop it! Get a grip.* Her life was already complicated enough.

He quit stirring and held her gaze. 'So, where's what's-is-face?'

Talk of the devil, or major complication number one. 'Oh, he's gone on a fishing trip with Shamus. He won't be back till after dark.'

'Porridge, there y' go. Help yourself to apple and honey.'

'Thanks.' She smiled. The oatmeal tasted wonderfully sweet. She ate with relish, but after a while she could sense him studying her, scrutinizing until it made her uncomfortable. She tried to find something to look at, anything but him. 'I see that you like travelling.' She pointed at the artefacts from all over the world with a sweeping gesture.

'Yeah, isn't that what Gypsies do?'

'Oh, was I being patronising? Sorry.'

'Don't worry about it.' He looked at her directly. 'Well now, does he know you're here?'

She took a deep breath. 'Matt?'

'Mmmm…'

'Of course,' she muttered, feigning indignation.

'Good. I think it's important to have honesty and integrity in relationships.'

'Yeah, me too,' she agreed, fidgeting.

She looked up at the ceiling where bunches of assorted herbs hung to dry from hooks. She took a deep breath and drank in an assortment of pungent aromas. It smelt like the countryside throughout the seasons, the heady aroma of lavender and mint and the sharper notes of sage and thyme cut with scents that she didn't recognize. *He probably makes up potions to seduce his latest love interest or casts spells like a witch. Silly,* she thought, laughing at her own fancifulness, *everyone knows that males are wizards or warlocks, not witches.* Nonetheless, "witch" stuck in her mind. 'What're the herbs for?'

'I use different herbs for different things. We Pavees, as we call ourselves, use natural remedies. We don't have much store by doctors and the like. Have you ever tried nettle tea?'

Juliet made a face. 'No, and I'm not sure I want to.'

'Ah, but my nettle tea is a potent brew. It keeps irate clients away for one thing. Works like a charm. I've not had one of those nice letters from his solicitors for – oh, let me see – well, several weeks now. So, the tea must be working.'

The notion of spells, charms, and potions, popped into her head. How weird. 'Oh dear, I'm sorry. Matt was pretty upset about the mares,' she said.

'To be sure,' Tommy replied with a wicked grin. 'But, was it honestly me own fault if old Pa Riley's gelding, that I only took in out of the goodness of my heart, mind, turned out to be a rig? And a right randy old rig at that. I ask you now, was it my fault?'

Juliet tried hard to suppress a giggle. She shouldn't laugh, but little droplets of oatmeal splattered down her chin. 'Well, it was bad enough that it was a rig, I guess, but worst of all, if the foals are anything to go by, it was a huge black and white carthorse of a thing.'

'Oh aye, and what's wrong with coloureds, then?'

He looked offended, and she couldn't tell if he was joking. 'Nothing, I mean nothing until Matt gets warmed up on the subject. They're not his favourite things.'

'That's just horse snobbery.'

'Well, there's not much demand in England for...' Juliet picked her words carefully, 'that certain type. I believe Matt's considering exporting them back to Ireland.'

The pantomime played out between them, back and forth.

'Ah, interesting idea. Over here there's demand, of course, for isn't every Irishman a Gypsy at heart? But there is, as you can imagine, an issue of over-supply.'

'Indeed, particularly if Pa Riley's rig hasn't been properly gelded yet.'

'Gelded? Good heavens, no. He is, alas, no more, passed away peacefully on the job, as it were.'

'What a way to go,' she said chuckling.

'Mind you,' Tommy said when the chuckling eventually died down, 'I do have a really cracking mare for sale.'

'How old?' she asked a little breathlessly.

'Four.'

Not a horse to take to Badminton next month then, she thought with a twinge of regret. Even at the lowest levels, Intro and Pre-Novice, the horse had to be five.

'Please, spare me,' she groaned.

Her mobile trilled, and she rummaged in her handbag. Probably Todd, she thought. Bless his heart. He was always stressing about her. She glanced at the caller ID. *Shit.* Not Todd, Matt. *Shit!* She picked up.

'Um, shopping,' she said when he asked what she was doing.

'Shopping?'

'Uh-huh.' Her head bobbed up and down like a nodding dog in the back of a Cortina. *Quick, think. Be convincing.* Tommy was staring at her, one eyebrow akimbo. She tried not to look at him. 'Hmmm… fabulous Waterford crystal,' she enthused. 'You know, for… mother's birthday.'

Tommy's eyebrow took off.

'Ha, hum,' she coughed. 'Well, gotta dash. *Ciao.*'

'I take it that was Matt?' Tommy enquired with a broad grin.

'And, so what if it was?'

'Well, so much for honesty and integrity,' he said with a smirk.

'Well… I…' she spluttered, her face feeling hot. 'How long have you lived here?' she asked, in order to change the subject.

'Let me see now, hmmm… I've been here for…' he squinted as he tried to calculate, 'like sixteen and a half years, since I was eighteen. Come on. I always take the dogs for a walk around this time.' Tommy raised his hand for a high-five. He let out a shrill whistle, and the assorted mutts bayed and barked in delight, practically knocking Juliet off her feet in their rush to get near Tommy.

It was Juliet's turn to do the math. So, he was thirty-four or five. Not too old. Relief surged through her.

They all spilled outside. Juliet was quiet. She hadn't shown herself in her best light, getting caught out like that. What would Tommy make of it? Of course, she didn't really care what he thought.

'I hope you don't believe that I'm shallow and devious. I mean, it was only a little white lie and…'

'Those are the worst kind, don't you think?'

Juliet didn't know what to say. She looked mortified and gulped. 'What a handsome dog,' she said, pointing at the Wolfhound.

'Yeah, Gulliver's a rescue dog.'

'Ah. What happened to him?'

'He belonged to a lady who had two other dogs. He was fine with them, but he became increasingly aggressive towards male dogs. And so, the lady called Pa to try and cure it. When he got to the house, one of the small dogs rushed over and said, "I know what the problem is." Pa introduced himself and replied, "Thank you for communicating with me. I'd really like to know some more about this."

"Well," the little dog confided, "he attacks the other dogs because our owner is terrified of men. He feels her emotional pain, and he wants to protect her."

"I see," Pa said. "That's interesting. Do you know why your owner is afraid of men?"

"Oh yes, she's been like that ever since the age of seven." Whereupon Pa had an impression of a dark, sinister figure and the overwhelming feeling of sickening abuse. So, he told the owner what he'd learned from the little dog, and she broke down, sobbing uncontrollably.'

Juliet stared at Tommy in astonishment. 'You mean Pa's an animal communicator? I've heard of them but… what happened?'

Tommy shook his head. 'Pa worked with the woman over several healing sessions, but it was too painful for her to continue, and all the while, Gulliver's behaviour grew worse and worse.'

'And, you rescued him?'

Tommy squirmed a fraction. 'Not exactly, he's here for a few months and after that he'll return to his owner to be put down.'

Juliet came to a halt with a jolt. 'You've got to be kidding. Why? He's perfectly fine here with all the other dogs.'

'It's hard. God knows I've become attached to him myself, but it's what Gulliver wants.'

'No, no. There must be some mistake.'

'You know what? Dying is allowed, that's what he told Pa. Gulliver believes that it's his path to sacrifice himself for his owner, so that she can get the help she needs going forwards. He sees it as her gateway out of emotional pain.'

'How touching,' she said, looking at the dog with tears shining in her eyes.

A little subdued after hearing Gulliver's story, she watched Tommy as he walked up the track. He had a stick in his hand that went with a swish as he beat the overgrowth back. His movements came fluid and easy in the manner of a poised man, a man happy in his own skin. It reminded her of a childhood game, trampling through the long grass which parted underfoot. It was so satisfying, leaving tracks. She plucked at a long, curled frond of rye grass and chewed the end, savouring the perfect peace and harmony. Ahead, she spotted an old barn with an ancient roof that sagged in the middle, the sort of barn that in the South of England would make property developers delirious. It had a wonderful aspect, as it looked out over rolling meadows for miles, and beyond into the distance. She stopped and listened to doves cooing from under the eaves.

'It's really pretty here. Do you own all this?' She made a sweeping gesture with her arm.

'No, it's rented. That way, I can come and go as I please.'

'Oh, how can you stand to leave, not knowing where home will be, and when you'll come back? I'd hate that.'

He shrugged. 'It's better, I reckon, not to get too attached.'

When he spoke, he held her gaze in a pointed way as if telegraphing her a message.

She took it as a warning.

Surely, he'd just laid out the parameters, and let her know he didn't do commitment? Juliet licked her lips. The more he came across as cool and elusive, the more she wanted to catch him.

'You must get attached to something right? Okay, maybe not to people or places, but then what about dogs or horses?'

He shrugged.

'Dogs, perhaps, horses no. It would be a bit difficult, don't ya think, as buying and selling is my livelihood? Besides, you're on the road, no fixed abode yourself an' all.' He paused and stared into the distance.

'Maybe, but I have a house, a yard…' *And a live-in lover who I'm now engaged to,* she thought with a tinge of regret.

'We're different, you and me. I move on, you stick at it. Your line of work requires tremendous courage, and commitment. Regardless of falls or setbacks, you carry on. Like now after you've lost your top horse. And no one appreciates all the hard work that goes on week in, week out. It's a long, gruelling journey to the top. And then with horses it can be gone,' he snapped his fingers, 'just like that.'

'True, but I love what I do. It's been a bad run lately, but that can't last forever. Eventually my luck will change. Meanwhile I've got good backup, and lots of support. There's Franz, my dressage instructor; Jenny, the sports psychologist; Marcia and Matt for show jumping; my pupils. The other riders, oh, and Todd, he's a total sweetheart. He…' She paused and gulped, suddenly aware of the treachery that she'd contemplated. How could she steal his rides? No one deserved such betrayal, but especially not Todd. Yet, she had to win at all costs, and if she didn't, something inside her would die.

'Oh yeah, you're every Pony Club kid's idol.'

'Well, actually, I think it was Gothic they loved. We're still getting stacks of sympathy cards from his fans. He's even got his own

Facebook page. What about the mare you mentioned? Does she have a name?'

The doves cooed in the background.

'For sure, she's called after someone very special.'

Juliet's stomach felt knotted, it began to hurt as if she'd been punched. What a disappointment. So, there was someone, a woman. Could it be his wife?

'Oh.' Her words escaped like air from a punctured balloon. He had a perfect right to be married, of course, but that didn't fit with the image she had of him. Her lips formed a tight, thin line, and the arching of her eyebrows signalled her disapproval. Her shoulders sagged, and she felt deflated.

'Yeah.' His eyes brightened. 'Her professional name's Sky Catcher, but she's always Aoife to me.'

Juliet sniffed, her cheeks forming two hollows of indignation. 'How nice, are you sure you can bear to part with her, then?'

'Well, no, it won't be easy.' He set off down the track again.

They passed the first field, where the geldings grazed contentedly. A robin bobbed along the wire fence, his head on one side, and his beady eyes following Juliet. She wondered why robins came in pairs on Christmas cards, but she'd only ever seen them individually in the wild. Tommy slowed down, and she caught up so that they walked side by side. He turned, his head cocked slightly to one side like the robin. The synchronicity of their movements made her smile.

'Are you wondering who the mare is named after, now?' he asked with an impish grin.

'No, I wasn't wondering anything like that,' she spluttered as her cheeks coloured.

'Oh, well, I'll not bother to be explaining, then.'

She stiffened. Of course, she desperately wanted to know, but it was not a good thing for a man to get a whiff of desperation from a woman. Besides, he had the look of a man who was a hard dog to keep on the porch. So, she said nothing, and tried to appear uninterested.

After the walk, they stood in the kitchen side-by-side in front of the sink. 'In our tradition, only the women do housework,' Tommy explained. 'But as I live alone, like, I've no choice. Mind you, according to our rules, we can only bathe in running water, so don't ever wash your hands in the washing-up sink, or you'll be contaminated.'

'Really.' She raised an eyebrow. 'I'm surprised you live here alone.'

'Ah, so did you expect a caravan full of kids, then? Wouldn't that be right grand?'

'No. I…' She decided to play it cool. 'Whatever.'

She washed. He dried.

Something so mundane, and yet she felt so content.

'Tell me something, why didn't you ever get married?' she probed, burning to know more about his past relationships.

He put the dishcloth down and cocked his head. 'Our custom is that you marry young, in your teens. The girl must be a Traveller, and a virgin, otherwise she's deemed impure. The parents pay a bride fee, then you live with the in-laws until your first child is born.' He licked his lips, and chuckled. 'That seemed far too restrictive for me.'

'So, you can never marry outside the Traveller society?'

Tommy's eyes widened. 'Never say never.'

When they had finished, Tommy set off out of the back door with the Irish Wolfhound, two Lurchers, three Border Collies, a Greyhound, and Juliet all trailing in his wake. After twenty paces or so, they reached the pristine stable yard. Compared to the house, the stables looked immaculate. She interpreted it as the hallmark of someone who spent most of their time outdoors, someone not too dissimilar to herself. The horses snorted and kicked their doors, impatient for their feed.

'I know I'm late. Don't get on about it. We've got company today, and I got a little distracted. Whoa, Jack, steady boy.'

'Can I help?' She cocked her head and licked her lips in little darting movements.

'Sure. I'll mix the feeds, and you can dish them out. Only watch out for Jack Wolf. He bites.' He leaned towards her, and she could smell his hair. It smelled like fresh spring rainwater, and all natural things outdoors.

'I'm used to that. So does Icon. Gothic doesn't. He's the perfect gentleman. I mean, he was, oh…'

'Ah, I'm sorry to hear about the terrible accident. I was in England at the time, and I read about it in the papers. I offer my condolences. That horse was your Olympic horse 'n all?'

'Yes.' After the funeral, she had begun to cope with the trauma. Little by little, day by day, the pain, the guilt and bitterness had begun to ease a fraction. She didn't want to think about it, to be reminded. She only wanted to forget, forget and move forward to a happier place.

His eyes searched her face. He looked concerned, as if he really cared.

'It wasn't an accident. They were taken out, murdered in cold blood.'

'I'm really sorry. Have the police caught who did it yet?'

Juliet shook her head. 'No, I don't know what's taking them so long. In America, they'd be in there, guns blazing like in the movies.'

Tommy looked at her more closely. 'Wow, you're American? I thought –'

Juliet laughed. 'I know the accent confuses everyone. Too long hanging out in the UK, I guess.'

'D' you have a replacement horse yet?'

'I'm looking.' She bit her lip. For a while, captivated by Tommy's aura, she'd forgotten, but now all the unpleasant memories broke the surface again. A wave of cold oppressiveness came about as if the sun had ducked behind a cloud.

'Tell ya what, once we've finished up here, how's about we go for a drive, find a nice quiet pub, and you can tell me all about it over a spot of lunch?'

'Well…'

'Come on, live a little.'

'Yes.' She brightened a fraction. 'That would be nice. Will you excuse me a minute while I go upstairs and freshen up?'

'Sure.'

In the bathroom, she called DS Barrett for an update. The detective wanted Katya's contact details to try find out more about the Apache vision she'd related to Juliet.

'I'll text them to you after we hang up,' Juliet said. 'Have there been any developments?'

DS Barrett paused, then after a while she exhaled. 'There were two men walking their dogs on the Heath on the morning of the incident. We've interviewed both of them, neither of the two men are suspects at this stage, but it seems they saw an as yet unidentified man running away from the burning car.'

'Did they give a description? Do you have anything useful?'

'Not really, but obviously we're following up all leads. Oh, one other thing, the insurance company has just rejected the claim for Gothic.'

'What?' Juliet exclaimed, 'Why, and on what grounds? How fucking well dare they?'

'The Bot says no.'

'Wait, what do you mean?'

'Insurance companies, banks, recruitment agencies, they all use robots to do the leg work. And they sometimes come up with illogical conclusions, crazy inferences, and sometimes humans are not even allowed to use their common sense to override the robots.'

'That's crap!'

DS Barrett sighed. 'I know, tell me about it. It bugs the hell out of me. This whole area has to be tightly regulated now, before AI really takes hold and impacts every aspect of our lives.'

'What can I do?'

'Don't worry, it's in hand. However, don't discuss this conversation with anyone. Do I make myself clear?'

Juliet caught her reflection in the mirror – her brow was furrowed, and she looked weary. 'I guess so.' If the insurance company refused to pay up, how would she ever afford a replacement?

'Good. Anyway, I've got to hop. My other line's ringing,' the detective announced.

With that, they hung up.

What else can go wrong, Juliet wondered? *What the heck did I ever do to deserve this?*

* * *

Tommy Rafferty drove a battered old army Jeep with a canvas roof that was ripped in a thousand places. He turned the ancient engine over and pumped the accelerator until it finally started. In one practiced motion, he turned the steering wheel, and the Jeep shot off down the driveway. The potholes and the lack of suspension didn't make for a comfortable ride, but Juliet didn't mind. She enjoyed just being with him.

Tommy's elbow poked out of the open window. The T-shirt that he wore looked as if it might have been white once upon a time but wasn't entirely any more. She stared at his strong and sinewy arms, fascinated by the well-defined muscles, not huge but definitely honed. He had tanned skin, weathered to a deep olive colour from an outdoor life, she supposed. Interesting hands too, long tapering fingers – nice hands, with neat nails. These must be artistic and sensitive hands for patting dogs, stroking horses, and caressing women.

'A penny for them,' he said softly.

'Oh.' Juliet gasped, and her heart gave a flutter. *What if he could read her thoughts?* Tommy had something, some indefinable quality that set him apart from other men.

'You were going to tell me about Gothic.'

189

She paused for a moment, wondering where to begin. 'Gothic was more than a horse; he was everything to me, the bond between us was telepathic. Losing him was devastating, and yet I now think it was for Totem – who was never buried.' Juliet stared at her feet.

'Who's Totem?'

She took a deep breath. This wasn't going to be easy. 'Totem was my first top eventer. He taught me everything, but I... betrayed him.'

'What d' you mean?' His brow furrowed, and his thick dark eyebrows disappeared beneath his tumbling curls.

Reluctant to continue, she looked into his eyes as if trying to read his thoughts. She saw kindness, and genuine concern, and falteringly she continued. 'He got colic – a terrible colic attack. He was too weak to stand, but when he saw me he struggled to his feet, trying to be brave for my sake. The vet came out throughout the night and gave him shots for a suspected twisted gut. In those days, they didn't always operate. I had an important event the next day. If only... if only I'd stayed with him.' Juliet gasped. The memory was too vivid, too painful.

She took a deep breath and shook her head. 'I wanted to stay with him, but there was nothing I could do, so I went to the competition.' Juliet buried her face in her hands. 'And I'll regret that decision for the rest of my life.'

Tommy reached out and squeezed her hand. 'There now, steady. It's okay.'

Juliet gulped and gave a sniff. 'Not really. I'm so ashamed of myself, I left him to a terrible fate and I was so ashamed that I lied about it.' Juliet flinched as she recalled the conversation with DS Barrett when she came to the stable yard. 'I told someone that he'd just vanished. Does that make me a bad person?' She turned to him, so desperate for forgiveness.

'No, of course not. Come here and let me give you a hug.'

CHAPTER TWENTY-SIX

Juliet

Tommy drove in silence. Neither of them spoke a word. Juliet felt emotionally and physically drained. Gently, he gave her knee a reassuring squeeze, which she appreciated more than she cared to let on. But, even Tommy's comforting presence couldn't shift the all-encompassing sadness.

The sight of the pub perched high on the cliffs overlooking the sea did nothing to lift her spirits either. Tommy touched her on the arm, not taking hold, steering her the way that Matt would have done, but just empathizing quietly. He parked the Jeep and gave her a few moments to compose herself.

'Ready?' he asked.

Nodding, she slipped down from the seat that time had worn hard and smooth and landed on the grass. It felt coarse and springy under the soles of her shoes. She took a deep breath and tasted salt on her lips. The air smelt of seaweed and fish. In the distance, keen-eyed gulls were hovering on the eddies, then swooping and diving on scraps.

Another deep breath and she began to feel better.

She felt grateful to Tommy for being there while knowing how to give her some space of her own. He looked concerned, and she felt that he really cared enough to listen without making any judgements. His movements conveyed the calmness of the polished-mirror surface of a lake on a perfectly still day. She felt that his gentleness came from some deep inner well of confidence, or a deep lake, dark in its intensity, a silent pool. Here at last was a man who understood her perfectly and possessed the confidence to just let her be herself.

Tommy slipped his hand in hers. A sensation like a spark rushed up her arm. She trembled, and he gave her hand a comforting squeeze.

'There now,' he exhaled, his eyes searching hers. Vibrant blue shadowed by thick, inky lashes. She thought that her knees might give out. The energy between them crackled with delicious anticipation.

They sat outside under a parasol looking out to sea, and Juliet felt some of her guilt dissolve and drift away. He made her feel alive and free just by being himself. For a while they sat in silence, savouring the moment. Eventually Tommy spoke. 'I can recommend the wild boar sausages or scallops if you prefer.' He sounded husky, as if something interfered with his breathing.

'Sausages for me,' she said.

It occurred to her that he felt the same way about her too. An instant, mutual, and inescapable attraction had them both enmeshed.

'Me too, and two pints of cider to wash them down,' he said to the waitress. Then, after she'd left, he probed again. 'Losing both your top horses and seeing Isabella crushed must have been devastating. Do you want to talk about what happened to Totem?'

'Oh.' Juliet stared out to sea. 'I was such a fool.' Her voice trailed off, and for a moment, she couldn't speak. It took a while for her to compose herself. 'I should have told them to phone me or left explicit instructions for him to be put down at home. But instead, when it looked hopeless, my groom called out the knacker-man.'

'Well, that would've been a humane end.'

'No,' Juliet swallowed, her shoulders sagged, and she shook her head. 'I would do anything, anything, to undo my mistake.'

The drinks arrived, and Tommy sipped his cider. He appeared to be mulling this over.

'It doesn't always do to look back. You've got to keep moving forward.'

Their food arrived at last. Starving, she licked her lips at the prospect of sausages and mashed potato, awash with a thick tangy gravy.

'Yes, but they eat horses in some countries, don't they?'

'What?' Tommy looked puzzled.

She thought of Chateaubriand, red and bloody on some French Madame's plate, and shivered with revulsion. 'The French eat horses.' And she pushed her food away untouched.

'They do, that be right. But, let's not think about that now. Well now, can you think of a nation more sentimental about horses than the Irish? I mean, for us, horses are in the blood. Petting, betting, buying, and selling. Oh, and art of course. Don't you be worrying about the French.'

It felt good to get it off her chest and the tension in her neck and shoulders eased a little.

Tommy had the most captivating way about him. Juliet raised her glass and sipped the last of the cider, slowly savouring each mouthful. It tasted like honey and apple blossom, and a perfect spring day, like today. Something as simple as an ice-cold glass of cider seemed so elegant and fine. Why didn't she and Matt live like that? Instead, they went to endless champagne receptions and cocktail parties, and lived beyond their means.

* * *

On the way back, they took the coastal route, miles of country road parting the blue-green grass that rolled off the edge of the cliffs toward the endless sea. Juliet inhaled deeply, savouring the scent of new-mown grass and the smell of a thousand dusty roads. She had a curious I've-been-here-before feeling, and she wondered if that came from the place or Tommy or both. The wind wafting through the open window caught her hair so that it streamed out behind her in thick black tendrils. Her cheeks glowed. How long had it been since she'd felt so alive? Now that she had met Tommy, everything seemed easier and more relaxed. Just being near him gave her a warm, contented feeling. If only life could be a series of days just like this one.

Tommy stared straight ahead at the road and way into the distance, as if he was searching for something – soul secrets that were carried by the wind. He didn't look at her, but she knew that he could find her in his peripheral vision whenever he wanted to. They drove along with the windows wide open, filling the Jeep with the smell of the sea. Not saying anything, just thinking and being. Thoughts of him filled her mind. She wanted to know more, everything about him.

She turned towards him. 'Were you ever married or engaged? I get the feeling that you're alone.'

He didn't answer immediately. 'Alone is not necessarily lonely, if that's what you mean.'

'No, I just wondered.' How come someone as attractive as him hadn't been snapped up and devoured whole by some predatory female?

'At heart and by heritage, I'm a Traveller. Never happier then when I'm on the road. The ties that bind a man to a person or a place aren't for me. So, Travellers make difficult husbands for ordinary people, see. And living in the Traveller community, well, I find it too small and restrictive after a while.'

'You mean you like your freedom and space?'

'Yes, space.' He smiled. 'That reminds me of a poem:

Let there be webs in your togetherness,
let the winds of the star galaxies dance between you.

'Yeats?'

'Good guess. It's by Gibran.'

'Sorry, never heard of him. Are you a poetry fan, then?'

'I guess.' He laughed. 'That's the Irish for you. We drink, we sing, we recite poetry, we get emotional. It always seems to me that poetry's the place where words and silence meet to create music, this is the place where all the longings of the ancient words can be heard.'

'Hmmm, that's profound.' She looked at him, her eyes wide and shining, trying to fathom the aura that radiated from him. She didn't understand why she found him so alluring. Did he have this effect on every woman he met? She flushed a little as flames of passion burnt her cheeks, heavens above and all things below. *What was it about him?*

When they got back to his smallholding, Juliet gulped with relief. She couldn't wait to escape from the Jeep, to put some distance between them both and give herself chance to think.

'Right,' Tommy said, only just audible over the din of the dogs barking as they rushed out to greet him. 'Well, if you'll excuse me, I must be getting on.'

Juliet tried to disguise her disappointment. She didn't want to leave, but she didn't like the way he left her feeling so needy and vulnerable. So perhaps, it would be better to go. She couldn't trust herself around him. Who could say what might happen? She had no control over her feelings any longer. Part of her knew it would be better to walk away and move on with her life as before. And part of her cared nothing for that. If only he would reach out and take her in his arms, drawing her close. That thought flashed through her mind, but it made her feel bad all the same. She hadn't done anything to feel guilty about – yet – but she knew that if he asked she'd be powerless to resist. *Enough,* she told herself. *This is absurd.*

'Well, I guess I'll be making tracks. Thanks for lunch – your company.' Juliet shuffled her toe in the gravel. 'Oh, and thanks for listening too.'

'My pleasure,' he said softly, with a lingering look. 'Before you go, would you tell me what happened to Totem?'

Juliet stiffened. She turned away and stared into the distance.

'It might help you to talk about it,' he persisted.

'Yes.' Some of the tension in her shoulders eased. 'The knacker-man didn't put him down when he got back to the slaughterhouse. Instead, he had to endure the most horrible fate, dying a slow lingering death but still able to walk – barely. They… loaded him on the cattle ship, you know as horsemeat for Europe.'

'Don't be so hard on yourself. Maybe you're mistaken. After all, they don't allow live exports from England.'

'I know that's the theory, but there's no mistake… if only. You see, sometimes he comes to me at night. His trusting eyes had turned into flashbulbs of terror. His coat's matted and thick with foamy sweat. He's in agony, agony within and hell all around. No water, no air to breathe, everything disgusting and vile.' Juliet covered her ears, her face contorted. 'I can't stand it. I can't stand the sound.'

'What is it?' He reached out and touched her arm.

'It's a horse screaming. A horse trapped in hell. Screaming for me to make the pain stop, and I can't do anything to save him. Eventually he ceases; silence comes. He's quiet now. Exhausted and subdued. The silence is almost worse, damning. He knows that I've failed him. And his trust, his trust is betrayed for all eternity.' Juliet bit back the tears. 'And heaven knows if that isn't bad enough, I couldn't save Gothic or Isabella either.'

Tommy shrugged. 'Sometimes it makes no sense. Sometimes it's just that God's busy, perhaps?'

195

CHAPTER TWENTY-SEVEN
Juliet

Somehow, after she'd told Tommy about Totem, she felt lighter, as if a cloud had lifted. He possessed well-developed listening skills. He was so quiet and attentive. Like a poet, he heard the words both spoken and unsaid. *Could he understand? Really understand?* He seemed to have an open mind. And the aura about him, the thing that she found so irresistible, had an indefinable spiritual quality. Juliet reached for the gold unicorn around her neck and chewed her lip, uncertain whether to risk it or not.

He might take her for one of those hippy-dippy chicks who went around chanting. This reincarnation thing was a real speed bump. She had hit it with Matt, and it had thrown their relationship off-track. What if Tommy closed his mind against her too? Honesty wasn't always sensible, and she didn't know what to do, but she had to talk to someone, to share. She realized that she was shivering.

'Look at you, come on inside and get warm.' He ushered her into the kitchen and they sat on stools in front of the hearth. Tommy lit a fire. She listened to the logs crackling as a delicious smell of pine filled the air. She stared, captivated by the orange and red flames that flickered in the hearth.

'Feeling better?' Tommy enquired.

She nodded and smiled, wondering if she really could come out with what was on her mind.

'Juliet?'

'I don't want you to think that I'm a candidate for a straitjacket.'

He grinned at her reassuringly. 'I'm not exactly Mr. Average Joe myself now, am I?'

'Well, maybe not. Oh, I don't know.' She chewed her lip as he cocked his head and studied her with those piercing blue eyes. 'Well, this might sound a bit strange, but I have this notion that when Totem died, he came back as Gothic. And you know what happened to Gothic. Somehow, I can't shake off the idea that I'm to blame, as if I'm being punished for something.' She waited, trying to gauge his reaction.

'Let me get this straight. Are you saying that Totem and Gothic were one an' the same horse?'

'Yes.'

'Sweet baby Jesus in a manger,' he chuckled. 'Well, ancient Gypsy wisdom says that when you discover you're riding a dead horse, the best course of action is to dismount.'

'This isn't some crazy notion. I'm serious.'

'On the other hand, you can always harness several dead horses together for increasing speed.'

'Tommy, please.'

'Sorry. It was meant to be a joke.' He stood up and put another couple of logs on the fire.

'Ha-ha.'

'Okay. I guess then that the horse returns to kind of rework the ending, until you get it right?'

'I'm not sure. Something like that, until the debt of karma is repaid, I think. It's pretty worrying, I mean...' Although they were alone, she glanced over her shoulder to make sure that no one was listening. Then, she leaned forwards towards Tommy. 'If he comes back to teach me a lesson, maybe there's worse things further back that I can't recall. It's there all the time, this nagging worry that I did something really unthinkable.'

'What, like in past lives, you mean? Are you warm enough now?'

'That's it exactly.' Relieved, she let out a sigh. Tommy seemed to understand. 'There are several theories about animals reincarnating. Some people believe there's an over-soul for the entire animal kingdom and, on passing, the animal becomes part of the group soul. But that can't be right, because it means that animals don't have personality or character, only instinctive behaviour. I think we can create karmic situations with animals just as readily as with humans, and I have this powerful, inescapable feeling that Totem and Gothic aren't really dead, that their spirit carries on.' She paused and licked her lips. 'Then Katya told me that my son, an Apache Indian, wanted me to help him with a mission, and that he was sending me a replacement horse. Do

197

you have any experience of this sort of thing?' She felt the fierce heat from the fire on her legs and quickly moved her stool farther back.

'Not personally. No. But Pa contacts animals both dead and living, and he reckons that time is just a concept, and space doesn't actually exist.'

'He sounds like a real character.'

'Oh, he's a character all right. Let's just say that he and the authorities here didn't always see eye to eye. That's why he moved to England. But really, it doesn't matter what anyone else believes. If it feels right to you, then let it be your truth. Just live by that.'

'Yeah,' she breathed. 'At first, I really resisted the idea, completely closed my mind, but the similarities between Totem and Gothic were uncanny, spooky even. Fran, one of my grooms at the time, was a really down-to-earth Northerner, but even she became convinced that the two horses were one and the same. Everything, their quirks, their way of going, likes and dislikes, oh and their talent, of course.' She was feeling relaxed and cosy as she watched the fire flickering.

Tommy scrutinized her closely with a look of concern. 'When did you first embark on this spiritual path?'

'In my teens, I guess. I was raised a Catholic, but I always found it so restrictive, unbearable in fact. I read a lot, especially anything metaphysical. Then, when Totem died and I found Gothic, the whole idea of reincarnation just resonated.' She paused, wondering how far she could go. 'It's not really the sort of thing I can discuss every day. A couple of my friends on the eventing circuit might understand. Todd and Louisa are both superstitious, but generally it's not something that I want to develop. You probably think I'm nuts?'

'No, you seem perfectly fine to me. Riding's truly an instinctive sport, and greatness is all about a sense of timing that can't be taught.' He stared at her long and hard.

A philosopher as well as a poet, she thought. In Tommy's company she could reveal another dimension of herself that otherwise had to remain hidden. 'Matt thinks I'm insane,' she sighed, 'what about you?'

'Well.' Tommy looked uncomfortable, as though he didn't want to get drawn in on the subject. He hopped off the stool and stoked the fire. 'That's his problem, I guess. It's understandable that you're distraught after what happened.'

A diplomatic response, but not really the encouragement she'd hoped for.

'You don't feel then, not even a tiny bit of you, that what I'm saying might be feasible?' She was aware that her tone betrayed her neediness.

'No two people share the same reality. I try to keep an open mind. Do you want to share something else with me?'

She watched him closely, anxious to gauge his reaction.

He paused for what seemed like age, then stood and paced the room. 'I don't have any first-hand experience of these kind of things myself. I think I need to go outside and get some air.'

Juliet's shoulders drooped. She'd gone too far, rambling on like a lunatic until she blew it and completely alienated him.

'What about Pa? Does he believe that animals have a higher awareness when it comes to death?'

Tommy stopped pacing and pondered a moment. 'No. He reckons some animals, like Gulliver, are enlightened and some are not. He was called out once to see a Doberman that had seriously injured its back. The prognosis was not good. The dog had recently been rehomed with a family and after years as a guard dog was just beginning to learn what is was like to be loved and touched. Pa asked him if he knew that his time had come and if he was ready to pass on and the dog started howling. He wasn't ready. He didn't want to go, and he had no comprehension of what lay ahead. But really, what does that prove? Hey, I almost forgot, do you want to take a quick look at the mare? I think she might be what you're looking for.'

Juliet stood up, strode across the kitchen, and reached for her coat. She ought to leave before she said anything else that she'd regret.

'Well, I guess I'd better be going. Thanks for listening.' She hesitated. Even as her words rang in her ears they lacked authenticity. By now she'd become addicted to his company, like the last drag on a cigarette before quitting. She wanted to stay, to savour his company so badly, but there was no way that Matt would ever do business with Tommy again. 'I'm afraid I don't think looking at your mare's such a good idea. I'm sure she's very nice but...'

'It's not a horse for Matt. It's a horse for you.'

Could he really read her mind? 'Hmm, but name me one top-ranking mare in eventing,' she said with scepticism.

'The Wexford Lady, Hotshot Hayley. In fact, Preci-Spark only had event mares, but that's not the point. You're just closing yourself off to possibilities. Slamming doors shut that haven't even opened.' He looked at her as if trying to judge whether she'd been swayed or not. 'Besides, I love riding mares. If you build up a good relationship from the start, they'll try their heart out for you. Plus, her breeding is perfect. Her mother was by Sky Boy, out of a cracking King of Diamonds mare.'

'Sky Boy?' Her heart skipped a beat and she warmed to her favourite subject – bloodlines and competition horse breeding. 'What an amazing coincidence. Gothic was related to Sky Boy. I've always liked him. I think he's up there with Just-A-Monarch, my absolute favourite TB stallion.' She hesitated. The mare had a superb pedigree and Juliet could barely disguise her interest. 'How old did you say she was?'

'Four.'

'Has she done anything?' she said excitedly. The same age as Gothic when she'd bought him. What incredible synchronicity.

'No, she was backed at three, hunted last winter. After that she was turned away. She's really special, and she jumps like a stag, very talented.'

Tommy bent to pat the dogs, and they responded by covering his arm in sloppy licks. One of the Border Terriers leapt in the air, desperate for his attention.

'Actually,' Tommy paused to consider his words, 'she jumps like a comet with a mane full of stardust. Bred her myself out of me grade A show jumping mare. But I have to say, she's not exactly a horse.'

'What do you mean?'

'Well, more otherworldly.' Now, it was his turn to look embarrassed. He shrugged and seemed lost for words. 'Oh, I don't know. You'd better see for yourself.'

CHAPTER TWENTY-EIGHT

Juliet

As they walked along the track towards the mares' field, the black clouds gathered ominously like ravens circling the remains of a road accident. She found the stillness unbearable and oppressive.

'There's a storm brewing,' Tommy said as they reached the gate. A quick calculation revealed nine head collars hanging over the gate, each with a lead rope attached.

'Yes.' She could feel the charge of static crackling in the atmosphere.

'We need the rain to clear the air a bit.' He selected one of the head collars and drew back the latch. The field stretched over twenty acres at least, and Juliet strained her eyes to make out the shapes way off in the distance.

'Where are they?' she asked, craning her neck.

'They're all out of sight. There's a hollow about halfway. Don't worry, they'll come.' Tommy cupped his hand around his mouth and called, 'Kai, kai, kai, come-anah, kai, kai, kai.'

It sounded old and primitive, like an ancient chant. Before very long the horses responded. Juliet heard their hooves thundering in the distance, and then the herd broke into sight.

'Wow,' she said in amazement as the mares galloped across the plain. All shapes and sizes in assorted colours. These once-settled horses had reverted to their wild and natural state. Out in the front, her mane and tail streaming, she caught a tantalizing glimpse of the leader of the herd.

The head mare.

She looked like a skewbald, but she couldn't be certain. In the distance, a grouchy old man, the thunder rumbled. The horses galloped faster than the wind, approaching at such speed that Juliet feared that they would never stop in time.

'Oh my God, it's Espiritus!' Juliet's voice crackled with excitement.

It had never occurred to her for a moment that the horse in her dream was female. Then, doubt set in. Could it really be Espiritus? Suddenly, almost imperceptibly, the skewbald signalled to the herd with a flick of her ears. The pace eased off, dropping first to a canter, then a trot, and finally for the last few strides to a walk. Juliet sensed that some of the mares had foals at foot, long-legged and gawky with Bambi eyes. But, she had no interest in these. The skewbald alone drew all her attention, holding her gaze in her thrall.

The rest of the herd hung back. They were ever watchful and obedient while the lead mare broke ranks and strutted forward. As Tommy approached, the thunder roared, and a flash of lightning forked across the sky in a silver arc. The horse reared, her forelegs pawing at the air in a gesture of defiance. Then, with a sudden twist, both powerful and athletic, the mare tossed her head and set off across the field.

'We'd better hurry back. You'll get soaked,' Tommy said.

The rain drove in across the plain so fiercely that it stung her cheeks, but she held her breath, unable to speak in case it broke the spell.

'Come on.' His hand tugging at her arm brought her out of the trance. The rain had plastered his hair to his forehead and his shirt was sticking to his chest. 'Come on. You were miles away.'

'No, not yet. Let's stay a while longer. Can you catch her?' Her stare fixed beyond him, across the field. 'I need to get a closer look.'

Tommy shrugged. 'I don't know. She's wild and high-strung at the best of times, and in this weather –'

'I'm not going anywhere.' Juliet stared at him so that he felt the full force of her will.

'I guess we can at least try.' He looked doubtful.

The horse made it perfectly clear that she did not wish to be caught. Exhausted and infuriated, Tommy flung the head collar to the ground.

'Damn you!' he cursed.

The mare stopped and stared at him with her sides heaving.

'Whoa, Espiritus, whoa,' Juliet said, reaching forward. The mare snorted, and then stretched her muzzle towards Juliet's outstretched palm. The mare gave it a sniff. Juliet moved quietly and slipped a head collar on, talking to her all the time. 'There, my beautiful girl, there, steady now.'

By the time they reached the stable yard, the rain had eased off, a typical April shower. Soon the sun poked out from behind a cloud. Tommy held the mare by the halter and scratched the spot between the ears that horses find so hard to reach. She settled a little, but it soon became clear to Juliet that this horse had barely been handled. Each time Juliet ran her hand down the skewbald's leg, trying to persuade her to pick her foot up, the mare stomped and thrashed about. The mare had lumps on both her forelegs: splints. When Juliet tried to check the hind legs, an almighty kick sent her flying across the yard.

'Are ya okay?' Tommy fretted.

Winded but not seriously, Juliet picked herself up. The rain had penetrated through all her layers of clothing, and her teeth chattered. 'I thought you said she'd been backed?'

'Did I now? Well, I must be getting meself confused.' He looked up at the sky as if searching for divine inspiration.

He had slipped into a thick Irish brogue. Close up in the wet, hauled straight out of a muddy field, the mare did not look much like the horse of her dreams. She had her tail tucked up, and the ears remained flattened against the skull in a scowl. Yet, Espiritus or not, the mare had spirit and a bold attitude, the crucial quality for a decent event horse.

Over the years, Juliet had developed an instinct for which horses had what it took. Above all else, they had to be bold. She would need a lot of polish, but this youngster had potential. And part of her, that instinctive part she tried to heed more and more, told her that she must be Espiritus.

'Tommy Rafferty,' she warned, 'don't you dare give me any of that old kissing-the-Blarney-stone nonsense.'

He laughed. 'Okay, I confess. No, she's not been backed.'

'She hasn't even been handled, has she? Well, there's no way she could make the trip to England in this state. She'd go berserk. So, you have to promise me that as of tonight she's brought into the yard and handled regularly every day until she's calm and well mannered –'

'Yes, ma'am.'

'And don't interrupt. I'm not finished yet. And promise me that you'll get her used to loading and travelling in a horsebox. I've seen horses coming off that ferry and believe me, they're not a pretty sight.'

Her face crumpled as she thought about Gothic after he'd been imported, and she turned away briefly.

'Juliet.' He reached out to reassure her. 'There now, it's all right.

I promise you on my dog's life that she'll be the best-handled five-year-old that Shamus ever did export. Okay?'

'A five-year-old?' Her eyes narrowed. 'You told me she was four. Is this how it is with all your dealings? You know… a little bit dishonest? I thought…' She had assumed it would be different with her, but it seemed not. 'I'm beginning to think that Matt was right about you!'

He winced and held his hands up, palms towards her in a gesture of surrender. 'Okay, okay. I'm sorry. I promise I'll never mislead you again, but –'

She didn't let him finish. 'No buts, thank you, and while we're on the subject, who is this Aoife woman?'

'Ah, well…'

Juliet shot him a warning look that said *I am not in the mood to be trifled with.*

'That would be my sister, like.'

'Of course,' she said airily. Then her face darkened. 'Oh, poor Isabella, her sister Orla was a good friend. We used to chat for hours on the phone, but now we don't even speak. She unfriended me on Facebook. And I miss her so much. Grief just rolls out like an oil slick out at sea, doesn't it?'

Tommy reached over and gave her arm a squeeze. 'There now, of course, that's only natural that you're upset. But don't close your mind or your heart to this horse. She's the perfect type, brave and bold, and why… didn't you see the way she moves?'

Juliet sniffed, and her face brightened a shade. 'Oh, she moves well enough, although I don't know how with those splints. How did an unbroken five-year-old get splints, for heaven's sake?'

'That's her. That is… she takes herself on expeditions.'

Juliet looked puzzled. 'What do you mean?'

The horse tossed her head in pure agitation, anxious to be free. She nudged Tommy as if to say, "Come on, come on, get a move on. Let me get back to my field."

Tommy scratched his head. 'It's kind of hard to explain, but she jumps out of the field, and takes herself off on jaunts. I've no idea where she goes or why, and I've long given up trying to stop her as it's pointless. No matter how high I raise the fences, she still clears them. It seems like she's searching for something.'

'Well, lots of horses jump out of their fields.' She caught her breath in excitement. It must be, surely? Juliet looked at the mare, a striking-looking horse and powerful for a mare too. She glanced up at the sky, blinking at the rainbow and all the colours of light. She closed her eyes and made a wish.

'Sure, but how many horses do you know disappear at night like a comet trailing the moon? Out all night. Then she comes back by the light of dawn, all dripping in sweat and foam as if she's run the National or something.'

'Oh,' Juliet murmured as she gently reached out and touched the horse's nose. 'It's her. It's really her.'

'What?' he enquired, raising one eyebrow.

In spite of her damp clothes, a warm inner glow suffused her body, and she remembered the vision that had visited her in the still of the night. She gasped as she recalled the brown and white horse that had come, a skewbald. The vision had been a truly magical creature with stardust in its mane, surrounded by enchantment. Its proud bearing, the spirited swish of its tail, reminded her of her favourite poem. 'It's the horse that jumped into my dream,' she gasped, her eyes brimming with excitement. 'My wish came true.' And a wide grin spread across her face.

They returned to the house. Juliet did not notice that her wet clothes were sticking to her. Nothing mattered now that she had found Espiritus. Tommy gave her a towel, and one of his old shirts to wear, as he hung her clothes in front of the stove to dry. In the kitchen, the dogs milled this way and that, hungry and upset. Tommy had to feed them quickly and make amends with pats and apologies. Meanwhile, Juliet made herself useful by raiding the fridge. She rustled up some grilled bacon and fried eggs. 'How do you like your eggs cooked, over easy or sunny side up?'

'Whatever you're having,' he replied.

'Here we go. It's a calorie attack.' She served the eggs with thick wedges of brown bread and butter. She grinned as she put a plate in front of him. Since she had found Espiritus, she was back to her old Jennifer Aniston, *Sound of Music, Friends* self.

'Great, thanks.' He wolfed down the food with relish. 'So, you'll be taking her then? Believe me, it's a decision you'll never regret.'

'I think I like you better when you're not trying to sell me something,' Juliet said as she mopped up egg yolk with her bread. A hard-to-suppress smile tugged at the corner of her mouth.

Tommy laughed. 'Actually, I wasn't intending to sell her. I was thinking more along the lines of a gift.'

'I... oh, that's very kind, but that's not kosher. We'll need to agree on a price.'

Tommy laid his knife and fork together on his plate and scraped his chair across the floor as he got up. 'You realize that it's bad luck to refuse a Traveller's gift?' He moved so easily, so naturally towards her, and laid his hands on her shoulders. Thumbs outstretched, he slowly massaged her neck. A space had opened between them, and intimacy as smooth as silk poured in.

Juliet began to relax, but for no apparent reason, she suddenly thought about Matt, and what he would say about the horse. That was too bad to contemplate, and she screwed her eyes tight shut. A gift was out of the question. She hated being beholden to anyone. Tommy stroked her neck, sending little shivers of delight down her spine. Part of her wanted to yield to him and sink against his chest. But she knew that this had to stop before they went too far. It took every ounce of willpower that she possessed, but she shrugged and squirmed.

Tommy stopped and returned to his seat.

'But it's a horse that you bred yourself and named after your sister. So…' It came as a surprise to her when she realized just how much she craved his touch.

'Precisely. That's why I'd like you to have her. And surely, the fact is that, she's been looking for you and you've been looking for her. Well now, that must mean something, to be sure?'

Juliet gasped when he said that. True enough, she wanted that horse so badly. At least as badly as she wanted him. 'I don't know what to say.'

'Say that you'll come back tomorrow. There's something I want you to see.' He stared at her, holding her gaze until she looked away.

His words made her take a sharp, short breath. 'I… I can't. We're leaving tomorrow. Going back to England.'

'Ah.' He looked at her with a fierce intensity, his eyes burning. A Jack Russell whined and scratched at the door to be let out. Tommy did not seem to notice. 'Do you have to go?' he murmured.

'Oh,' she croaked, not knowing what to say. 'How about a cup of tea? Real tea though, none of that nettle stuff. You do have real tea, don't you?'

'What me, a Gypsy, not have any tea? How would I do my readings?' His smile was thin and watery.

'Do you… do readings, I mean?' She did not try and hide her relief that the subject had settled on smaller matters. Things had been getting too intense, too complicated. And she had an overwhelming urge to keep the conversation safe and neutral.

'No, that's an art that passes down the female line. Daughters are highly prized in Traveller families.' He filled the kettle and switched it on.

'Ah, my father would never make a great Traveller, then. He prefers boys – the whole passing on the family name thing, I guess.'

'Do you have any brothers?' He seemed subdued.

'Yes, one, Charles, I'm the oldest, how about you?'

'A sister, I'm the oldest too. No doubt there are a few more of us scattered around. Travellers are a dying breed, and Pa… well, he felt that he was doing his tribal duty, I expect. You know sort of keeping the numbers up.'

'Like Papa Riley's rig that was doing his part for the carthorse population.'

'I guess.' He poured the tea and set two mugs down on the table.

They both leaned forward at the same time and reached for the milk jug.

'Sorry,' she said, feeling awkward.

'After you,' he offered, looking uncomfortable.

A long silence ensued. Juliet hoped he'd know what do.

Finally, Tommy said, 'I like your perfume. It reminds me of hippies and open-air rock concerts.'

'Wow.' She laughed. 'I guess I know what you mean. It's made from patchouli oil, lavender, orange, and pine. I got it in the Maldives.'

'The selling point is?'

'Well according to the advertising blurb from a Japanese New Year wish: "Hear the rustling in the pines: let your prosperity be as constant as the greenness of my mantle, and may your friends stand as I do, steadfast against the adverse winds of change." '

'Poetry and perfume, hmmm, that's nice. What's it called?'

'Karma,' she said with a giggle.

He laughed. 'Ah, right, of course, how apt. Have you thought of a name for your new horse yet? I heard you call her something that I didn't quite catch.'

'You mean Gothic? Yes, her name's Espiritus.'

'Hang on a minute.' He put his cup down so suddenly that tea sloshed over the table in two muddy coloured pools. 'I bred that horse myself. The mother, my show jumper, kept me up all night for over two weeks. What you're suggesting, well, that's not reincarnation. That's possession!'

Juliet shrugged. 'I don't know, I try not to analyse it. Reincarnation is the belief that upon death the soul exits the body and then begins the preparations to come back within another physical form. I don't know how Gothic returned as Espiritus, your Aoife. It has something to do with acceptance. Accepting things that we can't always understand or rationalize.'

He looked at her for what seemed like an age. At last he spoke, softly, in his melodious, lilting tone. 'Well, I can't be pretending that I truly understand, but I can catch a vague impression. Get the gist of it, maybe. I'd like to understand some more. What do you think about tomorrow?'

'Yes,' she said in a voice that came from the heart, and her face brightened at the prospect. 'I think that would be great.' *What would such a day be worth?* Such a short time really, but where would she rather be than right here with Tommy? It occurred to her that perhaps she had wasted too many days already, and "now" would only appear this once.

CHAPTER TWENTY-NINE
Juliet

Later that evening, Juliet left Matt in the bedroom watching Sky Sports, and she headed down to the bar. As an athlete, she didn't often drink. But she felt like celebrating, so she ordered an exotic-sounding cocktail. As the bartender was shaking and mixing it, her phone rang – she glanced at the screen. DS Barrett came up on the display, so she accepted the call.

'Hi, it's after nine. Are you working overtime?'

'As ever,' DS Barrett confirmed. 'I spoke to Katya, and just wanted to fill you in. The details are still patchy, but here's what came up…'

Juliet interrupted her. 'Hold on, let me just take my drink and find a seat somewhere a little quieter.' This was easier said than done in Ireland, and in a bar. Talk about a challenge indeed. 'Thanks,' she said to the barman, and she headed for a quieter spot at the back. 'Okay, that's better. Fire away.'

'Well it goes back to the mid-eighteen-hundreds, in Apache territory in New Mexico.' Rosetta explained. 'The Mexicans frequently raided the Apaches, massacring women and children, scalping the men, and stealing their horses and belongings. In one such raid the chief's daughter was captured, exactly what happened to her is unclear, but she had a son, who subsequently witnessed the horrific death of his Mexican father, and his prize horse, in a bloodcurdling, brutal revenge attack by the Apaches.'

Juliet exhaled. 'Jeez, that's gross, but what does it mean exactly?'

Rosetta paused. 'I'm not sure. It will take some unravelling, I suspect. Obviously, I'll keep you posted, and if you discover anything which you think might be relevant, call me.'

'Sure,' Juliet agreed, wondering how all the strands would knit together.

There was a longer pause, until DS Barrett cleared her throat and recommenced. 'It would really help if you'd agree to past life regression, that –'

Juliet scowled. She didn't know why she was so averse to the idea, but it left her cold. 'Okay, got to go. Enjoy what's left of your evening.' She hung up and then she called Todd and told him all about Tommy and Espiritus.

'Slow down,' he said as her garbled words spilled out in a rush. 'What is it that's got you so animated?'

'An amazing skewbald… and Tommy's totally gorgeous. He laughs at all my jokes and puts up with my smart-ass comments.'

'Lord above,' Todd groaned, 'it must be lust. Your jokes are crap.'

'Thanks a bunch!'

'Hmmm, so this good-looking Lothario… what exactly does he do, apart from setting women's hearts alight, of course?'

'He's a Traveller, a horse dealer, a poet, oh, and so much more. And Pa, who brought him up, he's an animal communicator.'

Todd let out a low whistle. 'Jeez, this just gets better by the minute. And no doubt this Tommy is hung like Colin Farrell crossed with a Shire horse?'

Juliet chuckled. 'I've no idea.'

'Ah, my dear, and you're not planning to find out?'

'I'm not planning anything.' She feigned indignation. 'Really!' Then she added with a sigh, 'I never believed in this before, but I think he might be The One.'

'Oh my God, not… not *the One*. I so know all about this. As your friend, please let me give you a piece of advice.'

'What?'

Todd paused for emphasis. 'Just shag him and get it out of your system.'

'Todd! You're totally insufferable.'

'Oh, I know.'

'What happened with Barrie? Did he get the part?'

Todd let out a delighted cackle. 'No, thank heavens, so I can sleep at night for a while. Whoops, someone's at the door, got to dash. Keep me posted.'

* * *

That night, Juliet could not sleep, and she couldn't find the words to describe the rush of conflicting emotions that she felt. Whenever she thought of Tommy, his image filled her mind, and all the empty spaces in her heart. The man lying next to her in the bed, the man she thought she loved, simply was not the man she wanted to wake up with any more. Mentally, she had to detach from Matt, in order to move forward with someone else. She would never forget how her heart had fluttered the first time she'd heard Tommy's sing-song voice, so rhythmical and lilting.

She wriggled, looking for a warm, comfortable spot in the curve of the mattress. As he came to her in her mind's eye, a strange tingling sensation electrified her body. Imagining how it would be, the two of them together at last, she caressed herself with longing. Her eyes closed. Her lips parted in delicious anticipation. *Oh Tommy, Tommy,* she thought, her heart beating as skittishly as a girl's.

He took her in his arms.

She moaned.

A sigh escaped her lips. Finally, all the tension evaporated, and she felt herself relax. At last sleep finally came.

* * *

Later, when she stirred and woke at dawn, she turned the possibilities over a million times in her head. The spark between her and Tommy could not be denied. It was an itch that had to be scratched. Pure lust, perhaps? Yet, she sensed that she had reached a crossroads, a pivotal moment in her relationship with Matt. In her entire life, in fact.

Juliet found it impossible to resist the lure of the man who had replaced the horse in her dreams. She decided that it would be best if she slipped out and simply left Matt a note. No way could she risk her plans being derailed.

Juliet inched out from under the hot and clingy covers, desperate not to wake Matt. The bedclothes formed a soggy mass drenched with perspiration. She let out a sigh of relief. *No need to worry,* she thought. Matt snored in the leaden trance that went hand-in-hand with a serious overindulgence of alcohol.

Then to her horror, he stirred, his right arm flailing across the bed. It landed on her with a thud. A dead weight as heavy as a corpse.

'Argh… get offa me,' he muttered in his sleep.

He opened his mouth wide, and moaned. His breath smelt awful and rancid.

Juliet froze, paralysed with fear and hardly daring to breathe. If he woke up, she would be finished. Slowly and ever so gently, she lifted the arm off her chest and gave him a sharp poke in the ribs.

Matt grunted.

She held her breath for what seemed like forever. Then, at last, he rolled over, dragging the comforter with him. Juliet mouthed a silent prayer of thanks and slipped out of bed.

She couldn't risk a shower in case he woke up, so she doused herself in perfume, applied a quick coat of mascara and a dash of sheer lipstick. In a flash, she wriggled into her jodhpurs, grabbed her riding boots and handbag, and tiptoed across the room, praying that the floorboards wouldn't creak. She propped the note against the lamp on the bedside table for him to find:

I didn't want to wake you since you looked as if you needed your sleep. I've gone to look at a horse, changed flights to tomorrow.
I'll be back around tea time.
Juliet x.

She tiptoed out of the room, closing the door softly in case it squeaked. It did, setting her teeth on edge. She glanced over her shoulder to check that the coast was clear. *Please God, don't let him wake up now.*

She burst out the front door.

The cool morning air hit her hot cheeks, and she sighed. *Nearly there, almost made it,* she reassured herself. The sharp chunks of gravel underfoot hurt her feet, and she wondered if she should stop to put her boots on.

'Wait,' a man's voice commanded her.

Juliet hesitated, and her heart gave a lurch. She turned, hardly daring to breathe.

Kevin, one of the waiters, waved at her. 'Y' dropped something.'

'Oh, yes how careless of me.' She forced a smile and retrieved the lost riding boot.

Kevin eyed her up and down. 'Where y' off to so early an' all?'

'Riding, gotta run. Thanks.'

'Would ya be going out by Tommy Rafferty's place, by any chance? I saw ya out there yesterday.'

Juliet's jaw dropped open in disbelief. She mouthed a reply, but no words came. In a small town like Inis Cara, it would not take much to fan the flames of intrigue. All the atrocities in far-flung places across the world, why, who cared about those? How could they compare to a juicy nugget of scandal? She imagined that a betrothed horse-woman from England taking up with a local Gypsy might set a few tongues wagging.

'It's all right, an' all.' Kevin winked. 'Tommy's a mate o' mine.'

'Ah,' she said in a strangled voice. 'Well, thanks.' And she sprinted over to the car. Did Tommy make a habit of seducing women who were already spoken for? Bag, boots, and coat all got thrown into the car. Then, she scrambled into the driver's seat and turned the ignition key.

It will be just my luck if it decides to act up. Start, please start, she silently begged. The 4x4 obliged, and she sped off out of the parking lot, wheels spinning. She took the road across the heath that headed out towards Tommy's place.

Once the Silent Inn faded to a tiny speck in the rearview mirror, Juliet allowed herself to smile. It felt good to be spontaneous for a change. She had spent all her life playing a part – the perfect oldest child desperate for approval, the ambitious eventing rider, the dutiful partner. Somehow, since meeting Tommy, none of that mattered much anymore. For now, she could just be herself. Chewing her bottom lip like she'd done as a child whenever she had been naughty or fallen a little short of perfection, she wondered what Matt would do when he found the note. He would be furious, especially if she went ahead and bought a horse without his permission: especially Tommy's horse.

Oh well, she decided. She couldn't help it, and if Tommy turned out to be a notorious womaniser, so what? The moment alone mattered, and in the rush of exhilaration that swept over her, she was determined to give herself over to it.

She turned into Tommy's driveway, abandoned rather than parked the car, and ran barefoot, boots in hand, across the driveway. She couldn't wait to see him again.

Tommy stood in the kitchen, feeding the dogs meanwhile they waited obediently in a line. He turned and, when he saw Juliet, a smile broke across his face.

'Hi, you're an early bird.'

His tousled hair flopped over his forehead as if he had just got out of bed, and he looked so sweet and seductive.

'Oh, I thought I'd never escape,' she gasped. 'And then, just as I got to the car park, Kevin came after me and he asked me if I was on my way to see you.'

'I know I've had a phone call myself.' He shrugged. 'That's the trouble with small towns. They're a magnet for small minds.'

'What can we do?' Frown lines etched across her brow.

'Kevin won't say nothing. Besides, if the tongues are already wagging, why don't we give them a proper run for their money?'

He opened his arms and she tumbled towards him, scattering the dogs, who shot higgledy-piggledy across the room. She reached out and touched his cheek, relishing the feel of the unshaven stubble. He ran his fingers through her hair, teasing the tresses that curled around her face.

In an instant, their lips touched, and she knew that she never wanted to be parted from him. They kissed for a long time. The smell, the taste of him was better than the finest champagne. Here in the kitchen, he in a shirt, she barefoot. It felt like the most natural thing in the world. At last, she broke free and leaned away from him, breathing hard, overwhelmed by her hot, hungry desires, but worried where they would lead.

'How about something to eat?' she gasped.

'Later,' he murmured. 'I'll be dressed in a jiffy. Then there's something I want you to see.'

Juliet smiled as he went upstairs to get changed. She followed him upstairs to the restroom. As she washed her hands at the sink, she froze as she caught sight of the woman's lipstick left so casually on the shelf under the mirror. What was he up to, and more to the point, who had he spent the night with? She returned to the kitchen, lipstick in her pocket, wondering if she should confront him.

Tommy came down dressed in faded jeans, walking boots, and a sheepskin gilet over his shirt. He handed her an ancient leather flying jacket with a sheepskin collar. Outside, they went along the thicket, a procession in single file. Tommy and the dogs went first, with Juliet following. She wondered if she should ask him about the lipstick now. He would probably just tell her to mind her own business. After all, she thought with a sigh, she hadn't known him long enough to stake any claims.

She didn't like the thicket. The undergrowth was so dense that it seemed as if very little sunlight could penetrate it. The brambles snatched and grabbed, tangling themselves in her hair.

'How's Espiritus?' Juliet said. The thought of him spending the night with another woman made her feel miserable.

'She's fine, which is more than can be said for the stable.'

'Oh dear,' Juliet said with a faint grin. 'Where are we going?'

'Exploring,' he said and beckoned for her to follow him deep into the thicket. She hesitated.

It smelt disgusting, and it looked dim and airless.

Her feet felt glued to the spot. Tiny beads of perspiration broke out on her forehead.

Tommy stopped to look back at her. 'Are you okay?' His voice reflected considerable tenderness and concern.

She shook her head, looking for an alternative route. *I can't do this,* she thought, trembling. *I can't, it's too dark.*

No air.

Tommy called her name and reached for her hand, coaxing her to take a few steps. The stagnant air cloyed in her nostrils, making it difficult to breathe. A spider's web snared itself in her face, heavy with decomposing flies. As she inhaled, it slipped, silken and slimy, into her mouth.

She gagged.

Oh, god, how repulsive. The thought of those thick hairy legs made her skin crawl. Her arms flailed, and she screamed a bloodcurdling sound.

Tommy rushed to her side. 'What's wrong?' But Juliet continued to utter panic-stricken shrieks. Tommy took her in his arms and stroked her hair. 'There, don't fret there.'

'Spiders, I-I can't stand them,' she sobbed. 'At boarding school, they… they used to put them in my bed.'

'Here now, let me help.' He brushed her cheek lightly and wiped the cobweb away.

'I can't stand this place. It gives me the creeps.'

'How old were you when you were sent away to school?'

Juliet bit her lip. 'I was seven, I hardly ever saw my parents. They were in the Far East a lot of the time. The… the other girls went home during the holidays, but mother thought it wasn't safe in Bangkok and I was too young. Even when I was older, she said the same thing. And I got farmed out to relatives. Once, I came to Ireland to stay with my aunt. That was fun. Then, I had to return to school, and at school, the matron wasn't very nice. I was difficult… angry, I guess. It felt like I'd been abandoned.'

'Okay, so what happened?'

'She… she used to lock me in the cellar in the pitch-black with the insects… spiders…' Juliet shuddered in a convulsion-like spasm. 'And rats.'

'Oh, come here, you poor thing.' He enfolded her in his arms and kissed her tenderly on the forehead.

Tommy handled Juliet with considerable skill, as if she was a young horse confronting water where unimaginable sea monsters lurked beneath the surface. He made it clear that he would wait for as long as it took.

'Yikes,' Juliet said, still hesitant. What if there were more spiders crouching in the undergrowth, ready to ambush her as she went past? She simply couldn't bear it.

'Come on. It's not much farther, and you'll be glad you came, I promise.'

'Maybe,' she said as she dragged herself forward. Out of the corner of her eye she saw something move. A fat hairy spider squatting in the middle of its gossamer trap. 'Oh help, there's one. Kill it!'

'Don't worry, I've got it. There,' he said, flicking the spider and its web to the ground. 'You're safe now.'

'Yes.' She trembled.

After a short distance, her face registered relief as the narrow, gloomy track fanned out into a woodland clearing. Juliet blinked, her eyes adjusting to the sunlight that streamed through to illuminate the space.

She sneaked a glance at Tommy out of the corner of her eye. He appeared composed and carefree. That was what she loved about him. Tommy had stopped, his back pressed against a gnarled old oak. He threw sticks for the dogs to retrieve casually, as if they had all the time in the world. She watched him, so absorbed and at ease with himself, finding such immense self-assurance enthralling. Why didn't he take her in his arms and sweep her off her feet? Couldn't he see the passion in her eyes? And how could he mistake the hungry desire of her body language?

The silence made her uncomfortable. She didn't know what he had planned or what he was thinking. 'Shall we get moving?'

'Shush.' He raised a finger to his lips. 'Listen now, can you hear that?'

Juliet heard the sound of water, faint and muffled in the background. 'Is there a stream or something?' she asked.

'To be sure, it's a waterfall. I thought you might like to see it.'

'Oh.' Her voice quavered.

'According to local folklore, this is a fairy dell.'

'Wow that's incredible.' She smiled to herself. After all, yesterday, she'd arrived unannounced and asked him if he believed in fairies. It seemed that he did indeed.

'Can you feel the ancient rhythms pulsing beneath your feet?'

'I'm not sure, but it feels…' She searched for that perfect word. The one word that would capture her feelings for the place and most of all for him… 'Magical.'

'Well now, it's time for my morning swim.' His eyes twinkled as he added, 'And you know how us Gypsies are about our superstitions and our rituals.'

She threw her head back and laughed. She hadn't laughed that way for a long time.

'Come on.' He reached down, took her by the hand, and led her across the clearing. And beyond that, about a hundred and fifty yards down a well-worn track. The track ran alongside a stream, which twisted and turned around a sharp corner until it spread into a pool at the bottom of a waterfall. Across the mouth of the waterfall, a rope bridge swayed a little in the gentle breeze.

The waterfall was magnificent, with cascades of foamy water which spilled over like a three-tiered wedding cake. A wedding cake very similar to the one she'd imagined for her and Matt's wedding. She thought of Matt and all his worldly experience. He could make love all night without tiring. Juliet bit her lip. She wondered why life was so darn complicated. If anyone could, Matt could deliver her the horse to get her Olympic goals back on track. How long would it last – the cake, her and Matt, her feelings for Tommy? And it occurred to her that an affair was a temporary, transient thing. But guilt would remain like a stain on her heart.

Alongside the rock pool, the path climbed steeply towards the pitch of the waterfall. They picked their way across the huge grey slabs of rock that had been worn smooth with the passage of time. The dogs tried to follow, but Tommy sent them back, and they obediently turned around and trotted off homewards.

'Come on, shoes off,' Tommy ordered, turning back and grabbing her hand. 'And be careful, the stones are slippery and covered in moss, pretty treacherous.'

They scrambled uphill over rocks and fallen trees until they reached the rickety old bridge. It swayed across the yawning mouth of the waterfall. It looked as if it had been crafted by Peter Pan and the Lost Boys out of bits of driftwood and string.

She had a sinking feeling about this. It had to be the most decrepit bridge that she'd ever seen, like the ones in action movies which always collapsed just as the enemy got to the halfway stage.

'Is it safe?' Juliet enquired as she tested the first part with her toe.

'Yeah. It's a replica of the rope bridge at Carrick-a-Rede. You have to run across without stopping though. At any rate, that's what I've been doing ever since I was a boy. It always reminded me of a cross between a spider's web an' me old granny's crocheting. You first, there you go.'

'Thanks. Sending the woman across first in case it isn't safe, I presume? How gallant of you,' she said with a faint-hearted laugh.

'Away with you now, where's your spirit of adventure?'

Juliet tossed her head and jutted out her chin. There was no way she would be outdone by a man. No way. When she stepped onto the bridge, it emitted an ominous creak, and she touched her unicorn pendant for luck.

She steeled herself. Then with gritted teeth, she took off, pausing from time to time to steady herself on the ropes. When she reached the middle, the timber slats groaned, and the bridge creaked towards the waterfall. Her stomach lurched, and she grabbed the frayed rope handrail. The wooden struts had long ago rotted in places, and she could see the dark, still water of the pool way below.

Not a good idea to look down.

She raised her chin and set her jaw in determination. Her legs felt leaden as she willed them into action. This old bridge couldn't get the better of her. Tommy came up close behind, and at the end they collapsed together in a heap, giggling and exhilarated.

'Wow, so fun. Should we do it again?' she said.

He shook his head and gestured for her to follow him, a slow descent until they came to a large flat rock about halfway down the track. Below them the final tier of the waterfall spilled out, all bubbles and foam, into the large rock pool.

'Do you know the legend of Tír na nÓg?' he asked.

'No, but why do I get the feeling that I'm about to get a lesson in Irish folk history?'

He laughed. 'Well, it happens I'll be telling it to you one o' these days when you're in the right mood. Anyhow, this is the place where the unicorns come to watch the young virgins bathing. That's what I wanted to show you.'

'Seriously, unicorns? That's incredible.' Juliet stared into the depths of the rock pool, imagining a beautiful girl swimming naked as the unicorn, timid and quivering, approached with its muzzle outstretched.

'Don't you mean virgins, how incredible?'

She looked up and saw him grinning. 'Oh, you're joking. I'm such an idiot.'

'No, it's true. There are hoof prints at the edge of the water. Come on, I'll show you.'

She looked at him, and, in one swift movement that made her gulp, he had removed his jacket, and then his T-shirt to reveal a washboard-hard torso. *Holy shit, that's some six-pack,* she thought, with an admiring glance. The sun had heated up the day, and she felt hot and flushed.

'What are you doing?' She stared at him disapprovingly, her hand resting on her hip.

'Skinny-dipping. Come on, get a move on.'

Juliet's jaw dropped a fraction. They were heading into dangerous territory. Trouble – *big* trouble – was brewing. 'You can't just dive in and… well, it doesn't look deep enough.'

'Are you planning to go swimming with your kit on?' He unbuttoned his jeans and inched the flies down a fraction.

Juliet held her breath, and then with unbridled eagerness that Miss Roberts, her school form mistress, would have described as "unseemly haste," she removed her jacket and unbuttoned her shirt to reveal her bra. Tommy grinned encouragingly as she let her shirt trail from her fingers and fall in a heap onto the rocks.

She checked him out like a farmer scrutinizing a herd of prize beef. Not an ounce of fat in sight. He had an all-over tan, bronzed and swarthy, with a little shadowing of hair on his chest. The hair looked soft and dark, and she had the urge to reach out and touch.

God, she wouldn't say no to that.

Growing bolder, she stared at him, and he stared back, holding her gaze for a long time until, in the end, she grew flustered and glanced away.

'Your forfeit,' he said.

It seemed like a childhood game in the woods. Stick thin skinny, she was not. In fact, her stomach had a mind of its own. She sucked it in a bit to compensate, and thrust out her chest, hoping that he liked a little soft, womanly flesh. Tommy studied her slowly, not like a boy now but a man who knew what he likes and liked what he saw. She wondered if Tommy Rafferty had ever really been young. It seemed to her that he had been born all-knowing, especially in the ways of horses and women.

He reached out and drew her towards him, slipping his arm around her until her chest was in close contact with his. She could feel his breath on her cheek, steady and even. The smell of him, clean and masculine yet earthy too, made her light-headed. She burrowed her nose in his armpit and drank in the smell. Not earthy exactly, but musky like an animal's lair. It was a smell that made her skin tingle, stirring something deep within. She tilted her face towards his, and they kissed hungrily. She never wanted to be parted from him.

How long they kissed, she couldn't say. But it felt like an awakening, as if she had always known the taste and the feel of him. They leaned apart to catch their breath and look at each other, their eyes shining.

'Can you feel it?'

She reached out and caressed the bulge in his jeans. 'Hmmm.' She sighed.

'No.' He grinned. 'I meant can you feel the magic of this place?'

'Yes. Oh yes.'

He leaned towards her and drew her to him. They kissed, and he placed his hands, one lightly supporting the small of her back, and with the other he unhooked her bra so that it fell in a heap at her feet. Juliet closed her eyes as he caressed her breasts, relaxing into the moment and giving herself over to it. She knew that they had crossed the line, beyond the point of return. He nuzzled her earlobe, and slowly caressed her neck with his tongue. She quivered. He nibbled her ear, her neck, her lips, and finally her nipples, which stiffened and gathered at his touch. Through her half-closed eyes, she watched the bull rushes, as tall and majestic as Busby soldiers, swaying gently in the breeze by the water's edge.

Tall and majestic – tall and erect, she thought, stroking his chest and tracing the outline of his ribs. Travelling with deliberate slowness, she inched down the zipper of his jeans and slipped her fingers inside. He reciprocated, gently caressing between her thighs.

Eventually, with considerable reluctance, they moved apart. She held her breath and licked her lips as he removed his jeans. His body looked coppery against the backdrop of the forest foliage, and the jade of the ancient trees mottled by the fresh lime of new spring growth. Then she sat down, and he pulled off her boots. Unassisted, she wriggled out of her jodhpurs, tugging and pulling at them until she was free. He watched intently, his eyes glazed dark with desire.

He knelt down on the flat grey rock, which nature had somehow rendered up from the riverbed, and arranged their jackets ready for them to lie on. After a while, he gently coaxed her down until they lay side by side. The surface of the rock was hard and unforgiving. For a moment, she wished they were indoors, in bed to be precise, with a sheet draped artfully over her modesty.

The spring sun failed to heat the air very much, but she felt hot even as her back pressed against the jackets forming a thin layer over the cool, grainy surface of the rock. In response to the arousal, her skin had flushed red and mottled as strawberries and whipped cream. As delightful as this image was, it was ruined by the furry black forest of her pubes. *Shit,* she thought, *why didn't I get a bikini wax?* Not that Tommy seemed to mind.

'You know, I've wanted you since the moment we first met,' he said.

'Really? But you always seem so uninterested.' Cue angelic hosts and fluttering doves. He'd noticed her from the very onset.

'Hmmm.' His breathing came in heavy bursts as he lowered himself on top of her. His chest brushed her nipples, and his erection teased and tantalised. 'Do I seem uninterested now?'

'Hardly.' She groaned as he kissed her with little darting movements. Her skin tingled in delicious anticipation. She licked her lips and traced her fingertips lightly across his buttocks.

'Oh, please, I want you,' Juliet moaned arching herself towards him and closing her eyes. 'Oh yes.' She gasped at the first potent thrust. She drew him inside, all-encompassing like a shoreline that rushes to greet the sea. She imagined a seagull high above the sea, hovering in a cloudless sky. The air was filled with the zesty scent of pinecones. The bird was soaring higher and higher.

His breathing came in shallow bursts, and all his movements had an urgent edge. But Juliet knew that he would hold himself back. He would wait and let her choose the moment, no matter how long it might take. Somewhere deep in the core of her being, she sensed that he had already been waiting for a very long time.

Forever, perhaps?

CHAPTER THIRTY

Juliet

The second time they made love, it flowed. Less hurried, less frenzied. Afterwards, they lay together for a long time, wrapped in each other's arms, listening to the waterfall and basking in the slow-fading sun. Eventually they stirred, and she watched in admiration as he dived from the rock into the pool. As she poked her nose over the edge of the rock, Tommy surfaced and waved, beckoning to her to join him. She held her breath, screwed her eyes tight shut, and jumped off the rock ledge into the unknown. The cold water knocked the air from her chest. Juliet gasped as she came up to the surface. Her teeth were chattering, and it took some time for her body to acclimatize.

'Keep moving. You'll soon warm up,' Tommy said. 'Come on, I'll race you to the other side.'

Her dainty breaststroke made no impression on Tommy's powerful crawl, and he won by miles.

'How deep is it?' She peered into the indigo water, which seemed dark and unfathomable, rather like Tommy. He did not appear to live on the same plane as everyone else. He had this curious air of detachment that suggested he operated on his own terms, a law unto himself. She had an impression, not exactly an instinct, of a core of pure titanium. She sat on a rock under the waterfall with the spray cascading down her neck and shoulders and watched him swimming.

Tommy flipped over onto his back and called out, 'You look like a mermaid.' His words echoed.

She laughed, warm and glowing from their lovemaking. She tried to pinpoint her feelings, to tie them down in some tangible way. The rush of an illicit affair, indeed. But somehow, as she turned that notion over, it did not seem right. The word *inevitability* popped into her head, as if, after thousands of years in separate galaxies, a shooting star and a comet had fallen into the same constellation at last.

It felt so natural being with Tommy and so right.

She knew in a strange, unfathomable way of knowing, that they'd met before, eons ago.

Together, they left the pool and clambered back to the rock, their rock, to dry off in the watery sunlight and get dressed. They lay down together, and Tommy had his head resting in his hands as he stared at the sky with a faraway look in his eyes.

'What're you thinking about?' she said.

'A poem, I'm saying it over in me head.'

'Is there any chance of you reciting it out loud? What's it called?'

'Ah… *The Bright Field*.'

'Who's it by? An Irish poet?'

'No, the Welsh poet, R. S. Thomas. It's about looking back on life and feeling, maybe, that you ruined something or regretted something that you never did.' He paused. 'I was wondering, you see, if that's how it'll be for us.'

'Did you learn it at school?' Juliet's heart quickened. She did not want to get drawn into the matter of their future together. Why spoil things? *Oh*, she sighed internally, *why was life so complicated?*

'Yes, but my education was from life. Part by Pa, and the rest self-taught. Maths and science had no interest for me, only things of beauty – art, literature, and poetry, especially poetry. In this day and age, with everything in hyper-drive, it's becoming a dying art, and that's a great shame, because if we lose poetry, we are all in danger of losing the sense of rhythm in our lives.'

'Why yes, you're right. I'd never really thought of it like that. These are sound-bite times, where website hits have replaced minutes, although the internet has some positive aspects.'

'Such as?'

'Well, amazing access to unlimited information, and some bad news too, of course. Did you hear about the latest ISIS attack in Rome?'

Tommy shook his head. 'I don't know why they go to Syria, or wherever – for training, mind. They could come over here to Ireland. We could do a first-rate job of outsourcing terrorists.'

Juliet looked thoughtful. 'The provisional IRA didn't invent terrorism though, did they?'

'No, they merely elevated the scale and methods of execution.'

He sighed. 'I've no time for such things. How much strife, war, and information do we need to blow our minds? I reckon computers and televisions are bad news for human relationships. They prevent us from reaching out and connecting with one another in a deep or meaningful way. With computers and televisions as false prophets, small wonder that we're turning into a load of spiritual junkies.'

'We're getting into soapbox territory, what's the answer?'

'Oh, I don't know. Maybe I'm just out of tune with the times, but I'd like to slow the world down a little, I guess.' He sighed. 'Ah yes, that reminds me of my favourite verse about the passage of time:

> *Time is all we possess and in the end time ravages all*
> *Like as the waves make towards the pebbled shore,*
> *so do our minutes hasten to their end.*
> *Each changing place with that which goes before,*
> *in sequent toil all forwards do contend.*

'That's a Shakespeare sonnet. It's one of my favourites too.' She shivered as the sun disappeared behind a cloud.

'Wow, remind me never to play Trivial Pursuit with you.'

Tommy caressed her arm and reached for her hand. 'Come on, we'd better be getting back.'

* * *

Back in the kitchen, it felt a little awkward. Juliet made small talk, while Tommy made nettle tea sweetened with honey. She crinkled her nose, convinced that it would taste gross. Hesitantly, she took a sip. To her surprise, it tasted much better than she had expected. She looked around, and her eyes were drawn to the dresser which was filled with trophies and cups. A random thought popped into her head, and she remembered the ruby-red lipstick. What kind of a woman wore that?

She cleared her throat. 'I couldn't help noticing that one of your visitors left something behind. I found a lipstick in your restroom.' She waved it at him. She couldn't breathe. She couldn't speak. Her heart clattered furiously against her ribs. His eyes followed her outstretched arm. She couldn't contemplate the thought of losing him to another woman.

'Ah, it's not how you think.' He squirmed, and she could swear that for a split second, before he managed to compose himself, the expression on his face had been one of pure guilt.

'How is it, then?' Juliet closed her eyes momentarily, the mere thought of him seeing someone else constricted her chest until it hurt.

'It belongs to a friend of mine.'

'Really?' Her voice was even, but it took every ounce of control that she possessed.

Tommy smiled. 'You can trust me on this. There's no one else. I swear to you.' He looked at her, the cup pressed against his lips until he spoke at last. 'So, you're leaving tomorrow. What're you going to do about the horse?'

Juliet squirmed. 'I don't know, I don't know. It's so difficult.' He seemed sincere about the lipstick. She decided to give him the benefit of the doubt about other women, but she didn't know what to do about Espiritus.

'That can't be it? Are you just going to turn your back and walk away?'

'Oh, you know how it is with Matt. He's never going to let me have the horse anyway.' She wanted that mare so much. Maybe she could lie about where the horse had come from. Anything to avoid an almighty scene. Right now, with so much at stake, and Matt on the brink of getting a four-star horse already entered for Badminton, and then with the World Equestrian Games ahead, she couldn't risk upsetting him. She sighed, knowing deep down that she would tell Matt the truth just as she had always tried to do.

'Well, what's it got to do with him?'

'Everything. We're engaged, and he's my business partner. We're a team.' She felt like a stalked animal desperate to take flight. Matt had a powerful hold over her, and she couldn't explain it. When they had first met, he seemed so streetwise, whereas her background had been so protected. Matt could take care of himself. He could take care of things, take care of her. Why would she trade certainty and security for an unknown future with Tommy?

'Sounds like a mighty fine cage to me. Now that I'm beginning to get to know you better, I think what you'd really like is to be set free.'

Juliet slid off her stool and paced the kitchen. She didn't want to hear this at all, especially because it struck a chord somewhere. 'I can't, I can't. It's too much, too soon.'

Tommy drained his cup and shook his head. 'If you don't mind me saying, I think you're getting in the way of yourself.'

'Oh,' she said through gritted teeth, 'you're so… infuriating.' Deep

225

down, his words resonated. But no way would she admit it. *Oh, Earth, moon and stars, what had they had set in motion?*

'I don't get it. What's holding you back? What're you afraid of?'

'I told you. Matt.'

'Not really. You're erecting barriers all over the place. It just seems such a waste to let your fears, and someone else's expectations set the frontiers of your destiny. You owe it to yourself, and the horse.'

'Yes,' she sighed. 'You're right. I'll ask Shamus to make all the arrangements.' She would have the horse at any price, and she thrust out her chin in determination. *To hell with the consequences,* she thought.

'Great.' He flashed a dazzling smile at her.

Juliet glanced at her watch and bent to scoop up her handbag. 'Damn, I'd better get going.' Yet, leaving him was proving too difficult. She felt as if they were entwined, his edges blurring into hers. She sighed and forced herself to draw away.

'Right.' Tommy escorted her to the driveway, and to her car.

She jumped in behind the wheel all brisk and purposeful, and then she crumpled.

'What are we going to do?' Juliet sighed.

'Let's not fret about that now. Just get a good night's sleep.' He kissed one eyelid at a time, then the tip of her nose, and lightly on her lips.

'Bye.' She gave a little wave out of the open window and moved off at a crawl. In the mirror, she watched him watching her until he receded into the distance and disappeared.

CHAPTER THIRTY-ONE

Rosetta
Yorrex

Saturday evening arrived, and outside a sweltering blanket of humidity descended, which seemed to be pervading all corners of Rav's tidy-freak flat. The windows were open, ostensibly to let some cool air in.

It ain't working, Rosetta thought as she swatted her hair off her face and tucked it behind her ear. She'd been invited round for supper, a vegetarian curry. A nice thought, but was it a date, or something else? There had been another terrorist attack in Rome. Thank heavens they'd managed to get Ed extracted from that whole scene. Rosetta turned her attention back to Rav as he emerged from the kitchen.

'Do you want a hand with anything?'

'It's, fine thanks. Well now, what is EPIS, and how did you get involved?' Rav asked as he set their plates down on the dining table.

'Cheers,' she said. 'It smells delicious.' *So, it was not first and foremost a date, more of a fishing expedition,* she deduced with a tinge of disappointment. Unless of course, that was just his way of breaking the ice. 'Well, it's a bit like the Freemasons. My father's a Freemason, all gloves, aprons, initiation ceremonies, and tight-sealed lips under threat of death or something.' Rosetta paused, she had to be careful, as EPIS was hot on issues of unauthorised disclosure of information. 'What did the commissioner tell you when I was seconded?'

He gave her a querying look, before shaking his head. 'Not a great deal, and every time I try to find out more, he raises his hands to cut off the imminent line of questioning.'

'Right,' she laughed, taking a forkful of curry. 'But you know I'm a witch, a psychic, and I work for the global intelligence service?'

Rav swallowed and nodded. 'But I'd like to get a better understanding of what exactly it is you – and they – actually do.'

'Ah, well I'm not going to be able to go into much detail.' Her voice dropped to a loud whisper. EPIS, just to make certain their employees held their tongues, did prolific background checks, kept files on them all, going right back to birth. With the files maintained current right to the minute. And similar files held on family and friends – as an insurance policy – perhaps? Rosetta pondered a while. She wasn't keen to find out. 'Well, it's not the first time that programmes have been set up using psychics to help the American intelligence services. Remember when they found out that the Russians were taking a close interest in parapsychology?'

Rav scrunched his forehead, trying to recall. 'Vaguely,' he muttered.

'There was a team set up to investigate telepathy – extrasensory perception, or ESP. Professor May was the research director of the Pentagon's ESP programme. They were conducting experiments to see if it had validity for psychic spying missions, for instance. The unit was disbanded to a great media fanfare: End of an *Aura* for CIA Mystics, and so forth. Back in the nineties, there was also a spoof book and a film. Do you remember *Men Who Stare at Goats*?'

Rav looked blank.

'It was about the US Army, using psychic soldiers to explore New Age concepts, and the military applications of the paranormal. The title refers to attempts to kill goats by staring at them and stopping their hearts.'

'That's fiction, right?' Rav shot her a querying look which said: *please tell me it's not real.*

'Sometimes the truth is stranger than fiction.' Rosetta tucked into her curry and set about tearing off a strip of naan bread, which she quickly demolished.

The colour drained from his face, and he assumed a grim expression. 'How much further out there does it get?'

A hell-of-a-lot, she thought. Apparently, even the President had been rebuffed when he tried to get the UFO files opened, and when he tried to make enquiries into aliens. EPIS told him that his security clearance wasn't high enough to warrant any disclosure, which suggested to her that the military and the intelligence agencies were in control and actually called all the shots.

In Rav's case, it would be best if she bombarded him with innuendo and rumour to throw him off the scent.

'In America, conspiracy theories abound. In 1979, an engineer who specialised in explosives claimed that he had helped build an underground base close to Dulce, a quaint town in New Mexico near the border with Colorado. Dulce is not really a tourist destination. There's a motel, a petrol station, and a few stores, and its setting of rocky mountains covered with pine trees and orange scrubland. It is also the tribal headquarters of the Jicarilla Apache Indians. The population, including the Indians on the reservation, is around three thousand seven hundred and fifty in total. It's claimed that underneath the tangled bush, craggy cliffs, and steep rock formations, there are labyrinths and a deep underground mega-complex where strange experiments abound, reminiscent of the Netflix series *Stranger Things*. Have you heard of that?' she asked.

Rav shook his head, fork poised, about to put food into his mouth.

'OMG, you must watch it. It's amazing, kind of an EPIS-world with kids and a retro theme.'

'I don't have Netflix.' He sounded rather bored and supressed a yawn.

'Right.' Rosetta grinned. 'Well, you can come around to my place for a return supper date, and we can watch it then. It's old but awesome.'

Rav looked a tad less than enthusiastic at the prospect. 'So, you were saying?'

'Right, where was I? Ah, yes, telling you about Dulce, although, I'm just using that as an example, of course. There are some fifteen, secret, supposed military bases in the USA alone. Do you remember Area 51 in the film *Independence Day*, or *Star Gate* in Colorado Springs?'

Rav laced his fingers on top of his head, as if to help him think. 'But these are places in films – fictional, not real, right?'

Rosetta sucked in her cheeks. 'Of course. I'm just being illustrative, so you can get a gist of what EPIS is, and why I joined.'

He frowned, and he scratched his forehead. 'Sorry, please go ahead.'

Usually, the best way to sow confusion was to spin a far-fetched version of the truth. She continued with the description.

'Stories and rumours of aliens, UFO sightings, strange lights, and aviation phenomena abound. Curious tales spread, describing sightings of genetically engineered animals such as the "Cabbit" – a half-cat, half-rabbit creature – and local police have investigated curious incidents of mutilated cattle. On one ranch near the Navajo River, some thirteen miles east of Dulce, cattle were attacked, left half-devoured and covered in a strange translucent slime which glowed in the dark.' Rosetta paused to allow time for this to sink in. 'I guess over the past few decades or so, Dulce seems to have attracted a higher than usual concentration of paranormal activity. But this could just be like a magnet attracting conspiracy theories – none of which are conclusively proven to date. But watch this space, perhaps? Do you follow conspiracy theories? There are lots about 9/11, for example?'

Rav shook his head. 'I don't watch news channels on the basis that's its invariably bad stuff – and who needs that?'

Rosetta continued. 'Dulce mainly attracts UFO tourists who claim that people abducted by aliens have ended up there and are being experimented on. British conspiracy theorist Clive Speight believed that people were being subjected to mind-control experiments, and after his untimely death in Poland a few days before he was due to give a lecture on UFOs and cover-ups by the American and other governments, his family believed that he was murdered as part of a cover-up.'

'I see… no, actually, I don't.' Rav got up and cleared the table. He looked bemused. 'But what does EPIS really do, and how did you get involved?' Rav returned from the kitchen armed with a cloth to wipe the table. He looked concerned, sat down, and then got up again, this time to get dessert – Eton Mess – which he set down on the table. 'It seems potentially quite dangerous. Too many vested interests, perhaps?'

Rosetta gulped down a sweet mouthful. 'Delicious, thanks,' she enthused. 'Okay, what I'm trying to convey is there's always huge controversy, swirling conspiracy theories, secrecy and subterfuge, claims, denials, and counter-claims. There are forces out there that will not hesitate to discredit you, destroy you if necessary, to cover up what's really going on. Mark my words. Remember Dr. Kelly and Tony Blair's weapons of mass-not-destruction? The powers that be won't hesitate to strike against you if it serves their ends. So, things are never quite what they seem.'

'Is EPIS kind of like sci-fi spooks?' Rav asked.

Rosetta shrugged. 'I'm not entirely sure what you mean. EPIS are the good guys who hold the forces of darkness in check. AI and robots will be programmed with the values EPIS upholds and all the data is block-chain based, so no one person, or central authority, can take control. What's important is to keep an open mind. Remember, there's always a huge division between the sceptics and the believers.

Then, you have the undecided. They, the powers that be, are particularly hostile to theories about aliens. They'll say things like "It's UFO hogwash!" or, "Here comes another conspiracy theory from the UFO nuts." And then we respond by wondering what they're trying to cover up.'

'What do you reckon about UFOs and aliens?' Rav polished off the last of his dessert.

'I'm open-minded, of course,' she said, waving her arm dismissively. She had to duck this one. If the President didn't have ET clearance, sure-as-shit Rav didn't. Rosetta cleared her throat and continued. 'My mum says she's seen spaceships in her backyard on a few occasions. Our relative, Sir Fredrick Hoyle, was the royal astrologer of big bang theory fame, and he missed out on the much-deserved Nobel prize because he queried Darwin's version of evolution, wrote sci-fi, and suggested that life on Earth was sparked from cosmic dust or viruses. He was ridiculed over this. He and his colleague, Chandra – hang on a moment...' She did a Google search on her phone. 'Chandra Wickramsinghe, developed a theory or hypothesis called panspermia – that life here was seeded from outer space.'

'Aren't they exploring that – the astrobiologists? I mean, they're like trying to find out if carbon-based life is universal, somewhere out there?' Rav made a sweeping gesture with his arm.

'Hmmm, so many out-there's, so little time, eh? Where are they looking, exactly?'

Rav perked up. 'I don't watch much TV, as you probably guessed, but I do love the Discovery channel. I gathered that when it came to the shortlist for life-supporting exoplanets, or moons, the favourites are Mars, Europa, and Enceladus. That last one's particularly interesting as it's an ocean world. There's some sort of inter-disciplinary group called SETG looking into life out there.'

Rosetta shook her head. 'Don't you just love acronyms? What's SETG when it's at home?'

'Or away.' Rav laughed, scratching his head. 'I think it stands for Search for Extra-Terrestrial Genomes or something.'

'That's cool. It reminds me of the song: "*We are stardust, we are golden, we are billion year old carbon.*"'

'Ah, yes,' Rav exhaled. 'Joni Mitchell, I've got that track. I'll put some music on.' He stood up and activated the surround sound system.

Rosetta paused, relaxing into the mood music. Rav's place was quite minimalistic but the music system, like the fittings and furnishings, was high-end and top of the range. 'Just wondering, but has anyone warned Mars?'

Rav cocked his head on one side and arched an eyebrow. 'About?'

'Musk and the takeover bid!'

'Ah, yes, he's going to colonise it, isn't he?'

Rosetta rolled her eyes up to the ceiling. 'First, he sends a dummy in a spacesuit called Star-man, plus a cherry red electric car.'

'Yeah.' Rav laughed. 'You have to admire his chutzpah. Whatever next, eh?'

'The Big Fucking Rocket fuelled by liquid methane, that's what's next. Stick it to 'em, Elon and BFR.' Then, she lowered her voice and leaned across the table, closer to Rav. 'This next bit is confidential, so you can't disclose it, otherwise, something really bad might happen. Promise you'll never repeat it.'

'Then don't tell me.' Rav looked startled.

'Man up. Just don't go blabbing,' she said with a chuckle. 'I trust you, and your total discretion.'

'Thanks.' Rav nodded appreciatively.

'UFOs are not *per se* the primary concern for EPIS, although the linguist researchers and the digital innovation teams are working with telepathy, to facilitate alien communication. That's profoundly advantageous, don't you think?' She didn't mention that not long ago she'd had a call from the delighted Gandalf breaking the news that he'd had a major breakthrough and cracked some of the Blue aliens' code.

Rav rolled his eyes and remained silent. 'I don't know what to make of what I'm not supposed to know.'

'Right.' Rosetta laughed. 'Sorry, but you asked. So, to answer your question,' she continued, 'I was recruited four years ago by a top parapsychologist called Prof James Randell. We met at Senate House in London. We were both there studying the Harry Price material, arguably one of the most important collections of occult and magic literature in the world. Afterwards, we went for coffee. I'm a coffee addict but it was Starbucks... yuck!'

'Sorry, I'll get you some,' Rav said, looking eager to escape. He sauntered off to the kitchen.

'Black, no sugar please,' she called. 'Thanks.' She accepted the steaming cup he offered. 'Do you have any liquors, to go with it? Baileys, brandy – whatever?'

Rav shook his head. 'I'm starting to think I've opened Pandora's box.'

'Well, hardly Pandora's bar. Remind me next time to bring my own booze to your dry watering hole.' She took a sip of coffee, which was hot. Although the humidity levels had dropped a little since the thunder and lightning had let rip, she would have preferred an iced-cold version. 'Now, where was I? Ah, yes, how I joined EPIS. Well, James and I soon made this a regular get-together, albeit at different venues, at least once a week. His breadth of knowledge is fascinating, and at the time he was researching scientific examination of psychic phenomena. He explained that investigators generally fall into two camps, believers and sceptics, as I mentioned earlier. He pointed out that some guy had set up a foundation offering a thousand dollars to anyone who could prove a paranormal claim under controlled conditions. The reward has since risen to a million dollars, and it still goes unclaimed. Many celebrity psychics refuse to take the test. One very commercially successful UK medium issued a statement via her lawyer saying: "I'm too busy to take a test." James also noted that, of the few mediums who have taken the test, they all came up with excuses after they failed. This, he felt, proved the point that they were cheats, fakes, showmen, or magicians, deluded into leading people astray.' Rosetta leaned back in her chair and stared at Rav. 'So, where do you fit in? Are you a believer or a sceptic?'

Rav hesitated a moment. 'I'd say I'm probably an undecided at present.'

'Okay, I see there's work still to be done with you.' Rosetta let out a long sigh of fake exasperation. 'Obviously, I'm a believer, so I said that many people are ready to believe in the paranormal. James countered that the majority of psychics are simply illusionists. They use shrewd guesswork and broad generalisations. He pointed out that the British Psychological Society was interested in putting claims to contact the spirit world and receive information from the other side to rigorous and empirical investigation. Currently, they operate on the assumption that human personality and consciousness depend on a living brain – if mediums and psychics can demonstrate that that the dead can communicate, then this challenges the baseline psychological assumptions and it has profound implications for bereavement and grief. James had a notebook full of fake and discredited mediums across the world who he reckoned were all con artists to some extent.'

'Well, it doesn't look too good does it?' Rav sighed. 'I mean, common sense suggests this stuff is all dubious, fake gurus, cult leaders, and so on.'

Rosetta laughed and took a mouthful of dessert. 'Rav, come on, please. You see all sorts, all kinds of people from all walks of life and sometimes they defy belief! Actually, being a criminal has a few undeniable attractions it seems to me – fucked up thinking that denies accountability, plus zero guilt or remorse. I'll have some of that. You know things are rarely what they seem at first. There's crime solving by hunches *and* dogged donkey work, and that's how it works. Would we solve as many cases if we never thought outside the box?'

Rav grudgingly conceded that she had a point as he sipped his tea. 'Maybe, just, maybe.'

'Here's the most important thing in all of this. EPIS, first and foremost, is committed to the exploration of the power of the human mind, and that remains a vital and highly important endeavour. Their mission statement is to use this knowledge for the advancement of mankind, and sometimes, when necessary, for the ultimate protection of mankind. Think how awesome it would be if we could predict and prevent the vast majority of crimes?'

Rav looked crestfallen. 'I'm thinking P45 and twiddling my thumbs. So, yeah that's terrific, thanks.'

'That's why I joined them, to put you out of a job.' She slapped her forehead. 'Yikes, that's one of the benefits I almost forgot.'

'You're too kind. I'm lost for words.'

Rosetta detected the hint of sarcasm in his tone and deduced that Rav was disengaging from the subject. A lot of people did that when their core values or beliefs were challenged. She would try to get him back onside. 'There have been cases where psychics have helped the police. I was involved with the Met in helping to solve the Ratchet murders in Battersea, London.'

He put his elbow on the table and rested his chin in his hand whilst staring at her. His eyes were large and dark with thick black lashes. It occurred to her that Rav was undoubtedly attractive. Not as tall or earthy as Daniel, but more refined somehow. *Maybe too refined for me*, she thought? *We'll see*, a small voice chattered in her head. She wondered if he would be quite so restrained and controlled in the bedroom. *Enough of that*, Rosetta admonished herself.

'I know,' he sighed. 'The commissioner used that as one of his bonus points when trying to sell the idea to me.'

'I take it that you weren't convinced. Cheers for that.' She reached across the table and gave his arm a nudge.

'Ouch,' Rav quipped with a shrug. 'Well, now I've got used to the idea I can see some benefits, I guess.'

'Right, and the use of psychics in solving crime often goes un-reported, but the Pittsburgh police, for instance, have unofficially used mediums some five hundred and fifty times to date. Not all the paranormal stuff is woo-woo, is it? After all, the Book of Revelation uses prophetic visions as a literary device, and there are numerous well-documented studies on children who remember past lives, and some who spoke fluently in ancient tongues which couldn't be at-tributed to the parents, relatives, school, or nannies –'

Rav interrupted. 'I don't have a problem with the past-life bit, or reincarnation, as that's consistent with my belief system. But I'm re-ally not convinced about all this psychic power stuff.'

'Well, how do you explain me calling Juliet to warn her about her accident?'

He leaned back in his chair and crossed his arms over his chest. 'I… I can't.'

'Just keep an open mind, perhaps?'

'I guess so.' Rav covered his mouth politely to stifle a yawn.

'So, it's my position,' Rosetta said decisively, 'that the sceptics will always try to disprove the unexplainable, while the believers may have bias the other way. Professor Randell is a renowned sceptic, which is vital, I reckon, to ensure balance in the process. EPIS has recruited many experts like him to hold us in check, I guess.' Rosetta finished off the last of her dessert. 'Thank you, that was delicious. I accept that there are frauds, con men, and so on in all walks of life. Not just when it comes to the paranormal, surely? So, in the realm of the unknown, the jury is still out. Ultimately, we can all make up our own minds.'

Rav yawned again, only more obviously this time.

'Sorry, I'm keeping you up. Would you like a hand with the wash-ing up?'

Rav smiled. 'No, that's fine. Thanks.'

'Well, I'd better be on my way home.' Rosetta drained her coffee. 'Thanks for a lovely evening.'

She was desperate for a cigarette and getting turfed out into the gar-den to smoke didn't hold too much appeal. Particularly now that the storm had broken, and it was pouring rain that bounced from the gutters with an audible whoosh. So, she thanked Rav for his hospitality, found her thick coat, and aimed for the door. Rav insisted on escorting her to her car under cover of a big umbrella which was struggling to cope with the deluge. That was very thoughtful and considerate, she felt.

'Rosetta.' He leaned forwards, and for a moment she thought he was going to kiss her on the cheek, but then he drew back and cleared his throat nervously. 'Text me to let me know you got home safely.'

Rosetta grinned. 'Sure.' It had been a long time since anyone even cared. 'Go inside now, you're getting soaked. Oh, do you fancy supper at my place next time?'

'Yes, that would be great.'

Rosetta drove off, pleased that he had accepted with enthusiasm and without hesitation.

CHAPTER THIRTY-TWO

Juliet
Inis Cara

Yesterday had been glorious, hotter than the height of summer at the beach, but merely a day later, it had changed, and the rain came down in sheets of silver and grey, driving across the moors. To make matters worse, Matt looked as black as an impending storm cloud.

Juliet toyed with her cereal, trying to pluck up the courage to break the news about Espiritus. She stared out the window and sighed, then took a deep breath. *Oh well, here goes,* she thought, clearing her throat. 'I've found a horse.'

An excruciating silence prevailed.

Maybe he hadn't heard? She tried again, and this time she got a response.

'So that's why you've been skulking around, leaving notes, disappearing all day and half the night. You think you're so clever, don't you? I know what you're up to.' His words flew accusingly in her direction, making her gasp.

'I'm just drinking my coffee.' She tried to sound nonchalant, but what if he suspected there was something going on between her and Tommy? 'Why are you so angry? I thought you'd be pleased? She's a youngster, really talented.'

'You're joking. A youngster, wow, and let me guess... not only is it a useless mare, it's probably un-backed as well?' Matt snarled, his voice dripping with sarcasm. 'Am I right?'

Her stomach flipped. *Oh shit, how she wished they didn't have to go into this.* Either he was guessing, or he knew more than he was letting on. 'Well...'

'What the hell are you playing at, going behind my back, sneaking about? We're supposed to be a team, a partnership. Haven't I always got your best interests at heart?' He looked as if he had swallowed a wasp or two.

'Of course, but I'm perfectly capable of buying a horse on my own.' She squirmed guiltily and dropped her spoon with a clatter.

'You did what?' His face flickered with disbelief, and his eyes narrowed. 'Where did you get the horse from, exactly?'

'You aren't my keeper, you know. And what difference does it make where I got her from?'

'It's a perfectly straightforward question. Where did you get the horse from?' By now he was scowling, his eyes dark with repressed rage.

'Gosh, what difference does it make? From Tommy Rafferty, so what?'

'You idiot.' He spat as his arm shot across the table and he grabbed her wrist. 'You bought a horse from that Gypsy scumbag. Jesus, he's not even a real Gypsy. He's just a BUFD.'

'A what?' she gasped, struggling against his grip.

'A bricked-up fucking *diddicoy*. What the hell are you playing at?'

'Let me go, you son of a bitch.' Juliet shoved his hand away and sprang to her feet, trying hard to compose herself. She spun around and sprinted towards the door.

'Right, that's it!' Matt sprinted after her, glaring and hostile. 'No way will I have another of Rafferty's mares. Christ, look at the trouble the last lot caused. I'm not having it. So, you're going to have to choose. It's either the horse or me.'

Juliet whirled to confront him, her long black hair practically lashing him in the face. 'Frankly, there's no contest. Espiritus is staying.' With that, she stormed out of the dining room.

Matt took the car, but first, he yanked her suitcase out of the trunk, and threw it across the parking lot. The suitcase flew open, scattering the contents: panties, bras – all her personal things. They lay in forlorn heaps, damp and bleak and fingered by drizzle.

Matt drove off at speed – to the airport, she presumed. He left muddy tyre treads imprinted across her underwear. Wearily, she stooped to retrieve her clothes. She felt nothing, nothing for Matt, only a profound sense of weariness. She didn't have the strength to argue any more.

She crammed the dirty, damp items into the suitcase and hauled it back into the foyer of the Silent Inn.

'Would you like a cup of tea or something?' Kevin asked in a soft, soothing tone.

'Oh,' she said. 'That would be nice. Thank you.'

Kevin reached out and offered to carry the suitcase. 'I couldn't help overhearing the row with your man over breakfast, and I hope you don't mind, but I've called Tommy.'

'Ah. Thank you.' She managed a weak smile. She sat for a while, wondering what to do. She decided to send DS Barrett a message telling her she'd found Gothic's replacement, Espiritus, and how she felt there was a link between her and Totem too. Juliet stared into the cup that had already seen its umpteenth refill and thought how tempting it would be not to go to the airport. Maybe she could just walk away from her old life, which had been filled with power struggles, and the endless square dance with a man who seemed a stranger to her now.

It would be so much simpler to give it all up.

But deep down, it wasn't that simple. She couldn't give up at the first major setback. *Damn Matt, damn him. Why did he have to make everything so difficult?* She'd gotten this far, and with his help, the next Olympics, another gold medal, could still be within her grasp. Nothing, no one, must derail her plans. She thought of Tommy and Espiritus. An unbroken horse would never be ready in time. It took years to bring an unmade horse up through the ranks to the very top levels of competition. She had to find another ready-made four-star horse and start the process of developing a partnership in the short time that was left, before Badminton next month. All her hopes of getting Chi-Chi Charlie in time rested with Matt. She hated to admit it, but she needed him, and he knew it. Right now, her personal life would have to take a back seat to the bigger objective.

That turned out to be a fleeting thought when she looked up and saw Tommy striding across the room. His face was lit up with concern and his eyes blazed. Her heart skipped a beat, as light and eager as a girl's. He looked so dark and dashing. Juliet sprang to her feet and threw herself into his arms.

'Saints preserve us, are you all right? Kevin phoned me. I came as soon as I heard.' His breath came in short, sharp bursts, and he stared at her with an almost demonic intensity. *Byron turned Heathcliff.*

Juliet nodded. He had hold of both her arms, and his grip tightened. She sensed in him something strong and full of purpose.

'If he so much as harmed a hair of your head, I swear I'll kill him.

Did he lay a finger on you?' He searched her face for a sign.

Juliet swallowed and shook her head. She could feel the leashed power straining beneath the surface. She jerked free and took a step backwards. This Tommy was no longer so cool and detached, and she knew then that he cared for her deeply. He'd said he'd kill Matt, and she had no doubt that he meant it. All the heat and passion of the Irish had risen in his blood.

Juliet caught her breath. 'Please, I'm fine. He lost it when I told him about Espiritus. But I'm fine. Just a little shaken, that's all.'

'You're sure?' His words came thick and deep, and she wondered what she had unleashed.

The curse of the Gypsies?

'The lowdown, good-for-nothing bastard. That man is toxic. You're sure you're all right?' he spat.

'Yes,' she whispered, taken aback at the force of his outburst. 'You really don't like Matt, do you?'

'I've no time for a man who mistreats women or horses.'

Juliet tilted her chin and stared at him in surprise. 'What do you mean about horses?'

'That's right an' all. We go back a few years me and him, to our junior show jumping days. Did he never mention it?'

Juliet's hand flew to her mouth. 'No.' If Matt knew Tommy from his past, why on earth had he never said anything? *Why the need for secrecy?* Then, with a sinking heart, she remembered what Orla had said about his mother. She claimed that his mother had defrauded many people in the equestrian set. At the time, she'd dismissed it. She hadn't believed her, because she thought that Orla was just trying to cause trouble. Perhaps Orla had been right about Matt. Oh Lord, what a fool she'd been. She knew a little, the stuff he'd chosen to reveal, but she'd never really asked him about his past in any detail.

'What did Matt do to cause such animosity between you?'

Tommy looked at her, but he glanced away, unwilling to meet her eyes.

'Please, I need to know.'

'You'll have to ask him that. If I badmouth him, you'll only suspect my motives.'

'I… Oh…' Her mouth snapped shut. True. She'd made the same mistake by not trusting Orla. She felt cold and clammy, full of remorse. She'd betrayed Orla's trust to keep Matt, and now she was betraying Matt with Tommy. Right now, she really didn't like herself very much.

'For now, don't worry about it.' Tommy folded her in his arms and caressed her hair. With his touch came a surge of warmth that left her limp. Her head fell back, and she closed her eyes. He pressed his hard and insistent lips against hers as he drew her into his powerful embrace. He moved away a little, and when he spoke, his voice was calm, and his breathing had returned to normal. 'So here you are, abandoned in Ireland at my mercy.' He smiled. 'What time's the flight?'

'Oh, around 3:00 p.m.,' she said in a robotic tone.

'Come on, cheer up. There's plenty of time to say your goodbyes to Espiritus, and I'll drive you to the airport.'

* * *

When they got to the Jeep, he reached inside and removed a bouquet. He held out a small bunch of wildflowers – bluebells, lilies of the valley, and forget-me-nots, and he smiled that crooked little smile of his. Her heart fluttered and something deep inside her stirred.

'Thank you. They're lovely,' she said, accepting the bouquet with a huge grin. Her mood lifted instantly.

'It's my pleasure.'

Tommy made words sound sunny and melodic, but she'd seen a different side to him today, deep, passionate, and brooding.

Not long afterwards, back at his place, Espiritus looked up from her breakfast and poked her nose over the stable door as Juliet and Tommy approached. Juliet drew back the bolt and stepped inside. She slipped her arms round the horse's neck and buried her face in her mane. No matter how many times she smelled it, she would never tire of the smell of horse.

It was a good smell. Honest, true and uplifting.

They stayed like that for a long time until Espiritus gave her an impatient nudge and charged off to the manger to polish off the remains of her food.

'She looks like she's lost some weight,' Juliet said, eyeing the mare's ribs with concern.

'Not much, and anyway, she'll put it back on now that she's calmed down at last.'

'Has she been wormed? Her teeth might need checking.'

Tommy arched one eyebrow. 'Stop your fretting, now. She'll be fine. Come on, I've got something for you inside.'

She slipped out of the stable, and he reached out and took her right hand with his, drawing her close until she could feel his shoulder blades through the light cotton fabric of his shirt. He felt warm, and the scent of him filled her nostrils, the smell of soap and horses.

She could no longer tell where his aroma ended, and her own began.

They moved closer together, his hand on the small of her back, pressing her against his chest. She wondered if he could feel the firm contours of her breasts through the flimsy material of his shirt and her dress. The dark and purposeful look in his eyes suggested that he could. And then he kissed her. A long and lingering kiss, and she felt that she had been falling towards him all her life.

Always.

Indoors, in the cool whiteness of Tommy's room, they made love, talked, then made love some more. Afterwards, she lay in his arms, naked except for a sheet draped across her lower half, with her head nestled in the crook of his shoulder. Tommy stared at the ceiling, his head resting on a pillow. After a while, he stirred and raised himself a fraction until he rested on one elbow. He looked at her with a fierce protectiveness that took her breath away.

'You know, Juliet, that you and I could spend forever searching for what we've found?' he said in that lingering voice of his.

His words echoed her thoughts, and she gasped in surprise. To think that he too would subscribe to such notions. And she smiled to herself. It must be the universal language of love. Then she knew... this feeling of perfect unity that they had somehow stemmed from the past.

'Yes, I think we've already been searching for one another across many centuries. There's a karmic theory, a concept maybe, about twin souls based on Isis and Osiris, who spend countless lifetimes trying to find each other.'

He laughed. 'Well, my Egyptian princess, come and take a look at my pyramid.'

'Egyptian queen, if you don't mind.' She giggled and dived under the sheet. 'Oh, my word, it's the Great Pyramid of Giza,' she said as she emerged.

He held his finger to her lips. 'Shush,' he said softly. 'I can hear something.'

She listened intently and heard a latch lift and fall, followed by a door creaking open. She covered her mouth and held her breath. What if Matt hadn't gone to the airport after all? A downstairs door shut. *Oh no, what if he'd come to catch her in bed with Tommy?* There'd be a terrible scene, a fight. She must hide. She looked around the room, desperately searching for a way out. The sound of footsteps approaching sent her heart racing. The footsteps were getting closer. Heaven forbid there was someone at the bottom of the stairs. What on earth was she going to do?

'Caitlin?' Tommy called out. 'Is that you? Did you get them?'

'Yes,' someone replied. A woman's voice, Juliet realized with a surge of relief.

'Great,' he said. He wrapped a sheet around himself and went scuttling out onto the landing. 'Would you mind cleaning them and popping them in the fridge? The ironing's in the utility room. Can you come back tomorrow to do the cleaning?'

'That's fine.' The footsteps receded as she retraced her steps, and Juliet burst out in a fit of nervous giggles as he explained that Caitlin helped him around the house, but she'd just got back from a month's vacation.

* * *

Tommy showed her the bath and pointed out that he never used it, as Travellers must use running water. She declined, there might be a spider lurking in it. So, they took a shower together in cold and invigorating water, and afterwards, Tommy rubbed her dry on a huge bath towel that then became a turban for her hair. Downstairs in the kitchen, Tommy had put her flowers in water and there was a bottle of champagne in an ice bucket.

'Gosh,' she exclaimed, 'a champagne breakfast. What are we celebrating?'

Tommy eased the cork, and it went off with a *whoosh* across the kitchen. She grabbed the glasses to catch the foamy bubbles that spilled from the bottle like volcanic lava.

'I've a notion that it's your birthday. Cheers,' he said. He raised his glass and clinked it against hers. 'To us, and many happy returns to you.'

'It is. How nice of you. Cheers.' Their glasses clinked again. *How thoughtful and sensitive he is,* she thought, and wondered how he'd found out. From Shamus, perhaps?

He moved to the fridge in that easy, almost languid, way of his and removed a platter of oysters garnished with black pepper, parsley, and wedges of lemon.

243

'Here you go, fresh from Galway. Only they're not at their best at this time of year, so I hope you'll forgive me. There's a festival in September – the foodies' eighth wonder of the world. Ever tried oysters washed down with Guinness?'

'Not yet.' She tilted her head back, allowing the oyster to glide down her throat. It tasted of sex, seaweed... all things illicit and potent.

'I thought, maybe...' His tipped his head to one side, like a guilty little boy who'd been caught stealing in the apple orchard. 'Well, I was wandering if you could maybe take a later flight? There's an Aer Lingus flight to Heathrow at eleven this evening.'

'Were you now?' She smiled. 'And why would that be?'

'Well.' He gulped down another oyster. 'As it's Easter Monday, it's the Jameson Irish Grand National today, an' I've a horse running.'

'A racehorse owner, my, oh my, you're full of surprises, aren't you?'

'Well, it's not exactly mine, for sure. He's owned by a syndicate, so I've a thirty-third share, like. Come on. We'd better get a move on, or we'll miss the start.'

CHAPTER THIRTY-THREE

Juliet

As they approached Fairy House racecourse in Ratoath, County Meath, long, slow-moving queues of traffic snaked towards the car parks. Tommy drummed his fingers on the steering wheel and checked his watch.

'Get a move on, you eejits!' he yelled out of the window and honked the horn for good measure. After an intolerable wait, they turned into the owners' and trainers' parking lot, where he rammed the Jeep into the first available space.

'Come on, come on,' he said, like a sheepdog worrying a delinquent lamb.

'Aren't you going to lock up?'

He shot her a withering look. 'Be honest with me now. Who'd be stealing that?' He shooed her along with one hand, his camera and binoculars in the other.

The weather continued to brighten until the final shower cloud was burnt off, and the sun made a welcome appearance. Officially, the going was described as good to soft.

'That,' Tommy fretted, 'is not good. Not good at all. Bygone Times prefers the going good to firm. All that mud at the take-off in front of the fences. It'll be treacherous, you mark my words.'

Juliet nodded, trying to pacify him as best she could.

As they reached the owners' stand, Tommy disappeared into a sea of friends and well-wishers, all slapping him on the back and kissing him on the cheek. She couldn't help thinking that the Irish were an altogether more emotional and sentimental race than the English, and that, together with their enormous capacity for enjoying themselves and their obvious love of horses, made them very appealing.

She felt so at home, so relaxed.

Perhaps, after the Olympics, she could relocate to Ireland. Not super convenient, as all the big events were in England, but she really wanted to be near this man. For a moment, she indulged herself in a fantasy of their future together, filled with dogs, horses, and maybe even children one day.

Eventually, Tommy returned to her side, looking hot and red in the face. *Oh heck, he's handsome,* she thought, admiring his smart jacket and tie and brogues the colour of peat. It was only supposed to be a brief fling, but somehow this man had got completely under her skin. The drinks flowed: beer, wine, and spirits, as Tommy yanked his tie loose and sprang onto a bench to deliver a speech.

'Okay, quit your racket. I'd like to introduce you to Juliet, my good-luck charm. Although I'm sure you all agree we've no need of charms and talismans today. Ours is the best horse in the race.'

'Juliet,' came the chorus from the stands.

She blushed at this unexpected announcement and raised her glass in response.

'To dear friends, and...' She looked at Tommy imploringly and hissed, 'What's the horse's name?'

He whispered the reply.

'And to Bygone Times.' Juliet sat down with a big grin. Then her mouth dropped open. 'Oh, but isn't he the favourite?'

'He is an' all.' He beamed. 'And you know what? I can't think of anything finer than watching him win with you by my side.'

'Ah.' She looked up at him, her eyes shining. It would be a sad moment whenever he was out of her sight. She liked the look of him so much that it hurt.

Wow, this is really it.

What she had felt about Matt simply didn't compare to this, not even in the beginning when they'd first met. *It must be love* she thought grabbing hold of the railing for support. *That once-in-a-lifetime sort of love most people only dream about.*

What would such a love be worth?

How tempting it would be to stay in Ireland, where she felt so at home, but at what price? She'd been aiming to go to the Olympics ever since she was a kid. Yes, she'd achieved gold once, but that had just made her hungrier. Her whole life depended on proving that she wasn't a one-hit wonder. She wanted to be remembered as the best of the best. She wondered how close Matt had come to securing Chi-Chi Charlie, and she sighed. *How could she choose between Matt with the horse, or Tommy without?*

Oh, life could be so complicated, and she decided not to think about it right then. Instead, she turned her attention to the race.

The field approached the fence, a huge oxer with a ditch on the landing side, tightly bunched together. Juliet spotted Bygone Times in the middle and in the thick of it. She strained her neck and stood on her tiptoes. *Where was he?* Her heart sank as he was swallowed up in the sea of horses and she lost sight of him. By her side, Tommy grew agitated. Juliet closed her eyes, crossed her fingers and prayed silently. *Please, let him get around safely. Please.*

At each fence, the big field thinned out until only a handful of horses remained in contention. There he was. She let out a sigh of relief. Inextricably buried at the back, but at least he was intact. Then, as the runners approached the second last, Juliet gasped, and her hand flew to her mouth. Out of the corner of her eye, she caught a glimpse of a loose horse veering sharply to the left. It went at full pelt, cutting in front of the onward-bound horses just as they came to the fence.

'Oh Jesus,' she groaned. Is it too late? The horses and jockeys were all fully committed to take off and had no time to take evasive action. She buried her face in her hands. A few terrible, heart-stopping moments later, she looked up to find that total carnage had unfolded, with a sickening tangle of hooves and arms sprawled across the track.

'Ouch, is he down?' she muttered, desperately trying to make out his colours amidst the chaos on the course.

'Jesus, Joseph, and Mary, that was a mother of a fall.' Tommy grimaced as he peered through his binoculars, his knuckles white from gripping them so tightly.

'Is he all right? Is the jockey on his feet?'

'Struth, he's up. Thank the Lord, and… so is Brendon, what's more. Hang about, the blighter – he still kept hold of the reins and I do believe… Yes, he's remounting. Go on, Brendon. Go on, my man!'

A deafening roar went up from the crowd, and they surged forward in one motion, almost sweeping Juliet off her feet.

'What's happening?' she squealed.

'He's back in the saddle, and they've just cleared the last…' An almighty roar from the crowd swallowed his words as Brendon gave a decisive shake of the reins and Bygone Times responded with a powerful surge. Juliet could hardly believe her eyes.

As the contenders passed the distance marker, the commentator's voice rose in pitch.

'And it's Esprit d'Espace that takes up the running, followed by Nemesis making up ground with a strong run on the outside. Then Man-in-the-Moon, and then the favourite, Bygone Times, in fourth.'

'Just look at him.' Tommy beamed. 'He's as fit and fresh as when they led him out of the collecting ring.'

The horse's big ground-covering stride ate up the gap between him and the leaders. Juliet bit her lip. Was it possible for him to come from behind and win? She held her breath as he drew neck and neck with Man-in-the-Moon.

'Yes,' she yelled as he eased past and into third place. 'Come on!'

Juliet squealed in delight as Brendon urged the big horse on with hands and heels flying like a demon's. The gap was shrinking. The crowd sensed a fight, and they let out a roar.

The two leaders hung together, tightly bunched on the rails. Bygone Times had no way of passing unless he switched to the outside to make his run. And that would lose too much precious time. Brendon sat tight on their heels with the big horse underneath him like a coiled spring.

The finishing post loomed into view.

'Shit. Holy shit,' Tommy cursed in total exasperation.

'Why can't he just barge through?'

'Tempting, but it's not allowed. He must have free passage. Brendon can't come up on the inside to make his run unless there's room, damn it. Otherwise he'll forfeit the race or maybe even get disqualified for the rest of the season.'

'Oh.' She cupped her hands over her eyes to get a better view. She couldn't bet on it, but it seemed that the horse on the rails was losing speed and drifting backwards. In a deft movement that took less than a second, Bygone Times overtook the trailing Nemesis and zigzagged like a cobra striking at its prey towards the gap that the defeated horse had left by the rails. Now two thoroughbreds galloped nose to nose round the home corner and up the final straight in a desperate battle for first place.

'I don't know if he'll get away with that. It was bloody tight, and if he wins, they're bound to argue that he interfered with at least one of the horses.' Tommy grimaced. As he spoke, Bygone Times poked his nose out in front and Tommy leapt in the air. 'Come on, come on, my beauty.'

With one shake of the reins from the diminutive jockey, Bygone Times surged convincingly ahead. The crowd let out a collective gasp of amazement. Then, as the favourite launched himself forwards and practically took off, the crowd erupted.

'Come on, my son, come on.' Tommy sprang to his feet, leapt in the air, and shook his fist. The Irishmen's passion for horses had set his eyes alight.

'Yes! Yes!'

A deafening roar went up as the big black colt flew past the winning post. Bygone Times, born, bred, and trained in Ireland, was truly one of their own. Brendon stood up in his stirrups, punching the air in unrestrained delight. Then, he sat down and thumped the horse's neck. He had every reason to be overjoyed. He had just won the richest race in Ireland, the nation of horses and horse lovers.

Tommy could hardly contain himself. He grabbed Juliet by the hand and practically dragged her to the winners' enclosure, where he introduced her to Brendon.

'Pleased to meet you,' the jockey said, wiping the mud from his eyes so that it streaked across his flushed red face. 'Well, there's no mistaking that you two are related. The likeness is uncanny.'

Juliet looked puzzled, and Tommy stepped in. 'No, Brendon. This is Juliet, not my sister, Aoife.'

'Well, now, Tommy, I swear she's the spitting image of you,' he said.

Juliet laughed 'Oh, so now I know what you see in me – yourself.'

'Absolutely. Originality was never my scene. Even Kevin commented on the similarities between us.' Tommy grinned. He reached out and patted his beloved colt's steaming neck, and as he did, Juliet became aware of a presence close behind her. Someone hissed a low warning in her ear.

'If you carry on seeing Tommy, you'll regret it for a very long time.'

Juliet spun around frantically, but there was no one there. In spite of the warm spring air, she felt a sudden chill.

CHAPTER THIRTY-FOUR

Rosetta
Yorrex

Sweetpea was a Wiccan witch who lived in a converted shed on an allotment near the River Eizel. She was also a member of EPIS, but more on a consultancy basis than an active member, since she had an aversion to technology. In fact, her aversion to technology was what made her so valuable to them. She led a simple life, without a television. She occasionally listened to the radio, usually BBC4, but generally she was free from undue outside influences, and maintained a pure connectivity to nature and paganism. This made her a good foil for the complexities of fast-evolving life in the increasingly technological world. Sweetpea could reflect back some of humanity's old, original unsullied morality and values, which was crucial in order to program deep robots so their A.I. couldn't turn and destroy humanity.

The shed had solar panels for hot water, a wood-burning stove, and a composting toilet. It was painted a flamboyant pink with jaunty bunting draped under the awning. Out front, her old bicycle was propped against a tree.

Rosetta smiled at the sign on the door: "One nice Witch lives here, and a grumpy old Wizard."

She knocked, a soft rap with the brass bee knocker, and let herself in. The shabby-chic theme continued inside as well, as Sweetpea had created a very homely effect from rescued recycled materials and cheap rugs and knickknacks from charity shops.

Sweetpea had her radio on and she was swaying to some kind of waft-away music. She had her eyes closed but gestured to her friend to take a seat. Sweetpea held a pivotal role at EPIS, as she and many other native and indigenous peoples from across the globe were formulating the human values that would be instilled into all AI to ensure that the robots created never turned against humanity. A vital undertaking, in an era where even narrow AI, as deployed in Alex and Siri, were teaching children to be nasty to their parents.

Actually, she thought with a small sigh, *mine don't need much help. It was a toss-up. Which was worse – being cut off or getting lippy abuse?*

'Morning,' Rosetta said, a little disgruntled to discover that her friend had company, as she really needed to discuss the implications of the email that she'd received from Juliet, and the case in general. 'Are you meditating?'

Sweetpea opened her eyes and laughed, flicking her long grey plait behind her back. 'No. Not my thing, but those two are.' She pointed to the man and the woman sitting on the mismatched wooden dining chairs. 'I don't go there myself. I've seen folks sitting in the half-lotus position, emptying their minds. They convince themselves that they're communicating with their higher power, or whatever their God or Goddess is called.'

'Well, what's wrong with that?'

'Nothing at all, but I'm too old to sit in the lotus position. It makes my bones creak. Once, I got stuck and my legs locked, and I had to call the ambulance.'

Rosetta laughed as she pulled the door closed behind her and took a seat next to the portly middle-aged gentleman dressed in an old-fashioned suit with wide lapels, and a thin, anxious-looking woman wearing jeans and a T-shirt.

'Okay,' Sweetpea said. 'I have a question for you all. How many animals of each kind did Moses take onto the Ark?'

'Two,' Miss Anxious replied.

'I reckon it's none.' Rosetta ventured.

Mr. Business thought for a while, and the delaying tactic helped him to resist the instinctive response. 'Wasn't it Noah and the Ark, not Moses?'

Sweatpea let out a cackle. 'Indeed, but see how when it's a familiar context and you slip in another Biblical character, our suspicions aren't alerted because it's not something unusual? Susan answered intuitively. Rosetta stuck to the facts. And Sam, you slowed down and allowed your rational thought processes to figure it out.'

'Oh.' The anxious woman looked crestfallen. 'So, my answer was –'

'Predictable.' Sweatpea laughed, but not unkindly. 'As we learn

251

and develop, some mistakes are made with even greater confidence.'

'You mean we think we're right, but they're still mistakes all the same?' Rosetta asked.

'Yes – moving on now. Well, Sam is here today to share his story. Sam, can you tell us something about yourself that we wouldn't have guessed?'

'Yes, sure. Well, I'm actually a recovered anorexic. Too well-recovered, as you can see.' He laughed, and so did Rosetta and Sweetpea. Susan looked unsure.

Sam cleared his throat. 'I was only joking, you know, to break the ice. The first time I came here, the idea of being in the same room as a witch terrified me.'

'Understandable,' Rosetta agreed, 'as the unconventional spiritual path is often misunderstood and the very word *witch* arouses prejudice and intolerance. Sorry, Sam. I interrupted. Please continue.'

'Well, it was my daughter who kind of nudged me gently, until curiosity got the better of me and I called in one day after work to buy some of Sweetpea's organic produce. We got chatting over a cup of tea, and gradually I stopped being afraid of labels. I realised that Sweetpea is simply someone who doesn't comply with established rules. I'm an accountant, quite conventional, so her way of thinking is quite novel from my perspective.'

'Ah,' Susan said. 'So, you prefer maths and formulas and readily solvable problems? Isn't that about control as well?'

'Exactly, but I come to see Sweetpea regularly to explore that repressed part of me. I realised that Sweetpea always tries to reach out beyond the rules, conventions, and boundaries, to express love and joy and celebrate the simple things in life.'

'What do you think holds most people back?' Rosetta asked.

'Fear, always fear. Some people accept their sixth sense, but sadly many don't.' She sighed. 'Love is a classic case of fear getting in the way.'

'Not quite following,' Sam said, with a puzzled expression.

'Well, love is invariably associated with loss and suffering, so that makes us scared.' Sweetpea turned her attention to Susan. 'Do you have a question for me?'

'Yes.' Susan squirmed, her voice faint and a little quaky. 'I'd like to know if…'

Sweatpea made encouraging noises, as if trying to coax a reluctant horse over a fence.

'My sister passed away two months ago.' Susan's lower lip trembled. 'It was so sudden. One minute she was playing tennis, and the next minute she collapsed and died. An aneurysm, they said. Now I'm looking after my three nieces, and it's all up to me. I'm worried that I'll mess it up and that I won't be able to cope... and then what? Social services will take them into care.' Susan started to cry.

Rosetta passed her a box of tissues.

'There, there. You cry all you like,' Sweetpea said.

'Well.' Sam cleared his throat. 'On my third visit to her, Sweetpea laid her hands on my forehead. It felt as if she was sending out a wave of energy. Afterwards, she told me I had to go to see my doctor immediately and ask him to look at my back. Sure enough, he found a lesion which he removed and sent for biopsy.'

Susan stopped sniffling and looked curious. 'What was the outcome?'

Sam shook his head. 'My worst fears were confirmed. It was malignant melanoma. But thanks to Sweetpea, it was detected early. With melanoma, the farther it invades the layers of skin, or if it gets into your lymph nodes, the worse the prognosis. Thanks to my visit to the witch, my chances of a full recovery are over ninety-five percent.' He laughed.

'That's fantastic. I'm pleased for you. But I'm wondering how things will work out for me?'

Sweetpea looked thoughtful. 'It's how it is meant to be. You can't have your own children, correct?'

'No.' Susan looked taken aback. 'I went through menopause in my early twenties. But –'

'Your sister was a single mother?' Sweetpea asked.

Susan nodded.

'You were always destined to be a mother, and your sister is always at your side. You're not replacing her. No one can. But she always intended for you both to raise them. She made you their guardian, didn't she?'

'Are you saying that she... she knew she was going to die young?'

'I believe so. It was sudden, but she was prepared. Don't feel guilty. Just be full of the joy of living and teach the girls to be positive and grateful, and that will be plenty enough. That's what she would have wanted.'

Sweetpea got up from her chair and handed Susan and Sam each a bunch of lavender bound with silver cord. 'That's it for today's session. Same time next week and please send your friends along if they need a little help.'

'How much do you charge?' Susan asked.

'I don't do money, but gifts are always appreciated; such as kitchen and toilet rolls, biodegradable bin liners, ah, and cat food is always appreciated. They appear to be multiplying. I'm a vegan, but they eat meat, of course. Although they do seem rather fussy. The Lidl and Aldi own-label brands do not go down too well, even with my strays.' Sweetpea laughed. 'Consumerism has gone mad even amongst cats, it seems.'

Sam threw a couple of logs on the wood burner before he left. 'I've got an order of logs and coal being delivered next week for you. Cheerio.'

He and Susan headed for the door and departed.

'Well, dear friend, how are things?' She smiled at Rosetta.

Rosetta was relieved. It was so great to be able to unburden herself to someone who genuinely understood and was on the same wavelength. 'Police investigation, past life, or personal?' Rosetta began.

'All three, I guess. I'll put the kettle on.' Sweetpea stood up and busied herself.

'Where do I begin?' Rosetta pondered. 'Well, I could do with your help with the police investigation. I need to reframe things. The stolen car belonged to my ex.'

'Peter? That's interesting,' she said, returning with the tea and passing a cup to Rosetta.

'Thanks. His alibi stacks up. But there's no CCTV footage at the station where the car was parked, so we haven't been able to identify the driver. How bloody typical, that. Then there's the horse dealer. An Irish Traveller called Tommy Rafferty, who was at the scene when the car was torched and abandoned on Farley Heath.'

'Do you think he did it?'

Rosetta took a sip of tea. 'No. Well, I'm not sure. It doesn't feel quite right, timing's out, and he's alibied by another dog walker.'

'Okay.' Sweetpea hugged her cup of tea close to her chest for warmth. 'Let's try to eliminate intuitive bias. It's hard for us witches, but necessary for a detective. So, here's an example: there's an American man. He's tall, slender, quiet, polite, and considerate, and he rarely raises his voice.'

'Is he single? He sounds like my ideal date.'

'Shush. He wears spectacles –'

'Oh, I'm going off the ideal now.'

'Is he a farmer, or a librarian?'

'Hmm.' Rosetta pondered. 'Well, the average person, including me, would say he's a librarian, but that's obviously the wrong answer.'

'Correct. Statistical bias suggests there are thousands more farmers than librarians in America, so the odds favour a shy, quiet farmer.'

'Okay, I see. I need to re-examine the statistical probabilities, starting with the road rage attack?'

'Exactly,' Sweetpea said in between sipping her tea. 'It happened on a Monday, outside the rush hour, on a quiet country road, in wintery, icy conditions. What are the statistics for that?'

'Extremely rare, virtually unheard of… ah… Do you think it's just staged to look like a random road rage attack?'

Sweetpea nodded. 'Who had motive, and where do the statistics point?'

'If it's not a random act committed by a stranger, then the statistics point to the fact that sixty-seven percent of murders are committed by someone the victim knows, such as a friend, relative, or someone close. This is not your standard killing. I think the Olympic gold medal horse was the intended target. The poor teenage girl, Isabella, was a tragic case of collateral damage,' Rosetta said.

Sweetpea stretched her legs then crossed her ankles. 'I used to be a keen rider in my youth. I had horses at my uncle's farm.'

'Really? I never knew that.'

'A horse of that calibre would be insured for a lot of money. Was the rider the owner? A lot of top competition horses are syndicated.'

'Juliet owned the horse, but – hang on a minute, the boyfriend or fiancé, Matt Lebaine, handled all the financial affairs. But he was out of the country in America at the time.'

'Ah.' Sweetpea perked up as if they were on the brink of cracking something significant. 'This is low-tech crime solving at its best. Absence doesn't necessarily absolve motive, though, does it?'

'No, and he's the beneficiary of the insurance policy. So, he's the obvious candidate and I've a hunch that the groom, Tracy, is involved too, since she conveniently called in sick on the day.'

'There you go, crime solving by hunches. That's a first.'

'Yeah.' Rosetta laughed. 'Alas, there's still a lot of hard grunt and donkey work ahead. We simply haven't got the hard proof to convict. It ain't over till the fat lady sings – or in this case, the fit boy sings. The lovely would-be murderous Matt is a personal trainer. Well, actually, he's a jack of all trades. He does a bit of horse dealing and runs the finances for Juliet. But for all he's fine in the looks department, he's not a particularly nice person. He's definitely not my type, but as for Mr. Rafferty... phew!' Rosetta made a face, and mock-panted like a thirsty puppy.

'Mr. who?'

Rosetta laughed. 'Sorry, I'm getting ahead of myself. Tommy Rafferty's an Irish horse dealer who was on the Heath the morning the crime took place. A potential witness, so I went to Ireland to interview him, which was very interesting.'

'Hmmm. Aside from work, how are things with you?'

'There is no me, aside from work.' Rosetta sighed. 'But Peter relented, and I finally got to see my kids, but the contact is in danger of tailing off again. Presumably they still think I'm mad, deranged, that I have borderline personality disorder, that I'm bipolar, or all of the above. Actually, Peter's latest idea is that I'm a psychopath.'

'Really?' Sweetpea raised one eyebrow. 'How does that work, exactly?'

Rosetta gave a low growl of frustration. 'Well, first and foremost I'm charming –'

She raised her hand, her palm gesturing for Rosetta to stop. 'Fail, at first base,' she cackled.

'Cheers, for that. Also, I'm manipulative, emotionally ruthless, without empathy, gifted at hiding my true self, and always acting a part, such as the model citizen, which is totally a front. I'm a prolific liar, but totally without guilt or shame if I get caught out, and my primary concern is me, me and my image.' Rosetta shrugged. 'So, thanks for that, Peter.' She gritted her teeth and spat, 'He's such a wanker. Do all ex-husbands go to the great School for Wankers? And if so, mine's got a bloody PhD first-class, no contest.'

'Well, he was never quite my cup of tea, I have to say. He used to look at me as if I was doggy doo-doo on his shoe, or something.'

Rosetta laughed. 'Yes, I remember that look of utter disdain, like the bad smell of a noxious fart was wafting his way.' She narrowed her eyes, flared her nostrils, and mimicked Peter's face. 'One is not amused. How do I score on the psycho scale? Did I pass? Should I now crack on and start a cult?'

'I'm afraid not. Not enough ticks on the check list.'

'You mean, I don't even cut it as a psycho-psychic? Ah well, must keep practising, eh?'

'How's your love life? It sounds to me as if you could do with a little distraction.'

'Love, that was the thing that you said was linked to loss and suffering. Correct. That's my assessment too.'

'So, it's not going well with you and Daniel? But you seemed so well-matched.'

'Who?'

'Sorry. I didn't mean to pry.'

'That's okay. There's nothing to tell. He's gone underground, doesn't communicate.' Rosetta frowned. Suddenly, she felt tired and deflated. 'I don't know what I've done or, then again, what I haven't done. It's the lack of closure that hurts the most, I guess. Why can't he just find the balls to man up and explain? I deserve that at least surely?'

Sweetpea gave Rosetta's knee a friendly squeeze. 'I'm sorry. Relationships aren't really my area of expertise. He's working on my eviction and defending the case for me against the allotment governing body. I could ask him to get in touch?'

'Thanks, but Ritchie already tried that, and still radio silence.' Rosetta covered her face with her hands, took a deep breath, and gulped. 'I feel like one of those rescue dogs that no one wants. Rejected by the husband, my kids, the boyfriend – and, with Daniel, the paranormal thing wasn't an issue, so I can't even use that as an excuse. It's just me. I suck.' Her voice trailed off, and there was a long silence as she processed this latest bit of information. 'Great. I mean, I'm pleased he's helping you, but he's an employment lawyer, so what's that all about? EPIS has got hot-shot lawyers on speed-dial. They either discredit the opposition or sue, and they literally have an army of litigation specialists, so why Daniel? I don't get it.'

'He offered as a personal favour. I don't possess a PC or anything like that, so he's appointed a solicitor, and lined up a barrister if it goes to court, which I hope it won't, but this is an old-boys network and, apart from Arnold and Gilbert a few plots down, they all want me kicked out.' Sweetpea sighed. 'Someone sprayed obscenities on the front door last week, and there's a peeping Tom who comes around late at night and shines a torch through the window. I feel quite vulnerable here on my own, but that's what they want. They're trying to intimidate me, so I'll leave.'

'Right, the bastards… how dare they. You leave that one with me. Why didn't you tell me sooner? I'll send two undercover police officers out to keep you under surveillance. When we catch the person responsible, that'll send a warning shot over the bow to the rest of them. What time does the peeper usually show up?'

'Usually around nine or ten at night.' Sweetpea looked relieved, and absentmindedly stroked the tabby cat curled up on her lap. 'Thank you. I'd appreciate it. Now, what's going on with the past-life problem?'

Rosetta thought for a while. 'It's definitely horse-related. When I ran my visons, the Eclipse system came up with Gothic, the horse who was killed, and before him, Juliet's top horse was called Totem, which links up with the Native American theme. Juliet's in Ireland at the moment, and she went to see a Romany fortune teller who mentioned Apaches. With curious synchronicity, she's in Inis Cara right now with a horse dealer –who seems to have found her a replacement horse – and the dealer is the one and only Tommy Rafferty. Juliet sent me an email and I'm trying to tie up some loose ends. Ah, and my beloved ex, remember, it was his Range Rover. He's somehow mixed up in this. He was even in my dream.' Rosetta shuddered. 'I can't seem to get away from him, can I?'

Sweetpea shook her head. 'I'm getting a bit confused. Horses seem to play a pivotal part in all this. Has Juliet found a replacement horse?'

'I think so. It's one of those painted pony things, called – hang on a mo.' She removed her notebook from her handbag and flicked through the pages. 'Ah yes, Espiritus.' Rosetta glanced around and noticed another of Sweetpea's signs: "My other car's a broom." No wizard around for sure. As far as she knew, her friend had never had a serious relationship, she certainly didn't own a car, only a bicycle. She couldn't drive… but what the heck?

'Spirit, that's a nice name,' Sweetpea said. 'Is that the registered name, or the stable name? Is it a piebald or a skewbald?'

'I haven't got a clue. But there's something else I ought to mention. As Rafferty's a potential witness, and he was at one time a potential suspect I guess, I went to Ireland to interview him.'

'And?'

Rosetta's mouth went dry and she squirmed. 'It's a bit tricky, this. He's not directly involved, but he may be protecting someone, so he knows more than he's letting on. Anyway, I ended up in bed with him.'

Sweetpea let out a loud cackle of laughter, and the cat shot up in the air and scooted under Rosetta's chair. 'Priceless! So, we've got your ex-husband, your lover, Juliet, plus an as-yet-unidentified potential hit man. What an intoxicating mix. You couldn't make it up if you tried.'

'Aren't you forgetting something? What about the bloody reincarnating Apache horse? And since someone cocked it up big time and sucked aliens in via the time portal, I can't go back in time that way. So, now I'm pretty much groping in the dark,' Rosetta said with a sigh.

Even WTF didn't really cut it, did it? Plus, the whole investigation was practically on hold until the insurance company paid out the claim and they could follow the money trail.

'Ah yes, the ETs. I'd love to see one before I die, but flying's not for me. Now, where were we? Ah yes, Spirit. Okay. Here's what to do. Get hold of Juliet, or the Rafferty chap. Are you still in contact with him?'

'No. That's hardly appropriate. It was just a one-night stand, although –' Rosetta paused. She really had to take herself to task and stop thinking about him. She was about to add that she felt the attraction wasn't entirely new, and he was divine, but she had to keep her professional distance.

'Okay. Well, get hold of the horse's passport, either the breed society one or whatever. That will give you the date of birth, which may narrow things down a bit.'

Rosetta sprang to her feet and kissed Sweetpea gently on the forehead. 'That's a brilliant idea. What a star.' She took her phone out and sent Juliet a quick message:

Hi, can you get hold of Espiritus' official passport asap?
I need to know her date of birth. Thanks.

'Now, don't fret,' she said to Sweetpea. 'I'll send the boys out tomorrow to sort your Peeping Tom problem. Anyway, gotta dash, take care.' She waved goodbye and flew out the door.

On the way to her car, her phone pinged as a WhatsApp message arrived. Rosetta glanced at it, the message was from Juliet:

Sorry, I forgot all about this.
It's a recording of my session with Katya. Hope it helps.

CHAPTER THIRTY-FIVE

Juliet
Inis Cara

The drive to the Dublin airport would take half an hour or so. Not far, but too far considering the effect the celebrations had on Tommy's brain. He swayed slightly and slurred his words. Juliet sighed as she shoved him into the Jeep on the passenger side. She decided not to mention the strange threat. It was probably one of his jilted lovers who'd had too much to drink. *Not the only one*, she thought with a shrug.

'I'm perfectly-perfect capable of driving,' he insisted, to no avail. 'An' you'll never manage this temperamental old girl.'

She laughed. Although she didn't find inebriated men particularly attractive, she couldn't be pissed off with him for long. He looked so like a little-lost-boy. Sure, he had well and truly pickled his liver, but then today his horse had won the local Grand National.

'I'll handle it. I've got my HGV license and I'm used to driving horse-boxes the size of houses. Now can you just quit bitching and concentrate on where we're going.'

'Aye-aye, captain.' He had the window open and his elbow poked out. The breeze ruffled his hair so that it flapped gently against the collar of his jacket.

'Why don't you put your sunglasses on and hide your bloodshot eyes?' She double-declutched, but the gearshift still jumped, screeching in protest at her attempted change.

'Charmed, I'm sure. I can't look as bad as all that.'

'Worse.' She laughed. Then she looked up and saw the sign saying two miles to the airport – only two miles until she left Ireland,

Espiritus, and Tommy behind. Her laughter disintegrated into the hollow emptiness of her stomach.

Half an hour later, they sat lingering over a cup of coffee in the airport restaurant, which had huge sixties-style windows that overlooked the runway. Her phone pinged as a message came in. She glanced at the screen and read the text from DS Barrett wanting to know Espiritus' date of birth.

'Can you tell me when Espiritus was born?' *It was a long shot,* she decided, given the alcohol-addled state of his brain, but as usual he surprised her.

'Of course, I can. It's 17th February 2017. It was a long night, a long labour, and bloody well freezing. But it turned out grand in the end an' all.' Tommy grinned.

'Cheers,' she said, texting the detective back with the details. 'Can you let me have a copy of her passport? I'll need it for the import paperwork.'

He nodded. 'I'll email it as soon as I get home.'

'Thanks.' Juliet sighed. Then, she stared out the window. The light had faded, and the runway was lit up, so she could just make out a plane about to take off. The announcement system called the gate number for the Aer Lingus flight to Heathrow, and her heart sank. She glanced at her watch, willing the second hand to stop. In less than half an hour, she would be boarding a plane back to England.

'It's almost time,' she said, unable to meet his eye. 'What gate was it again?'

'Seven?' He seemed better after the injection of caffeine, but his voice still sounded dull and listless. 'So, what are we going to do?' He looked her straight in the eye, his meaning direct and personal.

'I don't know,' she said, turning away. She had been dreading this moment.

'Stay,' he said as he reached over and held her hands. 'I mean it. Oh, I've never been one for settling down, and I can't make any promises about the future, but I think this time it could be different.'

She hesitated. Her doubts came not from the tremendous strength of her feelings for him but from a more practical and mundane level. Ireland was an inconvenient platform to underpin her eventing career, and she'd come too far, worked too hard not to maximize her chances of success.

'The timing's not right. I need to focus on securing a ride for Badminton. There might not even be enough time left for that, so it might be Burghley for the next big outing.' She paused. 'I need to get a string of four-star horses in order to qualify for the next Olympics.'

'But after that, surely you can move your horses and make your base here with me?' His eyes blazed with passionate intensity.

She gulped, not trusting herself to speak. Right now, her ambition to win another gold medal transcended everything. She had to go back home to Matt, at least until she had the horse, and yet she wanted Tommy so badly.

'Maybe. It's a way off. Let's see.'

'Matt will never understand you like I do. Never in a thousand years.'

'Please.' She pulled herself free. 'It's all happening so quickly. Don't you think we ought to wait a while?'

'I know it's what you really want. Damn it. Just say yes.'

'Oh,' she whispered, and her answer rose from her heart. 'Of course, I want us to be together. It's just that… well. Maybe you could move to England?'

Tommy shrugged. 'I'm an Irishman born and bred. No offence intended, but I don't set much store by England and most of the English. Some o' them look down their noses as if we're only fit for tarmacking driveways and the like. But for you, since you're an American and they love the Irish, I'll think about it.'

At that moment, the sound of a phone ringing came shrill and insistent from the depths of her purse. Juliet jumped. She looked down and snatched up her cell phone.

'Don't answer it.' Tommy leaned over the table and grabbed her arm with an unexpected roughness. As his face moved closer, she could smell the whiskey on his breath.

'Tommy, please…' He loosened his grip and watched every move as she picked up the phone and took the call. 'Hello?'

'Juliet, good news,' Matt said without any hint of animosity or anger. 'We got full planning permission and Land Development Ltd. have just improved their offer by half a million. I think I can increase that to three-quarters of a million more. It's the chance of a lifetime.'

'Oh, that's great,' came her flat reply.

'And that's not all. Chi-Chi Charlie's in the bag.' He paused. 'They'll get him moved to our yard next week, but with one proviso. Soon, we'll need to find a base near the M1. When are you coming home?'

Juliet bit her lip. 'I'm at the airport.' She looked at Tommy and registered the pain and confusion in his face. She screwed her eyes tight shut.

'Hello, did you hear me?'

Juliet took a deep breath. 'Yes, I heard you.'

She turned the phone off and replaced it in her purse. 'Matt found me a four-star horse that's entered for Badminton. I have to go back. It's my last chance to qualify.'

'Right you are, then,' Tommy said, his tone even, but the look of desolation on his face told a different story. She felt his pain as sharp and keen as if she owned it.

'Tommy, please. Right now, I have to do this, but we can work something out. We can –' she started, but he raised a finger to her lips.

'Shush. You know that we're meant to be together now. Don't you?'

They both stood up and took a few steps. He drew her in his arms and held her close. 'Well then,' he said at last. 'It's time to be making tracks. Now, you have my mobile number?'

'Yes.' She forced herself to walk slowly towards the departure gate.

'And you'll be sure to phone me about the arrangements for Espiritus, and anything else? You won't hesitate to call me, anytime, if there are any problems?'

Juliet turned. She wanted to speak but she couldn't. She said no with a shake of her head and tried to swallow the lump in her throat. She stopped. Neither of them moved. She didn't want to let him out of her sight.

A loudspeaker announcement called for the last passengers on her flight to board immediately. Reluctantly, she set off, wondering how it would feel without him. But right now, she had to be tough. She had to make sure that she brought home another Olympic gold.

Aim straight and keep your focus. She gave herself an internal pep talk.

'Juliet,' he called, sprinting after her. 'There's something that I must tell you. I –'

Juliet waved. 'I'll call you when I land.'

And she continued briskly to the gate, wondering what he had to say that was so important.

CHAPTER THIRTY-SIX

Rosetta

On a foul, stormy day just after noon, Rosetta drove out to Minsterford, a neighbouring village. Peter was waiting in the car park, sheltering from the rain. Through the window, he gestured at her to head inside. They'd chosen a remote country pub, so they weren't spotted. *Good choice,* Rosetta thought as she glanced around the typical scene of oak beams, exposed brickwork, and an open fire filled with crackling logs. She scanned the room and aimed for a corner table near the fire. *Out of earshot,* she thought, peeling off her scarf and coat while Peter went to the bar to order food and drinks. Typical of him, he hadn't checked what she wanted. He'd just assumed.

He tucked into steak and chips with all the trimmings while she toyed with a chicken and avocado salad. *Why do men always assume you're on a diet?* she wondered. She eyed his plate with interest. If they'd still been married, she'd have nicked a few of his chips. But post-divorce, she assumed chips were now off-limits.

'How's Patricia?' she asked, making small talk. *I mean, it's hardly as if I give a shit about that cow. Shut up, you sound deranged.* She ran the silent internal monologue with herself and fell silent.

Peter stared at his plate, cut a piece of bloody red meat, and forked it into his mouth.

A red wine-coloured rivulet of juice seeped across the plate. *Not a good omen, this,* Rosetta decided. He chewed methodically. *Nothing new there, then,* Rosetta observed. Peter was a creature of habit then and now it seemed. He didn't respond. *All in his own good time,* she supposed. Behind him, through the window, the wind had picked up and the rain was slashing against the glass. In her pocket her phone trilled. She checked the screen. Shirley calling.

'Hi,' Rosetta said. 'What's up?

'Where are you? Rav's told me to summon you in, urgent-like.'

'Out of town, I've got something important to attend to. So, can it wait?'

'I dunna think he's gonna buy that,' Shirley replied. 'Apparently, he's been trying to get hold of you all morning and you have nay picked up.'

Rosetta waited a moment, gathering her thoughts, then she made a reassuring noise. 'Okay it's okay. I'll handle it when I get back.'

'It'd be better –'

Rosetta ignored the note of warning in Shirley's voice. 'Gotta go, bye.'

With that, she hung up and turned her attention to Peter. 'Right, where were we? I met with the kids and I gather that Ed's interested in religion, particularly the Koran.'

'Yes, they mentioned that they'd seen you.' Peter stared at her, impassive as a poker shark.

Rosetta gave an exasperated gasp. Her heart was beating fast as she wondered how bad things were. Of course, she suspected the worst. Worry came as a non-negotiable part of the maternal landscape. *Why did Peter always have to make everything so difficult?* She licked her lips. 'I gather you told him to break off all contact with his Muslim friend. For the record, I backed you up on that. Has he been… radicalised?'

Peter narrowed his eyes and his shoulders dropped a fraction. For a moment, she thought he looked defeated. But he set down his knife and fork and lowered his voice. 'Regrettably, yes, but…'

'For fuck sake, Peter, how could you let that happen? It all went on right under your bloody nose and what about the goddamn boarding school, they weren't exactly on the ball?' A wave of nausea rose inside and she recoiled at the sight of her salad. She reached for her wine, her hand tightening around the glass.

Peter sighed. 'Believe me, I'm as shocked as you are, but luckily it was caught early, and things are being…' He held his hands out in an impassioned plea. 'Hopefully, things are being turned around.'

'Turned around how, exactly?'

'There are counter-radicalisation programs –'

Rosetta interrupted. 'You mean like Prevent? Well, in the Muslim community they're not too impressed with that, are they? Don't they call it "MI5 Islam" or something?'

'I couldn't involve a government agency, for obvious reasons,' Peter said, looking rattled. 'But my contact got Ed involved with a group of young Muslims from Dewsbury in West Yorkshire that he was working with, to try and turn them away from a destructive path. He showed them an amputation saw and pictures of a fighter with a leg, an arm, and part of his gut missing.'

Wincing, Rosetta moved the bloody steak plate and the remains of the salad to a neighbouring table. 'Lovely, but was it effective enough?'

'Well, then he showed them cesspits and buckets of vomit, festering fly-infested wounds, and he explained how unsanitary jihadi battlegrounds are – awash with diarrhoea and mucus.' Peter paused, looking tired and much older than she remembered him. 'That seems to have frightened the hell out of Ed and stopped him in his tracks.'

'So, what do we do? Sit back and keep our fingers crossed? This is our son here, and you denied him a mother's influence.' Rosetta shuddered, horrible images churned inside her head.

Peter raised his palms out in a pacifying gesture. 'Fair cop, ha-ha, but let's just try and pull together on this. We're all in a tricky position, which needs handling with the utmost care.'

'Too true,' Rosetta agreed. *I'm shirking my duty right now by being here and any time soon I'm going to be crossing the boundaries of professional ethics.*

Actually, she was not so much crossing boundaries as blowing them up. Deep down, doubt was niggling. If she went any further with this, there'd be no turning back. Yet, Ed was her son, her firstborn.

Meanwhile, an over-zealous waitress appeared, cleared the plates, and took their coffee order as Peter shooed her away with a brusque wave.

'The jihadi label won't do anyone any favours, I guess.'

'Quite.' He rolled his eyes towards the beams. 'It's hardly the irresistible hook in one's personal statement for one's Oxford application, eh?'

'Like fuck.' The more she thought about this entire episode, the more she felt sick. Teenagers, what are they like? They just screw up and expect the parents to wave a magic wand and clear up all the mess. 'So,' she continued, 'how's Pa Riley involved in the accident?'

Peter glanced around to make sure they couldn't be overheard. 'He's not. His boy went off the rails.'

'Handy, that,' Rosetta said with a shrug. 'Did he cough up anything useful? I don't need to tell you, of all people, that we really need a name, a diversion, a conviction, and pronto.'

Peter paused as the waitress appeared with the coffee and Rosetta waved her empty wine glass.

'I think I need something stronger, another sauvignon, please.'

'Chilean or New Zealand?' the waitress asked.

'He's paying, so make it a large New Zealand, love.' She followed the girl's back as she shimmed her tidy butt, encased in a tight black skirt, towards the bar. 'This is a bloody mess, and I'm due back at the station as we speak. So, do you have anything for me or not?'

Peter laughed, emitting a deep throaty sound. 'You never change, Rosetta. You totally lack finesse.'

Rosetta flinched. *What a cheek.* After all, she was bailing his ass out of boiling water, not the other way around. He looked past her, obviously eager to get on his way and put some distance between himself and his darling ex-wife.

'Actually, what you call finesse I call arse-licking, and at this you are consummate, of course. While you're brown-nosing, I'm solving crimes and clearing up humanity's great ugly cock-ups. I conclude that you are not in my league, you never were, and you certainly never will be.' Rosetta smiled as the waitress appeared with the wine, and she took a gulp. 'Hmm, and I'm not sure exactly how finesse applies to a man who can't keep his flies zipped up. Do you have any ideas about how to mitigate such very undiplomatic incidents and boorish behaviour, huh?'

Peter's nostrils flared a fraction and his cheek twitched. He glared at her across the table.

Rosetta typed "finesse, meaning?" into the Google search engine on her phone. 'Ah,' she said, feigning surprise. 'Google's definition of finesse is: *impressive delicacy and skill.* Well, you and Patricia at it on your desk in your office, that's a peachy bit of a Bill and Monica moment of finesse indeed. Well, shall we just leave it at that?'

'I'm sorry,' he muttered. 'I... I...' Peter looked almost contrite. Almost, but not quite.

'Apology gratefully accepted.' *It had been a long time coming,* she thought. 'Okay, so I need the name of Pa's accomplice.'

'You can't drag Riley into it. I promised there'd be no come-back. He –'

'For the record, you dragged that unsavoury piece of shit into it, not me. However, I take your point.' She took another mouthful of wine and swallowed. 'Okay, plus I need the number of his burner.'

He reached for his cappuccino, which left a trail of froth around his upper lip. 'What on earth's a burner?'

'What are you like? You've got one yourself. A pre-paid phone with no registered owner. I need the hit man's number and the service provider.'

'Is that all?' Peter leaned forward and met her eye, irritated.

'The name will do for now.' Her pulse quickened, and she held her breath.

Peter reached in his coat pocket, removed his phone, and brought up a picture, which he showed to Rosetta.

She took a long hard look at the photograph. The man was thick-set, tall, probably over six foot two, she'd guess with dark curly hair, and probably in his late thirties. *Finally.* She breathed a long sigh of relief. At last, she was getting somewhere with this investigation.

'His name's Baron O'Neil.'

Rosetta frowned, deep in concentration as she typed the name into the notes section of her phone. 'So, did he screw up, or did Riley put him up to it, or what?'

Peter shrugged. 'I can only speculate, but I don't think Riley had anything to do with the road rage attack. In fact, he's bloody livid.'

'Right,' Rosetta said, her mind racing through the possibilities, but the most important thing was that they were now on the brink of solving the case. 'Okay, thanks. Look, I've got to dash, my boss wants me back like yesterday. Plus, I've got to figure out some plausible explanation as to where this lead came from.'

'Good luck with that one.' Peter wheeled round and snapped his fingers at the waitress.

Still as arrogant as ever, Rosetta thought ruefully. 'Now, don't forget I need the phone details.'

'Really,' Peter hissed, wearing a grim expression. 'And how exactly am I supposed to come up with that?'

Rosetta shrugged. 'You'll manage, your sort always come out on top.' She felt her phone start to vibrate in her pocket. She glanced at the screen: Rav. *Oh shit, now I'm really in for it,* she thought.

'I'll see what I can do. No promises, mind.' There was the chink of ice in his delivery.

By now, her phone was hopping. She and Peter had started a conversation that needed to be finished. But it would have to wait for another time.

'I've got to head back now,' she said. 'I'm AWOL.' Rosetta pulled her coat on and wrapped her scarf around her neck.

She made her way to the exit and turned her collar up as some protection against the shitty weather. *Jesus Christ,* she thought, bracing herself to try stay on her feet. Deep in thought, her hair taking off in the fierce wind, she battled towards her car and the realisation hit her hard. She was about to take a crooked path, a very crooked path, indeed. *But what choice do I have?* she asked herself. She thought of Ed. She shuddered at just how bad it might have been, and she blinked back the tears from her rain-soaked cheeks. How far would a mother go to protect her son? *My family life's a wreckage. All I have left is my career and my reputation, both of which are now also on the line. Fuck it, I really need a fag,* she thought. But in this foul weather, that would have to wait.

Rosetta scrambled into her car, dripping so much that a puddle formed in the driver's seat. She reached for her phone, turned the car ignition on, and set the heater to work. She peered through the windscreen wipers as they went at it in overdrive. Rosetta did the unthinkable and lit a cigarette. She never smoked in the car.

Never.

Her heart beat hard and heavy until the nicotine kicked in, gradually the pounding slowed a little. Outside, it continued pissing down. Inside, puffing it up, she chuckled at the contrast. If she called her boss and told him some cock-and-bull story about Tommy agreeing to talk in return for immunity from prosecution, and she got caught out, then her career could spiral out of control. *Should I take the leap from elite officer to bent copper? If I go down this route, there's no turning back.* Rosetta took a long hard drag on the cigarette and reached for her phone. She called Rav. He picked up immediately and gave her serious grief, demanding to know why she'd taken so long to respond and when on earth she planned on getting back to the station. Rosetta remained silent and took the tongue-lashing. Eventually, Rav calmed down somewhat.

'Sod it,' she muttered, putting the car into drive, releasing the handbrake, and heading out of the car park with the windscreen wipers going ten to the dozen. At the junction, she wound down the window and threw out the cigarette butt. *I could do with another one,* she thought, *to calm my nerves.* Now, she had crossed the line and there was no turning back. She'd just entered a new phase: bent cop. *Gone bent for all the right reasons,* she told herself. But still… what if she got caught?

CHAPTER THIRTY-SEVEN
Rosetta

Rosetta was working in her study at home, she had drawn up index cards with all the past life links and associations. She was studying the patterns when an email from Juliet pinged into her inbox. She strummed her fingers on the desk as she waited for the scanned attachment to download. *At last.* She breathed a sigh of relief as she opened it and studied Espiritus's passport. Her registered name was Sky Catcher, and the mare had been born on 17th February. Rosetta exited the emails and logged into Eclipse. She typed in the date: *17th February Apache Indian, horse* and hit Enter.

Eclipse whirred into action and came up with:

> Geronimo, a Chiricahua Apache from Bedonkohe band, was born 1829 in upper Gila County in New Mexico. He was named 'the One Who Yawns.' In 1851, his mother, wife, and three children were massacred in a Mexican raid while Geronimo was away from the camp. This tragedy steeled him for a life of conflict. After this, he hated Mexicans and killed them indiscriminately. He would later become revered as a war shaman with seemingly supernatural powers. His name became legendary and he died from a fall off his horse when pneumonia set in on 17th February at age seventy-nine. He was buried at Fort Sill, in Oklahoma. His horse wandered off and was appropriated by the Mexicans.

Wow, wigwams and tipis, that's it! Rosetta could hardly contain her excitement. But what did it mean? She asked Eclipse to elaborate, and soon the system displayed an interesting narrative:

Geronimo's descendants believe that his grave was desecrated, and that his skull, femur bones, and funeral artefacts, including riding equipment, a silver bit, a hunting horn, and other effects, were stolen by members of a top-secret society called the Elite Order of the Skull and Bones, formed by students at Yale University. The fifteen seniors each year who are invited to join the society purportedly perform an initiation ceremony which involves kissing Geronimo's skull. It is rumoured that the skull is kept in the Temple, the society's clubhouse at New Haven, Connecticut. The story goes, that nine years after Geronimo's death, some of the Bones men dug up the grave and removed relics. This version was given some credence in 2006, when Marc Wartman was doing some research at Yale's Sterling library and found a letter dated 1918 tucked inside a book and written from one Bones man to another.

Using this letter as evidence, Geronimo's descendants claim that the skull of the worthy Geronimo the Terrible was exhumed from its tomb at Fort Sill, by the club, and is now safe inside the Temple, together with his well-worn femurs, bit, and saddle horn. Geronimo's descendants want the remains returned, together with his funerary objects, so that he may be reburied in his birthplace with an Apache burial ceremony and his spirit may be released. Some years previously, they mounted an unsuccessful legal challenge saying, "Everyone knows that to desecrate an Indian burial ground is to invite the wrath of the spirits."

'Phew,' Rosetta said, letting out a soft whistle. 'That explains why we're still feeling the karmic ripples to this day.' She got up and went into the kitchen to make a cup of tea, wondering what the relevance of the re-incarnating horse could be.

Atone popped through the cat flap and shot across the room, meowing as he wrapped himself round her legs.

'Okay, I'll feed you. Just a minute,' she said as she topped up his milk, ripped open the foil packet of cat food, and added it to his dish. 'Thank you for the delightful present you left on the mat this morning, my furry friend. I trust you'll be retrieving it later for your supper.' Rosetta shuddered and made a mental note to call the vermin catcher.

Mice she could just about cope with, but rats? It was a big one too, and as she made the tea, she wondered how the Dickens he'd got it through the cat flap. *Determined little soldier, this one, she thought,* giving another involuntary shudder. Christ, what if it scarpered out from its hiding place and ran out of the kitchen on some kind of ratty rampage? 'Yuck,' she muttered as she hurriedly grabbed her tea and closed the kitchen door with a slam.

Atone started mewling and staring at her through the glass panel.

'No, sorry, mate,' she said, thinking about his trophy collection over the last few years. 'That's all yours, that one.' He'd caught rabbits, all manner of birds, a pigeon once, which squawked and shit all over the place – just what she needed after a bad day at work.

She continued back to the study, laughing to herself about the bat that he'd kindly deposited in her bed one time. Thank heavens it wasn't a vampire one. Still, it had sent out weird sonic sounds that had scared the living daylights out of her till she'd made a run for the spare room. Bernard, the chap from the Bat Protection Society, came around and caught him. It had been an adolescent male apparently, although how he could tell still remained a mystery to this day. He'd nursed him back to health in a large, aerated jam jar, complete with a tea towel. A month later, with much ceremony, Bernard returned after dark and released little Batty-Boyo in the garden.

Terrific, I've got bats in the belfry, rats in the kitchen and still no nearer to solving the horse situation. She sent Dr. Ashworth the file via Eclipse and asked her to take a look and see what she thought. Eclipse, unlike email, was totally secure and un-hackable.

Rosetta decided to do a bit more general internet research to see what that came up with.

The searches were quite illuminating. There was a massacre – the Kas-Ki-Yeh massacre – where his mother, wife, and three children were slain by Mexicans. This started years of tit-for-tat revenge and retaliation and underpinned Geronimo's hatred of Mexicans.

Rosetta grabbed her notebook and a pen and scribbled, *themes are massacre, revenge, desecration, and wrathful spirits.* Then she searched the site to investigate about Apache burial rites and discovered a piece where an Apache described his grandfather's death:

We dressed him in his best clothes, painted his face, and wrapped him in rich blankets. Then we saddled his favourite horse and took him to a cave where the horse was slain and laid with him. Now the winds in the pines sing a slow requiem over the dead warrior.

'That's it!' She leapt out of her chair and did a jig around the room. 'Geronimo's horse needs to be returned, and I know just where to find the horse's remains.' Scooping up the index cards she'd prepared, she sat cross-legged on the floor and spread them out in a fan to create a mind-map of themes and sub-plots in order to reconstruct the past life story:

TERRORISM:

Definition

Use of indiscriminate violence and mayhem as a means to create terror to achieve financial, political, religious, or ideological aims.

Possible links

Tommy – Ireland home of Provisional IRA. Ed, who was recruited [almost] to join a jihad-by-the-sword radical Islamic group. Geronimo, who also became linked to ISIS when US troops invaded Afghanistan and established Camp Geronimo as a forward base. After 9/11 posters and T-shirts sprang up picturing Geronimo and fellow warriors with the caption: "Homeland Security – Fighting Terrorism Since 1492." Then his name was used in conjunction with the killing of terrorist mastermind Osama Bin Laden – when Navy Seals finally killed him, they sent back the message: Geronimo EKIA.

Was Geronimo a terrorist?

The association of his name and Osama's did not go down well and resulted in angry backlashes, numerous hearings about racial stereotyping of indigenous peoples. Geronimo's relative Harlyn said: "Obviously to equate Geronimo with Osama Bin Laden is an unpardonable slander of Native Americans and their most famous leader in history."

Mexicans/Apache Indians/US Army

The Apaches were not the invaders. Instead, their territory was invaded by the Spanish, the Mexicans, and then the US army, who viewed them as pagans of the promised land – like heathens, living outside their laws and conventions. The inappropriate codename made Osama the 21st century equivalent of Geronimo and perpetuated the "Indians are enemies" stereotype. Geronimo was undoubtedly an amazing warrior and guerrilla fighter whose quest for revenge

273

began after an unprovoked attack – the Kas-Ki-Yeh massacre – perpetrated by Mexicans. Many Apache women and children, including Geronimo's entire family, were brutally slaughtered by Mexicans, who also stole their horses and provisions.

So, one man's terrorist is another man's freedom fighter. Geronimo is a warrior's name, invoking courage, incredible stamina, endurance, and uncompromising ferocity. In the territories of New Mexico and Arizona, and across northern Mexico, it was a synonym for terror throughout the 1870s and 1880s.

Geronimo was not a terrorist

Geronimo was a leader who took his people down the path of war in self-defence. He was a heroic defender of native rights. Terrorism seeks to have a psychological impact by attacking an unarmed adversary. This was not Geronimo's modus operandi, and his motives were survival and preservation, not financial/political/religious or ideological.

THEMES: REVENGE

Geronimo's motivation was retaliation for the horrific atrocities committed against the Apaches by the Mexicans, and the US Congress sent a quarter of their military forces to destroy him. On 13th November 1882, the Apaches plotted an ambush and they went on to Galeana, where Mexican commander Juan Mata Ortiz was garrisoned with his troops. The Apaches stole some horses, knowing the Mexicans would chase them, next they set up an ambush on the road between Galeana and Carsas Grandes, known as Chocolate Pass. When Ortiz and his troops realised they'd been trapped, they retreated to higher ground and dug in, waiting for reinforcements. But the Apaches picked them off one by one, with the command: 'Do not kill el Capitan. *Sin bala, sin flecha, sin lanza, pero fuego.*' The same as in Katya's vision and as confirmed by historical records: "You're not going to have a quick death – no bullet, no arrow, no lance – but fire."

Mexican commander Juan Mata Ortiz was burnt alive over a pit at the top of a small hill just north of Galeana. After the ambush, the garrison folk ran to the church and, from the bell tower, they watched the smoke coming from that little hill with sinking hearts.

PAST LIFE:

People

Peter was indirectly involved in the road rage attack and had previously regressed to an Apache in a past life. Was Ed linked somehow via the tenuous terrorist link? In Katya's visions, the Apache son tells his mother [Juliet?] that he will forgive her for what she did to his father. What does this mean? The boy also says that Geronimo's horse must be returned as part of the righting of wrongs committed, and for past deeds to be atoned. This part currently can't be linked together. Too many gaps. Who did what to whom, and why? What is the negative karma playing out here?

Horses: Totem/Gothic/Espiritus

A totem is a spirit being, a sacred object, or symbol that serves as an emblem of a group of people, clan, or tribe. Espiritus, which means spirit, is a painted horse who was born on the same day that Geronimo died, and the same day that this favourite horse was taken by Mexicans: its fate is unknown. The horse should have been buried with his master, the famous Apache warrior. The three reincarnated horses all belong to Juliet, so we have to assume that her past life role is somehow pivotally connected. Gothic's remains need to be returned to the Apaches as a symbolic peace offering and to lay the spirits to rest. Technically, Gothic should be buried with Geronimo, technically at Fort Sill, but his relatives may decide on a preferred site closer to his place of birth, as is their prerogative.

Satisfied with the progress she had made, Rosetta scanned the index cards and sent them to her boss, arranging a mutually convenient time for a catch-up call.

Thirty minutes or so later, Rosetta called her boss. She had been keeping her fully briefed since the onset.

'Hi,' Dr. Ashworth said. 'Great work. What a fascinating case.'

'Yeah.' Rosetta gave her the update about the convention in some Apache funerals, where the favourite horse was laid to rest and buried at the same place. 'I can locate the horse. Although Juliet may not be too keen on exhuming Gothic's remains, I think I can persuade her. Can EPIS locate the funerary effects?'

'That should be possible, but where we'll have difficulty will be trying to locate Geronimo's skull and femur bones, if in fact they're not in the grave

275

at Fort Sill. If the Bones men did take them, they'll have removed all the evidence when Geronimo's descendants issued the court case. If not, we'd have to go back in time to reconstruct events, and that will take a while. As you may have gathered, we're having some problems right now.'

Rosetta arched one eyebrow. 'Sorry, problems such as?'

'The attempt to return the aliens didn't go entirely according to plan.' Dr. Ashworth sounded deflated. 'Instead of them going back from whence they came, more of them arrived.'

'Oh shit.'

'Quite.'

'I guess that means that T-Portal transportation is still suspended until further notice?' Rosetta paused. 'How many more exactly?'

'Don't ask.'

'Okay, just curious. But what do you make of the terrorist angle?'

Dr. Ashworth paused. 'I'm not really following the link with your ex-husband or your son, but I'm presuming this is somewhat off-limits until further notice?'

Rosetta breathed a sigh of relief. 'Yes, appreciated. I meant regarding Geronimo.'

Dr. Ashworth paused. 'I did a module on Westerns as part of a film studies course, so I've sat through quite a few.' She laughed and then continued, 'It seems to me that, for Hollywood, Geronimo as a warrior became too dangerous from a PC perspective, for them to tackle with any realism. So, they swung over to elevating his spiritual side until he practically became depicted as an Apache Moses and old prophet.'

Rosetta laughed. 'How myths are made in the cutting room, eh?'

'Indeed, but as far as enemies go, in today's ultra-PC climate it seems Apaches are off-limits, producers can't risk making ethnic groups look bad. Far better to have orcs and aliens cast as your movie villains.'

'Ah.' Rosetta shook her head. 'No doubt the aliens are getting unionised as we speak, so that only leaves orcs, I'm afraid, and maybe robots of course. They have terrific fiendish potential, don't they?'

'Yes.' Dr. Ashworth sounded grave.

'Okay, on a lighter note,' Rosetta said, 'how about we contact some Apaches from Geronimo's tribe, and they can organise a reburial of the horse remains and the funerary effects if they wish? It's not total completion, but at least it gives some degree of closure, surely?'

'Yes, it would be an improvement, I guess. Okay, let's go for it. I'll be in touch.' With that, Dr. Ashworth hung up.

276

Rosetta and Professor Romanoff had a regular weekly catch-up on FaceTime. Shortly after the call with her boss, she connected with her friend.

'Hi, how're things? I've just spoken to Dr. Ashworth, and I gather the LGM posted the details of the party on Facebook, and the parents aren't too happy at the hordes of unexpected guests turning up.' Rosetta laughed as her friend looked puzzled.

'The what?' he asked.

'The Little Green Men,' Rosetta giggled and shook her head.

'Oh.' He groaned. 'Right, well... no, mom and dad aren't too impressed. Full on pissed off, in fact.'

'I bet.' Rosetta shook her head. 'What happens now?'

'Beats me.' Ritchie shrugged. 'They aren't green, though, I feel I ought to mention that. So far only White, Blue, or Grey, and the 'Grey' ones are a real pain in the butt, quite frankly. They keep causing havoc with Jobs-Worthy and short circuiting the electrical circuits – then everything shuts down. I swear they're playing games with us.'

Rosetta reached for her mug of coffee and took a sip. 'I take it they're more technologically advanced than us, then?'

'Definitely,' he said with a sigh. He scratched his head and looked thoughtful. 'Actually, they're vastly more advanced than us. But as far as I can tell the Greys are programmed to create havoc, resist change, and generally preserve the status quo. The Whites are variable, some are positive towards humanity others not so.'

'So, like the Establishment here on Earth?'

'I guess. We're not having much luck communicating with them, but the Blues are far more receptive.' His face lit up with joy. 'In fact, we've had a breakthrough with some of their communication codes.'

'Wow, that's incredible.' Rosetta beamed, she knew how many years and how much of his life he had devoted to this mission. 'Well done, you must be thrilled.'

'Yes,' he chuckled with glee. 'They sent me telepathic images of crop circles, hieroglyphics, and dolphins. Dolphins and orcas can communicate when they're miles apart.'

'Like a kind of watery telepathy?' she interrupted.

'Yes, back in twenty-eighteen there was a killer whale taught to mimic human speech, which puts them on a footing with humans. While birds mimic each other, the skill is exceedingly rare in mammals other than people. Their speech patterns are complex sequences of bleeps and squeaks, and we can say that killer whales and other cetaceans have highly developed social intelligence. When we played dolphin recordings, the Blues responded. Mind you, the code's not anywhere near cracked. There's a long way to go, but finally we're on the right track.'

'Brill – so any luck with the big questions, like where do they come from and why are they here?' Rosetta asked, delighted for her friend.

The professor's eyes gleamed as he spoke. 'Well, there are at least four different species, from different planets, and they all appear to have different agendas. The Blues are mainly from the star, Sirius, and their mission seems to be to raise human consciousness and stop us destroying the planet. They appear to have some kind of spiritual mission and want us to recognise that we are spiritual beings having a physical experience on Earth, and they want to get us to evolve and vibrate at a higher frequency. But really the how, who, and what remains unclear.'

Rosetta nodded. 'But let me guess… you're working on it?'

'Yeah, and as far as I can determine, they've been visiting Earth for a long, long time. There are too many unexplained sightings. They seem to pass through warp drive and worm holes, but crucially, so far, they've shown no hostile intent. In fact, quite the opposite, as they seem to only intervene near nuclear bases, to stop us blowing ourselves up.'

'Wow,' Rosetta said, taking a deep breath. 'Well, the next thing we know we'll have the powers that be tweeting, *"The truth is out there."'*

'Or, the truth is right here under our noses and we're working on it.'

'Yeah.' Rosetta chuckled, raising her mug of coffee. 'I'll drink to that. Just a thought, but is it possible that we learned to communicate from them, the… what did you call them, the cetaceans?'

'Affirmative, that's entirely feasible.' He chuckled.

'Cool, well, I've got to say bye now. See you same time next week?'

Ritchie blew her a kiss and the ended the video call.

CHAPTER THIRTY-EIGHT

Juliet

Espiritus arrived after a long trip by land and sea. She was stressed and sweaty when she came off the lorry, and when she went into her stable to settle down, she proceeded to box walk, which was technically deemed to be a bad habit. Juliet left her to settle in the isolation box, but the mare objected to being separated from the other horses. She stomped her feet, went round and round in circles, and whinnied loudly to create a real racket. Juliet felt bad and deflated by her distress, but it was a necessary precaution for any new horse in a new yard, in case they were carrying the strangles virus, which was highly contagious. It affected the lymph nodes and caused fever, swellings, abscesses, and a thick nasal discharge.

So, Espiritus, whether she liked it or not, would have to be kept away from the others for at least two weeks to ensure that she was symptom-free. Juliet knew that if strangles took hold in a stable yard, it would spread like wildfire and the whole yard would have to be put into quarantine, and sometimes, special hygiene and disinfection measures will be in effect for a few months. As a top competition rider, Juliet had to take precautions for the horse's sake and to avoid being grounded. She couldn't afford to take the risk of cross-contamination. Espiritus continued snorting, shaking her head, and whinnying so that everyone got the message.

Juliet sighed. *The lady doth protest too much.* She called Tommy via WhatsApp, great for free international calls – to tell him that Espiritus had arrived safely.

'Hi, she's here safe and sound but in isolation, so she's pretty vocal as you can probably imagine.' She held the phone in the mare's direction, so he could hear her complaining.

'Ay, she's a mouthy mare all right. Glad she's in good voice, and how about you? How're things?'

'I'm okay.' Juliet twiddled with a long strand of hair. 'I'm missing you like crazy, though.' She left the stable yard and headed to the kitchen via the back door, the phone nestled to her ear.

Tommy sighed. 'Me too, shall I come over and help you back herself?'

'Yeah, that would be great. She needs to settle in here first, so should we say in three to four weeks?'

'That seems so far away,' he said tutting. 'How will I manage without you?' He paused for a while. 'So, what did you decide about the four-star horse? I forget the name…'

'Chi-Chi Charlie,' she said with a chuckle. 'It's kind of a mouthful.'

'For sure, and are you going for it or not?'

She heaved a sigh. 'However, much I want to get to the top, I can't do that to Todd. I simply can't drop my pal up shit creek. I wouldn't be able to live with myself. He's always been there for me through thick and thin. So, it wouldn't be fair, and any success that I had would kind of be tainted. Does that make sense?'

'For sure now. I had a situation like that with one of the other Travellers, a tricky one. But we're supposed to stick together through thick an' thin. How's Matt taken it?'

'Badly. As in very.'

Tommy laughed. 'That's a fret. Mind you, he's such a prat.'

Juliet laughed, and it came out as a snort. 'Well, you're biased, of course. Actually, now that I think of it… do you remember when Matt and I fought, and you came to my rescue at the Silent Inn?'

'That bloody eejit!'

'Yeah,' Juliet agreed. 'You mentioned that you knew him from your teens and you didn't seem too impressed. Why, and what exactly did he do to make an enemy out of you?'

'It was on the junior BSJA circuit when I was in West Yorkshire training with Nigel Simpson. Matt was one of my main rivals…' His voice was so quiet that she had to strain to hear him.

'Yes, he's my main coach for the show jumping phase. He's darn good…'

'Well, his techniques back then weren't so darn fine. Pretty soon, the rumours started circulating about him and his mother's unconventional training methods.'

In the background, the washing machine finished its cycle. Juliet unloaded the contents with one hand and moved them into the drier, the smell of fresh linen wafting by until she closed the door and started the program.

'Unconventional. What do you mean?'

'Bloody barbaric as it turned out. Not just bog-standard rapping but rapping with wire mesh spikes under the front bandages.'

'No.' She gasped. Her hand flew to her mouth. She couldn't believe what she was hearing. 'Matt wouldn't do something like that.'

'Really?' Tommy continued. 'Well, one owner removed his entire string of ponies and found a row of infected puncture wounds on the inside of both forelegs on two of them. Another came away totally head-shy, terrified of humans and still is to this day.'

Juliet swallowed with a gulp, trying to process this. Rapping involved hitting the front legs so that the pony would associate hitting a pole with pain. And with spikes impaling the flesh, the pain would be excruciating. 'What happened?'

Tommy paused. 'As I recall, they were banned for a while but then they carried on. Cruella De Vil, the mother and her psycho son carried on business as usual for a year or so. Then, she left for Australia under a cloud.'

Juliet poured herself a glass of water and slumped on a chair. 'You should have told me all this before.'

There was a brittle silence. 'Well, you were pretty wrapped up in your own stuff, how to get an Olympic horse. And if I'd told you sooner, that would have made acquiring Chi-Chi Charlie more complicated. So, I figured it wasn't my place.' He paused as if he was chewing carefully over his next words. 'Plus, I wanted you to choose me for me self like, not as some consolation prize when you twigged what a two-faced twat he was.'

'The asshole,' she said, resting her head in her hands. 'Seriously though, how could I have gotten it so wrong?'

'Fricking hell,' Tommy spat. 'Well, you weren't the only one. Old Ma Bates ripped off half the equestrian circle and most of the show jumping set with her scams, frauds, and you name it.'

'Ma Bates?'

'Yeah, Lebaine is just a posh made-up name they changed by deed poll.'

'What?' Juliet spluttered, struggling to make sense of these revelations. It felt as if a huge yawning chasm had opened right before her eyes. It felt like a big black sink hole, in fact. 'You knew all this, but you still did business with him?'

'Whoa, hold it right there,' his voice bristled with irritation. 'He was Shamus's client, not mine. Besides, if I ruled out all the dodgy sorts there's be very few horses exported from Ireland an' all.'

A surge of fury rose in her. 'Really. So, business is business, and anything goes?'

'Excuse me,' Tommy growled. 'But aren't you missing the point? It wasn't me sleeping with the enemy, getting engaged an' all that.'

His words hit her like a punch in the ribs. 'No.' Her first instinct was to defend herself, but that soon subsided. 'Well. Yes. I... I... shit. I'm sorry. I totally misjudged him.' The room began to swim a little as the solid foundations of her life went hurtling off into quicksand.

'Look, I need to say this because I care about you, so don't take it the wrong way.' There was a long spell of silence while Tommy worked on what to say. 'Well, there's no beating around the bush. He's a dangerous bastard, is what he is. All the while, he's been pretending to be someone different, to get you to love him. He's a devious, lying cheat and then some. There, I've said it.'

Juliet felt the colour drain from her face, and her hands grew clammy with nerves. She gripped hold of the edge of the table to steady herself as a terrible thought flashed through her mind. *What if Matt had something to do with the accident?* She closed her eyes, trying not to think about it. If she went down that road it would be like the aftermath of a napalm bomb – leaving nothing but shattered dreams and destruction in its wake.

She needed to park this for now and get the conversation back on a more neutral track. 'So, what've you been up to?' she said, trying to sound cheerful, but deep inside, all the while trying to push the nagging doubts about Matt back down.

'Ah, busy bringing on Tick and Tock, a couple of nice Connies, to sell on as kids' BSJA ponies.'

'Aren't you kind of heavy to ride ponies?'

She recalled that Matt was the beneficiary of the insurance policies. *No,* she screamed at herself internally. *How could I have allowed that?*

'Well, they're strong, solid sorts. But, no, you're right. I've got meself some help, a young groom, and she's grand an' all.'

Juliet inhaled sharply. 'I'm not big on the idea, actually.' She stuck out her lip in a pout.

'Aren't you, now? Well, you're over there with Matt, having a whale of a time, no doubt.'

'I'm going to get him to leave.'

'Ah, go away outta that. You're having me on, for sure.'

'I'm serious. I've been in the guest room ever since I got back. The way I feel about you, I can't be with him. I can't stand it anymore. The thought of him makes me feel sick. I nearly asked him to go when I got back from Ireland.'

'Well, well, well, how nearly brave of you. Nearly, well done then, eh? So, what stopped you?'

Juliet breathed deeply. Her initial reaction was a twinge of guilt. She needed Matt to get her back on track for another Olympic gold. The twinge turned into a pang as she realised how selfishly she'd been behaving. 'I... I couldn't draw a line in the sand and end the relationship until... well...'

'Come on, spit it out.'

'You're just making this difficult on purpose.' She flipped her hair off her face. 'Well, with less than two years to prepare for the next Olympics, I needed to secure the right horse without any more delay. And... and, Matt had the key, so...'

'So, you were hedging your bets?'

Juliet sighed, irritated at being exposed. 'Yes, but I'll tell him he has to move out by the end of the month.'

Tommy let out a soft low whistle. 'By-jabbers, that's grand. Tonight, I'll be out getting ossified.'

Juliet groaned. 'Okay, well, let's catch up on Skype tomorrow evening around six, or we could do FaceTime, as long as you're sober. I don't want to be looking at you if you're wasted.'

'Deal,' he agreed. 'I'll be on the mineral by then, stop your fretting. Give Espiritus a hug from me. And by the way, I got the girl groom, so I can spend more time with you over there.'

'Ah, it must be love. Take care.' She felt pleased at how things were going with her and Tommy. They had a future together and it would all work out. 'Bye,' Juliet said, ending the call.

But the situation with Matt just lurched from bad to dire. She didn't know what to think as a fog descended clouding her perception. How had she been taken in by him? Was she completely deluded? Her world kept on shattering piece by piece. Whatever next?

With that, she dialled Todd and told him some of what she'd just learned.

'It's a total nightmare.' Juliet sobbed down the phone. She was breathless and choking and making little sense.

'It is,' he echoed. 'It's a total nightmare indeed. Let's talk about it over lunch.'

* * *

An hour later, they met at the White Hart for lunch. Todd wore a pale baby blue T-shirt under a striped navy shirt, immaculate jeans, and tan coloured Vans. Aware that she looked and felt far from immaculate herself, Juliet sighed as Todd went to get drinks. Her mouth tasted metallic and nasty and the sip of wine reminded her of lemon sours. She quickly brought Todd up to speed with the latest developments and what she'd discovered about Matt.

He looked shocked. 'Oh my, oh my… whatever next?'

Juliet gave a slight shudder. What indeed? One morning not so long ago, she'd been on top of the world at breakfast, only to end up wallowing in grief by lunchtime. Now she felt humiliated and a total failure. It occurred to her how transitory happiness could be, and how control was an illusion at best. She'd been so wrapped up in her achievements and ambition that she'd gotten it all wrong. She'd completely taken her eye off the ball.

'I let Matt into my world, my life, my house… '

'Your bed,' Todd finished off her sentence.

'Yes, thanks for reminding me about that,' she muttered, 'and all for what?'

Todd studied his soda and lime as if searching for inspiration. 'For love, I guess. You wanted to be rescued from your past, the feeling that your parents had abandoned you, perhaps?'

She thought about it and groaned. 'Well, this just taps into all that pain. It hurts like having a root canal drilled. The feeling deep down is that I'm not worth it, that somehow, I'm not worthy of love. And all the Olympic gold medals were supposed to fill the void, but really nothing could. Certainly not Matt. I see that now. He's a fake, a low-grade con man. I've been so freaking blind and stupid.' Juliet bit her lip and sniffed.

Todd held her gaze for a second, until he reached across the table and gave her hand a squeeze. 'Shall we order something to eat?'

Juliet shook her head and ran her fingers through her hair. 'I'm so furious with myself. I've lost my appetite. What do I do?'

Todd took charge. 'Right, you go home and put anything and everything of value under lock and key, phone the police, and fill them in on Matt's past. Then you give him his marching orders, pronto. I'll send Barrie over to help with his packing.'

For the first time in a while Juliet laughed. Barrie was serious beefcake who'd done a few undercover survival stints with ex-SAS personnel. At six foot three, and with a physique that looked as if he snacked on steroids, there was no way Matt would want to mess with him.

'Perfect.' Juliet jutted out her chin.

'Glad you approve, darling. We'll send a couple of our grooms in to cover, and meanwhile you can move in with us, till this all settles down a bit.'

Juliet threw her arms round his neck and gave him a big hug. 'You're simply the best.'

'Yes,' he agreed, 'better than all the rest.'

'But hold off for the time being, until I can speak to the police and run it by DS Barrett.'

Todd raised his palm. 'Deal,' he said. 'You just say the word.'

CHAPTER THIRTY-NINE

Rosetta

When Rosetta took Juliet's call, she counselled her not to make any rash decisions when it came to Matt. It was nearly six months after the accident, a significant delay thanks to the robots holding up the claim pay-out. *So much for AI advancing crime detection,* she thought ruefully. The insurance pay-out was imminent, and they needed him in-situ and unsuspecting for now.

Rosetta drove to Juliet's house and knocked on the door. Juliet took her coat and indicated for her to follow her and make herself comfortable in the enormous, stunning kitchen. As she entered, Rosetta took a deep breath, gasping with admiration at the high apex ceiling with gnarled beams which looked as if they'd been reclaimed from an old wreck dragged up and recovered from the deep, off the sea bed. The floors were continental slate, a dark-grey colour with orange and blue veins running through. It felt smooth underfoot, not too highly polished, and Rosetta imagined that if she walked over it barefoot, she would feel the natural indentations. The ebb and the flow of life captured and recreated in a perfect-imperfect flooring.

Rosetta glanced greedily around, taking it all in. The walls were half-tiled in beautiful dove-grey marble. The kitchen work surfaces were dark-grey granite, with gold flecks which glittered in the morning sunlight. The kitchen opened into a conservatory worthy of interior design dream territory.

'Wow,' Rosetta said appreciatively. 'This is something else.'

Juliet smiled. 'Glad you like it. I do too, but it took a while to get it just right.'

'You obviously have a great eye for design. If you don't mind me asking, how much does a kitchen like this actually cost?'

Juliet laughed. 'Don't ask, too much.'

'I bet,' Rosetta agreed. 'Well, there are a few things we need to catch up on. You mentioned that you had some information about Matt?' she said, still surveying her surroundings with a detective's keen eye for detail.

The kitchen had an AGA, but the overall design blended old with extremely high-tech, and overall, it looked very expensive. The surround sound system was Bosch, the hi-tech security alarm no doubt top of the range with gizmos, and everything from the heating to the lighting could be remotely controlled. But, the new technology was carefully hidden from plain sight, so it didn't clash. *Old, all modcons,* was how Rosetta mentally summed it up. The kitchen and the conservatory overlooked the picture-book paddocks where horses were grazing.

Juliet stood at the sink, dressed casually in black leggings with fluffy pink leg warmers over top, and a long black and pink jumper thrown over to finish it off. She looked as if she'd been to a yoga class or something. She busied herself loading the dishwasher. She was enviably slim and had a way of moving which combined elegance with grace.

Horse riding must be great for core balance, Rosetta concluded.

Finally, Juliet spoke and told her what she'd learned from Tommy.

'Well, that's interesting. What did you say his real name was?'

Juliet rubbed her forehead. 'Brian – no – Bates, I think.'

Rosetta typed that into the notes section of her phone. Alice had taught her how to use it: "my mother, the techie-dumbo," she'd said, and they'd both had a laugh at that. 'We'll follow up and keep you posted. I know it's going to be tricky, but you need to carry on as usual. Don't do anything out of the ordinary that might make him suspicious.'

Juliet spun round, looking stunned. 'Are you saying he's... he's a suspect?'

'I can't comment right now, but there are a few other matters to catch up on.'

'Such as?' Juliet enquired, glancing round uncomfortably.

'Well,' Rosetta said, taking a deep breath. 'You know I work on past lives to try and unravel the original causes that lie behind more recent events?'

Juliet stared at her but didn't say anything. Then she blinked as if she wasn't entirely convinced. 'What're you getting at? You're obviously leading up to something.' She plonked herself down on a kitchen chair at the opposite end of the table.

No point waffling, Rosetta decided.

'Yes,' she agreed. 'In this case there's a link, a strong link to the Apache American Indians.'

'That's pretty far-fetched.' Juliet waved her arm dismissively with a sweeping gesture. Then, she stood and leaned back against the kitchen unit, folded her arms across her chest, and stuck out her chin in defiance.

'Not really,' Rosetta persevered. 'You had a horse called Totem.'

'Try just a coincidence.'

'Actually, synchronicity is common in past-life situations. Think of déjà vu for example. Also, you believe that Totem came back as Gothic, don't you? There's always a past-life story. Stories are in our blood, in our bones. I investigate the stories which raise their voices to make us sit up and take notice. Yours is one of those.'

'Well, I… well… I don't know what to make of it.'

'That's fair enough. It's head vs heart vs gut instinct, but my point is that you have a strong sixth sense about this. Psychic things can't always be proven, but nor should they be totally dismissed. Actually, the organisation I work for is making great strides with obtaining evidence.'

Juliet looked more resigned than convinced. 'Go on, then.' She sighed. 'Hit me with your grand theory.'

'There's a past-life connection to this, the death of a horse and a rider. In the present, that's Gothic and Isabella. But almost a century ago, a famous Apache warrior fell from his horse and died not long afterwards.'

'Who do you mean, and what's that got to do with me?'

'I don't know the full backstory yet, but it certainly has to do with Espiritus, Gothic, and Totem. When Apache chiefs or shaman warriors like Geronimo die, their favourite horse is slain and laid to rest with them; sometimes in a cave, sometimes on the wide-open plains. Most often, as many bands or tribes are nomadic, the burials are on the open plain. In Geronimo's case, he was captured and kept prisoner at Fort Sill, Oklahoma, where he was finally buried. His descendants believe that subsequently his grave was robbed.'

'I don't like what I'm hearing.' Juliet shivered. 'I'm confused, and it's making me feel freaked-out.'

'I'm sorry, I know it's all new and it's difficult to get your head around it. But the Apaches believe that when a grave is desecrated, the spirit is not at rest. They want Geronimo and all his funerary effects to be recovered and reburied with a proper Apache ceremony at his birthplace at the tribute of the Gila River, in what is now New Mexico.'

Juliet swallowed and stared at Rosetta, aghast. 'If you're suggesting what I think you are then stop, right now. I'm not having it, no way!'

Rosetta turned her palms upright and held Juliet's gaze. 'It's the only way. The only way to break the cycle. It's like a chain reaction. At some point, only atonement will halt the destructive consequences. The link is irrefutable. I've investigated many similar cases. I know the signs to look for. Espiritus was born on 17th February…'

'Is that why you wanted a copy of her passport?'

Rosetta nodded and gave Juliet's hand a squeeze. 'That's the day that Geronimo died. He died from pneumonia after a fall from his horse. Subsequently, the horse was taken by Mexicans. Now it needs to be returned,' she said softly. 'I need you to trust me on this, but we have to repatriate Gothic to New Mexico where he belongs.'

'No,' Juliet wailed. 'He's my horse. He belongs with me. I couldn't bury Totem. I have to keep Gothic safe. Totem came back so I could get the ending right this time.'

'Exactly.' Rosetta gave a faint smile. 'It is all about getting the ending, the burial, the farewell ceremony, right. There's a saying…' Rosetta wracked her brain. She'd memorised it, or so she thought. *Wait, and it will come to me in a minute. Ah yes,* she finally remembered. 'As I recall, "No heaven can heaven be, if my horse isn't there to welcome me." Gothic is your horse, but then again, he isn't. We have to take him back to the Apaches who've suffered so many losses and terrible wrongs. It's the right thing to do and what Gothic would want.'

A tear trickled down Juliet's cheek. 'I need some time to think about it.'

'Of course,' she said soothingly. 'My boss will pick up the tab and make all the arrangements. You can come to New Mexico and see him reunited with his tribe, if you like?'

Juliet thought a moment. 'Yes. I'd like that. It feels right.'

'Good.' Rosetta stood up. 'Shall I make us both a hot drink?'

At Juliet's nod, Rosetta busied herself making two mugs of green mint tea. 'So how are things going? How's Espiritus?' she asked, setting the cups down on the kitchen table and taking a seat.

Juliet joined her. 'Thanks. She's a handful. She's very temperamental. But Tommy's coming over to help me back her soon.'

'What do you mean by back her?' Rosetta blew on the steaming tea.

'That's where you train a horse, first to get used to the weight of the saddle on their back, then the saddle and the rider. Then they have to learn the commands. We call them aids.'

'Oh right, and how long does that take?'

'It depends how much handling you do in preparation. She's already used to the bridle and a bit in her mouth, and she's been around the school with a roller around her middle and long reins. That's where you stand behind them at a safe distance, so you don't get kicked. That way, the horse learns to go forward and to change direction according to the signal via the bit. She's a fast learner and very bold too, but they need to be brave to jump top-class fences, as some of them are huge. Espiritus means "spirit" and when I watch her move, she reminds me of the spirit of the wind. She moves beautifully, and she has such free-floating paces.' Juliet's face lit up with a fleeting look of love and pride, indicating a strong bond had already formed between the horse and owner.

Rosetta sipped her drink, which was still too hot to take a gulp of, so she blew on it again for a while. 'Are you and Tommy quite close, then?' This was all getting extremely complicated, more complicated by the minute in fact. It made her feel very uncomfortable, especially now it transpired that the investigating officer and the victim had both slept with the same man, and he was a crime witness. *Shit. Bitch, moan, whinge or what?*

'Yes. Obviously, it's finished with Matt. As soon as you give me the nod, he'll be moving out.' She looked anxious. 'How much longer will it take to solve this case? It's been dragging on forever.'

'Not long now.' They'd have to pick him up soon and bring him in before he had the chance to leave and, God forbid, disappear.

'Well, it's all getting very tricky around here. He doesn't know about Tommy, and its early days for us, but fingers crossed.' She made an optimistic gesture and sipped her tea.

'When's Tommy coming over to help back Espiritus?'

Juliet looked suspicious. 'In about three weeks. Obviously, Matt will have to be out of the way before then. Are you asking on a personal level, or is this police business?'

Rosetta ducked the question. 'Well, Tommy seems like a decent enough sort.'

Juliet folded her arms across her chest and put her head to one side while she scrutinised Rosetta. 'Meaning, you know Tommy. How do you know him, and since when exactly?'

'We met fairly recently.' She reached in her handbag for her cigarettes and lighter. 'May I have an ashtray, please?'

Juliet slammed her cup down on the table, sending splodges of pale green liquid across its gnarled surface. 'Where and in what capacity?' She sprang to her feet to retrieve something, then she begrudgingly passed Rosetta an old egg cup as a makeshift ashtray.

Rosetta pursed her lips. It might be better to come clean, but then again maybe not. So, she hedged. 'I was in Ireland last month, and I was introduced to him by a friend.'

'Strange, that he never mentioned it to me. Why would that be?'

Rosetta shrugged. 'No idea.'

Juliet fixed Rosetta with an icy glare. 'You're not answering the question, so let's cut to the chase. Now, what exactly is it that you're not telling me?'

Rosetta grew thoughtful as a tiny pang of guilt crept in. It would not look good to admit that she'd slept with a witness to the crime. Her brain flashed a warning signal. *Go slowly, take care, danger ahead.*

Juliet pressed on, as determined as a Jack Russell bolting down a rabbit hole. 'You still haven't given me an answer.'

'I appreciate how frustrating it must seem, but I'm not at liberty to go into details.' Rosetta stubbed out her cigarette.

Juliet stared at the cigarette butt in the egg cup. It had a rim of red lipstick on the filter. An image of the lipstick she'd found at Tommy's house flashed through her mind. 'Your lipstick, is it Estée Lauder?'

'Yeah,' she said, nodding with a short self-depreciating laugh. 'I should probably change it. Upgrade my image, get my colours done. I've been wearing the same colour combinations for almost a decade.'

'I know what you mean,' Juliet agreed. 'Some riders go out in full makeup. I can't be bothered. I mean, who's got the time? What colour is it, anyway?'

Rosetta thought for a moment. '*Racing Red*, I think. I had to buy a replacement only a while back.'

Juliet sprang to her feet, pointing her finger at Rosetta in a gesture of outraged accusation. 'You were at Tommy's house, in his bathroom, and I'm betting in his bedroom too, weren't you?'

Rosetta exhaled as the unexpected question packed a punch which sent her reeling backwards in her chair. Her cheeks grew hot with embarrassment, but she decided it would be better to brazen it out.

'Excuse me. Put the finger back in its holster, please. Yes, it was a one-off, and before your trip. I didn't know you two were an item until today, so I don't know what you're getting so worked up about.'

'Because there's more to this than meets the eye. Why would you go to Inis Cara, and why would you just happen to bump into Tommy? It doesn't add up.'

Rosetta weighed up the options, and on balance opted for the truth. 'I had him in for questioning.'

Juliet's jaw dropped, and her tone was incredulous. 'What on earth? Why…?'

Game over, Rosetta decided. 'He was on Farley Heath, dog walking, on the morning of 19th December. Remember I told you there were two men who saw the Range Rover going up in smoke? He was one of them.'

Juliet looked shocked and confused, a chill ran through her. 'He… he never mentioned that. I don't understand. I…'

'He didn't volunteer any information. We only tracked him down after following up on leads and some good police work.'

'Has he been charged with anything? Will he be?'

'No, and that's unlikely,' Rosetta announced, cringing internally at the prospect. That roll-out would be unpleasant for all of them. Tommy could be charged with obstruction of justice, and her conduct would be under intense scrutiny. *I might even get burnt at the stake… again*, she joked to herself. Then there was the Ed-Peter-Pa connection. A real mess, this. She forced a weak smile as Juliet sat heavily on the designer kitchen chair, glaring at her across the table.

'I don't understand.'

'It might be best if you got him to explain it to you in person,' Rosetta suggested.

Juliet nodded as Rosetta stood up and gathered her things, ready to depart. 'Yes, I'll be booking a flight to Ireland first thing, and see what he's got to say for himself. They're never lost for words, the Irish, are they?'

'No,' Rosetta agreed as she set off out of the kitchen and into the hallway. *Poor Juliet.* She'd been let down by Matt and now Tommy, in quick succession. *Bloody men*, she thought as she went out the front door.

As she stepped out of the porch, a blast of chilly air blew stinging rain into her face. *So much for the good old English summertime*, she thought with a shiver. *It must be a bank holiday.* Rosetta pondered on the date. It was always a wash out for the bucket and spade brigade on a bank holiday, wasn't it? But that was May and August, as she recalled, so Lord knows about weather forecasts anymore. Rosetta blinked and turned the collar of her coat up to keep the weather tentacles out as she hurried towards her car.

Still, at least Juliet would get some answers, which was more than Rosetta could bank on. Months had passed, and she'd still heard nothing from Daniel. No explanation, nothing. There was even a term for his behaviour these days, they called it "ghosting."

She pressed the remote which bleeped to open the car door, and she hurled her handbag onto to the passenger seat. As she settled into the driver's seat, Rosetta sniffed. There was a faint odour of junk food wafting about. She opened the glove compartment on the passenger side and sure enough, she discovered empty wrappers and plastic cartons.

'Thanks for that, boys,' she muttered under her breath and decided to berate the surveillance teams when she got back to the station.

She opened the window a fraction to let the smell out. She checked the rearview mirror as she started reversing. Then she remembered Daniel sitting next to her, smiling, on their way for a minibreak in Brighton. They'd had such fun, walks on the pier, endless ice creams, sitting on the beach in a pair of matching foldaway chairs, eating fish and chips and laughing. Rosetta replayed the highlights from the time they'd been together like a movie in her mind.

She missed him. The twinkle in his eye and the warmth of his touch. Tears welled up in her eyes. First, Peter had rejected her for a younger woman, then her own kids had cast her out, and now this. It felt like a massive punch in the heart. Despair rose up from somewhere deep within. She wouldn't cry. She wouldn't let the feelings of loss and abandonment drag her down. They'd been so happy, her and Daniel. Then it had all fizzled out. Communication with her children was patchy and hit-and-miss. She braked, reached across to remove a tissue from her bag, and blew her nose. *Right.* She took a deep breath, changed gear into drive mode, and pulled off down the long driveway. The uncertainty, the not knowing, that hurt like a festering scab, and the detective in her hated open ends, unanswered questions. But so far, closure – personal and professional – remained just out of reach.

Would she get some answers from the man she loved? Could they solve this crime and secure the conviction Isabella's family so deserved?

CHAPTER FORTY

Juliet
Ireland

Tommy picked her up from the airport. Juliet felt bad for the pain that she had caused him by returning to England, but she had to know the truth. They retrieved the car from the multi-storey airport parking lot and set off in silence, both staring out the window at the road ahead. After a while, she tried to engage him in some rather stilted small talk. Tommy became monosyllabic, glaring at her with an angry, puzzled expression, then returned his focus to the road. Their first fight was brewing, and she wasn't looking forward to it. Yet, she had to ask questions, even knowing full well that she wouldn't like the answers.

Juliet felt sick with nerves, her heart racing faster than the furies. Maybe she could ignore the nagging doubt that had taken hold, the twisting wrench in her stomach? They could return to normal, if only she could swallow back the unanswered questions. Pick up where they had left off, pretend nothing had happened. But where would that get her? It would fester… a scab itching to be picked at, for sure? Some women did turn a blind eye, bury their heads in the sand and hope the storm would pass. The conflict avoiders, the followers, the people pleasers, the co-dependants. She wasn't one of these types. She was an Aries, a cardinal fire sign, and Enneagram type eight: the powerful, self-confident, decisive, challenging type. Although her self-confidence was beginning to ebb somewhat right now. She glanced at Tommy, who didn't look too happy.

'Well, I've had enough of this, so out with it,' he snapped.

Juliet sniffed. Where would she begin? She hadn't really worked up the nerve to broach the subject. She didn't know where to begin, for fear of where it might end.

At last, she spluttered out the question that had been nagging her for so long. 'Did DS Barrett visit you?'

His knuckles tensed white on the steering wheel. 'Who?'

Juliet narrowed her eyes. 'Rosetta. You know what I'm getting at.'

He let out a breath and rolled his eyes heavenwards. 'So that's what this is all about?'

'And you admit that she did come to see you? Flew all the way over from England, in fact?'

Tommy shook his head. 'What's wrong with you, woman? For sure, you're off your head with jealous thoughts an' all.'

'Jealous?' Juliet shook her head. She noticed that he had reverted to the thick Irish brogue again like he always did when he was on the defensive.

'Well,' he huffed, 'you're acting mighty strange, mind, and it seems to me that you don't like the idea of other women finding me attractive.'

'Oh, I know how you are with women,' Juliet said darkly, in her most forbidding tone.

'Is that so?' He set his head at a jaunty angle and glared at her.

Juliet frowned, not sure how to respond. Of course, she didn't like it. How many women would the shallow jerk get through in a week when she wasn't around? A wave of jealousy had her in its grip. Inside she was furious, but she needed to seem calm and at ease while she decided how to play it next. 'I don't know what to think. I'm sincerely hoping that you'll come up with some plausible explanation about why you omitted to mention that she went to your house.'

'It's no secret that I like the ladies, now, is it?' His tone seemed jokey and dismissive as he continued, 'I've always thought that women are like racehorses.'

'Really?' Juliet struggled to keep her tone even, astonished that he could joke about such a thing. 'And why's that?'

'Hmmm, the odds are better in strings, chestnuts, bays, palominos, greys. I'm not fussy about the colour –'

Juliet reached over, snagged his ear, and gave it a sharp tug.

'Ouch… bloody hell, woman! You nearly had us both in the ditch. Let-go-my-ear!'

Juliet glared at him, her eyes flashing a warning. 'I'll have a straight answer, or mark my words, you'll be sorry.'

'Oh, so now it's threats I'm hearing.'

Juliet bared her teeth, her temper rising very close to the surface. 'Don't you dare mess with me about this.' Her ribs hurt from the pressure of pent-up rage. 'I want the truth, now, so spit it out.'

'Jesus, I…'

'That's the wrong answer.' Juliet let fly a well-aimed punch in the soft folds of his otherwise taut belly.

Tommy let out a hiss, and the car swerved. Cursing under his breath, he pulled over and drew to a stop.

'Sweet Jesus, have you completely taken leave of your senses? You nearly had us both killed.'

In reply, Juliet raised a clenched fist. 'You're looking at a woman who won an Olympic gold medal in one of the very few sports where men compete against women. I took them all on and I won. So, if you wanna bullshit me, think very carefully and think again.'

Tommy raised his hands in surrender. 'Please, no more of your pummelling. My belly still hurts.'

'It's not your belly I'll be after next time, but your manhood!'

Tommy sighed. 'Okay, she did come to Inis Cara.'

Juliet nodded, encouraging him to continue. She rolled the window down, allowing the cool air to soothe her face a little.

'For the record I didn't find her attractive and nothing happened. There, are you satisfied?' Tommy growled.

'Definitely not. Keep going and this time cut the crap,' she barked.

'Is there no pleasing you at all?' He sighed even louder this time. 'She contacted the Garda in Kirk and they asked me to go to the station for some questioning.' He folded his arms across his chest and sucked in his cheeks.

'About the Range Rover that was involved in the accident? Why would they be interested in talking to you about that?' She detected something dark and sad lurking beneath the surface that he couldn't or wouldn't tell her about.

Tommy assumed the look of wide-eyed indignant innocence as he shrugged. 'I've no idea. A case of mistaken identity, I guess. I don't know anything about it, I promise.'

Juliet could barely disguise her astonishment. 'You were questioned by the police about the car that killed Issie and Gothic, that almost killed me too, that ruined my life, and you didn't even bother mentioning it?'

'Yes. No… well, it was tricky.'

'I bet.' Juliet gulped as tears began welling up. 'I'm going to get to the bottom of this come hell or high water, so it would be better if you told me yourself. Go ahead, get it off your chest.'

After a long pause, he spoke softly, his face resigned. 'I was in England on Farley Heath that morning, taking Gulliver for a walk.'

Juliet thought her head would explode. Maybe she had misheard. 'You were there when the car was abandoned?' Her tone became high-pitched and sharp as the ringing in her ears accelerated. 'Did you see anyone? Did you see Peter Marshall?'

A long pause.

'A murder investigation, but you never came forward to volunteer information, and you kept it from me – me, of all people. What's the fuck is wrong with you?' Juliet shook her head, moaning softly. She'd thought she knew this man, but his actions were incomprehensible. She started to sob.

'I didn't see anyone. I swear on my mother's life.'

When Tommy reached out and touched her arm, she recoiled. 'Don't touch me.'

'I wanted to tell you. I tried, at the airport after the race, remember?' His tone came low and plaintive now as he hung his head and fell silent.

Juliet shook her head and sniffed. She bit her lip and rummaged in her purse for a tissue and blew her nose. 'I left Matt for you.'

'Damn it, that's not true. Don't make me your scapegoat. You left Matt because he's a first-rate bastard.' His head snapped up and his eyes hardened. 'Don't you dare compare me to him. I'm having none of it.' His anger took her momentarily aback, unsure how to proceed, but she ploughed on.

'Why did you invite DS Barrett back to your house?'

He looked at her as if she'd sprouted an extra head. 'I never invited her. I don't know what you're on about.'

Juliet sighed. The weariness in her chest rested as heavy on her as a rain-sodden coat. 'You're not helping the situation. You have to be honest with me. Just tell me the truth.' She reached inside the handbag again and waved the lipstick under his nose. 'I found this in your restroom, remember.'

'That doesn't prove anything,' he spluttered. 'It could belong to anyone.'

'Well, it's not yours… or is it? And that lame excuse is supposed to make me feel better? How could you?'

'Mother Mary and baby Jesus, you've got this all wrong.' He

slammed the steering wheel with the heel of his hand. 'Enough! I've had enough of your nagging and interrogations. I won't stand for any more of it!'

'It's her lipstick and it was in your restroom. So, while you're damn good at spinning yarns and kissing the Blarney stone, I doubt even you can charm your way out of this one. And I won't be standing for any more bullshit.'

A strange gurgling sound escaped from Tommy's lips. 'All right, I slept with her, but so what? It was a one-off, and it happened before we became serious.'

Juliet grew limp, almost lifeless. The pressure on her lungs became intolerable. With supreme effort she spat, 'You son of a bitch! How could you?' Her voice cut through the air as sharp as a circus whip.

His face contorted with shock as the seriousness of the situation sank in. 'I never meant to hurt you. I love you.'

'Really?' Juliet stared out the window. Her voice sounded faint and far away. 'Maybe you do, but there's no point continuing with a relationship that's built on lies and deceit. How can I ever trust you again? I have to have the full truth.'

He hesitated, his face drained, and that pleased her. Right now, he deserved to suffer.

'Tommy, please, talk to me. What did you see on the heath that morning?'

He looked distinctly ill at ease as he searched for some escape route. After a while, he gave a long sigh. 'There was an old guy, walking his dog too. But I... I saw another man running away.'

'Marshall?' The muscles in her belly squirmed and knotted.

He fell silent and lowered his head.

'Well, you have to go to the police. Tell them what you saw and give a statement.'

Tommy shook his head. 'Believe me, I'd do anything for you, but I can't do that. Besides, I already gave a statement. If I change my story now, that's perverting the course of justice or something, and I could be prosecuted, and worse than that, if it got back that I'd cooperated with the police, I'd be completely ostracised.'

His words pierced her heart. Juliet's mouth opened to form a perfect circle, and a rush of air escaped. She couldn't speak, couldn't think straight. *Oh, God, what have I done to deserve this?*

'Don't do this, Tommy, please.' Her mouth twisted in agony and she wrung her hands. 'I'll speak to Rosetta, DS Barrett, and ask her for immunity from prosecution. That would work, but you have to help them catch the person responsible. You have to –'

A sharp hissing sound escaped his lips, and he shook his head. 'I gave an oath to the clan and to our chief. Breaking an oath will bring down a curse.' His eyes darted around, and he looked like a man on the edge of a fast-eroding cliff with wet slippery clay under his feet. 'I can't do that even for you. If you were one of my own kind, you'd understand. Besides, women always defer to the men.'

'Fuck that!'

Tommy shook his head. 'You're too aggressive. No Traveller man would ever tolerate your attitude or your feisty ways. You'd be tamed and come to know your place. I'm more enlightened in that regard but...' he hesitated, 'even I find your words, your conduct today, unacceptable.'

Her eyes watered, tears following. 'You're blaming me for your betrayal. How does that work?' *How can I ever forgive you?* How could they move on as if nothing had happened? The future seemed impossible.

Tommy looked thoughtful. 'You're far too headstrong, opinionated, and domineering –'

'How dare you?'

'Wait, let me finish. This is one of the reasons we marry our own kind, also to keep the bloodlines pure. When Kate married Will, there was no question that she must fit into his world. He's of royal blood and descent, and she's from middle England, but she knows her place, her role. Ultimately, her place requires deference,' Tommy observed with a grin, 'even when he's dad dancing.'

Juliet scowled. 'I've never heard such sexist trash in my entire life.'

'In any relationship between two different ethnic groups, there must be tolerance, acceptance and, as hard as it may be, the couple must work to understand each other and overcome their differences.' He sighed. 'I fear that you're not giving me – us – a chance.'

Little by little, Juliet raised her chin and summoned every bit of resolve she possessed. 'Then it's over. We can't continue with this between us,' she whispered.

His eyes grew dark and haunted as they widened in momentary panic. 'You don't mean that. You can't.'

'I can, and I do. You have to choose, me or them.' She paused and looked him in the eye, searching his face for clues. 'So, what's it going to be?'

Tommy buried his head in his hands, the silence deafening.

'Fine, turn the car around and take me back to the airport, please.' Juliet slumped back in her seat, her head resting against the window, too exhausted even to cry.

CHAPTER FORTY-ONE

Rosetta

Yorrex police badly needed a break, and as Peter had drawn a blank on obtaining the details of O'Neil's burner, Rosetta had to resort to a more indirect approach. Only yesterday she had, with EPIS's assistance, planted incriminating calls on Matt's regular mobile. It was now simply a matter of someone over here tracking the calls, putting two and two together, and making a connection between Matt and Baron. Rav had gathered the team together and apprised them about some new telephone call records which were of particular interest. Apparently, there were a batch of them logged as "B my Accountant," which didn't stack up. The officers were gathered in the incident room, waiting for an update on the identity of the caller. They didn't have to wait too long. Dennis entered the room, looking well chuffed with himself.

'Right,' Rav announced, 'what have you got for us?'

'Well, if I say it myself, I think we could be getting close to cracking this case.'

Shirley gave a whoop of delight. 'Let's hope so, for wee Isabella's sake!'

Dennis continued. 'The number belongs to Baron O'Neil, who's already known to us, thanks to his record for theft, armed robbery, and assault. He's served time and was released on probation a few months ago.' Dennis paused, presumably for dramatic effect. 'Here's the interesting bit. His address is the Travellers' settlement at Farley Heath.'

Rosetta pretended to seem surprised and she gave a loud whoop and punched the air. 'That means he's familiar with the area and he'd know the tracks that lead to the spot where the Range Rover was set alight. So, what next? Do we bring them all in?' She felt a bit bad as it obviously came as no surprise to her, but she had to play along.

Rav pondered a moment. 'No, not yet, we need to let this roll out. Let Matt collect the insurance money and then we follow the money trail, until hopefully we connect Lebaine to O'Neil. Next, Colin, can you get hold of Baron's bank account details then talk to all the banks involved? Once real-time online access is set up, so we can monitor the fund movements back and forth from here, call Equine Insurance and tell them to pay out on the claim, PDQ.'

'Right, I'm on it now,' Colin said, exiting the room.

Rosetta nodded. 'That's a good idea. So, we're working on the theory that Matt put Baron up to it for a cut of the insurance money?'

'That's right,' Rav confirmed. 'What we don't know is what Tracy's involvement is. Charlie, can you make some discreet enquiries about any connections that she has to Baron, as it seems likely that her job was to supply the hit man? After the failed search before Christmas, we don't want any of them getting spooked and tipping the others off. The last thing we want is Baron doing a runner.'

'Roger, boss,' Charlie said.

By now, Dennis had taken a seat, but he shuffled to his feet with a pained expression on his face. 'Can I have permission to be excused? I had a killer curry last night and it's giving me some right old gip today.'

Rav let out a long sigh. 'Very well, but when you're done, can you organise covert twenty-four-hour surveillance on all three suspects?'

'Aye.' Shirley chuckled. 'Put him on the night shift but ban him from takeaways, as our patrol cars are no equipped with potties.'

'Ha-ha, very funny,' Dennis muttered as he made a hasty exit.

Rosetta shook her head. 'Just thinking… it was a strange method though, wasn't it? But then I guess, if they'd done away with the horse by another method, the insurance company would have insisted on an autopsy.'

'Yes, you're right,' Rav agreed. 'It was set up carefully. That way, it didn't directly implicate either Matt or Tracy. Okay, folks, back to work.'

* * *

Rosetta returned to her office and chewed over the case so far. Matt's mother had left him as an adolescent and disappeared off to Australia where she served time for fraud – two stints, behind bars, one for investment scams and another for organising internet dating scams. *Hmm, like mother, like son, perhaps?* She stared at the silver-framed photographs of Ed and Alice and wondered if they were like her in any way. With a lump in her throat, she opened her MacBook and sent them both private messages on Snapchat and Instagram. Teenagers were so fickle nowadays, and it was best to figure out their main social media preference and ideally catch them online for any chance of getting a response. She sighed and lit up a cigarette. It never got any easier, but sometimes, when she was busy and distracted, she forgot for a while and the pain eased a little.

Her phone rang. Line one, so that was Rav.

'Hi, have you got a minute? Log onto the *Mail Online*.' He paused while she caught up. 'Found it?'

'Hang on, it's slow.' She scanned the headlines. *Yorrex Police Goes Harry Potter*. Yes, now they've hired a witch to help solve important cases...

'Shit,' she said. It was all she could think of, so she said it again. 'Shit.' Her head began to spin, and she sucked on her cigarette for comfort. 'WTF? Do they name me?'

Rav let out a loud sigh. 'Hmmm, not yet, but take a look outside your office window.'

Rosetta leapt off her chair and peered through the blinds. Outside, in the car park, there were about ten to fifteen journalists with mics, booms, and cameras, huddled in a group. *Waiting to pounce,* she thought. She plonked herself back in her chair and buried her head in her hands. 'What am I going to do? If this gets out, that will totally screw things up with my kids.' *Right back to square one,* she thought.

Rav commiserated. 'Well, we are now deep into damage limitation territory. The commissioner has summoned me upstairs, so I can't stay on the phone long, but I want you to go to my place. Go out the back way and stay there till all this blows over.'

Rosetta opened her mouth to protest. 'I can't. I... I've got no clothes, no tooth brush – no one to feed the cat.'

'Don't worry. I'll send a plainclothes female officer right now to collect your things and look after the cat.'

Rosetta baulked. 'But if they catch us together, that will just make your job even more complicated.'

'That's my problem, and I'm prepared to take my chances. Go out the back in twenty minutes. I'll send a delivery van to pick you up. Get in the back and it'll take you to my place.'

'Thanks. I owe you.' She paused. 'Why?'

'Ask me no questions and I'll tell you no lies.'

CHAPTER FORTY-TWO
Rosetta

Rosetta sat cross-legged on the floor of Rav's lounge, wearing Mickey Mouse pyjamas and a pair of mismatched hiking socks. *Thanks for that*, she thought, an image flashing through her mind of a vindictive plainclothes officer rummaging through her clothes and picking the least flattering things she could find. Females could be extremely bitchy, particularly when it came to attracting a man. She supposed, for the first time, that maybe Rav wasn't such a bad catch. He fully understood the pressures of the job and seemed to accept her for what she was. She blinked in the dimness. The curtains were drawn to shield her from the press, who so far hadn't realised who or where she was, but it was only a matter of time before they tracked her down.

Poor Rav had been hauled in front of the district commissioner and told in no uncertain times to get the situation under control. The media would go into a feeding frenzy over her involvement if they found out. EPIS wanted it closed down too. They didn't want any fingers pointing at them, putting them under scrutiny and getting in the way of the mission. At some point the general public might get it, the enlightened ones at any rate, but meanwhile it was better for all concerned if they were just left quietly to get on with the job of karmic clean-up and cracking ET communication codes in secret. Rosetta sighed. She'd phoned Peter to warn him and ask him to keep the kids off school until it all settled down. But he'd never responded, so there was no way of knowing what action – if any – he'd taken. She'd tried Alice and Ed but got no response, so she'd called the headmistress and asked her to hold an assembly about differences, different beliefs, and the importance of tolerance to others.

The headmistress, Mrs. Davies, had sent her a reassuring email, which she called up again on her laptop.

Dear Mrs. Barrett,

Thank you for your telephone call. I can confirm that I plan to hold an assembly along the lines you mentioned and we both discussed, without delay, although as a Catholic school we already teach morality from the Bible and the New and Old Testament. I have asked all my members of staff to be on the look-out for any instances of bullying, which as usual will not be condoned.

On behalf of myself and my staff, may I wish you and your family well in this difficult time.

Kind Regards.

Rosetta sighed. She had no idea if that would work. She really wanted to connect with her children to protect them, to explain, but she had no way of reaching them. From experience, she didn't hold out much hope on the bullying front. Schools, especially private schools, tended to mouth off a lot and spout policies, but at the end of the day the parents paid the purse, and he who pays the piper calls the tune, after all. They might make the odd serious example over drugs, with high-profile expulsions, at least two boarding schools she knew admitted to hiring security guards with sniffer dogs to search the dorms; but how did they stamp out bullying, particularly when it was endemic online? It was heart-breaking. Her two children wouldn't want a mother splashed all over the papers for no good reason.

Edward and Alice would be mortified. All they wanted to do at their ages was to fit in. They weren't like her in that respect. She'd always been different, a maverick. She never followed the pack or joined any clique, and all she could do was hope that her kids would come through it okay and one day they'd understand and forgive her. In the age of global communications and social media, friends had long since overtaken parents in the influence sphere. Now they grew up with followers and "friends," who weren't really friends, but just associates, and sometimes worse. How did they know the difference? *With presidents and celebs tweeting and chirping right, left, and centre, and reality TV more popular than a good documentary, where will the new ways lead us?* Rosetta wondered. When Alice had been around ten, her friend Pasha had been boarding at the senior school while her parents were in Nigeria. She had a laptop and a smartphone, and by accident Rosetta had come across her Facebook account after Pasha and Alice had been "chatting."

Horrified, she'd discovered men in their thirties who'd signed up as Pasha's friends, sending her messages such as, "Sex is like chocolate, are you ready to lick it?" She'd immediately reported it to the school, which also had been advised of something wrong after a senior girl had borrowed Pasha's phone and been disturbed by the messages being sent. The police had been called in and two known paedophiles intercepted and arrested. *Friends, right? How do schools, parents, police get up to speed and keep ahead of developments in fast-moving cyberspace?* With that thought, she typed Peter a WhatsApp message.

Peter, due to risk of bullying and online abuse, please block their phones, and I'll have their social media accounts temporarily shut down…

She was about to hit Send, then thought better of it. He would just show the kids her messages and use them against her. The sick, sad specimen. After all, that was what he'd done throughout the divorce, and nothing much had changed since then, as far as she could tell. So, for the next twenty minutes, she made some phone calls and called in a few favours. *When the furore blew over, their services could be restored, but for now, less is more,* she thought. As usual, she was cast as the bad witch in the pantomime, with no sign of reprieve any time soon. Stuck there at Rav's place like a goldfish tossed out of its bowl, she had no access to EPIS, which made progress on the backstory extremely limited. So now, she needed to keep herself busy. Meanwhile, she had to bend the Anglepoise desk lamps that were running on an extension lead so she could point them at the sheaves of paper spread out in front of her like a geisha's fan.

She had Baron O'Neil's prison file to plough through to see if any clues came up. Also, she wanted to understand a person's journey. What choices they made and where those choices led. Her EPIS contact had accessed the Inmate Information System and downloaded the hefty extract for O'Neil. He'd been a juvenile offender with a record of car theft, disturbance of the peace, and so on, to the extent that he was tagged at age twelve and placed on curfew: fat lot of good that did, it seemed from the notes. Baron acquired a drug habit and then it spiralled downhill, judging from the details of the prisoner's life which, behind her, the HP printer was spewing out in volumes of paper as thick as *War and Peace*. Rosetta rubbed her temples. The headache she'd woken up with didn't seem to be easing. Shifting through until she got the stack in numerical order, Rosetta first flicked through the contents page, then waded into the pile summarising the contents in her head as she went along:

Offense:

Baron attacked a man in a pub after an argument when he was eighteen. He was jailed for two years after he smashed a broken glass in a man's face. On his release, his behaviour worsened, and he was involved in several armed robberies where the victims were lured to a pre-arranged site, by a profile on Plenty of Fish, the internet dating website. It was a fake dating profile, using images of an eighteen-year-old girl, who didn't exist, of course. But *she* lured men out to meet her, so the dates were arranged and then the victims were ambushed by gunmen. One victim saw a woman who he believed was his date, and he excitedly got out of his car to meet her. Then two masked gunmen jumped out from behind the building and beat and robbed him. The victim was taken to hospital with serious head injuries.

In another scam, a man was left shot in a pub car park and the armed men drove off in his vehicle. When Baron was questioned by police, he denied any involvement, but they found several items that implicated him in a number of robberies. There were probably other victims who hadn't come forward. Baron was the registered user of the Plenty of Fish accounts which he used to lure the victims.

Sentence:

Baron was charged with two counts of armed robbery with a firearm, wounding with intent, online impersonation, and possession of marijuana. The details of the fraudulent Plenty of Fish dating site account were deleted.

Better get my profile off there, then, she thought, although Match.com was not much better. Really, these sites needed to do more to prevent scammers, fraudsters, and con merchants, and above all, the public needed to get wise and not assume everyone else thought like they did or shared their values. They didn't, and psychopaths came in all guises, professions, shapes, and sizes. There were far more of them out there, in all walks of life than anyone could ever realise: policemen and women, politicians, doctors, dentists, teachers, barristers. *Always do your homework. Check, check, and double-check, and remember trust always has to be earned.*

Doing some online research, Rosetta was surprised to learn that five percent of prisoners in jail considered themselves to be Gypsy, Romani or Travellers like Baron, who'd originally been raised in Ireland. This was a very high percentage of the population, and amongst Gypsies and Travellers, illiteracy rates were high. So presumably this must have something to do with the high number of offenders, since if they couldn't read or write, they couldn't pass the theory part of the driving test, for example.

Baron, she noted, while adept at hot-wiring and 'borrowing' cars, had never actually passed his test. Moreover, people like him couldn't claim benefits, register with their GP or for work, and so were pushed into the illegal economy to earn black money. When there was a choice of sentence between service in the community or jail, Gypsies and Travellers were far more likely to be sent to jail simply because their illiteracy prevented them from attending or enrolling in offender behaviour courses run in the community. Effectively, there was no alternative except a prison sentence. It shocked her to discover the links between offending and poor education. The statistics were dramatic, since the Gypsy and Traveller percentage of the population was way over-represented in proportion to the ethnic population size. Rosetta sighed and stretched her legs out in front of her. Travellers and Roma suffered undue public prejudice and discrimination in society. From bullying at school, on the rare occasions that they attended, to police harassment, discrimination in the workforce, and, startlingly, one in twenty of the prisoners in jail today were Gypsies. Not great and something needed to be done, surely? Rosetta felt bad about how she'd treated Brad, the Traveller welfare officer. She'd been rude and dismissive, and he actually had a far better understanding of both sides of the story. She made a mental note to get EPIS to increase funding for outreach literacy programmes for Gypsies.

Rosetta groaned. By now she had a massive headache but no co-deine and, worse still, no cigarettes. She'd have to pop out to the shops later. Rav had provided her with a wig – a ginger one! *Thanks for that, mate.* He'd also provided her with a run-around hire car. She turned to check out the noise. The throbbing noise from the printer was almost keeping time with the aching pulse inside her head. Her back ached from bending over. Either that or old age was setting in. After several skiing accidents and resultant operations, her knees now creaked like doors in a haunted house, and as for her eyesight, well, that didn't bode well, either. She held a piece of paper up close and then moved it farther away. It didn't seem to make much difference – all a blur. Knees knackered, eyes knackered – what next? So, she got up and went into the kitchen to put the kettle on.

The kettle whistled, but the sound was dimmed by the printer churning out sheet after sheet of paper, and, as the printer spewed out more, the sheaves fluttered down like autumn leaves, creating more chaos. Back in the lounge with a cup of tea in hand, she groaned.

The Inmate Information System contained everything about the life of a prisoner: personal details, offences, sentence, possibility of parole, relationships, movements, what wing they were assigned to, their case number information, risk assessments carried out, any courses taken, activities, paid and unpaid work, breaches of discipline, offender rehabilitation programs, and on and on…

Rosetta tiptoed across the white paper sea, leaping over the pile as her mobile pinged. She picked up the message.

How's it going? I'll bring you a takeaway and a bottle of wine tonight, although I may be late. Rather manic here at the mo. Rav. X

Rosetta stared at the message. Did he mean kiss, or was that his way of denoting a full stop?

Cheers, and good luck, she replied.

She reminded herself to take more codeine, alternating them every four hours with paracetamol. If she didn't move her head too suddenly, she could kid herself that the pain was receding, beaten back into submission. And as she tipped her head back and swallowed two tablets with a gulp of tea, she wondered what she really hoped she'd find from delving into life behind bars, and this vivid and depressing portrait of prison life. She exhaled to try to ease the tension that was building in her neck, then she carried on reading, eager to understand more about what made criminals tick and what made them repeat an offense.

The early years of a long sentence were the worst, until the prisoner adjusted, she supposed. New inmates were put into the induction spur, a separate wing for newcomers until they got acclimatised. Kind of like a prison kindergarten, but once in there they were most prone to crises, such as self-harming. Here were men facing fifteen, twenty, twenty-five years in prison without any hope of release. They must be desperate for meaning, beset by loss. Adjustment takes time. *Well, that's one thing they had, at least*, she thought. But since the ISIS and terrorist attacks, the public's attitude had turned more to punishment and retribution than rehabilitation, and the funding for courses that might have eased the passage of time was getting cut back every year.

Baron O'Neil, then in his late twenties, was no exception to self-harming. He cut his arms with razor blades when he could get hold of them, and blades appeared to feature widely in prison. Baron couldn't read or write, so there was no way for his family to communicate except by visits, and often it seemed these were banned for no apparent reason. Hardly unpredictable, then, that when he ended up in isolation for some minor indiscretion, he attempted suicide. In conversations with his personal officer following this attempt, Baron said: 'I'm worthless. Even pigs in squalor have a slaughter value, but no one gives a shit about inmates. We're not even raw meat.'

She discovered how the prisoners quickly learned not to express emotions, since that could be used against them. The inmate code was: don't laugh, don't look happy, don't look too glad or grateful either, because someone, Big Brother, was always watching on their monitor screens, trying to decide if the prisoner wasn't suffering enough, and what pain they could inflict to help him redeem himself.

And there was always someone watching, deciding when prisoners' sentence reviews would come up. *If you don't look as if you're being punished, they come up with new, inventive ways to make you pay. If you look like you're getting on too well with anyone, they'll split you up – it's divide and conquer all the way.* Inmates were moved to a different cell every twenty-eight days or so. This was intentionally disheartening, as all they had was their own bit of private space with their photos and posters on the walls.

O'Neil had a stuffed hedgehog on his bed, apparently, but after a routine strip search, the prison officers found a cannabis joint, and the toy hedgehog, which smelt of his kids, was confiscated. Apparently, they set fire to it outside his cell and forced him to watch it go up in flames. *Forget* Orange is the New Black-*style friendships*, Rosetta thought, in this men's prison the aim was to prevent the formation of gang relationships or, in fact, any relationship, it seemed. The inmates were constantly challenged with uncertainty and the threat of constant change. They got shuffled around like a pack of cards just to disorientate them and make them easier to manage, she assumed.

Rosetta drained the last of her cup of tea and whooped in delight when, after a rummage, she found a half-full packet of cigarettes in her jacket pocket. She grabbed a disused plant pot from the utility room to use as an ashtray and lit up. *Ah, bliss. At least they were allowed smokes on the inside,* she thought with a sigh of relief. But otherwise, as she was beginning to gather, life inside was a pretty brutalising regime. Baron was incarcerated in a high-security prison, where violence and drug addiction were rife. Other things had changed over the years too, particularly the relationship between prisoners and staff. Prisons now were overcrowded, and prison officers felt they were scrutinised constantly on matters of human rights and political correctness.

Rosetta lit up another cigarette. Rav would not be happy about this, so she opened a window. Peering through it, she breathed a sigh of relief. No sign of the press pontificating about freedom. *Hilarious, this,* she thought, as she found herself holed up in Rav's house like a sardine ready for canning, basically in hiding and under siege. What about the freedom of the people on the other side of the paparazzi flashbulbs? People like Diana and Dodi? Hunting had been banned in England, so foxes were protected. But famous humans who made headlines, which sold tabloids, were still fair game and anyone's quarry.

From what she'd read, the jail community used to function on a kind of recognised gangster-gentleman's code, where the inmates and the prison officers knew where they stood and had some mutual respect. But now, seemingly, the modern multicultural population of the prison was viewed with intense suspicion by its staff. Perhaps prison officers were frightened by the growing Muslim population, and beyond the prison walls, the public, with the press fanning the terrorism flames, seemed to be growing less liberal by the day. It was claimed that the jihadi behind the Westminster attack was radicalised in prison, and that he came out from behind bars obsessed with Islam. Nationalism was taking hold across Europe and in the United Kingdom, with the Scots demanding independence.

Now the mood had shifted, and it seemed that prison should be for punishment, not rehabilitation. From time to time, the press gave the mix a stir, reporting how offenders had Sky, with back-to-back *Game of Thrones*; lucky things. What an easy ride they were having on the back of people's hard-earned taxes. When public opinion turned significantly, politicians tended to react, particularly when there was an election or referendum on the horizon. So, funding for courses, self-development, life and future work skills – things which made the inmates' lives more bearable – was axed, little by little.

Baron seemed to be making pretty good progress. There were few behaviour issues affecting his chances of parole, no problem incidents save a handwritten note saying the prisoner was watching *Les Misérables*, and this DVD had been confiscated as it contained violent themes and images.

Rosetta looked up. The printer was growling, seemingly hell-bent on turning itself inside out. The red light flashed, stopped. She knew what was coming next. She didn't have to be a prophet to guess. *Epic paper jam.* She got up, opened the printer's various drawers and fiddly flaps and pulled out an inky black drum. Her fingers looked as if she'd been rummaging through coal. Then she couldn't get the drawer thing closed again. Helpfully, the printer brain said that there was a paper jam. Handy this, stating the bloody obvious, but she could not locate it. She wrestled with a corner bit of virgin paper, tugging and pulling like a dentist trying to extract a molar. There, out it came.

Phew. She breathed a sigh of relief. Then, she poked the screen and turned the printer off. Of course, when she then turned it on again, it was not satisfied. Oh no, it kept saying the same thing like a demented R2D2: *paper jam, paper jam.* It went all Dalek with all its lights flashing, not just the red one. Rosetta buried her head in her hands and was tempted to exterminate the printer by hurling it across the room. Where was the dear Doctor when you needed backup? Ah yes, he had vaporised in his Tardis, terrific.

So, there she was stuck with the malfunctioning black printer that was now only fit for the great scrap heap in the sky. She would have nipped out to PC World to grab a nice new one in a fancy box, but she hated instructions and it would be a nightmare to set the thing up. Probably men put viruses in printers, PCs, and laptops to keep mere women in their place. *That and make our passwords invalid just to really make our hair fall out. Well, guess what, it works. I give up. Take me to your leader. Please remove the paper guzzling monstrosity. I am going green and saving trees.* She could see the headlines now: *Rosetta the Psychic Witch Goes Eco-warrior – last seen living in a treehouse somewhere near Glastonbury.*

She gave the printer a long hard stare. 'Fuck it, fuck you,' she said.

Time to get washed and dressed, she decided. *Tra-la-la-la.* Hands up, who loves modern technology? She snorted. *Not me, please bring back the abacus and the quill.* Actually, even carving images in stone would be better than this thing. After her shower she returned, refreshed and ready for battle. She glanced at her watch. 4:00 p.m. So, the school kids next door would be home soon, and if all else failed she could bribe one of them to help with the Dalek if needs be. *After all it's the young people, the Millennials, who rule the planet today, isn't it? Experience no longer counts.* She resumed her position, sitting cross-legged on the floor, where she picked up another page of the O'Neil report. She checked the contents page. Chapter Six: "Relationships." Now, that looked interesting. What pages did she need? She eyed the black beast and willed it not to have devoured this bit – pages sixty-two to sixty-five. Ah, mercy of mercies, there they were.

Relationships:

Baron is married. His wife's name is Katie O'Neil. They have two children, aged seven and nine, a boy named Paddy and a girl called Rosie. They live on the Travellers' camp near Farley Heath in a clan of about thirty to forty men, women, and children. His sister-in-law, Tracy Mathews, visits him often, at least once a fortnight, and she brings him toiletries, sweets, cake, cigarettes, and so forth.

Rosetta let out a loud whistle and thumped the floor. That was it. Why hadn't they come up with the connection before? *That's it!* She lit up another cigarette in celebration. She could murder a drink, but Rav only had vegetable juice in the fridge.

She grabbed her phone and dialled him.

'Hi, it's me, can you talk?'

Rav paused. 'Well, now is not exactly a good moment, but actually I need to send you a draft of the statement that I'm planning to release to the press later on today. Can you look at it and run it past your boss? We're in enough hot water as it is without adding EPIS to the bloodcurdling mix.'

'Sure, but actually don't worry, they're already on the case. I'll forward their version shortly. With an army of lawyers and PR gurus, they're experts at containment. They've already issued a super-injunction, you know, a gag order on the press and all the social media mob.'

Rav whistled. 'Wow, that's pretty impressive. Yes, let me have a copy ASAP.'

'Sure thing. Meanwhile, I've got some other good news for you. I've been ploughing through Baron O'Neil's inmate information file –'

'How the – how did you get hold of that so quickly?'

'Don't ask. Anyway, it's very interesting, and guess what I discovered in the relationship section?'

'Go on.'

'Tracy Mathews is his sister-in-law. How on earth did we miss that?'

'Phew… I've no idea. No birth registration records, perhaps? Okay, well done. Catch up later.'

'*Ciao.*' With that, she hung up and continued flicking through the paperwork.

Towards the end of his sentence, things seemed to be improving for him. Baron O'Neil moved onto the enhanced level of the incentives and earned privilege scheme. In 2019 he got a job in the gym, and a note said he was no trouble and seemed focused on serving his sentence and leaving prison at the earliest opportunity. O'Neil had learned how to make life better for himself. He followed orders, obeyed the rules, and played the game. Most of the time, while he was out on parole, he kept his nose clean. So why, after all this, after everything he'd been through, did he turn to crime again? Was it greed? Was the amount of money on offer simply too tempting to resist?

CHAPTER FORTY-THREE

Rav

Rav had been summoned to the commissioner's office. When he arrived, his boss was staring out of his large window at the dark, brooding sky. Rav took in the scene, *that about sums up the prevailing mood,* he thought. Meanwhile, he silently prayed that Rosetta would do as she promised and forward him the copy of the EPIS super-injunction, or anything to pacify the boss. The Big C began pacing up and down, like a ravenous tiger on the scent of a fresh carcass. Rav had been chewed up and spat out by the commissioner once before, and it was not an experience he cared to repeat. He knew his boss well enough to know that he was obsessive about finances and hitting crime targets. Bad news with either would invariably set him off. He was slow to anger, but once he got himself really wound up, he would blow a head gasket. Rav fervently wished that the boss would sit down. The pacing was beginning to make him feel nervous.

'Do you realise how much we've spent on this investigation?' The commissioner fixed him with a cold-eyed glare and an expression which reminded Rav of his headmaster. He had the sinking feeling that he was about to fail this maths exam.

'Well, I guess the six officers on twenty-four-hour surveillance is racking up a large overtime bill –'

'Damn right, it is.' The commissioner sat down heavily in his chair. 'And it's not six. It's eight. What on earth are the other two doing? Carry on at this rate, and we'll have a ruddy football team.'

Rav paused, wracking his brain. 'Oh, the two extra men are staking out the Brightside Allotment in relation to a Peeping Tom and a hate crime incident.'

The commissioner's eyes bulged. 'Struth, what does that have to do with the Levine case, for crying out loud?'

Rav noticed the boss's foot tapping under the desk. *What a fidget,* he thought, watching the foot go *tap, tap, tap.*

'Well?'

Tread carefully, Rav thought, *dangerous territory ahead.* 'It's not directly linked, but the victim is a… a witch.'

'*What?*' the commissioner spat. 'I don't believe I'm hearing this.'

'Well, I have given this some thought, and I've put the related line expenses under a separate code and I thought we could charge this back to EPIS. She's another one of theirs, apparently.'

The commissioner sprang to his feet and gazed out the window again. The rain was driving in and leaving silvery snail trails down the window. 'CIA mystics, pre-cogs, more bloody witches and weirdoes than Hogwarts. When and where exactly will it end?' He turned to face Rav with a thunderous expression and his arms folded across his chest.

Not good body language, this, Rav thought, and he resolved to stay silent.

Not so the commissioner. 'The expenses on this inquiry are out of hand. Forensics, surveillance, TV appeals, the next thing we know, they'll be asking questions in Parliament, and heaven forbid they send another force in to bloody investigate. I'm not having it on my record that I'm financially bloody incompetent. Do I make myself clear?'

'Yes, perfectly clear sir.' Rav pursed his lips and blew out, wondering how he could pacify him. 'The insurance company has completed its investigations and it should be settled soon. Its accounts department processes payments on the twentieth of the month, so any day now. Then we'll track the bank payments and receipts by way of proof, so we can move to arrest the three suspects, and wind the surveillance operation down.'

'That's assuming that charges are brought imminently.' The commissioner glared at Rav. 'Otherwise we'll have to step up the operation to cover ports, airports, and the like. So, you'd better pull your finger out and make bloody well sure that you get this nailed pronto.'

Rav nodded.

There was a knock on the door. 'What is it?' the commissioner yelled.

Shirley bobbed her head around the door and handed Rav a few sheets of paper. 'Sorry to interrupt, but this just came in.'

Rav felt a wave of relief. 'Thanks, Hodges.' She closed the door as he placed the EPIS gagging order on the commissioner's desk. 'Good news, sir. Take a look at this.'

The commissioner sat down and skimmed the page. 'Pretty impressive, I suppose,' he said. 'The last thing we need is a pack of journalist sniffer dogs doing our job for us and, worse still, letting the bloody black cat out of the bag before we're ready to make arrests.'

'Indeed, sir.' Rav licked his lips and let out a grateful sigh. 'The press can move quicker than us on occasion as they're not bound by the same protocols. Mind you they have been making up their own stories, so I scheduled a question and answer session this afternoon at 4:00 p.m. That kept them all on ice for a bit. However, now that EPIS has slapped the injunction on everyone, I think I'll just read the statement.'

'Have they approved it?'

'I guess so. They wrote it.' He retrieved the copy of the order as he'd need it later. 'Okay, sir, will that be all?'

The commissioner nodded.

* * *

Later that day, Rav met the waiting press and media journalists in the big hall at the station which doubled for office parties and the like. He stood up and tested the microphone. He'd had the young techie lads set it up, and they were standing by in case of any problems, such as the hard drive in his brain malfunctioning, which seemed to happen more often as the years advanced. They'd also rigged the room to prohibit live broadcasts from the film crews.

'Good day, everyone, thank you for coming,' Rav cleared his throat. 'May I remind you that this briefing is strictly confidential, and live broadcasts are strictly forbidden. Please turn all cameras and recorders off immediately.' He paused to give them chance to comply. 'Now I know there's been a good deal of speculation in the rumour mill, and first of all, what we'd like to prevent is a witch hunt.' A few people in the audience sniggered as Rav continued, looking at his notes. 'So, please, don't spread panic, misinformation, and misunderstanding. The word "witch," taken out of context, is a derogatory term, and terminology, as you all know, is very important. Sensationalism may make headlines, but it can also have a detrimental effect on people's lives. Witches are pagans. This is a very old religion based on a reverence for nature. Paganism is nothing to do with dark magic, rituals, or sacrifice. Some ancient sites, such as Stonehenge in Wiltshire, are gathering points at important festivals such as solstices. Witchcraft in ancient history was known as the craft of the wise, because most who followed the path were in tune with nature, had knowledge of herbs and medicines, and they were valuable members of the community as healers and leaders –'

Jack Ford of Sky News interrupted. 'No disrespect, but how much longer is the history lesson going to last? Our audiences want to know what the police are doing, getting themselves bewitched.'

A chorus of laughter, and another hand shot up.

'Let me finish please,' Rav said. 'The fundamental tenet of witches is "Harm None." Yes, there are a number of officers, male and female, in forces across England and Wales who list their religion as pagan, and I stress that an individual's personal beliefs have no bearing on their professionalism. We employ officers from all walks of life and religious orientations. Missionaries demonised the old nature-based deities and witches too, to persuade people to convert. Indeed, witches have been persecuted for centuries, and sadly persecution on religious grounds still continues to this day. Take anti-Semitism, for instance.'

A hand shot up again. 'Jackie Sterling, *Daily Telegraph*. No disrespect, but we didn't come here for an RE lesson.'

A few journalists clapped and muttered, 'Hear, hear.'

Rav shook his head. 'Personally, I'm a Hindu, but whether an officer is an atheist, a Muslim, a Christian, a Jew, a Buddhist, a Sikh, a Wiccan, a Taoist, or whatever, has no bearing whatsoever on their abilities at work.'

'Are you seriously suggesting that witchcraft in the middle of a high-profile investigation has no effect on the outcome? What planet are Yorrex police on?' Trevor Banks asked. 'And what do Isabella's parents think? It seems, for all the psychic-witch crap, you're still no nearer to solving the case, are you?'

'I'll take questions at the end,' Rav said firmly. 'May I remind you that any attempt to make inflammatory or derogatory remarks to belittle a person's spiritual beliefs, or to incite or persecute them, will be treated as a hate crime and will not be tolerated.'

'My-oh-my, we are getting defensive, aren't we?' Rav studied his name badge with a frown: Bill Starkey, *The Sun*.

'Obviously, we know you've got something to hide, and our readers deserve to know what exactly that is. So, can you quit the sanctimonious PC twaddle and cut to the chase here, please?' Starkey growled.

The crowd erupted, soon the room echoed with wolf whistles and catcalling.

'As we've seen with internet trolls on social media sites, the digital age creates new battlegrounds for the worst aspects of human behaviour. May I inform you, in case word hasn't filtered down from up top yet, that all newspapers, media broadcasting companies, and social media sites and channels have been served with a super-injunction or gag order?' Rav indicated for the techies to show an enlarged version of the order on the whiteboard behind him. 'Feast your eyes on it.'

With that an uproar broke out. 'What the f–' Starkey spat.

Rav raised his palms in a request for calm. 'I'm sorry this is such a disappointment, but may I remind you that all films, photographs, and recordings of this briefing must be destroyed. And all reporting on this investigation is banned until further notice.'

Rav unclipped his microphone, gathered up his notes, and left the room as chaos erupted in his wake.

His father, Sanjeev, had always wanted his son to be a doctor, a lawyer, or an accountant. Certainly not a policeman, as there was no kudos in that. And as the crowd started baying in protest, he began to think his father might have been right. This job was a thankless, soul destroying task, and he had an inkling that it was about to get way more difficult. He headed for the bathroom, there at least he could have a bit of peace and quiet to gather his thoughts.

CHAPTER FORTY-FOUR

Rav and Rosetta

It worried Rav that the commissioner looked depressed. No doubt it was all the overtime and mounting expenses, not to mention the twenty-four-hour surveillance that was draining his budget. After all, he was judged not only on catching criminals, but these days more than ever on hitting financial targets and budget control.

The commissioner was always banging on about pursing-the-police, that and how long it had taken to wrap things up. Rav had given up trying to point out that the hold-up had been due to getting the insurance company's robot overruled, that took EPIS threatening to launch a legal challenge, plus agreeing to underwrite any unre-covered claim pay-out losses. Still, Rav was relieved to see that his boss cheered up when he put the evidence under his nose proving that the insurance company had finally paid out and they'd traced the funds into Matt's account, and then out to Tracy and Baron. The commissioner swiftly gave the necessary authorisations, and they moved quickly in a coordinated arrest pattern. They were going to crack this one, at last.

* * *

In interview room one, Rosetta set her clipboard down on the table, while Rav fiddled with the recording machine. *Technology is definitely not his thing,* she thought, and that endeared him to her somehow. He didn't even have a DVD or Blu-ray player in his house, and that was ancient technology these days. As for iPlayer and TV Catchup, he'd looked at her goggled-eyed when she'd mentioned them. A bit of a bookworm was our Rav.

At last, the green light flickered on and she said the names of every-one in the room. The looker with not much else going for him, Matt Lebaine, leaned back in his chair, his legs wide apart in his smart but casual Superdry joggers, T-shirt, and top-of-the-range trainers. *Good-looking, physically fit, and eye-catching, this one,* she thought as he clocked her with a condescending smirk. She thought of poor Isabella, her life cut so tragically short, and gave a shudder of revulsion. Having to sit opposite this egotistical bastard would be difficult, as just looking at him made her want to puke, but she'd do it for Isabella's sake. Anything to get those responsible brought to book. Next to him, his smartly dressed solicitor looked at his expensive watch and rolled his eyes towards the ceiling as if he was bored already. After the divorce from hell, she wasn't exactly in love with lawyers. Daniel had very much been the exception to the no-lawyer rule, and that hadn't worked out well either. Rosetta blew out through her lips in exasperation. She should have trusted her instinct and given lawyers a wide berth. But no, she had to go dabbling, didn't she? And now here we go. Behold not one, but two arrogant twats to contend with. A double whammy to kick-start the day.

Then, Mr. Supercilious spoke. 'What were the charges against my client, again?'

Rav looked unimpressed. 'Didn't you bother to read the admission notes?'

'My client called me from another case, so I'd be grateful if you'd reiterate for my benefit.'

'The charges are conspiracy to commit murder and conspiracy to defraud an insurance company. That's just for starters,' Rav said.

'So, what's your relationship with Tracy Mathews?' Rosetta asked.

'She's my girlfriend's head groom.'

'Oh, I thought you and Juliet were engaged? Has she called it off? I can't say I blame her if she did.' His smug conceit irritated the hell out of Rosetta. He was devious and manipulative, but she was not going to fall for his charms.

'That's none of your goddamn business.'

Rosetta stared at him. His cocky couldn't-give-a-shit attitude only expedited her desire to vomit, preferably all over him. Still, she had to rein herself in, keep neutral and professional. 'Well, if she hasn't yet, she will when this gets out. Right, on the 12th December you were in Miami. Why?'

'I'm a personal trainer, a coach and mentor. A client paid me to accompany her.'

'That's not what you told Juliet, is it? Why did you lie?'

Matt let out a long sigh. 'It was just easier. There was nothing going on. The client is like… ancient. Oh my God, she's about your age.' He gave her a long, challenging look.

'And rich,' Rosetta continued, increasingly rattled by the smartarse across the table, but summoning all her control so that it didn't show. Damned if she'd give him the satisfaction. 'How much did she pay you for your services in the bedroom?'

'That's slander, and you know it. She bought me some aftershave at duty-free. That's it.'

'We have a series of messages that she left on your phone.' Rosetta put a small hand-held device on the table and played one of the messages. There was silence as they all listened:

'Ah, my cheeky chappie, you make me so happy. I've sent a big thank-you to your bank account. See you tomorrow. I can't wait.'

Matt scrutinised the surface of the desk, and Rav and Rosetta scrutinised his face. Then he looked up, his eyes full of defiance.

'You can't prove anything,' he said.

'Actually, we can,' Rosetta said. 'For the tape, I'm showing the suspect Exhibit 34RR, his bank statements. There are a number of payments and receipts highlighted. But right now, I'm pointing out to the suspect a receipt of twenty thousand pounds on 16th December from a Mrs. Annie Robinson. This sum, we gather, was in addition to the all-expenses-included trip to America which she also paid for.' Rosetta gave him a withering look and added, 'I gather us old ones are always the best. So, do you still deny that you were paid for sexual services rendered?'

'No comment.' He scowled at her in disgust.

'Okay.' Rav took over. 'We've established that you're not really a personal trainer. That's just a front for male prostitution services that you provide to dissatisfied middle-aged women, isn't it?'

Matt sprang to his feet. 'How dare you?' His eyes flashed dangerously. 'They're trying to discredit me. This is character assassination. They can't be allowed to get away with this.' He turned to his solicitor and demanded, 'Do something to stop this, now!'

His solicitor touched his arm. 'They can, and they will. So, sit down now, please, and try to remain calm.'

Rosetta passed Rav a note on a yellow Post-it note. *Oh dear, poor baby boy narcissist.*

Rav nodded. 'Right, moving on, according to the same Exhibit

322

34RR, we see that on the 21st June, roughly six months after you conspired to have Gothic killed, you collected the insurance pay-out of just under a million pounds, and then you paid out one hundred thousand pounds and two hundred and fifty thousand pounds to your partners-in-crime, one Baron O'Neil and said Tracy Mathews. What exactly are these payments for?'

Matt squirmed a fraction, but he quickly regained his composure. 'We were all working together to try and secure a replacement four-star horse for Juliet.'

'Right, so we'd like to see a copy of the contract proving that. Where's it kept?'

'There isn't a contract. Baron's illiterate, so it was all done by way of gentlemen's handshake. That's how Gypsies and Irish Travellers operate.'

'You did it with a gentlemen's handshake?' Rosetta threw her head back and laughed. 'He's an ex-con with a record as long as your arm. Give me a break.'

'Precisely,' Matt agreed. 'That proves my point. You don't need contracts with his sort as if you break your word, you'll bloody well pay the price with a knuckle sandwich in the face.'

'Ah, so you know that he's capable of violence? And what makes you any better than him? You're a rent boy, and your mother's in jail in Australia serving ten years for fraud.'

'Ah, I've long wondered where my dear mother was. Do you have a forwarding address?'

Rosetta sucked in her cheeks, and her nostrils flared. 'Enough of this, stop being a –' she nearly spat out "wanker," but she stopped herself just in time. They had to ensure that everything went according to plan, they didn't want any possibility of this sick piece of shit getting off on a technicality. He had snuffed out a life, left a family bereft. Heavy, avoidable debts don't simply get written off, they always have to be paid.

Rosetta composed herself and continued. 'A young girl died in horrific circumstances, thanks to you. And mark my words, you will go down. We have more than enough evidence to convict the lot of you. So, now's the time for you to get your head out of your backside, do I make myself clear?'

Rav gave her ankle a sharp nudge under the table.

'Let me rephrase that. It's time to cooperate with the police.'

'You've got no proof, because I've not committed any crime. You're just bluffing, and not very convincingly.'

'Okay. For the tape, I'm handing Exhibit 39RR to the suspect. These are transcripts of his WhatsApp group messages to the other two suspects, Mathews and O'Neil before, on and after the 19th December. For the tape, I quote:

18th December

T: [An 'Okay' emoticon] It's all Go [An Arrow pointing up emoticon] for tomorrow. I'll phone in sick.
B: [Thumbs up emoticon]

19th December

M: Nag down, dead not injured?
T: Job done, innit? [Thumbs up emoticon]
B: [Thumbs up emoticon]

The posh solicitor frowned. 'I'd like a moment in private with my client, please.'

Rav nodded. 'Do not leave the designated holding room. If you need to use the bathroom, call an officer to accompany you. Interview suspended at eleven fifteen, at suspect's solicitor's request. Detectives Barrett and Patel are now exiting the room, taking the exhibits with them.' He switched off the tape recorder, turned to Rosetta, and they marched out of the room.

In the corridor, Rav leaned back against the wall. 'To think he lived with Juliet, yet he was plotting to rob and murder her, cool as a cucumber. Not a shred of remorse.' he said, shaking his head in disbelief. 'Incredible.'

'Terrible, and he got dear Mrs. Robinson to pay whilst providing him with an alibi,' she agreed with a sigh. 'But meet the classic narc. Next, he'll play the publicity for everything it's worth. For his type, it's the ego fix he craves. That's all that counts. Don't get sucked in, just keep our case tidy and tight, then let the CPS do their bit with him,' Rosetta advised.

Rav shook his head and grinned. 'Are you telling me how to do my job?'

'Sorry, I guess I was just thinking out loud.'

Rav and Rosetta hit the coffee machine then they headed upstairs to the observation screen to watch interview room two, where Baron O'Neil was being questioned by DC Boyd and DS Hodges.

'He didn't exactly come in quietly, did he?' Rosetta asked in a hushed whisper.

'No. They started off reading him his rights; "Baron O'Neil, I'm arresting you on suspicion of using a vehicle as a weapon in the murder of Isabella Levine," and at that point he landed a punch.'

Rosetta looked at the suspect. He was well built, tattooed, and wild-eyed, with multiple facial piercings. Not the sort anyone would want to mess with, for sure. She pitied the poor arresting officers. 'What happened next?'

'"You do not have to say anything. But it may harm your defence."'

'I know that bit off by heart. I mean, what did he do?'

'Apparently, he kicked the other officer in the… the down-below area.' Rav winced.

'Seriously, he kicked him in the goolies?' Rosetta looked surprised. 'The bloody cheek, but then I guess he knew he'd be going down for a very long stint this time. How did they eventually bring him in?'

'Well, with difficulty and with a bit of assistance from our friends Mr. Taser and Mrs. Pepper Spray.'

'Right,' Rosetta said with a nod, feeling suitably impressed. 'Mind you, he's a bit of a thick-looking plank, this one, eh?'

'Definitely one of humanity's twisted trees,' Rav agreed.

'So much for the witness assessment of average build. He's bigger than bloody Hagrid, isn't he?'

Rav nodded and they turned their attention to the proceedings in the interview room. They watched through one-way glass and listened with headphones.

'So, you're an obsessive loser with an extremely short fuse, right?' Charlie Boyd goaded.

'Watch your mouth and show me some respect,' O'Neil growled.

Charlie leaned back in his chair. 'Otherwise you'll do what, big man?'

Baron leapt to his feet and raised himself to his full height. He was a good six-foot-four. He leaned across the table, nose to nose with the detective. 'I'll rearrange your ugly mug so bad that even your kids won't recognise your remains.'

The duty solicitor, Fredo, grabbed Baron's arm and urged his client to be seated. 'Baron, this isn't helping. Sit down now, please.'

There was a long pause until eventually Baron's ample backside got reacquainted with his chair.

'Look,' Shirley said softly, to try and diffuse the situation. 'You know how it works. We've got the complete evidence trail, including a witness who saw you breaking into the car at Shirley Heights station. There'll be an identity parade, of course, but you totally fit the description. We have phone records of all the calls and messages between you, Lebaine, and your sister-in-law, Tracy, plotting the attack which left a young girl dead. We have bank records backing up the conspiracy. We know that Levine plotted this with Tracy's help, and you were the hit man who executed the plan.'

She tried appealing to logic. 'It's really game-over. The other two are dropping you in it, right now, as we speak. It's time to come clean, make a statement, and cooperate. Then, we can maybe look at mitigating factors regarding the charges and so on. But, rest assured, those two are going to try nail it all on you, so this is your chance to get your version across. My advice, for what it's worth, is it's time to get real, mate – talk.'

Fredo, the slightly built solicitor in his mid-fifties who cut a sad figure in his ancient crumpled suit, processed this.

Looks can be deceiving, Rosetta thought. *His brain is as sharp as his suit is lived in.* He was sufficiently experienced and pragmatic, and the entire Yorrex force knew him well. So, he was not one to be reckless with his clients' prospects.

'Now, Baron, what was Pa Riley's involvement in this? He knows Marshall, the guy who owns the car that you stole. Did Pa get you to steal that car to order?'

Rosetta was surprised when Shirley slipped that one in. *Shit,* she thought, and she held her breath. If Baron admitted Pa Riley was involved, that would implicate Peter, and potentially he'd drop her in it too. *Shit.* She licked her lips and stared, transfixed, through the glass. *Don't go there, whatever you do,* she pleaded silently. The whole stack of cards could be about to collapse, taking her reputation and her career with it, all the way down to hell.

Baron's jaw dropped open and his eyes darted sideways as if looking for a way to escape. 'Nah, he didn't have nuffin' to do with it. It was that Matt geezer. He wanted the pay-out, and if it looked like an accident, the insurance company couldn't argue. That Juliet woman, she had a big whack of life insurance. Only...'

Rosetta closed her eyes and mouthed a silent prayer – *Thank you.*

'Only the wrong person got wiped out, right?' Charlie said.

'Yeah, happen so,' Baron agreed.

'Okay,' Shirley said. 'The suspect is looking at murder. He knew when the horse was killed that the rider could die too. In fact, the plan was to kill Juliet and claim her life insurance. That's pre-meditation and intent, and it was all for financial gain. Then, there's theft of a vehicle, used with intent to kill. Shall I continue?'

Fredo nodded.

'First, there's resisting arrest. Second, assaulting two police officers. One was admitted to the hospital.'

Baron sniggered. 'It serves 'im right.'

'So, Fredo, we are going to leave him to you to get this straight in his head.' Shirley stood up. 'You get my drift? We're going to leave you alone for a while to confer with your client.' She snapped the tape recorder off.

Fredo nodded again.

* * *

Tracy Mathews had big eyes, an ample chest, and she was heavily made-up. Her mascara was smudged, as if she'd been crying. She was represented by Leon, another duty solicitor from the same firm as Fredo. Their offices were just around the corner from the police station, and they were in and out of the station all the time. The interview, conducted by Detectives Johnson and Firth, commenced once the tape was rolling.

'Okay, Tracy, we've picked up the other two conspirators and they're both in custody. So, Baron's your brother-in-law, and Matt's the boyfriend?' Detective Johnson asked.

'No.' Her eyes widened. 'It's not like that. He's the boss.'

'He's the boss, I thought your boss was Juliet? She pays your wages, right? Well, I guess you mean he was the boss who hatched this neat plot? Or was it your idea to kill Gothic and collect the insurance money?'

Her eyes grew even wider. 'No! I never, I love horses. It was all Matt's idea.'

Detective Johnson continued, 'A funny kind of love. Did you have anything to do with Totem's death, as well? Did you ship him off to the knackers' yard?'

Her lower lip began to tremble, and she sniffed. 'I only did what I thought was best.'

'Best for Totem, best for Gothic, that's quite a track record, eh? What about Isabella?'

'Oh,' she gasped. 'That was a mistake, an accident.'

'So, Matt comes up with this plan to collect the insurance money.

He collects a cool million and you buy in?'

Her jaw dropped open. 'I didn't know it was that much. He told me...'

'Ah, so you've confirmed your involvement. Your job was to recruit Baron to do the dirty work, then?'

She looked at her solicitor for guidance. He remained silent and shook his head.

'No comment,' she said.

'We know you and Baron are close. You visited him regularly in prison. We have all your phone records. For the tape, I'm showing the suspect Exhibit 39RR, five pages of phone call and message transcripts where she's arranging for O'Neil to intercept the two horse riders on the morning of the 19th December. Now, Tracy love, why on earth did you get yourself involved in this?' DS Firth asked softly.

'I'm not involved.' Her chin jutted out to prove her point.

'Look, Tracy, don't mess with us. We've got all the proof that confirms your involvement, such as bank statements showing that Lebaine paid you one hundred thousand pounds from the insurance money. So, there are lies, damn lies, and now it's time for you to tell us the truth.'

Tracy looked worried as she tried to fight back tears. 'Matt convinced me that we'd be together. That we'd set up our own yard, and I could compete. I fell for it. I fell for him. It wasn't really for the money and I... I really wish it –'

'Okay, so are you ready to make a statement?'

Tracy nodded, tears spilling down her cheeks. 'I'm so sorry about Isabella, honest. I'll never forgive myself...'

DS Firth passed her a tissue, and she blew her nose. 'I know it's hard, but a few more questions please,' he said. 'Did Baron steal the Range Rover from Shirley Heights railway station?'

'Yeah, he's a complete car freak, and it was a really flashy motor with posh plates.'

'Right, we'll get your statement drafted, and Leon here can go through it with you.'

Outside the room, Rav and Rosetta punched the air and did a victory jig.

'Eureka!' she yelled.

'Finally,' he said.

CHAPTER FORTY-FIVE
Rav

The police station was buzzing with anticipation as Rav addressed the crowded room. 'Settle down now and be quiet, everyone.' He waited until the department quietened to a hush. 'As you know, all three suspects were arrested yesterday and brought in for questioning. They were held in custody overnight, and processed this morning: the usual stuff, DNA samples and fingerprinting, and they've all been charged. Stuart's informed the Levine family and they're being kept in the loop. An officer spoke to Juliet when Matt was brought in, and she's been told about recent developments. The preliminary hearing will take place in a day or two, and all three will be kept in custody until then. Obviously, with his previous record, Baron will not be granted bail. He'll go on remand. He's pled guilty to all the charges, thanks obviously to Fredo talking some sense into him over the sentencing. So far, Tracy's cooperating, and she's given a full statement and will most likely enter a guilty plea too, but Matt Lebaine is entering not guilty pleas for every count, so that will obviously go to trial. We'll be pushing the CPS to block any bail application, although it's his first serious offence. His mother's a convicted fraudster, and she slipped the net and did a runner to Australia, and we don't want a repeat performance.'

'Like all the original Poms,' Charlie cackled.

'Hmm, I guess a warped sense of humour goes with the job? Well, Lebaine's a slippery customer, so we don't want him disappearing in a puff of smoke,' Rav continued. 'Do you have any questions or comments, please?'

'How're the family, Stuart? How're they holding up?' Shirley asked, looking concerned.

A sad expression flashed across Stuart's face. 'They're not, really. Ann's falling apart and Patrick's falling down – literally. They're pleased and relieved about the charges. That brings some closure, and they're glad that there will be accountability, but they're not relishing the prospect of a trial. Can't say I blame them, and I'm doubtful that their marriage will survive this.'

Rav shook his head. 'Most marriages don't survive the murder of a child. Is their GP involved, and are they seeing a bereavement counsellor?'

'I'm on it,' Stuart said. 'The priest visits regularly. That's about all we can do at the moment, sir.'

'Good. Mind you we don't want any suicides. Are we sure there's nothing else that can be done? Are all the risk assessments up-to-date according to standard protocol? The last thing we need is a duty-of-care SWAT team descending on us, bleating on about our failure to deal with mental health issues. Stuart, get on the case with Victim Support. Pull out all the stops and get Patrick seen by a psychiatrist, and preferably shipped into rehab as soon as possible. Marriage breakdown, divorce, and alcoholism are things we have plenty of experience with in our profession, but we can really do without suicides.' Rav mopped his brow with a tissue. 'As a precaution, get the wife on board. Ask Ann to clear out the medicine cabinet, put the contents under lock and key and dish out the daily prescribed dose of any pills the GP's ordered. Technically, we're not authorised to do this, but see if you can get Ann on-side. That will be fine and above board. We seriously don't need any prescription pill addictions on our consciences, adding to the payload.'

Shirley sighed. 'That's so sad for that poor family. It's all looking a wee bit grim. What about the press? Are we going to broadcast our success yet?'

Rav shook his head. 'I'd prefer to wait till after the preliminary hearing. Meanwhile, anyone got any good news?'

'Aye,' Charlie said with considerable enthusiasm. 'My New Year's resolution was to join a gym. I'm not quite there yet, but I'm doing plenty of research on the internet, so that counts as a finger workout.' He raised his hands and wriggled his fingers about, and everyone laughed. 'And I'd like all of you to know, particularly those of you who are sponsoring my weight loss campaign that I am getting plenty of exercise. Why, only last week, I even pushed a shopping trolley around Waitrose.'

Shirley cracked up laughing. 'Steady on, man. I bet it was nay full o' salad, mind. Do you have the Lark app I recommended downloaded yet?'

Charlie ducked his head as Dennis aimed a scrunched-up ball of paper at him. 'You're a sad specimen. You're destined to remain a fat bastard, aren't you?'

'I'll have you know that my GP has diagnosed a serious case of hangry.' He looked suitably pious.

'Is it contagious?' Shirley's eyes opened wide at the prospect.

'It is anger caused by extreme hunger.'

'You could have fooled me,' Rav announced. 'Now, now team. First, I'd like to congratulate you all on your hard work. Terrific result. Give yourselves a well-deserved pat on the back.' A rapturous round of cheering and applause ensued. 'And I've decided to give the commissioner's budget a final heart attack, so I'm inviting everyone to join me down at the White Hart tonight. Stanmore's wallet might even stretch to a few packets of crisps, but obviously no pork scratchings, due to my allergy.'

'What allergy is that, gaffer?' Dennis looked curious.

'Religious,' Rav said with a laugh.

'Well, before you did the press statement thingy, I did'na even know so many religions existed.' Shirley looked bewildered. 'And talking of which, where is our very own wee-witchy?'

'Rosetta's on her way to New Mexico, and a bit later she'll be joined by Juliet.'

Shirley opened her eyes wide and folded her hands behind her head. 'I hope she's nay recruiting that poor lassie over to the dark side.'

Rav shook his head. Clearly the appeal for more tolerance had fallen on deaf ears. 'She's not like that. Anyway, you lot, time to get back to the coal face. Off you go and make yourselves useful.' He went to his office, closed the door, and turned the blinds' spindle till they closed. Then he sent Rosetta a WhatsApp message:

Hi. Hope you're okay? You're probably still asleep?
Anyway, just told the team. All three are being charged. Well happy.
Can't call you tonight as we're off to the White Hart, fornicating. Xx

Whoops predictive text!!!? s/b celebrating.

Shirley raised her chin and tilted her head in the direction of Rav's office. 'I reckon he's got the hots for her,' Shirley confided in a low

331

conspiratorial whisper. 'He's always so protective.'

'Who, Rav? *Our* Rav? The Patron-Saint-of-Self-denial? Nah, she's totally not his type. Potty mouth, heavy drinker, smoker, carnivore. I mean, they're total opposites. Rav's law abiding and conservative, she's a complete maverick, always challenging the status quo and breaking the rules.' Dennis laughed. 'I mean you have to admit she always sails close to the wind.'

'Well.' Charlie shrugged. 'They say opposites attract.'

'Nah, it's nay that opposites attracting stuff. I reckon she's put a spell on him,' Shirley said in a loud whisper.

They all laughed.

* * *

Sweetpea

Sweetpea looked around her new abode. It was the same, but different. The shed was the same, but it had been relocated. Sam had been so kind and had chopped off a section at the bottom of his vast garden. Her plot was screened off, and it had its own separate access down a side track, plus a lockable gate and a high fence to deter intruders and rubberneckers. She missed the river that ran along the back of the allotment, where she'd collect water and go for a dip sometimes. Still, Sam had installed a brick outbuilding with hot and cold running water, a shower, a posh composting toilet which actually flushed, and even a washing machine and tumble drier.

Totally unnecessary, of course, but she'd come to appreciate these luxuries which most people took for granted. Her shed still functioned conservatively, with solar power and the wood-burning stove, as she tried to abide by eco and green principles in accordance with her religious beliefs. She had been sad to leave the allotment, her friends Arnold, Gilbert, and Sam had put up a good fight with Daniel's help, but ultimately, they'd lost. Yorrex County Council had served an eviction notice, something to do with planning regulations.

Luckily, Sam had stepped in and drafted paperwork which Daniel sorted, so that part of his former garden plot was hers for life and any coven she formed could take over under the auspices of her nominated replacement. Sam was quite keen to ensure that witches could practice without ridicule or persecution. Sweetpea was hoping that one day he might even join them, but so far, while he seemed tolerant of naked women cavorting at the bottom of his garden, he had manifested zero enthusiasm to join in.

Generally, all was well that ended well, as the bard would say. Rosetta's officers had detained a man, the Peeping Tom. His name was Ernest Higgins, but they were reluctant to charge him as there wasn't an obvious sexual motive and he denied responsibility for the crude graffiti. Still, he had been taken into the station for questioning and told under caution to stay away from her, so she felt that he had learned his lesson.

By now, Sweetpea was well settled in her new home and her fruit and vegetable plot was thriving. The cats had settled on a spot with all-round sun, and they laid out on warmer days and did what cats did best: sleep. Boo-Hoo, her tawny owl, was particularly delighted, as there was a small wooded area behind the shed, and he had found a lady friend, little hatchlings expected soon, perhaps? Her friends visited once a month for bridge evenings and the occasional games of whist, but even she, with all her ESP talents, found that she couldn't beat Arnold. For a time, she suspected that he might be a wizard. However, it transpired that he was a Most Excellent Master in the Freemasons. He also grew wonderful dahlias and always brought her a bunch, which she put in a lovely old blue and white jug.

Lately, he'd been trying to persuade her to get a beehive, but for now Sweetpea was happy just to accept his jars of delicious honey, after all it would be quite a painful affair if the bees swarmed and got fractious during one of the dancing-naked-under-the-moon ceremonies. She pulled a face at the mere thought and carried on weeding.

* * *

Juliet

When Juliet had been informed that Matt and Tracy had been charged, she'd been devastated. To learn that people she knew and trusted, and in Matt's case someone she had loved, could betray her in such a disgusting way was hard to comprehend. The insurance company had reclaimed the money they had paid out, saying it was a fraudulent claim. *They're never out of pocket, are they?* They vacuumed up those monthly premiums like Dracula with his teeth locked on, and, as she discovered, no chance of a blood transfusion when she needed one at a later date. So, there was no prospect of buying a replacement four-star horse any time soon, give or take a lottery win. Icon was the only sound Intermediate horse on the yard. The other two were injured, and only an Advanced horse with a four-star track record would get selected for the Equestrian World Games or afterwards, the Olympics. Espiritus had long years of slow training and build-up ahead of her, so all Juliet's dreams of winning a second gold medal had spectacularly collapsed. But, in comparison to the Levine's she knew she'd got off lightly.

They'd lost a beloved daughter, a sister, and their lives had slowly imploded in the aftermath. Patrick had been shipped off to rehab, and when she'd bumped into Ann in the supermarket recently, she'd seemed dazed and completely out of it.

Heart-breaking.

Orla had moved away and started a new job, probably to escape all the attention and the commiserating stares from well-wishers. She hadn't left a forwarding address, and all Juliet's calls and messages had gone unanswered. Eventually, Juliet took the hint and stopped trying to communicate – too painful, she concluded.

During the long spaces, the gaps between sleep as she lay in bed at night, Juliet surveyed the landscape of devastation and destruction which had become her reality lately. How quickly her life had unravelled. How had it happened and derailed so suddenly? In a flash, it went from an exhilarating gallop up a gentle sandy slope to a crashing out-of-control bolt at breakneck speed into a dark, dangerous forest.

Once a horse bolts, it flees for its life and there's no turning back.

The betrayal caused her layer upon layer of excruciating pain. She felt foolish and naive. To think that she'd lived with Matt and not seen any clues about what really lurked beneath the surface. The person that she thought she knew had been just a façade, a charming construct designed to fool everyone. She couldn't even trust her own judgement anymore and gradually that began to affect her riding ability. Doubt and fear, these emotions could be transmitted from the rider to the horse, and when she set a horse up at the approach to a fence, she had to be totally confident and committed. In the dressage phase, the rider needed to remain calm and relaxed. Lately, out jumping, all her horses had put in stops, and on one occasion the pair of them had been eliminated. *Olympic eventing rider reverts to pony club novice.* It seemed that everything was spiralling down to the bottom, and the very bottom was still a long way off.

She went to visit Matt in prison to try and persuade him to plead guilty and spare them all the prolonged agony of a trial, and herself from the ordeal of the witness stand. Matt, however, batted the idea away as if he was shooing off a fly with a plastic swatter. Juliet stared at his bristly chin and she concluded that the rugged look suited him.

She could not bring herself to look him in the eye as she knew she'd hit him with a laser beam of pure contempt, so she avoided eye contact.

'Matt, please think about what the Levine family are going through. They're already on the brink and having to relive it all at the trial could push them over the edge. Please. I'm begging you to change your plea to guilty.' Her tone was shrill and beseeching. A sermon delivered with passion, but it fell on deaf ears, it seemed.

'Why would I do that? I've got a crack legal team, a ruthless female barrister, a total Rottweiler, and a hottie too.'

Juliet gasped. This man seriously deserved a slap. What in the world was he thinking? Did he really think it was all about him? *Bring on the Matt Lebaine show.* How could she have lived with this nasty man, eaten at the same table, slept in the same bed, and not realised the cavernous depths of his ruthless egotism? Looking at him now made her think of having a root canal on a tooth abscess, and then some.

'You set me up, you betrayed me.' Then, she remembered what Rosetta had told her about criminal psychology, how they'd do anything to get you on their side. They wanted to get you to sympathise, because they were radicalised in jail. They wanted to hear you say: *I know you killed because your background was so deprived. You poor thing, the victim provoked you.* Rosetta reckoned that the more deranged they were the more capable they were of covering up. Juliet took a long, hard look at Matt and concluded that he was one sick fuck. She tugged at her collar as her throat tightened, just being in the same space as him, accelerated the gagging feeling.

Matt continued, obviously unaware of or unconcerned by her horrified expression. 'Yeah, I think it'll be a big media trial with heaps of publicity. Which is neat as I'm planning on writing a book.'

Juliet's response was swift and instinctive, and she gave him a really hard kick on the shin.

'Ouch,' he yelped, rubbing the afflicted part.

'Nothing compared with what you inflicted on my beautiful, gentle horse. Nothing compared to what a young girl suffered, crushed and bleeding in a ditch. Don't you have any shame? You should be showing remorse, not bragging, you sick piece of shit.' Juliet sprang to her feet and scooped her purse off the floor.

'You always were a sanctimonious cow, a spoilt little rich girl.' His eyes blazed, and he put his thumb in his mouth and taunted her. 'Boo-hoo-hoo, go along now and run to your mommy.'

Juliet stood up and rose to her full height, so she was looking down at him. She froze, trembling with anger. 'I thought I'd hate you. But you're not even worth that.' She snatched up her handbag and spun on her heel, shaking with rage as she marched towards the exit.

* * *

Rosetta

Rosetta went on ahead to Dulce, leaving Juliet to fly out later. She would stay at the Jicarilla Indian Reservation nearby, as the base was off-limits. *Only conscripts were allowed at Dulce.* EPIS had located Geronimo's funerary objects – a horn, a silver bit, a very ancient bridle, arrowheads, and an assortment of ceramics. Gothic's remains would be flown over the day after Juliet left.

Watching him being dug up would be too traumatic, and she'd already been through enough. Now, she was fretting about Matt's idea of writing a book, and the base lawyers were investigating to see if it could be blocked. Publishing companies could be influenced, but these days he could just self-publish an e-book. They might have to let it fly, then get it banned for defamation or some other juicy legal loophole. Dr. Ashworth had been busy hiring an Apache translator to go with the representatives from the PR and legal departments, to meet with Geronimo's descendants and discuss arrangements for the horse's prospective reburial ceremony. Negations were still underway.

On her second day on the base, Rosetta ran into Daniel in the corridor leading out of the reception bay. He looked momentarily taken aback, but he recovered quickly and slipped on the lawyer mask.

'Rosetta. What a surprise, how lovely to see you.'

Rosetta sucked her teeth. *Every inch the lawyer,* she thought. *Smile to your face and shaft you in the wallet.* 'Hi Dan,' she said loud enough to attract attention. 'Well now, fancy meeting you here. I thought you'd passed away, that or joined a kibbutz, perhaps?' He hated being called Dan.

He frowned a moment before getting himself together again and rearranging his features.

'So, what're you up to?' He lowered his tone. 'I guess you heard about the aliens. It's getting kinda crowded, if you see what I mean?'

'I heard you were dating one. How's it going?' Rosetta said with irony.

He paused then fake-laughed. 'I forgot about your wicked sense of humour. So, what's occurring?'

'Oh, you know, Dan, this and that. How about you? Have you got anything interesting to report, apart from airbrushing people, loved ones, out of your life?'

He gulped and reached for his tie to loosen it. 'Busy as ever, I was helping a mutual friend of ours.'

'Yes, Sweetpea mentioned that. Aren't you just so kind and thoughtful?' She slashed at him with the razor-sharp edge of her neat sarcasm.

'Right,' he breathed, unbuttoning the collar of his pristine crisp white shirt. 'I better get back to work.'

'Hang on a minute.' She raised her palm to prevent him scurrying off. 'Not so fast. Don't you think you at least owe me an explanation?'

Daniel shrugged and licked his lips. 'Well, I'm Jewish. You're not. It could never develop into anything more serious, and besides, grandma's getting on now and my mother's keen for me to get married while she's still around.'

Rosetta shot him an incredulous glare. 'Ah, so I'm just a *goy*, a *shiksa* for you to play around with until the right wife material comes along, is that it? And it took you over four years to figure this out? Four years of giving me the run around and wasting my time?'

'No.' He looked around anxiously to check if anyone was listening. 'I loved you, but I came to realise that we weren't... well... compatible. You can't have children. Well, perhaps, but it would be difficult, and you'd have to convert to Judaism, and I figured that would never happen.'

'Fine, but why not just tell me? Why the silence? Didn't I at least deserve an explanation?'

Daniel shrugged.

'That's it? No apology, no nothing?'

He shrugged again.

'Have you read *Portnoy's Complaint* by Philip Roth?'

He shook his head.

'Well, I have. Now go screw yourself, you pathetic excuse for a man.' She set off, then turned back to face him. 'Oh, and if you've got any leave due, I suggest you take it, pronto. Because I don't want to be looking at your miserable, snivelling face while I'm here. Do I make myself clear?'

Daniel nodded and quickly extracted himself.

* * *

Rosetta and Juliet

A few days later, Rosetta went to Salt Lake Lodge on the Jicarilla Apache Reserve to meet Juliet. She looked well. Her long hair had been braided into two pigtails, and it looked very Hiawatha. Juliet explained that she'd been on a fishing expedition at the Navajo River, and she pointed to the trout and catfish trophies that were cooking on a spit over the campfire. They sat cross-legged outside their tent on woven mats and coyote and bobcat rugs.

'I kinda feel like sleeping in a tipi,' Juliet said. 'My guide, Ishkoten, is going to organise it for me. We were talking about respect for the seasons, and the cyclical flow of life. He said we should teach our children about the ground beneath their feet and how they walk on the ashes of their ancestors.'

'I guess that's a valid point,' Rosetta said. 'How're you doing?'

Juliet shrugged and took a deep breath. 'I could implode with all the loss and pain. The bond between Gothic and I was telepathic, so losing him is all the more difficult.'

Rosetta raised an eyebrow. 'You're a kindred spirit, then?'

Juliet laughed. 'Not exactly, but it's been wave after wave of loss and that shifts something deep. Gothic, Isabella, then Matt and even Tommy... a tsunami of grief. And if I'm not careful, I could just spiral into a bottomless pit of depression...'

'The long dark night of the soul. If it's any consolation, I've been there too. We all do, if not in this lifetime, then the next.'

'Yeah, I guess,' Juliet agreed. 'But I'm determined not to go under. I'm going to stay upbeat and make something positive out of the experience.'

'Great.' Rosetta made a thumbs up sign. 'And you're going to stay here a while? That sounds like fun. So, who's holding down the fort at the other end while you're away?'

'Todd. That man is a Godsend. He's covering everything. He's shipped in some of his staff over to my place, and he's even going to compete my string, so they don't end the season thinking that it's okay to stop and refuse. Horses have long memories, so they need to end the season on a positive note. Todd's taking care of everything.' She sighed. 'Nothing's too much trouble for Todd where his friends are concerned. He's a total star. It makes me cringe, to think that I was even considering taking over Chi-Chi Charlie, his horse. How could I have been so crass?'

'Well, you didn't do it. You wised up. You did what was right, and you grew in the process. So, give yourself some credit for that.'

Juliet looked thoughtful. 'Yeah, I guess, but why does it have to be so hard?'

'We all have to evolve, learn our lessons and grow. It's the same on all four levels, the planes of existence: manifest, astral, mental, and

338

spiritual.' Rosetta confided with deep conviction.

'Astral plane, what's that all about?'

'It's a boundary crossed by the soul, where we go to live out our non-physical lives after we die here on Earth.'

'Mind-blowing,' Juliet decided.

'Don't worry about it. Just to let you know, Gothic's arrived, and he's settled. My boss is just finalising the arrangements. We should have a date for the ceremony soon. So, what have you got planned for the next few days?'

'My guide's got someone to teach me how to shoot a bow and arrow, and we're going pony trekking Apache-style tomorrow. Do you want to join us?'

Rosetta rolled her eyes. 'Riding with no saddle? That sounds like my idea of torture. No thanks, I'll stick to armchairs.'

Juliet gazed up at the stars. 'I've been learning a lot about the wild Mustangs over here and how they're rounded up by helicopter, penned, and often sent for slaughter, basically they're under threat of being eradicated. The big interests, backed by large scale cattle ranchers and oil and fracking companies, are threatening their very existence, so –' she paused, 'I've given it a lot of thought, and I'm going ahead with the sale of Luckenham Park to the property development company. With the money, I'm going to buy a big ranch where the wild horses can roam free, and people can come and sleep under the stars in tipis, tell stories round the camp fire like we are doing now. Hopefully, as an American gold medallist I should be able to amass plenty of media attention to get behind the cause.'

'Wow.' Rosetta looked at her with deep admiration. 'That's an amazing dream to translate into action. How many people get to create such a legacy?'

'Yeah.' Juliet laughed, looking happier than she had for a long time. 'All those years of classic dressage training, and now I reverted to riding Western-style. Well, actually, maybe Apache-style. We'll see how it goes tomorrow. But once I'm settled here, Espiritus can be shipped over and she can be one of the foundation mares on the new ranch. How about you help me choose a name for the ranch?'

'Well, it has to be… Sky something… Blue Sky… Star Sky… Sky Blue…'

'I know,' Juliet said excitedly. 'How about Sky Catcher? That's what Tommy registered Espiritus as.'

'Perfect.' Rosetta laughed, and raised her glass. 'Sky Catcher Ranch, here's to my visit for the opening ceremony.'

'All right, watch this space,'

The smell of salted baked potatoes and roasting fish wafted all around and mingled with the smell of ponderosa pines. Overhead, in the vast blankness overhanging the plains, the moon cast a soft glow, a shaft of silvery light.

'Ah, I love the moon,' Rosetta sighed. 'It's all about fertility, grace, beauty, and intuition. I came out here with my partner Daniel once. We brought a collection of our favourite slow songs, and we smooched well into the night. Back then I believed he was my twin flame.'

They both stared up at the pink-tinged moon, and Rosetta was tempted to draw down its energy and create a magical pathway. But the time wasn't right, and she couldn't involve Juliet without her permission and the necessary preparations. As she stared at the cosmos, a shooting star arced across the magnificent sky. She pointed it out to Juliet.

'Look, make a wish,' Rosetta said excitedly. 'Actually, three wishes.' They both closed their eyes.

'What did you wish for?' Juliet took a big gulp of neat rum from her tin mug.

'Ah, I wished to really bond with my kids. I miss them so much. But on a positive note, Alice has been messaging me regularly, and occasionally Edward and I catch up on FaceTime, so that's positive. Also, I've put in a request with my boss to be permanently based in the UK, so I can buy a little three-bedroom cottage, and my friend Sweetpea can plant the vegetable garden out back and grow roses round the front door, and the kids can stay over from time to time. I need a base, so I can have some kind of settled life, and invest more in my relationships.' Rosetta paused. 'What made the break-up so hard was that I believed that Daniel and I were twin flames.'

'Like soul mates?' Juliet cocked her head with interest.

'Yes, kind of, except twin flames were originally one soul which got split. Energetically, each completes the other. Soul mates connect to teach each other essential lessons, whereas twin souls have a bigger, more universal mission to accomplish together.' Rosetta traced her finger in the sandy soil in a swirling movement. 'I didn't handle the breakup with Daniel very well. In fact, I was a total bitch when we met up just recently.'

'Well, you felt that there was so much riding on it, personally, professionally, and for the planet, so that's understandable.'

'Maybe, I ran into him a few days ago,' she paused. 'Perhaps we can be friends again further down the line. This place has good memories, we used to come out here dancing together. Anyway, we'd been together for over three years, we got on really well, and I got posted away. Suddenly I'm in the UK, he's here, he came over to visit me, returns, and then the silence starts. No explanation. Nothing. Not even excuses. Just mind-numbing silence. Anyway, I cornered him and finally he admitted that I got the elbow on religious grounds. He's Jewish, and apparently I'm not good wife material.' She chuckled. 'Can't imagine why he thought that. I'm a hereditary witch, born to a magical family, using gifts handed down through the generations. You might have thought some of that would come in handy, but seemingly not. So, I wish for more interracial and religious tolerance. Also, I'd like more positive open-mindedness about other planets, and visitors from other galaxies. The Hopi Indians call them Sky Beings, and they're here now. So, Sky Beings rock!'

'All right,' they chanted in unison. Juliet grappled with the rum bottle, topped their mugs up, and they raised them together in a toast. 'Here's to racial, religious, and intergalactic tolerance.'

Rosetta continued, 'Also, on a personal level, I wished for things to work out with me and Rav. He's a good sort, but –'

Juliet laughed. 'Why do "men" and "but" always go together in the same sentence?'

It was Rosetta's turn to laugh. 'No, the "but" is his wife. She's lurking somewhere in the background, ready to re-materialise, or whatever wives do when they get wind of another woman – a rival. Suddenly, the discarded husband begins to look much more desirable, right?'

'That's one man problem I haven't experienced yet, but don't hold your breath.'

'It's only a matter of time,' they said in unison.

'Oh man,' Juliet said. 'It just occurred to me that you work together, and he's your boss.'

'Don't remind me.' Rosetta groaned, taking a piece of folded blanket to help her remove the food from the heat. She left it to rest in two steel camping dishes. 'I'll probably have to be based at a different unit, and it gets even more complicated… he'll have to give up the wife, but god forbid, I'll have to give up cigarettes. At our first kiss, I can't forget how he recoiled slightly when he smelt cigarette smoke on my breath, so I'll have to quit. How about you, what's on your wish list?'

'Hmm.' Juliet stretched and kicked off her shoes. 'I've enjoyed the time I've spent here on the reservation so much. It's a really tight-knit community and everyone knows each other. It feels like home to me. I know this isn't Geronimo's tribe, but maybe I've connected with something from my past. Maybe this was my tribe. Anyway, I wished for Geronimo's spirit to finally be set free.'

'That's a great wish, and what else?'

Juliet stared into the fire. 'I guess through being here I've come to appreciate family ties. I've never been particularly close to my parents. I was raised by grandparents, nannies, and shipped off to boarding school. So, I plan on staying in the States after the ceremony to spend some time with my parents and see if it's not too late to form some kind of connection.'

'I'll drink to that,' Rosetta said and drained her mug. 'Third wish.'

'I miss Tommy. Again, since I've been out here in the stunning wilderness, I've had time to think, and reassess things, and I came to realise that he is the love of my life.'

'Well, I felt a deep connection too, so I can see the attraction, and he is pretty good in…'

Juliet gave her a friendly shove. 'That's not funny. He's my soul mate, not yours!'

'Sorry, off I go trespassing again. Or is it BF stealing? Actually, I'm trying to forget that little indiscretion.' Rosetta cringed.

Juliet sighed. 'Well, considering the past events, none of us came out looking that compassionate or magnanimous, did we?'

Rosetta chewed her lip. 'Well, shit happens, I guess. Men go astray all the time, and no one bats an eyelid. Besides, I wasn't planning on entering a popularity contest any time soon. How about you and Tommy, do you think you'll get back together?'

Juliet stared into the distance, and a comforting silence settled. She poked the fire with a stick, sending embers and sparks fluttering into the night. 'I called him. I told him that I understood what he did, and his reasons. I said that I forgave him, and that I wanted to try again, if he was willing.'

Rosetta handed her the steel dish filled with delicious marinated fish and garlicky potatoes. 'Well, he's got off lightly.'

'So why didn't you charge him?'

'Good question.' Rosetta shrugged. 'I didn't really see what point that would serve. I need to go back and unravel the past-life back-story – who did what, when, and why – to make more sense of it.

Betrayal is a key theme, but Tommy remained true to his beliefs and his duty as he saw it. What did he say about the idea of you getting back together?'

'He said, "Frankly, my dear, I don't give a damn." Juliet shook her head. 'I don't know what to think.'

Rosetta laughed. 'Well, remember, being with your soul mate doesn't equate to a walk in the park, and sometimes soul mates shake you up and leave. You're supposed to have challenges in order to grow. Meanwhile, he quotes from *Gone with the Wind*, eh?'

'Oh, he's full of words and seductive baloney all right, always spouting poetry and hot air. That's the Irish for you, I guess?'

'He must've snogged the Blarney Stone, and sucked the life out the poor thing, never mind kissed it.'

They both fell about laughing. Juliet gave Rosetta another shove. 'That's the love of my life you're making fun of.'

'Don't get too hung up on one man, you'll have many lives, many loves,' Rosetta said as she poured another tot of rum into their cups, which they raised in salutation to the heavens above. 'To us, to the starry skies, and fish and potato suppers,' Rosetta said.

'Single-hashtag-and ready to mingle,' Juliet joined in, both of them full of thanks and praise for the perfect evening.

With that, they both tucked in using fingers, forks, and a few paper napkins.

Meanwhile, their laughter continued to echo into the wilderness, long into the magical night.

AUTHOR'S NOTES

A new consciousness has been emerging throughout the Age of Aquarius, and a rapid spiritual awakening is occurring, which science, and organized religions have not yet fully tapped into. At soul level, not everyone originates from planet Earth. Some initially incarnate elsewhere in a star system by choosing a destination which matches their energetic vibration the closest. The different origins are collectively referred to as "soul groups," and around 80% are found within Earth's solar system, whereas the remaining 20% come from elsewhere in the galaxy. These are the Star Travelers, who perhaps, understandably, don't feel entirely at home on Earth. Indeed, some of you are Space Hybrids who carry DNA from other planets. This may resonate with you for some obscure reason that's hard to pinpoint, or perhaps you have already identified yourself as a Blue Ray, an Indigo, a Crystal, a Light worker, a Star Seed… to name but a few of the advanced soul kindred spirits. You sense that somehow you are different, and that you have an important purpose to fulfil, but somehow that role remains unclear, and just out of reach. It is hard being here on earth where you want to fit in, yet don't quite, and you sense you have something important to accomplish – but what?

As the Jedi in Star Wars said: Search your feelings about what you know to be true. Wake up, and get ready to step up, and take your place in the universe.

Why are you here? Where are you from? Where are you going?

So far you may have led a difficult life, fraught with considerable pain and afflicted with much struggle. You may have felt down, alone, and depressed – abandoned in a strange location like a foreigner far from home. Does that sound familiar? It has been hard, but necessary, as there were things that you had to experience, and lessons that you needed to learn. Now, congratulate yourself for getting this far, for showing courage, determination and above all, resilience. You will rise above your past, and those mistakes and abusive situations won't be repeated or perpetuated. Sometimes, hearts have to break in order to open.

The way forward arises through healing, self-love and love for others, and healing is facilitated by forgiveness and compassion. Create good vibes, smile, find things to laugh about, share jokes and hugs. Give and receive compliments. Practice positive affirmations and take ownership of your own results. What starts off as adversity often ends up as grace. Remember… as you heal yourself, you heal the world. Don't be afraid to shine and manifest your gifts. Put your unique talent forward. Let it go forth. It's time to enhance your individual spiritual development, and help the planet transition away from darkness, destruction, and ascend to a new level of illumination, awareness, and vibrate at a higher frequency.

The shift has already started. Help it gain momentum.

Like drops in the ocean forming a cascade, now the tide is turning. Let go of limiting beliefs. Decline all states of limited resources, request, and expect a quantum upgrade. You are living at the end of an era. You chose this period in history in order to play your part as a steward in the planetary transformation process. You sense the calling… it's time to ride the winds of change.

Hounds of heaven, wolves of the world… join your pack, follow your sky tribe. Whales and dolphins, take a joyous leap and connect with your pod. Stand in your power, open your heart, and shine your light. Live a life beyond limitation. Embrace new possibilities and move from struggle to ease and finding your flow. Your soul's blueprint is the map, now it's up to you to navigate new territory. To help humanity turn away from destruction, transcend old constructs / structures / timelines, and bring about a better world filled with joy and light.

You have galaxies inside your head.
Stop letting people tell you, you can't shine.
Unknown

Listen to your intuition and follow synchronicities. They will guide you. Trust the process, believe your prophetic dreams, develop your psychic skills, your healing abilities, and manifest your gifts! Look for clarity in mysterious coincidences and learn to recognize and trust the signposts to your purpose wherever they appear.

Always keep at least a corner of your mind open to possibilities. Whenever you feel low, lonely and misunderstood, never forget who you are, and always acknowledge your uniquely inspiring gifts. Learn from others, from masters, spiritual gurus, but don't give your power away to them: always trust your own inner wisdom.

Live on a frequency of gratitude and expectancy. Do what you can, with what you have, depending on where you're at. Live your dream one step at a time. Expect a degree of confusion, doubt, fear – these things are inevitable. You are a spiritual being having a physical experience, and gradually [or suddenly, in some cases] the disconnection to your soul and your original blueprint will end, and alignment will be restored.

Explore new ideas, find new pathways, make improvements. Be original, expand and accelerate. Help humanity evolve and progress along a more spiritual path simply by raising your own vibration. Upgrade the way you show up in the world. You have enough, and you are more than enough.

I'm further than I've ever been, from all I've ever known.
Yet it seems I'm drawing closer to a space to call my own.
Unknown

You are not lost, or alone. You have been located. Now simply reach out and tell your friends and family about this book. Word of mouth has an amazing ripple effect.

HEY EARTHLINGS, THEY'VE LANDED!

Free competition to name the Blue and Grey Alien, and win mugs, signed paperback copies of the book, plus the two overall winners will be credited, and they will have their alien chums named in the next book.

To enter, go to bit.ly/2H3hG8r

Hope you enjoyed this novel.
We'd really appreciate it if you'd take a moment
to leave a review:

Books2Read.com/sop
GoodReads: bit.ly/2LihFPJ

To consider the Earth as the only populated world in infinite space is as absurd as to assert that in an entire field sown with millet only one grain will grow.

Metrodorus of Chios, 4th century BCE

I'd like to tell the public about the Alien situation, but my hands are tied.

J. F. Kennedy, 1963

Can we and all nations not live in peace? In our obsession with antagonisms of the moment, we often forget how much unites all members of humanity. Perhaps we need some outside universal threat to make us recognize this common bond. I occasionally think how quickly our differences worldwide would vanish if we were facing an alien threat from outside this world. And yet is not an alien force already among us? And what could be more alien to the universal aspirations of our peoples than war and the threat of war?

Ronald Regan, UN General Assembly 1987

The only thing that scares me more than space aliens is the idea that there aren't any space aliens. We can't be the best that creation has to offer. I pray we're not all that there is. If so, we're in big trouble.

Ellen DeGeneres

Well I hate to admit it, but it is possible that there is 1) such a thing as telepathy and 2) that the SETI project's idea that we might communicate with extra-terrestrial beings via telepathy is possibly a reasonable idea if telepathy exists and if extra-terrestrials exist. Otherwise we are trying to communicate with someone who doesn't exist with a system that doesn't work.

Philip K. Dick

Remember to look up at the stars not down at your feet. Try to make sense of what you see and wonder about what makes the universe exist. Be curious. And however difficult life may seem, there is always something you can do and succeed at. It matters that you don't just give up.

Stephen Hawking

ABOUT THE AUTHOR

To find out more about the Author, who co-authored the No.1
Best seller 'Inspired by the Passion Test':

Visit her website:
www.MoneyMagnet.Global/BooksByJJHughes

Get your free bonus chapter at bit.ly/2pgEfiW
And discover who committed unspeakable atrocities in the past
and why. Things are not always as they first appear, as the current
day victims, villains and rescuers may switch roles.

Follow J.J. Hughes on
Twitter, Facebook, LinkedIn, Google+, Instagram and Pinterest
[@booksbyJJHughes]